RICHARD FOREMAN

PLAYS AND MANIFESTOS

RICHARD FOREMAN

PLAYS AND MANIFESTOS

*edited and with
an introduction by*

Kate Davy

THE DRAMA REVIEW SERIES
New York: NEW YORK UNIVERSITY PRESS
1976

Copyright © 1976 by New York University

Library of Congress Catalog Card Number: 75-27117
ISBN (cloth): 0-8147-2560-0
ISBN (paper): 0-8147-2561-9

Library of Congress Cataloging in Publication Data

Foreman, Richard, 1937-
  Plays and manifestos.
  I. Title.
PS3556.07225P6   812'.5'4   75-27117
ISBN 0-8147-2560-0
ISBN 0-8147-2561-9 pbk.

Manufactured in the United States of America

PREFACE

All of the photographs accompanying the plays presented in this text were taken during performances of the productions directed by Richard Foreman. The performers appearing in these photographs are listed (see page 225) according to the production and characters they played. With the exception of CLASSICAL THERAPY, which was performed in Paris and in French, all of the productions were presented in New York City. The sketches included in the three manifestos were taken from Foreman's production notebooks.

Since Foreman stages his own plays, some textual material is deleted during the rehearsal period while other material is added. Because these changes are minimal, the plays appear here as originally written and not as changed in production. The absence of certain punctuation, such as question marks, is intentional.

For their advice and help in preparing this text, I would like to thank Arnold Aronson, Susan Pochapsky, Michael Kirby and, especially, Terry Helbing.

CONTENTS

INTRODUCTION

Richard Foreman is one of the most important avant-garde artists working in the theatre today. Since he founded the Ontological-Hysteric Theatre in 1968, he has written thirty-nine plays and produced, designed and directed twenty-one of them. However, only twelve plays were presented under the title "Ontological-Hysteric Theatre." The others fall into a "commercial theatre" category, or were produced in another media (video), or by another producing organization.* Eight of the twelve plays produced by the Ontological-Hysteric Theatre are presented in this text in the order of their production.

While the traditional process of theatrical production usually involves cooperation among producers, directors, set and costume designers there is no collaboration in Ontological-Hysteric Theatre—every aspect of Foreman's art is done for and by himself. Although he is involved in every aspect of theatre art, Foreman points out, "Many people don't think the text is important in my pieces, but I am basically a playwright. There are many things that distract people from the text but the text is at the center." His work is significant because it stands in direct opposition to the various forms of physical, energetic expressionism adopted by experimental theatre artists of the 1960's. This is true partly because the impulse behind Foreman's work is fundamentally different than that of most of his theatre contemporaries.

In founding his own theatre, Foreman rejected the tendency toward emotionally "moving" the audience and searched instead for a "spiritual" quality. His goal was to replace the theatre of confrontation, emotion and "ideas" with what he terms a "mental," non-emotional, yet sensual theatre. He stated, "I wanted a theatre that did the opposite of 'flow'—a theatre that was true to my own mental experiences, that is, the world as being pieces of things, awkwardly present for a moment and then either re-presented by consciousness or dropped in favor of some other momentary presentation." Hence, the functioning of the consciousness became his preoccupation, resulting in work that deals directly with the nature, process and activity of thought itself. He discarded the conventional dramatic attributes of plot development and character interaction, replacing them with a kind of "atomic" structure. He explains that this structuring involves the breaking down of all the theatrical elements (story, action, sound, light, composition, gesture) into "the smallest building-block units, the basic cells of the perceived experience of both living and art-making."

It is in this approach that the use of the word "ontological" becomes clear. Ontology is "the science of being or reality; the branch of knowledge that investigates the nature, essential properties, and relations of being." In his writing, Foreman takes the fundamental conflict (hysteric) basis of most traditional theatre and renders it phenomenologically—retarding and breaking up the hysterical situation or state, and focusing on the moment-to-moment reality of things-in-and-of-themselves. Foreman shares this phenomenological esthetic with Gertrude Stein.

---

* See page 227 for a complete chronology of the plays written and produced.

The Influence of Gertrude Stein

Although the influences on Foreman are numerous, he has stated that Stein's theo-retical writings on literature and theatre are the primary influence on his writing method, technique or style. Because she believed in the primacy of phenomena over ideas and events, Stein's work, like Foreman's, seems to relate more to a phenome-nology of the mind than to literature. Philosophically, she posited a dualism of "being" and "existence." In her book entitled *The Geographical History of America or The Relation of Human Nature to the Human Mind,* she equates "being" with the human mind and "existence" with human nature. While being is eternal, existence is time-bound. This led her to differentiate between "entity" in relation to "identity" and "knowing" in relation to "remembering." The characteristics break down as follows:

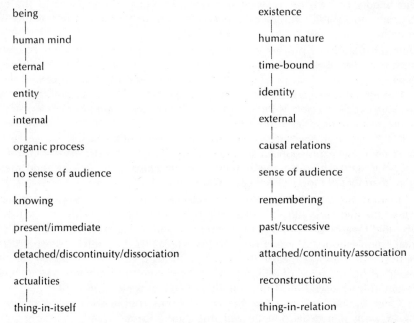

being	existence
human mind	human nature
eternal	time-bound
entity	identity
internal	external
organic process	causal relations
no sense of audience	sense of audience
knowing	remembering
present/immediate	past/successive
detached/discontinuity/dissociation	attached/continuity/association
actualities	reconstructions
thing-in-itself	thing-in-relation

This philosophical dichotomy formed the basis of Stein's approach to, and method of, writing. For her, "entity" and "identity" functioned both as states of mind and kinds of writing. "Identity writing" is audience writing and is intended to be popu-larly understood by a reading audience. The three Foreman manifestos included in this text are examples of "identity writing," while all of Foreman's plays fall into the "entity writing" category, which Stein refers to as "really writing" or "pure writing."

In practical terms, what precisely are the characteristics of "entity writing," what are its methods and why can Foreman's plays be labeled as such? Stein was a student of William James and the first one to realize the esthetic implications of his prag-matic philosophy. She translated James' notion of the "stream-of-consciousness" into an artistic expression of concrete phenomena. First, she insisted on the immediate, individual, concrete thing as final reality and then, rather than write "about" some-thing or explain it, she attempted to write the thing itself as she perceived it moment-to-moment. Her compositional device became the continuous, moment-to-moment progression of her own thinking process as she concentrated on present, concrete actualities. Using introspection as her means, the data of consciousness and its present moment as her content and the prolonged or "continuous present" as her structural device, Stein concretized James' concept of the "stream-of-consciousness," translating it into her literary genre. Her theory of the "continuous present" was one of her most important innovations and it constitutes the basic structural dimension of all Foreman's plays.

The use of the continuous present is one means of structuring a play in the absence of a developing narrative, story or plot. It eliminates what Stein referred to as "syncopation" in the theatre. By "syncopation" she meant that the emotional experience of the spectator never quite matched the emotional movement of the event on the stage. This syncopated time experience can be equated with the memory/expectancy structure of a play, which Stein linked to her notion of existence, human nature and identity, because it places the spectator in the position of remembering past information or events while anticipating future events, climaxes or resolutions. Being placed in such a position as a spectator made Stein very nervous because it forced her to "read" the performance in a specific, predetermined way, manipulating her emotions in an unnatural manner. After all, in real life, one's emotions always match the situation one is involved in at the moment.

To remedy syncopation, Stein conceived of the static or "landscape play." One perceives a landscape differently than a play because one reads them differently. The theatre experience is always going somewhere (progression) while a landscape is not. When reading a landscape or picture the eye moves from object to object, perceiving the relationships between individual elements presented simultaneously. In any landscape there are certain features which are always there and the relationships between these features are always, objectively, present. Like theatre, the landscape exists in time because it takes time to see a landscape as the eye moves from feature to feature in a definite order or pattern; the exact pattern is determined, subjectively, by the viewer.

Translating this into the theatrical event involves the presentation of certain elements—objects, people, words, scenery, actions—and the relationships between them, placed in a time frame with an order or pattern of reading or scanning them. A play as a landscape provides an example of the concreteness of experience versus the imaginative, intellectual qualities of a narrative, for a landscape play has no beginning, middle and end—it is simply there, it is continuously present.

In her writing, Stein used a device she called "beginning again and again" as one means of creating a continuous present within a landscape setting. A series of beginnings can create a picture in words or a total situation eliminating memory since a beginning has no history—it is simply "there," it is concrete—and a series of beginnings strung together do not go anywhere. In playwriting, Stein concentrated on the flow of individual images or "moments," taking the momentary intensity of each image and placing them next to each other in a sequence. In so doing, she created a series of present moments, by beginning again and again, resulting in a continuous present.

Foreman's Innovations

Like Stein, Foreman creates a continuous present in his writing by isolating his own present, internal time so that the words he writes exist in suspended time, moving as they move in each moment of his consciousness as he focuses on his own internal process or state. As Foreman points out, "The scripts themselves read like notations of my own process of imagining a theatre piece." Indeed, in the act of writing, Foreman incessantly documents his own effort at writing a play in an attempt, as he puts it, "to notate at every moment, with great exactness, what was going on as the 'writing was written.' " The result is a distinctive composition arrived at through a meticulous accumulation of subjective material and specific detail reflecting all the randomness, fits and starts, repetitions and surprise revelations that characterize the workings of the human consciousness.

When he writes, Foreman thinks about the "kind of room" and the "feel of the space" that the play exists in. He sees the props and other objects in the room and "the activities of the body." He does not think about the characters' personalities or faces, because "I really think they are all me." The characters are shades, "like De Chirico figures with the faces wiped out," that come and go in his consciousness. In one line, a character may be a "real flesh-and-blood Rhoda, who is someone I know, saying a real thing to me" and in the next line "Rhoda may become an echo, sort of a memory in my mind, of a certain aspect of the woman." Often, a line spoken by a character is actually Foreman's reaction to the line he has just written.

VOICE
Oh, it says what happened to Max's red
feet.
RHODA
—Why am I thinking about it now.
VERTICAL MOBILITY

Foreman's texts are very personal and self-referential, because they are a documentary of his consciousness in the act of writing.

One of the many distinctive features of Foreman's plays involves the extensive use of repetition leading to a kind of "cinematic" style. Stein, also, employed this technique which she characterized as the "continuous succession" of a statement. Each statement, formed in the present, is succeeded by another, slightly different statement, like the consecutive frames of a film that create an image that seems to extend itself in the present for a given period of time. Thus, Foreman's writing has a contemplative quality, in that it does not have the rapid "flow" of facts added to facts, as in an information structure.

In his method of generating texts, Foreman shares yet another artistic approach with Gertrude Stein. The method involves meditation, not in the sense of hypnotic trance, but rather a kind of "esthetic meditation." Meditation, for Stein, included a technique of contemplation and isolation, or a shutting out of external reality while concentrating on her own subjective responses to a given objective reality. She developed a highly disciplined power of immediate, intuitive perception through repeated acts of contemplation and concentration. The aim of her meditative activity was focused on capturing the moment of heightened perception and expressing that moment of greatest perceptual clarity. Through severe discipline and choosing, she managed to exclude memories, resemblances and past associations, including only the immediate, unique and vivid aspects of things seen, heard and felt in the present.

Esthetic meditation can also involve an act of complete detachment, discontinuity or dissociation at the moment of creation. Stein intentionally sought a state of mental deceleration or a moment of mental suspension, similar to that experienced when one is dozing or approaching the sleep state. The moment of creation becomes this moment of dissociation when the mind is so detached that focus, time, place, memory and identity sink into nothingness. Like Stein, Foreman's writing is not "about" consciousness; on the contrary, it directly reflects the operations of the author's mind employing a meditative process of composition.

Another exceptional feature of Foreman's plays is the fact that many of the same characters (Rhoda, Ben, Sophia, Max, etc.) reappear in all of the texts. However, it is extremely difficult to identify with any of these characters, no matter how familiar the reader becomes with them, since they are not presented in definite, recognizable situations and they do not, except momentarily, have feelings, needs, goals or ambitions. They function more as self-enclosed units than characters responding or reacting to situations of conflict or encounter. Occasionally, they refer to themselves in the third person. This is only one example of many devices used to "distance" the reader/spectator from the work. Like Stein, Foreman emphatically rejects "identity" or the desire to impress, flatter, coerce or persuade the audience. Both writers avoid "emotional traps" or the intentional manipulation for an audience's emotional responses. Every effort is made to resist psychic projection on the part of the audience into the experience by reducing the possibility of emotional involvement in terms of empathy, sympathy, identification and projection. Both artists hope their audiences will realize an "esthetic emotion," similar to their own detached, dissociated state in the act of writing, when experiencing their work.

By eliminating clearly developing situations, involving imaginary people in imaginary places, Foreman creates a world into which the reader has great difficulty projecting himself—thus, throwing the reader, as it were, back onto himself, startling him into a fresh awareness of his own mind. For Foreman, esthetic emotion occurs at this moment of "mental awakening." In order to make the activity of perception present to the spectator, Foreman retards rather than facilitates it by taking ordinary people in mundane situations and placing them in a context that breaks down stale associations producing a kind of "vibration." This "mental awakening" or perhaps, "consciousness altering" is realized when, given a number of possibilities, the audience "vibrates" between alternatives. Foreman explains, "Ontological-Hysteric Theatre is a form of 'concrete theatre' in which the moment-to-moment resistance and impenetrability of the materials worked onstage are framed and re-framed so that the spectator's attention is redistributed and exhilaration slowly invades his consciousness as a result of the continuous presentation and re-presentation of the atomic units of each experienced moment." His intention is to refocus the spectator's attention on the intervals, gaps, relations and rhythms which "saturate the givens (objects, words and actions) of any particular play." "In doing this, I believe the spectator is made available (as I am, when writing) to those most desirable energies which secretly connect him (through a kind of resonance) with the foundations of his being." It seems clear that some kind of "consciousness altering" composes the desired effect.

Although a detailed description of how Foreman translates his scripts into the theatrical event is not possible here, it may be helpful for the reader to know some basic characteristics common to all of the plays in terms of staging. Before the rehearsal period begins, Foreman records all of the music, noises and most of the dialog on tape. All of the lines spoken by the "Voice" and many of the "legends" are Foreman's own voice while the voices of individual characters are those of the performers designated for each role. During each performance, Foreman sits at a table, directly in front, or above and in back, of the audience seating section. From this table, he operates the various tape recorders and lighting instruments thereby "conducting" the performance since he controls all of the lighting and tape-recorded cues.

Different rules are used for delivering dialog and they vary within each production as well as from one production to another. Sometimes the performers speak their complete lines from the stage. Other times, the dialog is played over loudspeakers while the actors repeat a word or two quietly along with the tape, slightly echoing the line. For the most part, the performers read their lines slowly and clearly, delivering them in an uninflected manner. The lines are loud but unemotional.

Using the tape recorder as a vehicle, Foreman functions both as a commentator, by directly addressing the audience, and as a character, through the "Voice," speaking to other characters onstage. While most of the speech delivered by Foreman is written into the texts, much of it is improvised and added during the rehearsal period to clarify sections that Foreman feels need explanation. For example, during rehearsals for *PAIN(T)* and *VERTICAL MOBILITY,* Foreman added a tape of his voice to the beginning of each play: "This play is about making art (pause) from a certain energy (pause) which most people use (pause) most of the time *(PAIN(T))*," and, "The play focuses on Max who has given up writing . . . *(VERTICAL MOBILITY)*." Often, sentences labeled "legend" in the text are mounted on slides and projected onto both stationary and movable projection screens, providing a reading experience for the spectator as well as the aural experience.

In addition to the six or so titled characters, Foreman uses a number of unnamed performers that function as "crew people," carrying furniture on and offstage, participating in the composition of stage pictures and the "dances" that usually occur in a Foreman production. Occasionally, they are used to produce "live," nonrepresentational sound effects that accompany the taped score.

The use of specific devices to deliberately disrupt the play's "flow" constitutes another unique feature of a Foreman play. In the texts, he repeatedly calls for "pauses" and particular kinds of "noise." The single most commonly used line of character dialog consists, in its entirety, of the word "what." The interjection "huh" is often tacked onto the end of a character's line for verbal punctuation.

MAX
(Pause, tiny bells tinkle.)

Take a load off my feet, huh.
BEN

Do that
MAX

What

ALL
(Pause. Tinkle stops.)

Shhhhh.
BEN

I could be quiet when I do that or else
(A thud.)

Try it again.

HOTEL CHINA

Foreman has said that the important thing is "not to succumb to the easy tendency to get carried away in some kind of emotional flow, to pull oneself to a stop at every moment and re-examine what is there (in the mind as one writes, or in the physical presence of actors and decor as one is staging the piece) and to be true to that found 'arbitrary' moment."

The use of visual and aural "framing devices" constitutes a recognizable stylistic feature of every Foreman production. A framing device is anything that punctuates, frames, emphasizes, or brings into the foreground a particular word, object, action or position. For example, in *VERTICAL MOBILITY* a crew person attached a string to one wall, about three feet from the floor, drew it horizontally across the stage, parallel to the floor, and attached it to the opposite wall. The character, Max, was lying on the floor, and raised his leg so that his toe touched the string. A "frame" was added to the foot when a crew person attached a rectangular piece of white material to the string directly behind the foot—framing the foot (see page 173).

Although there are many examples of visual framing, the primary vehicle for framing lines and activity is the tape recorded words, music and noises that accompany every performance. While most of the noises are specified in the texts, many are added during rehearsals; they include foghorns, thuds, pings, boings, glass shattering, drumrolls, bells, whistles and screams. For example, the following sounds were added to the final lines of *VERTICAL MOBILITY*:

> RHODA
> *(Pause.)*
> He cannot speak openly, huh.
> *(Pause.)*
> Oh, Max, I do not recognize—
> MAX
> What.
> RHODA
> the room.
> *(A "ping" against the word "room.")*
> MAX
> Look.
> *(Pause.)*
> It became very beautiful. Oh, Rhoda.
> *(A "thud" against the word "beautiful.")*
> ALL
> Shhhhhhh.
> *(Pause.)*
> We are now in Paradise.
> *(A "thud" against the word "Paradise.")*
> RHODA
> I know it.
> MAX
> Is it beautiful enough.
> RHODA
> No.
> *(A loud "NO!" immediately after RHODA's "NO.")*

There is much that can be said about Foreman's staging techniques.* It will suffice to point out here that Foreman uses picturization or tableaux, employing the traditional "picture-frame stage" viewing arrangement for the spectators. In staging, he presents almost all of the scenes as sequences of static pictures. The performers are relaxed yet posed and motionless, creating tableau compositions. They usually gaze steadily at or toward the audience. In so doing, the performers force the spectator to notice where he is by implying with their stare, "I am here, where are you." Foreman explains that, "Having to notice where one is is very exhilarating." This technique is

---

*See Michael Kirby's article "Richard Foreman's Ontological-Hysteric Theatre," in *THE DRAMA REVIEW*, June, 1973, pp. 5-32.

related to Brechtian alienation and provides a concrete example in staging of a device employed to distance the viewer from the performance. In describing his staging concerns, Foreman acknowledges the influence of Brecht: "Everything shakes. Is about to break apart. A post-Brechtian alienation technique of theatre, applied upon spiritual rather than social concerns." As in reading the texts, Foreman wants the spectator to savor the work from afar rather than become involved with it as he is involved with events in life.

Gertrude Stein eliminated internal punctuation in long complicated sentences because she felt each sentence should impose itself upon the reader, forcing him to notice himself working at comprehending the whole. Foreman also uses various devices, in his staging, to put pressure on the mind, asking it to work at perceiving the experience. An example is the use of differences in scale. Often, a miniature box-set (like a room in a doll house) that represents a room seen earlier in the play, will be placed in a later scene. This is also worked in reverse—a miniature set of a scene to appear later will be placed in an earlier scene. In his production of *SOPHIA=*
(WISDOM) Part 3: THE CLIFFS, the faces of the performers are revealed in houses on the "cliff." The spectator can perceive the houses as in correct proportion, making the performer's heads seem gigantic; or the heads can be accepted as in correct proportion, dwarfing the houses. In any case, the spectator is challenged to a greater, more active collaboration in the experience of the piece.

In addition to staging the scripts themselves, Foreman attempts to stage the process of writing. "I'm basically interested in staging what's going on in my head while I'm writing the play." Although he is most often described as primarily a visual artist, he personally feels that his scripts are complete and self-sufficient. The words of the text do not function as mere background for the visual placement of the performers but are an integral part of his staging of how the mind operates when writing a play.

Although the emphasis and style have changed somewhat over the years, Foreman's basic intention and approach, in the texts and in the staging, has remained distinctively consistent. Because many of the same characters reappear in all of the plays, and because the absence of a developing narrative gives each play an open-endedness, all may be considered as parts of one developing whole. The fact that the plays can be regarded as "thought plays" or "monodramas," representing the inner workings of one person's mind, emphasizes this continuity. The characters can be seen to represent the various aspects of Foreman himself, personifying his attitudes and desires.

The reader of this text should keep in mind that the "experience" of reading and viewing the plays is more important than "understanding" them. Foreman is not interested in having his readers think along specific predetermined pathways to arrive at the "correct" intellectual conclusions. Instead of "explaining," the plays document as well as create or provoke thought. The reader will find that the plays are, as P. Adams Sitney suggests, "like rivers they simply repeat their existence."

Kate Davy
New York City
March, 1976

RICHARD FOREMAN

PLAYS AND MANIFESTOS

ANGELFACE

1.

(MAX sits alone in a chair in the center of the room. Throughout the scene, he doesn't move. His eyes are glazed. He smiles.
The door opens. WALTER is seen. Silence. WALTER is frozen.)

MAX
(Finally he laughs once.)
The door opens. I don't even turn my head.

WALTER
Does it turn?

MAX
What?

WALTER
(Laughs once.)
Heads turn.

MAX
Heads turn. My head is a head. Therefore: my head turns.
(Silence. He smiles.)
Open the door a second time.

WALTER
Why?

MAX
Find out if my head turns.

WALTER
I can't.

MAX
What?

WALTER
An opened door cannot be opened.

MAX
All doors can be opened!

WALTER
(After a pause. No one moves a muscle.)
All right. I'm staring at it. Staring at it is opening it a second time.

MAX
(Low.)
What is: opening it a third time.

WALTER
(Turns his head once. Pause.)
. . . A third time, a fourth time, a fifth time—

MAX
—Staring at doors cannot be repeated.

WALTER
I'm staring at Max.

ANGELFACE was the Ontological-Hysteric Theatre's first production in April, 1968. There are no extant photographs of the performance. The title photo, by Kate Davy, is of Richard Foreman at a rehearsal of PAIN(T) in 1974.

MAX

It's impossible to stare at Max.

WALTER

(Staring at MAX.)

Why?

MAX

(Pause.)

Because Max is never in the same place. He's always in different places.

WALTER

—My penetrating glance follows him to different parts of the room.

MAX

No.

WALTER

I have flexible eyes.

(He laughs.)

MAX

Paralysis of the eyes.

(Silence.)

Are you a mutant?

WALTER

No.

MAX

Then your eyes are in paralysis, like the rest of us.

WALTER

(Pause. Laughs.)

Where am I standing?

MAX

(Laughs.)

Where am I sitting.
The odds for every possibility, always the same odds—

WALTER

A hundred to one: five to one:—

MAX

—One to one: those are the only odds.

WALTER

What are the odds, eventually we come upon each other.

MAX

In this room?

WALTER

(After a pause, he calls out sharply.)

Max!

MAX

(Calling back his position.)

Walter!

(Pause.)

Walter! Follow my voice!

WALTER

(Low. Smiles.)

I can't follow people's voices. It always seems to me as if people's voices . . .

(He trails off.)

MAX

Yes?

WALTER

(Pause.)

You have a beautiful voice.

MAX

I have beautiful eyes.

WALTER

—It comes from all directions at once.

MAX

I have beautiful hands. I have beautiful ears.

WALTER

(Low.)

I will now try to point my head in the direction . . .

MAX

(Pause. Laughs.)

My voice comes from all directions at once: therefore.

WALTER

My head turns in all directions.

(His head doesn't move.)

MAX

My head may or may not turn.

WALTER

The door is open.

MAX

(Low.)

Close it and find Max, somewhere in this room.

WALTER

I'm doing it with my eyes—

(Holds up his hand, palms out.)

—with my hands, with my voice—

MAX

(Laughs.)

I don't have to turn my head to feel a draft.

WALTER

(Pause.)

My hands in full view. I could walk backwards through the door.

MAX

—Would suction make it shut tight?

WALTER

Try it.

MAX

What?

WALTER

Try it.

> (Silence. Hands still up.)

Would suction close the door?

MAX

> (Low.)

Twelve o'clock and all's well.

WALTER

Who's present?

MAX

Max. Walter.

WALTER

Twelve o'clock, remember.

MAX

—Rhoda's asleep.

WALTER

> (Counting the hours.)

One, two, three—

MAX

Our clocks are silent.

WALTER

Four, five, six—

MAX

—Are you looking for somebody?

WALTER

Seven, eight, nine—

MAX

> (Laughs.)

My door is ALWAYS unlocked!

WALTER

Ten, eleven, twelve.

> (Silence. Laughs.)

Where's Agatha?

MAX

Try turning the head, as if the head were on a swivel.

WALTER

I tried opening the door.

MAX

Open it again.

WALTER

> (Turns his head.)

I'm opening it.

> (Turns it again.)

I'm opening it.

> (Turns it.)

I'm opening it—

MAX

Am I visible?

WALTER

> (Looks at MAX.)

No.

MAX

Yes, I'm visible. You didn't recognize me.

WALTER

I'm looking for Agatha.

> (Pause. The closet door opens, AGATHA takes a few steps out as if sleepwalking.)

She just . . .

MAX

> (Pause.)

Yes?

WALTER

Just.

MAX

Just.

> (Pause.)

Open the door for the fifth time.

WALTER

> (As AGATHA stands silent.)

Agatha appears and disappears into the closet.

MAX

> (Pause. Laughs.)

No. If anybody locks themselves in the closet—

WALTER

—Yes!

MAX

> (Pause. Laughs.)

People who lock themselves in closets suffocate.

WALTER

People who put—

MAX

Yes?

WALTER

—hands over their eyes.

MAX

> (Pause.)

Yes?

WALTER

> (Laughs.)

I want to cross the room but I'm afraid of bumping into the furniture.

> (AGATHA starts backing into the closet, closing the door.)

The door's open!

MAX

Open it.

> (Pause.)

Open it for the seventh time.

WALTER

With my eyes. Turning my head.

> (He turns to the door, it closes.)

Opening the door.

MAX

Twelve o'clock. Why I can't sleep.

WALTER
I believe . . . that Agatha . . . is—
MAX
Yes?
WALTER
I believe it.
(Pause.)
Open the closet.
MAX
With my eyes?
WALTER
(Pause. Laughs.)
Max, are you capable of moving?
MAX
Certain muscles, yes—
WALTER
Which muscles, nailed to the floor of course—
MAX
(Laughing.)
—Floor, walls, doors, tables—
WALTER
Which muscles?
(Pause.)
Which doors are opened by which muscles?
MAX
(Pause, low.)
The eyes, always the eyes.
(Closet door opens.)
Rhoda's sleeping in the bedroom.
WALTER
(Laughs.)
Agatha's in the closet.
MAX
All my closets are empty.
WALTER
I got eyes, Max.
MAX
—Rhoda has eyes.
WALTER
(Pause.)
I step toward the closet.
(He doesn't move.)
MAX
What happens.
(Pause. WALTER takes a step.)
"One step." Each time Walter takes a step, I turn my head a bit more in a certain direction.
(WALTER takes another step.)
Two steps.
WALTER
(Stops and laughs.)
I can see from here.

MAX
What.
WALTER
(Pause.)
It's empty.
MAX
(Low.)
I have nothing to do with girls.
(Pause.)
Walter!
WALTER
(Laughs.)
The closet eats people.
MAX
—I have nothing to do with girls. Walter.
(Pause.)
Walter, I have nothing to do with girls.
WALTER
(Calls.)
—Rhoda!
MAX
She's sleeping.
WALTER
—Rhoda!
MAX
She's safe. Closets don't eat people, Walter.
WALTER
(Calling.)
Is Rhoda sleeping!
MAX
—Everytime you shout—
WALTER
(Didn't hear.)
—What?
MAX
(Pause. Then he calls.)
Rhoda!
WALTER
—Rhoda!
MAX
Walter!
WALTER
Rhoda!
MAX
Walter!
WALTER
Max!
(Pause. Laughs.)
I'm Rhoda's guardian angel.
MAX
(Laughs.)
I am.
(The front door opens and AGATHA gets pushed violently into the room, so violently that she

falls in the middle, on the carpet.
Pause. MAX laughs.)
See? My head turns.
WALTER
Which muscles are moving?
MAX
None.
AGATHA
*(Looking away from them, looking
at the floor, crudely.)*
Help me up!
MAX
Your uncle's invisible, eh?
WALTER
Where's Agatha?
MAX
(Barks out.)
Somebody help!
(Pause.)
Poor Agatha. Unfortunately I'm both
watched and held under suspicion. Walter
watches the muscles of my body: the mo-
ment they start emitting a certain light—
WALTER
*(Points with his finger, arm out-
stretched.)*
There she is.
MAX
(Pause, laughs.)
Walter is waiting. As soon as light shines
from my muscles, he feels his way across the
room.
WALTER
(Pointing.)
A beam of light, connecting my hand—
MAX
—Amazing!
WALTER
—Agatha's hair.
*(AGATHA, without rising, starts
dragging herself across to the door.)*
Look at her. Look at her, Max.
MAX
Inhuman, huh?
WALTER
Look at her, Max. What kind of animal?
MAX
(Low.)
She's trained.
(She stops, looks at MAX. Pause.)
Are you TRAINED, Walter? Look at that
arm.
WALTER
LIGHT!

MAX
Who trains those muscles?
*(WALTER stops pointing, looks at
MAX, whose eyes never blink,
never turn from the front.)*
He turns. Who trains the muscles?
WALTER
We found the girl—
MAX
—Maybe Walter invokes her!
WALTER
—Maybe Rhoda isn't asleep, and is hiding
behind the door.
WEINSTEIN
(Off.)
HEY!
WALTER
—Listening perhaps, in which case we
oughta take Rhoda's feelings into considera-
tion?
*(He turns angrily, goes and tries the
door to the bedroom, it's locked.
He turns back and laughs.)*
What happened when my back was turned?
MAX
(Low.)
The door is locked.
WALTER
What happened?
WEINSTEIN
(Off.)
HEY!!
MAX
Agatha's uncle whispers secrets.
WEINSTEIN
(Off.)
HEY-HEY-HEY!
MAX
—But I grip the arms of my chair. The
harder I squeeze . . .
WALTER
Yes?
MAX
(Pause.)
My arms glow in the dark. What do you see.
WALTER
(Pause.)
No change.
WEINSTEIN
(Off.)
HEY!!
AGATHA
(Still staring at the floor.)
My uncle's calling me!

MAX

—I don't even cover my ears. Agatha leaves a trail on the carpet.

WALTER

I don't see it.

MAX

I don't move. I touch nothing. I keep my body carefully separated.

WALTER

(Pointing at the carpet, low.)

—Where she's moved, it's wet.

MAX

—Agatha leave a PATH!

(Pause.)

Now she's vanished, right? See? Everything was in Walter's imagination.

(The lights start to dim.)

Rhoda has TWO guardian angels.

WALTER

(Frowns.)

I can't see.

(Pause. The lights grow dimmer.)

I can't see.

MAX

I am always . . .

(Whispers.)

Faithful.

(The lights are out completely.)

WALTER

I can't see.

MAX

(From the darkness.)

Point toward where you imagine Agatha.

(Pause.)

See? Agatha doesn't become visible.

WALTER

(Laughs.)

I'm pointing towards her.

MAX

Rhoda wakes.

(WALTER lights a match.)

She goes back to sleep.

WALTER

My hand is shaking.

MAX

Who loves her best?

(Pause.)

Which one of us?

WEINSTEIN

(Off.)

HEY!

(The match goes out.)

MAX

Rhoda wakes up again. How many people are in this room? 1-2-3-4-5-6-

(WALTER lights another match. This time he is sitting on the floor, attempting to set fire to the edge of a tablecloth hanging over the edge of a small table.)

What burns and what doesn't huh?

(Pause. The lights come up slowly. One match goes out and WALTER lights another. AGATHA is gone.)

WALTER

(Blows out his match, laughs.)

Caught in the act, huh?

MAX

(Laughs.)

Caught in the act.

WALTER

I visualize it. This whole room on fire.

MAX

I never encouraged anybody.

WALTER

—Who?

MAX

(Pause.)

I have nothing to do with girls, Walter.

WALTER

Teach Max a lesson.

MAX

(Low.)

Explain yourself, Walter.

WALTER

Everything in this room grows hair. Like Agatha. Falling out of Agatha's head, huh?

MAX

Fire.

WALTER

I visualize it.

MAX

The tables, the chairs, the carpet—

WALTER

(Holding up his hands.)

Not a match in my hand.

MAX

(Low.)

There she is Walter, behind you.

WALTER

—Rhoda?

MAX

No.

(Pause. WALTER doesn't turn.)

She's tempting you.

WALTER

Young girls don't tempt me.

MAX

—Now she's gone.

WALTER
(Low.)
—I'll kill you for that.
MAX
—What?
WALTER
(Pause. Laughs.)
The minute I threaten you, I see these walls
start shaking.
MAX
They put me to sleep.
WALTER
What.
MAX
The walls.
WALTER
These walls don't put ME to sleep. I'm
DIZZY.
MAX
I'm dizzy. That's when I fall asleep.
WALTER
(Shuts his eyes.)
I think of them on fire, I stop feeling
dizzy.
MAX
Set this room on fire, what happens? I'm on
fire, Rhoda's on fire—
WALTER
(Laughs.)
That's O.K. with ME.
MAX
—Now my head's MOVING, even.
WALTER
(Laughs.)
—Doors opening.
MAX
—Because it's on fire, it's capable of move-
ment.
(Pause.)
Only it isn't on fire, so light another match
please.
WALTER
(Laughs.)
I'm being encouraged.
MAX
Walter's out of matches, find some in this
room, hidden in hundreds of obvious
places—
WALTER
(Low.)
—Am I being encouraged.
MAX
—I'm helping you up.

WALTER
(Opens his eyes. Pause.)
I don't count on you helping me to my feet.
Agatha was on the floor in approximately
this position. Assume this is an imitation.
MAX
I don't help Agatha.
WALTER
(Laughs.)
I don't count on Max.
WEINSTEIN
(Off.)
—HEY!
MAX
(Laughs.)
He wants to know where she's hiding.
WEINSTEIN
(Off.)
—HEY!
MAX
HEY!
WALTER
Where is she hiding!
MAX
—CLOSET!
WALTER
(Pause.)
How many times . . . does she enter and re-
enter—
MAX
First, get Walter back on his feet.
WALTER
I don't count on Max—
MAX
—I'm alone in the closet. I turn my head to
the left.
(Pause. No one moves a muscle.)
On fire, my head turns slowly to the left.
(The table behind WALTER tips
over. No one moves.)
On fire, burnt to a crisp—
(A chair turns over.)
—my head falls, my chin falls onto my
chest—
WALTER
(Low.)
—Break something else.
MAX
(Pause.)
Get up from this chair, and in so doing, fail
to balance properly—begin falling to one
side—
WALTER
—Something behind me.

MAX

—Lurching to the left.

WALTER

—I stick out my left leg—

(Done.)

—Pieces of furniture, shattered by the blow from my foot.

MAX

(Pause. Laughs.)

Holes in the walls.

WALTER

(Low, smiles.)

Balance.

MAX

Balance . . .

WALTER

BALANCE!

MAX

(Laughs.)

Holes in the walls; pull me like magnets.

(Pause. Starts up again.)

There I am. Falling to one side. The weight of my body.

(Another chair turns over.)

—Break my fall—

WALTER

Crack!

MAX

—With an extended leg, but the momentum of the body; carrying me to the walls, where I BANG.

WALTER

(Pause. Low.)

Help me to my feet, Max.

MAX

I'm banging into the wall, Walter.

WALTER

(Pause.)

I break up the chairs for firewood.

(Off, a phone rings loud.)

If we don't get up now—

MAX

Let it ring, Walter.

(Pause. The phone stops.)

WALTER

HELP. ME. UP!

MAX

Shhhhh.

(Pause. WALTER starts crawling, like AGATHA, to a chair.)

Rhoda picks up the phone.

(WALTER starts breathing very loudly, very heavily, wheezing.)

No one answers.

(WALTER by a turned over chair,

still breathing, heaving, lifts himself.)

Shhh.

(Pause. WALTER starts—a hand on two opposite legs of the chair, trying to break them off, breathing very loud. Face reddening.)

Break, break, huh? A house full of firewood is a house of . . .

(Pause. Laughs.)

It's clean, huh?

(Outside door and bedroom door both open slowly. AGATHA in one doorway, RHODA in the other.)

Which one is sleepwalking and which one is imaginary.

(WEINSTEIN gives AGATHA a push and sends her tumbling into the room, where she falls in the same spot. Pause. Then MAX says sharply.)

Now. Answer the phone.

(Pause. Laughs.)

Lock the doors and windows.

(Pause. Laughs.)

First. Answer the phone.

(RHODA backs out slowly, AGATHA pulls herself out.)

Rhoda's sleeping. Can she answer a telephone in her sleep? Can she FIND a telephone in her sleep?

(RHODA and AGATHA are gone, MAX slowly and unsteadily rises. Stands there. WALTER, still frozen putting pressure on the legs of the chair, starts to imitate a phone.)

WALTER

Brrrring! Brrrrrring!

MAX

(Low, as WALTER continues.)

Oh boy, listen to those flames. What do those flames lick like, huh? Do those flames lick like tongues?

(Laughs, wiggles his hand like a flame.)

Tongues of flames, huh? Licking the carpet, huh? The walls, huh? The ceiling too, huh?

WALTER

(Stops, relaxes his grip on his chair.)

I'm gonna keep Max under observation.

(RHODA slowly and carefully walks into the room, backwards, careful backward steps.)

BLACKOUT

2.

(MAX sits in another chair. This time, the chair has its back to a side wall. MAX therefore in profile. He leans his head back, stretching his neck. The top of his head touches the wall. Silence. MAX laughs.)

MAX
Can Max listen to walls?
(Pause. Laughs.)
What are walls made of—paper—YES!
(He moves his head so his ear is now against the wall. He stares ahead, smiles.)
Glue human ears to walls. Yes.
(Slowly KARL opens the door from RHODA's bedroom, MAX never looks at him, but refers to him.)
Shhhh!

KARL
(Laughs.)
Max listens to walls.

MAX
Right.

KARL
(Low.)
Hello walls.

MAX
Both ears vibrating.

KARL
—My mouth is moving slightly.
(KARL slowly moves one careful step into the room, as if on a tight-rope. Stops midway.)
My heart, beating softly; blood—circulates—

MAX
Shhhhh.

KARL
(Stopped for good.)
I move so slowly. Max doesn't know that I move.
(MAX turns, looks at KARL. Pause.)
Now I'm not moving.

MAX
(Low.)
Karl is moving across the room to my chair.

KARL
Max's chair is empty.

MAX
(Low.)
One more step toward my chair, it flies to pieces.
(Pause.)
Don't move.

KARL
(Laughs.)
One more broken chair.
(Pause.)
Five.

MAX
—What?

KARL
—Five broken ones!
(Pause.)
I move slightly—

MAX
FIVE!

KARL
(Laughs.)
—Three doors.

MAX
(Laughs.)
—Two tables . . . Lights.

KARL
Offer me a seat, Max.

MAX
(Calls.)
—Rhoda?

KARL
(Shuts his eyes, smiling.)
Vis-u-alize my sis-ter! Lis-ten to voi-ces in-side MY HEAD!
(At this point, something happens in the rear, open window. WALTER's hand appears at the bottom of the sill. It pulls him up, and he rolls in, as it were, over the low sill, and then rolls down a ways into the room.)

MAX
—Rhoda?
(Pause.)
Karl has ears turned inside. I have ears glued to walls.

KARL
(Holds out his hand, eyes still closed.)
Place Rhoda's hand—

MAX
—Yes?

KARL
(Pause.)
My hand is supporting—

MAX
(Laughs.)
Two brothers; stretching out two hands—
WALTER and KARL
No—
MAX
(Pause.)
What hand goes into Karl's hand—
KARL
(Laughs, feeling its weight.)
Rhoda's hand.
MAX
(Pause. Low.)
Putting Walter's hand—
KARL
No.
MAX
—Into Karl's hand.
WALTER
No.
MAX
(Continues, low, quickly.)
—Asking Rhoda for Rhoda's advice, huh?
(Pause.)
Somebody; move my head closer to the wall, please.
WALTER
(From the floor, still, remember.)
Max talks too loud!
MAX
(Laughs.)
—Talk louder, more information or less information?
(Pause.)
How many brothers?
KARL
One. Eyes closed—
MAX
Walter, rolling in and out of the window, huh?
WALTER
Walter and Max, breaking furniture—
MAX
(Pause.)
Move your hand just a little—
(KARL does it, so slightly it can't be seen.)
—You broke something.
KARL
No.
MAX
Open your eyes, Karl.
KARL
No.

MAX
(Laughs.)
Lookit what's broke.
(Pause, laughs.)
There's a lot of broken furniture in this room!
(WALTER rolls back across the room, shoots up a hand at just the right time to pull himself up and as-if-rolling, back out the window he came in.)
KARL
I don't have—
MAX
(Not letting him finish.)
—What?
KARL
—No brothers.
MAX
—What brothers?
(Pause.)
Is Walter somebody's—
WALTER
(Off.)
"WALTER!"
KARL
(Simultaneously.)
What?
MAX
(Pause. Laughs.)
Is Rhoda's somebody's—
RHODA
(Off.)
"RHODA!"
KARL
(Simultaneously.)
—What?
MAX
(Pause. Puts out his hand.)
Here's my hand.
KARL
I can't see—
MAX
I can't see your hand, Karl.
(Pause.)
You see my hand?
KARL
(Laughs.)
No.
MAX
(Calls.)
—Rhoda?
KARL
Rhoda's invisible.

MAX
(Pause.)
Touch something.

KARL
—What?

MAX
I give you permission.
(Pause. MAX puts out his hand.)
Karl touches MY hand. Karl opens his eyes.

KARL
(Eyes still shut, laughs.)
—She's still invisible.

MAX
Where's all the broken furniture?
(KARL opens his eyes. MAX is staring at his (MAX's) hand.)
Chairs!

KARL
Broken.

MAX
Tables!

KARL
(Pause. Then laughs.)
Broken.

MAX
(Low.)
Blame Rhoda.

KARL
(Pause.)
. . . Rhoda?

MAX
Rhoda's invisible.
(The door from RHODA's bedroom opens. Pause. Then a chair is thrown out, into the room. MAX laughs, drops his hand.)
She's still invisible.
(WALTER rolls back in through the window.)
A chair breaks and Walter rolls in through the window.

KARL
(Laughs.)
Max has wonderful reasons.

MAX
No.

KARL
Max's house, Max's furniture—

MAX
(Softly.)
No—

WALTER
(Pause. Laughs. From the floor, his face pointing to the carpet.)
I'm not intruding.

MAX
Nobody in-trudes.

KARL
(Laughs.)
Is that Walter—?
(A loud bell rings.)
Who's pushing Walter out of the apartment!
(The bell is still ringing.)

MAX
—Rhoda has a guardian angel.
(Pause, bell still rings.)
He's on the carpet!
(The bell stops. The door is opened, just a crack, by WALTER II.)

WALTER II
(Calls in.)
—Agatha's present!

MAX
(Laughs.)
Nobody can see Walter.

WALTER
(Laughs, from the floor.)
Walter wants to be invisible.

WALTER II
(Off.)
This Walter!

WALTER
—This Walter!

MAX
(Pause. Laughs.)
Which Walter—

WALTER II
—YES!

MAX
(Starts again.)
Both of them—

WALTER and WALTER II
YES!

MAX
(Pause. Laughs.)
Each ear is attached to different—

WALTER II
(Off.)
—Walter is standing in the hall.

MAX
Rhoda is—

WALTER
(Interrupting, to carpet.)
—What!

MAX
(Pause.)
Rhoda is kept; in a different room.
(WALTER suddenly starts rolling across the room, rolls himself to the front door and bangs against it. MAX laughs.)
Walter is definitely looking for Agatha.
(WALTER succeeds in banging the door shut. Pause. WALTER, MAX, KARL all laugh.)
WALTER II
(Off.)
—Agatha!
WALTER
(Still on the floor.)
Not here!
MAX
Now who broke the furniture, huh?
(Pause.)
Max, Walter—
WALTER II
(Off.)
—Agatha!
MAX
—Rhoda!
KARL
(Low, laughs.)
Rhoda was not a participant.
MAX
Rhoda is participating right this minute. I NAME Rhoda—it makes the chairs and tables start shaking. "Rhoda." A word acts like a knife, huh? Look at the woodwork.
KARL
(Laughs.)
No.
MAX
(Pause.)
Which person is guilty—
(WALTER II pushes open the door, but WALTER is ready, and rolls against it, they struggle, WALTER panting heavily.)
—Rhoda guilty and Max.
WALTER II
(Pushing.)
Where— is— Where-is-she?
MAX
WHO!
WALTER II
(Continuing, overlapping.)
—Open-it-please!
(All freeze. Then WALTER laughs.)

WALTER
I look at the carpet. My face gets closer and closer—
MAX
(Laughs.)
Walter has wings.
WALTER
(Pause. Laughs and asks through the crack.)
Can I show my hand through the door?
MAX
Yes.
WALTER II
(Thrusting his hand in through the crack, fingers spread wide apart.)
—Yes!
MAX
Count the fingers—
(Holding up his own hand, fingers spread.)
Five.
WALTER II
(Laughs.)
Close the door on my hand.
KARL
(Pause. Laughs.)
Nobody moves toward the door.
MAX
Close the door on Walter's wrist, flames shoot from the fingers.
WALTER
(Still on the floor.)
Five!
MAX
(Low, looking at his own hand.)
Cut the hand at the wrist . . . the hand flies—
(WALTER, on the floor has raised one arm, showing five fingers spread.)
WALTER
Five!
MAX
Why doesn't Karl move into the room between Walter One and Walter Two—
KARL
No.
MAX
—Placing a hand, Karl. In each other hand. Walter One, Walter Two.
KARL
I'm waiting for Rhoda.
MAX
Hand?

WALTER II

(Now raising a second arm, he's awkwardly on his back, two hands stuck up in the air.)

—Two hands, ten fingers!

MAX

(Laughs.)

Look at Rhoda's guardian angel, huh?

WALTER

(Waving his fingers.)

Look at his wings, huh?

(Now WALTER II acts as if the door has been slammed on his wrist. He cries out in pain, falls to the floor in slow agony.)

WALTER II

My hand! My hand!

MAX

(Wiggling fingers.)

Walter's wing!

WALTER

—Can my wings lift me, huh? LIFT ME UP, WINGS!

(WALTER II falls completely to the floor now, and the weight of his body pushes the door open and he slides into the room. Stillness.)

WALTER II

(On the floor.)

I love Agatha.

WALTER

(On the floor, arms still up.)

Max!-Max!-Max!

MAX

I love Rhoda.

(Pause. Laughs.)

Consider me Rhoda's guardian angel.

WALTER

Lookit my wings!

(Lights out, except a back light remains, illuminating the window and the outdoors. AGATHA steps into the light.)

AGATHA

(Pause. Laughs.)

Can I talk?

MAX

YES!

AGATHA

(Laughs.)

I talk. Max turns out the lights.

MAX, KARL

WALTER, WALTER II

Yes!

AGATHA

I can imagine my father. I can imagine my uncle—

WALTER

—Brother.

AGATHA

Do I have a guardian angel?

MAX

(Pause. Laughs.)

No.

AGATHA

Is my uncle—

MAX

No.

(Pause.)

Max doesn't love her.

AGATHA

—I have a guardian angel! ME!

(Puts out hand, spread fingers, toward the window.)

—Can I break this window with my foot?

MAX, KARL

WALTER, WALTER II

(As she manages to shift quickly so her foot is up next to the edge of the window at the frame, high, revealing inside of thigh and underpants.)

NO!

WEINSTEIN

(Off.)

Lemme in!

MAX

(Turns to door.)

Hey!

AGATHA

(Foot still up, trying to balance.)

Hey! Can I put my foot here?

WALTER

(Laughs.)

No! I'm talking—

(She takes her foot in her hands, moves it over to the window space, it falls down over the ledge into the room, her body swings up after it.)

AGATHA

Hey! I almost fell into the room.

(Pause. Laughs.)

My uncle pushed me!

WEINSTEIN

(Off.)

HEY!

(Both WALTER and WALTER II roll furiously to the window and roll

out, both breathing heavily.
AGATHA laughs as they push past
her and she gets pushed out also.
WEINSTEIN then enters.
WEINSTEIN takes a chair and
moves it to the wall.)

MAX

Hey!

WEINSTEIN

(Stops, sits on the chair. Laughs
once. Still dark except at window,
remember.)

We gotta have some ROOM in here.

MAX

(Laughs.)

Clear the room.

WEINSTEIN

Clear the floor.

(Pause.)

Look, can we—

MAX

What?

(WALTER II rolls in the window,
hangs inside with his arm still
clutching the sill, so he's suspended
under it, facing the wall below the
window.)

WEINSTEIN

Can I—

WALTER II

Please!

MAX

—Hey!

WEINSTEIN

(Pause.)

Let's use this room, huh?

WALTER II

Please, can I—

MAX

Hey!

WEINSTEIN

HEY!

WALTER II

I love Agatha.

WEINSTEIN

Let's use this room, huh?

(Pause. No one answers him.)

Hey? HEY!

MAX

(Calls.)

Rhoda?

(WALTER II rolls back out.)

BLACKOUT

3.

(The room is empty: Silence.
RHODA enters. She stops next to
the door. Looks at the room.)

RHODA

(Laughs once.)

Can I sit?

(WEINSTEIN opens the front door,
comes in and stops next to the
door.)

WEINSTEIN

Have a seat.

RHODA

(Laughs.)

Don't offer me a seat.

WEINSTEIN

Have a seat for the wedding, huh?

RHODA

(Calls.)

Max!

WEINSTEIN

(Pause.)

Lemme kick a chair toward you, darling.

RHODA

Don't.

WEINSTEIN

—What?

RHODA

Don't kick any chairs.

(Pause. Calls.)

Max?

WEINSTEIN

Don't kick any chairs!

(Pause.)

I'm not close enough.

RHODA

—What?

WEINSTEIN

(Laughs.)

Move a chair closer to me and I'll kick it.

RHODA

(Standing still, she awkwardly ex-
tends a foot.)

I have a foot.

(Pause. Then WEINSTEIN puts out
his foot in the same awkward way.)

Two feet.

WEINSTEIN

(Laughs.)

Count feet, divide by two.

RHODA
(Pause. Laughs.)
Keep my feet separate from Mr. Weinstein's feet.
WEINSTEIN
—I walk like I had seven!
(Pause.)
That makes Rhoda confused, huh?
RHODA
I see two.
WEINSTEIN
I got more than two.
(Pause. Then the foot stuck out awkwardly, he starts banging it awkwardly on the floor.)
1-2-3-4-5 . . .
RHODA
(Pause.)
Go on.
WEINSTEIN
(Suddenly doubles over his leg.)
I got a pain in my leg now!
RHODA
(Laughs.)
I'll try to imagine it.
WEINSTEIN
—Ohhhh, my leg!
(He keeps moaning, falls to the floor in agony, clutching his leg, rocking back and forth.)
My leg, my leg—
RHODA
(Laughs.)
My leg hurts.
WEINSTEIN
—Oh my leg!
RHODA
(Closing her eyes, turns away.)
I see the leg; one. The pain; two.
WEINSTEIN
Oh—ahh—ahh!
RHODA
—Make a fist!
(She makes a fist and holds it up. Eyes still closed. Laughs.)
One pain in my fist, one pain in my leg.
(WEINSTEIN stops moaning. She opens her eyes.)
What happened?
WEINSTEIN
(Low, looking at the floor.)
Gimme a bite, darling.
RHODA
Lookit my fist, mister . . .
(She thrusts it out, looks at it.)

WEINSTEIN
Wow. It glows in the dark. Ha. What kinda fist glows?
(RHODA, standing where she is, blocks the door. AGATHA, in bridal gown, comes to the door but can't pass. Stops, frozen mid-step, behind RHODA.)
AGATHA
Excuse me.
RHODA
(Staring at her fist, laughs.)
I think; Agatha—
WEINSTEIN
(Low.)
Thanks.
AGATHA
Excuse me—
WEINSTEIN
Thanks.
RHODA
(Pause. Laughs and brings her fist before her mouth.)
My fist is an electric microphone.
OVER LOUDSPEAKER
(Everything over the loudspeaker is distorted and accompanied by feedback.)
THANKS.
WEINSTEIN
(Shouts.)
—Let's have the—
RHODA
—WHAT?!
AGATHA
(Pause, still frozen mid-step.)
Let me in.
(RHODA turns, three distinct wooden steps. Extends her fist toward AGATHA's chest.)
WEINSTEIN
Let's have the wedding.
AGATHA
(Laughs.)
I'm locked out.
WEINSTEIN
What?
AGATHA
(Laughs.)
Rhoda's fist.
LOUDSPEAKER
THANKS.
RHODA
(Pause. Laughs.)
Push it.

WEINSTEIN
Hey! She opened her—
RHODA
—What?
AGATHA
Eyes.
WEINSTEIN
—Eyes!
(Pause.)
Help me up.
RHODA
No.
(Pause.)
Two fists. One in my fist. One in my arm.
AGATHA
(Laughs.)
One in my FEET.
(She steps with each count, but is held in place by RHODA's outstretched fist. Like treading water.)
1-2-3-4-5-6-
RHODA
(Laughs over.)
—Nobody's moving.
AGATHA
—7-8-9-10.
RHODA
(Pause. Low.)
Agatha. Does Agatha have fists.
LOUDSPEAKER
Thanks.
RHODA
We both have the same fist.
WEINSTEIN
Help me up!
RHODA
(Low, quickly.)
Agatha can't move, her uncle can't, her uncle can, can Rhoda—
AGATHA
—What?
WEINSTEIN
I wanna thank you—
LOUDSPEAKER
THANKS.
WEINSTEIN
Look. For the use of this—
RHODA
(Overlapping his last sentence.)
—For the use of this wedding?
WEINSTEIN
This wonderful room. This wonderful place; this wonderful floor, this wonderful apartment—

RHODA
(Laughs.)
—Who's getting married?
WEINSTEIN
(Continues.)
—This wonderful carpet! HELP!
RHODA
WHO!
AGATHA
(Backing into the bedroom, vanishing. Counting her steps long after she disappears.)
1-2-3-4-5-6-7-8-9-10.
(As soon as she disappears, WALTER II comes in the front door.)
WALTER II
(As we still hear counting.)
Where's Agatha?
RHODA
(Her back to him.)
WHO!
(Long pause. Nobody moves.)
WEINSTEIN
Help me up.
WALTER II
(Overlaps, laughs.)
—Somebody's talking.
(Pause.)
I should have looked; to see who before I said it.
RHODA
(Laughs.)
I shouldn't be turning my back on Walter.
WEINSTEIN
Help me up.
WALTER II
I want to lift him off the floor because he's my father-in-law.
(Laughs.)
Not yet—
WEINSTEIN
Help me.
WALTER II
(To RHODA.)
—Help me?
RHODA
(Laughs.)
Make a fist.
WALTER
(Laughs.)
Two fists.

RHODA
I'm trying to face you, holding up two fists.
(She is lifting two tight fists.)

WALTER II
(Pause.)
You didn't turn.

RHODA
I don't make any fists—

WALTER
—YES!

RHODA
(Pause. Laughs.)
My fists are invisible.
(Pause. Tremendous tension in her fists, then she opens her hands and drops them. She and WALTER II abruptly exit, WEINSTEIN following them quickly on all fours. They are immediately followed by MAX and AGATHA entering from opposite doors and going to the center of the room.)

LOUDSPEAKER
Kiss the bride.

MAX
(Overlapping, laughs.)
What time is it.

AGATHA
Yes!
(Pause. Laughs.)
What time is it.

MAX
Watch.
(Pause. Low.)
Watch me.
(They both take steps, giant steps backwards toward their respective doors. Just before exiting they stop.)
Where's the bride.

LOUDSPEAKER
(Overlapping a word behind.)
—Where's the bride.
(WALTER II appears behind AGATHA, grabs her from behind and pulls her off, as WEINSTEIN re-enters on all fours and returns to his spot.)

WEINSTEIN
Help me up.
(Pause. The end of a rope falls to the floor, the other end invisible, tied above somewhere.)
Hey! Somebody on my side, huh?

MAX
Yes.

WEINSTEIN
(Pause.)
Put the rope—

MAX
(Laughs.)
Rope?

WEINSTEIN
(Pause.)
Look for the rope.

MAX
(MAX puts out his hands, as if to receive.)
Put a rope in my hands.

WEINSTEIN
I can't.
(Pause.)
Look for the rope.

MAX
(Spreads his feet, bracing himself.)
I'm ready.

WEINSTEIN
(Looks up, quizzically.)
Hey!

MAX
(Laughs.)
Kiss the bride, huh?

WEINSTEIN
Look for the rope.
(WALTER II appears. Stops inside the door. Pause.)

WALTER II
Agatha's waiting.

MAX
I'm ready.

WALTER II
—What?
(Pause. Laughs.)
Let's do it before—

MAX
(Interrupting.)
—What? What?

WALTER
(Continuing over.)
—Agatha changes her mind.
(Pause. He calls.)
Marry me!

AGATHA
(Off.)
Yes.

MAX
Walter should be kneeling.
WEINSTEIN
(Laughs.)
I'm kneeling.
WALTER II
(Laughs.)
I can't kneel.
(Pause.)
My knees are locked tight.
MAX
(Pause. Laughs.)
Kneel.
WEINSTEIN
(As WALTER II eases himself to the floor, keeping his knees locked, supporting himself on the doorknob behind him.)
Look for the rope!
MAX
I can't; my eyes glow—
WEINSTEIN
—Look up, god damnit!
MAX
My neck is stiff—
WALTER II
—MY neck is stiff.
WEINSTEIN
Walk toward me.
MAX
—Walk?
WEINSTEIN
WALK!
(Pause. No movement.)
He walks, he finds the rope hanging from the goddamn ceiling—
MAX
Come to me, rope!
(Pause. Laughs.)
Nobody answers.
WALTER II
(From the floor.)
Marry me!
WEINSTEIN
Yes!
(Pause.)
Yes. Yes. Yes. Yes.
(MAX takes one step.)
Yes, yes, yes, yes.
MAX
(Low.)
There it is.
WEINSTEIN
(Pause.)
What.

MAX
(Hands still out.)
I have the rope in my two hands. Do I still see the rope? Yes.
WEINSTEIN
Put it around my shoulders.
MAX
Yes.
(Pause.)
I make my head imitate my eyes.
(Shifts his empty hands from the horizontal "receiving" to the "outstretched.")
WEINSTEIN
—Yes!
WALTER II
(Laughs.)
My body is imitating me.
(MAX drops his rigidity, goes and takes the rope and ties it around WEINSTEIN's shoulders. At the same time AGATHA appears and unsuccessfully struggles with WALTER II, trying to lift him up to his feet.)
WALTER II
(Laughs.)
I have a prediction.
(Later.)
Agatha's dress—
MAX
(Turns away from WEINSTEIN.)
—What?
AGATHA
(Stops, working on WALTER. Pause.)
I tore it.
(Pause.)
I tore it.
LOUDSPEAKER
Kiss the bride.
(Wherever his head is, WALTER starts kissing the adjacent part of AGATHA.)
Kiss the bride.
(Pause. WALTER stops kissing, falls back to the ground. MAX is facing them.)
AGATHA
Is my dress torn.
MAX
Yes.
AGATHA
(Laughs.)
My dress is torn. Should I look at it or look at it in a mirror.

LOUDSPEAKER
Kiss the bride.

WEINSTEIN
(Over.)
Kiss the bride, fella.
(Pause. Then RHODA pushes out the door, through the barrier that is AGATHA and WALTER II. She stands looking as MAX finishes tying up WEINSTEIN. AGATHA goes out. The rope starts to pull and WEINSTEIN is lifted to a standing position, at which point AGATHA returns with flowers. WEINSTEIN hangs there. MAX goes and leans against a side wall. Pause.)

LOUDSPEAKER
Kiss the bride.

MAX
(Pause.)
Agatha has flowers. I count them. 1-2-3-4-5-

LOUDSPEAKER
Kiss the bride.

WEINSTEIN
(Laughs.)
I'm standing.

MAX
-6-7-8-(etc.).
(Pause.)
Is Agatha's uncle standing or hanging.

AGATHA
(Laughs.)
Maybe I'll hide my face in the flowers.

LOUDSPEAKER
(As she smells them.)
Kiss the bride.

AGATHA
(Face in the flowers.)
I can't smell them.

WALTER II
(Pause.)
I can't smell them.

AGATHA
(Face still hidden: laughs.)
Now I can smell them.
(WEINSTEIN closes his eyes and, hanging, goes to sleep.)
I ought to drop them.

MAX
No—

AGATHA
If I drop my flowers on Walter's face—

WALTER
(Interrupting, from the floor, laughing.)
I don't have a face.

AGATHA
(Extending the flowers, holding them over him.)
—Here's a face.

MAX
—Eyes, nose, teeth, lips, cheeks—
(AGATHA drops them as MAX continues, as they fall she says
"Excuse me"
over MAX's reciting. While WALTER puts his face in the flowers and vibrates his face in them.)
—Hair, mouth, nostrils, chin, mouth, nose, eyes.

LOUDSPEAKER
Kiss the bride.

MAX
One thing I like about Walter, he has a beautiful face.
(As he says this, RHODA turns and goes to AGATHA, puts her arms around her quickly and bends her back in a passionate kiss.)
Walter and I imitate each other.
(The front door opens, revealing WALTER I, who now has a pair of gigantic wooden wings, strapped onto his back, angel fashion. He stands—)
He pushes his face into the flowers and I push my face into the wall.

WALTER II
(Face still in the flowers.)
Help me up!
(AGATHA and RHODA now are standing facing each other, hands on each other's arms.)

WALTER I
WEDDING! Huh?

WALTER II
(Laughs, face in flowers.)
—Where's the wedding!

WALTER I
I can't get in—
(He thrusts his body forward, banging the wings with a loud smack against the doorposts.)
—My wings!
(As he bangs his wings a few more times to demonstrate, AGATHA

*and RHODA have a pushing match,
RHODA fairly quickly managing to
push AGATHA into the bedroom.
Before they are out of the room
even, MAX, face still to the wall.)*

MAX

Turn sideways.

WEINSTEIN

*(Moans in his sleep. WALTER I
turns sideways and slips into the
room, crosses toward the window.)*

RHODA

(Off.)

I'm winning!

WALTER I

*(Reaching the window, the light
outside goes out.)*

Hey! It's dark out here—

MAX

(Laughs.)

I'm invisible.

WALTER I

You are not invisible.

MAX

Walter is invisible.

WALTER II

Yes.

WALTER I

(Pause.)

I'm—

MAX

—Are you afraid of the dark, Walter?

WALTER I

(Pause, frowns.)

No. Not me.

(Pause, laughs.)

It's a problem to get out of a tiny window
like this.

MAX

Let it eat you.

WALTER I

(Pause, laughs.)

That's not serious.

(Pause.)

These wings—

WALTER II

YES!

MAX

They make it a problem.

(WALTER I frowns. Turns and exits.)

AGATHA

(Off.)

I can't see!

WALTER II

Where's Agatha.

MAX

In the closet.

WALTER II

(Pause, laughs from floor.)

Are we married, huh?

MAX

Open the closet door, lookit Agatha.

(Pause, laughs.)

Does that mean Agatha in the closet or
Agatha not in the closet.

WALTER II

I can't.

MAX

—What?

WALTER II

I'm on the floor.

MAX

Lookit Walter.

WALTER II

Yes!

MAX

He's headless.

WALTER II

—Flowers.

MAX

Flowers for a head.

WALTER II

Listen.

(Pause.)

I have two heads.

MAX

(Low, head still to wall.)

Hey Walter, stand up and show me two
heads at once.

WALTER II

(Pause.)

No.

MAX

(Pause.)

Get all the extra girls outa my house, huh?

WALTER II

(Laughs.)

No.

MAX

(Pause.)

How many extra girls in my house.

WALTER

Seven!

MAX

(Pause, calls.)

Hey!

RHODA and AGATHA
(Off.)
—HEY!

(Pause. MAX covers his eyes with one hand, puts out the other to feel his way as the lights dim, and he starts to cross the room to the bedroom door.)

WALTER II
Don't step on me.

(MAX stops. Pause, WALTER II shouts.)
Don't step on my two heads, Max!

(MAX crosses and exits into the bedroom. Pause. Then he comes out, dragging AGATHA.)
Don't step on my heads. Don't step on me, huh?

(MAX drags AGATHA to the closet. She doesn't resist, but goes totally limp. RHODA appears and watches, puffing a cigarette. She is standing over WALTER II.)
Step on my arms if you have to, but don't step on my hands. On the other hand, step on my legs if you must, huh? Step on my knees if you must, huh? Listen, step on my legs but don't blow a lotta that smoke in my direction.

RHODA
(Low.)
Everybody watch out for the flowers.

(AGATHA now struggles with MAX as he would shove her into the closet. It takes some time, but he finally gets her in.)

WEINSTEIN
(Wakes up with a start.)
I woke up.

(MAX is exhausted, leans against the door to catch his breath. Pause.)

WALTER II
Watch that smoke, everybody.
(Pause.)

MAX
(After a long time. Laughs.)
Everybody very happy about what I just did, huh?

(Three seconds more.)

BLACKOUT

4.

(Night: MAX stands in front of the closet. Back to door. One hand placed upon the closet door, the back of it against the wood.)

MAX
(Pause. Laughs.)
Unanswerable questions: is my hand burning. Is the door burning.
(Pause.)
My hand, glued to the door.

(The front door swings open to reveal WALTER I in his wings. He comes forward and smacks the wings against the frame. MAX laughs.)
Nailed!

WALTER I
Help me!
(Pause, laughs.)
Max—

MAX
Nailed by the hand.

WALTER I
I can't move.

MAX
Yes.

WALTER I
(Pause, laughs.)
Nailed.

MAX
Yes.

WALTER I
To the door.

(KARL appears in the window at rear, he also has a pair of wooden wings. He steps forward as if to thrust the top of his body through the window, and banging therefore, his wings on the sides of the window frame.)

KARL
Help me!

MAX
YES!

KARL
(Pause.)
I can't move.

MAX
Max on fire, Walter and Karl, frozen stiff.

WALTER I
No.

MAX
—Look at me.
(Pause. No one moves.)
Right. Walter's eyes put a shell over my body.

KARL
(Puts out a hand.)
My shell is HOT.

MAX
(Low, laughs.)
My shell is ice cold.
(Pause.)
My HAND is burning.

WALTER I
(Low.)
My shell is invisible.

MAX
(Pause.)
Can anybody hear me?

KARL
(Laughs.)
Thank God—

MAX
—What?

KARL
Thank God I can hear everything through my shell. Clear as a bell.

WALTER
(Laughs.)
I too. Clear as a bell. Through the shell.
(Pause. MAX turns so he faces the door. Keeping the back of the one hand on the door, he now places the second hand, back to door. Facing the door now, with the back of both hands against the door, he throws back his head.)

MAX
I still hear!

WALTER I
Hey, Max—

MAX
Yes!

WALTER I
Pull me into the room, huh?

MAX
What.

WALTER I
(Puts out his hands to be pulled.)
Pull me!

MAX
(Pause.)
My hands are—

WALTER I
—I'm stuck.

MAX
(Laughs.)
Can't you SEE?

WALTER I
(Pause. Hands still out.)
I see: every place at once.

KARL
Max!

WALTER I
(Laughs.)
Thanks to my wings, maybe.

KARL
Max!

WALTER I
The more I hear that name—

MAX
"Max!"

WALTER I
(Continuing over.)
—The more I'm capable of imagining an invisible person.
(Pause.)
"Max."—Now I'm seeing only his extremities.

KARL
(Putting his hands out also.)
Pull me into the room.

WALTER I
Hands and feet.

MAX
(Laughs.)
Wings.

KARL
Please!

WALTER I
Max wishes he had wings.

KARL
Please—
(He bangs forward, banging his wings against the window frame.)
Pull my wings forward.

MAX
(Low, laughs.)
Touch the magic spots on my shoulders.
(Pause.)
Touch them.

KARL
(Laughs.)
Yes.

WALTER I
(Pause. Ecstatic.)
Feel it!

MAX
Yes.

KARL
(Laughs.)
Max's shoulders: like ice.

MAX
(Laughs.)
Fire at one end of my arms.

KARL
Ice!

MAX
Ice at the roots: fire in the hands. The arms between—

WALTER I
(Laughs.)
Miles of arms.

MAX
Light!

KARL
Wings!

WALTER I
Rays of light . . . dotted lines between the three of us.

MAX
(Laughs.)
Invisible three, huh?
(Pause.)
Aren't we invisible?

WALTER
We can't move.

MAX
Not a ONE of us?
(Whistling from the closet. Lights dim, and bright light comes from the cracks around the side of the closet door.)
(KARL and WALTER clack their wings against the portals.)
Amazing? Light coming through the door?
(Laughs.)
I could read a newspaper.
(Pause.)

WALTER I
(Laughs.)
Agatha turns on a light, huh?

MAX
Who?

WALTER
Max is holding the door shut—

KARL
Max.

WALTER I
(Pause.)
Hold it!

MAX
(Laughs.)
I can't see.

WALTER I
We're helping.

KARL
My arms ache more than my wings.

MAX
(Laughs.)
Max holding the door, but he can't keep out the light.

WALTER I
(Low.)
Max, Karl, Walter—

KARL and MAX
Yes!

WALTER I
(Continues.)
—We open our mouths—the light pours in and vanishes.

MAX
(Pause. Laughs.)
Stomachs full of light.

KARL
Yes.

(The lights come up. All have mouths wide open, MAX looking at the ceiling. KARL's arms still out to let him be pulled into the room, as the door closes on WALTER I, laughs.)
My arms don't hurt.

WALTER I
(Off.)
Look how I'm shining!

MAX
(Lowering his head to look at the closet.)
It's still here.

KARL
—What?

MAX
This door.

KARL
—What?

MAX
What I wish. I thump on it with my fists.
(WALTER off, thumps.)
Bravo Walter, full use of the hands restored.

KARL
Mine also.

MAX
Mine also.

KARL
—What?

MAX
(Laughs.)
I'm thumping.

WALTER
(Off.)
I'm shining!

MAX
(Low.)
Place all chairs in a circle.

KARL
—What?

WALTER I
(Off.)
Hey Max!

MAX
(Pause.)
HEY!

WALTER I
(Off.)
I'm shining through my shell!
(Pause.)
See the door shining?

MAX
Yes.

KARL
See me shining?
(Pause.)
Max?

MAX
Move all chairs, please.

KARL
Max?

MAX
Go to work. Angels.

KARL
(Laughs.)
I can't move.
(Pause.)
Max, take me as I AM!

MAX
(Overlapping this last.)
Surround me, surround me.

KARL
—What?
(Pause. Laughs and lowers arms.)
Where's Rhoda.

MAX
Asleep.

KARL
(Laughs, puts one leg in through
the window.)
I'd like to test that.

MAX
Move the chairs; two angels.

KARL
—I can't move.

MAX
What parts of angels are still pliable?

KARL
I can't.

MAX
—What?

KARL
(Pause. Laughs.)
Help me into the room.

MAX
(Pause.)
Rhoda's guardian angel. Your eyes are in-
visible.

KARL
(Laughs.)
My shell—

MAX
—Find your eyes.

KARL
(Pause.)
How?

MAX
Point to your eyes with two fingers.

KARL
(Pause. Brings his second leg into
the room, so only his wide wings
catch outside, leaving him awkwardly leaning backwards, wings
outside lower half of body inside.)
I'm in the room.

MAX
All?

KARL
Look!

MAX
(Pause.)
Point to your eyes.

KARL
(Pause. Each index finger points to
an eye.)
Look.

MAX
Look.

(MAX slides his hands on the door,
keeping the back of the hand
against the door, he makes the
fingers point down. Then the front
door re-opens and WALTER II is
seen.)

WALTER II
Is Max really singing?

MAX
(Overlapping.)
What? Am I what?

KARL
Is Max singing?
(Pause. Laughs.)

Look, my shell has two openings.
(His hands still at eyes.)

MAX

(Laughs.)

My shell has seventeen openings.

WALTER II

Let me help by re-arranging the furniture.

MAX

Oh?

(WALTER II picks up a chair and carries it out.)

KARL

No place to sit.

MAX

Empty the room.

(Pause.)

All that remains—

(Bedroom door flies open, a chair slides across the room and out the door.)

—Doors, walls, floor, transparent windows.

KARL

Yes.

MAX

—Ceilings.

KARL

Light.

MAX

(Pause.)

I pull my hands away from the door.
(Pause.)

They move like shadows.

(He brings his hands together on the door. Then pulls them off, toward his face. The fingers fan like a mask in front of his face and he peers out through them.)

It doesn't move, huh?

WEINSTEIN

(Off.)

HEY!

MAX

Hey!

KARL

Help me out.

MAX

Where is she?

WEINSTEIN

(Off.)

HEY!

(Another chair slides out the door.)

KARL

(Laughs.)

Help me out the window.

(Pause.)

WEINSTEIN

(Off.)

HEY!

KARL

(Laughs.)

My wings are still outside.

MAX

That's because—wings.

KARL

I'm sitting on the windowsill.

(Pause. He laughs.)

I don't want to fall backward.

MAX

(Turns his head toward KARL, fingers still before eyes.)

Guard it.

KARL

What?

MAX

Guard it.

KARL

I can't see you.

MAX

I count to three—

KARL

(Laughs.)

My legs ache.

(Sits on the windowsill.)

MAX

—We uncover our eyes.

KARL

No—

MAX

One— Two—

KARL

—My eyes aren't covered.

MAX

Three!

(Pause. Low.)

Karl, fold up your—

KARL

—What?

MAX

—Wings. Guard the window.

(Pause. Laughs.)

Guard Rhoda.

(Pause.)

How many times has Rhoda fallen. Out of the window.

KARL

(Pause. Low.)

She's my own—

MAX

—What?

KARL

—Sister.

(Pause.)

Seven.

MAX

Seven!

KARL

When it rains.

MAX

What?

KARL

Seven times when it rains.

MAX

Guard it.

KARL

Rhoda—attracted by lightning.

MAX

(Low.)

Agatha.

KARL

—What?

(Pause, laughs.)

Who guards—

MAX

—Karl.

KARL

No. Who is guarded.

MAX

Rhoda.

KARL

Sisters.

(Pause. Laughs.)

Which one of us is speaking.

MAX

Both.

KARL

(Pause, laughs.)

Which one of us is concentrating harder.

MAX

Which one of us—

(Pause.)

Balanced.

KARL

Yes.

MAX

Are we keeping our balance?

(KARL falls backward out the window, so all we see are his legs waving in the window. At the same moment, the closet door opens, and bangs to a stop after six inches as it hits MAX's foot. AGATHA's hand appears around the edge of the door. The hand alone, it grips the edge of the door.)

Which really happened.

AGATHA

(Off.)

—What?

MAX

Karl falls out the window—

AGATHA

—YES!

MAX

(Pause.)

Somebody has—

WEINSTEIN

(Off.)

HEY!

MAX

The door has—

WEINSTEIN

(Off.)

HEY!

MAX

(Pause. Then he puts his hands back on the door and laughs.)

Three hands on one door.

KARL

(Only feet showing.)

My feet hurt!

WEINSTEIN

(Off.)

HEY!

MAX

(Pause.)

I look through a microscope, huh? Three hands at once: visible.

AGATHA

(Off.)

Is it raining?

MAX

Visible.

AGATHA

(Off. Pause, laughs.)

Is it day or night.

MAX

(Overlapping.)

—An angel is in the window: look.

AGATHA

(Off. Pause, laughs.)

Night.

MAX

It's so dark, all you can see: Karl's feet.

AGATHA

(Off. Simultaneously.)

I can't see!

KARL
My feet!

MAX
No wings on his feet, huh?

(RHODA comes and stands in the door from the bedroom.)

WEINSTEIN
(Off.)
HEY!

MAX
(Pause. Laughs.)
Rhoda's asleep. I'm guarding the door.

RHODA
Close it.

MAX
Yes.

RHODA
My— feet—

MAX
Close it.

(As RHODA puts her arms up as if sleepwalking.)

RHODA
Yes.

AGATHA
(Off.)
Four a.m. I'm not sleeping. 1-2-3-4.

MAX
(Simultaneously.)
I count to ten—

(Simultaneously, RHODA walks like a sleepwalker to the front door, and counts her steps. "One, two," etc.)

Then I close the door.

(Laughs.)
Something might break. 1,2,3,4,5,6,7,8,9,10.

RHODA
(Over, at the door, pushing against the shut door.)
—I'm sleeping.

MAX
(Pushing against his own door.)
Max reaches ten; pushes; can't close it. Breathes.

AGATHA
(Off.)
I'm dreaming.

RHODA
(Low, pushing against the door.)
Help.

MAX
(Pushing against the door.)
Help.

(Pause, laughs.)
I'm dizzy. I push harder still and for one or two seconds, my head clears.

KARL and RHODA
Help!

AGATHA
(Off.)
People are—

MAX
—My head's spinning. I push harder.

KARL
Help!

RHODA
(Simultaneous with KARL.)
Where's my brother I want help from my brother.

MAX
My head's spinning so I close my eyes.

AGATHA
(Off.)
—I push harder and harder.

RHODA
(Simultaneous with AGATHA.)
Where's my brother, I want help from my brother.

KARL
HELP!

AGATHA
(Off.)
—I hear something FUNNY!

(Silence. Hear MAX panting.)

KARL
(Pause.)
HELP!

RHODA
(Relaxes, stops pushing and laughs.)
I must be sleeping.

(MAX falls wearily against the door.)

AGATHA
—Help.

RHODA
—Is it raining?

(Pause.)
Max?

KARL
Help.

RHODA
(Pause. Laughs.)
I have to know if it's raining.

(Pause. Laughs. She doesn't turn from the door, but takes two steps backwards, hands out behind her, back to window.)

Lemme feel my way to the window, huh?

(Two steps, stops and laughs.)
I don't wanna break anything.
> *(AGATHA steps out through the door-crack. Pause. Then she suddenly exits quickly through the front door, leaving it open. RHODA moves, backwards, to the window.)*

Lemme see if it's raining.
> ### KARL and MAX
Help.
> ### RHODA
> *(Laughs.)*
—Help. I balance myself at the edge of the window.
> *(AGATHA throws a chair into the room, then her bouquet.)*

Why—
> ### MAX
> *(Low.)*
—Help.
> ### RHODA
—Back facing the window.
> ### MAX
Rhoda looks at the sky exclusively. Therefore—
> ### KARL
Help.
> ### MAX
Back to the window.
> ### RHODA
—Back to the window. Arch—
> ### MAX
Arch the back. The eyes point to the sky—
> ### WEINSTEIN
> *(Off.)*
Hey!
> ### AGATHA
> *(Still lingering outside the door.)*
I should be sleeping!
> ### WALTER I and WALTER II
> *(Off, as RHODA arches her back and sticks her torso out the window, looking up.)*
1-2-3-4—
> ### RHODA
> *(Laughs.)*
The rain is falling into my eyes.
> ### MAX
> *(Low.)*
Guard Rhoda.
> *(Pause. Laughs.)*
It's raining.
> *(RHODA falls backwards out the window. Pause. MAX pushes the closet door shut. Pause. Laughs.)*

Somebody left the—
> ### RHODA
> *(Only her feet showing, amidst KARL's feet.)*
—What!
> ### MAX
—Closet door open.
> *(Pause. He opens it again, now all the way. Looks into the closet.)*
I'm vanishing into it.
> ### RHODA
Help.
> ### MAX
> *(Pause, laughs.)*
The closet shuts my eyes.
> *(Pause.)*
My face is warm.
> ### RHODA and KARL
Help!
> *(Pause.)*
> ### RHODA
> *(Laughs.)*
I'm floating.

BLACKOUT

5.

> *(MAX alone in the center of the room. He is now tied up, a rope around his shoulders lifting him toward the ceiling, until only his extended toes manage to touch the carpet.)*
> ### MAX
> *(Pause.)*
What can I move?
> *(Pause. Laughs.)*
Which parts of my body are still mobile?
> *(The door opens. WALTER I comes forward. His wings bang clank! against the portals, stopping him.)*
> ### WALTER I
Hey!
> ### MAX
> *(Pause, laughs.)*
I can't even shut the window.
> ### WALTER I
> *(Low.)*
You want me to shut the window?
> ### MAX
Yes.

WALTER I

Yes.

(He extends one arm, at the same time turning away his head, closing his eyes.)

MAX

Which is the source of my air.

WALTER

Max.

MAX

YES.

WALTER

(Pause, feeling about with his arm.)

I can't—

MAX

—What?

WALTER

(Pause.)

How the hell can I get to the window!

WEINSTEIN

(Off, over loudspeaker.)

Hey!

(AGATHA walks by the window.)

MAX

The air I breathe—

WALTER I

It takes a long time—

MAX

—What?

WALTER

(Pause, laughs.)

What am I doing?

MAX

Answer me—

WALTER

—What?

MAX

(Pause.)

Walter. Reaching to the window.

WALTER

(Low.)

How long it takes my arm, huh?

MAX

Not enough arms. Walter.

WALTER

How SLOW, huh?

MAX

(Laughs.)

Yes. I turn my head back and forth between the window—

WEINSTEIN

(Loudspeaker.)

—Open.

MAX

And the door.

WEINSTEIN

(Loudspeaker.)

—Open.

MAX

(As AGATHA goes back past the window.)

—HEY!

WALTER I

(Shouts.)

My arm! Longer or not longer!

MAX

Yes.

WALTER I

(Pause.)

What? Max's opinion—

MAX

Yes.

WALTER I

Am I trying?

(Suddenly a rock is thrown through the window.)

MAX

(Pause, laughs.)

What is my source of air.

(Pause.)

The open window.

WALTER I

Yes.

MAX

The open door.

WALTER I

(Pause.)

Let's pick it up.

MAX

—What?

WALTER I

I'm reaching it.

(Pause. Laughs.)

My arm isn't long enough.

MAX

Close it.

WALTER I

What?

MAX

Close it.

WALTER I

—A rock came through the window.

MAX

Yes.

WALTER I

(Pause.)

Pick it up.

MAX

(Laughs.)

I can't reach it.

(Pause. Laughs.)
I'm afraid to touch it.
(Pause. Laughs.)
I'm afraid of an explosion.
                    WALTER I
           (Laughs, overlapping.)
I can't reach it!
           (Pause.)
Hey! Why isn't my arm longer?
                    MAX
Help!
           (Pause.)
Somebody get the rock.
                    WALTER I
           (Calls.)
Hey! We gotta rock lying on the floor!
           (Pause.)
Hey somebody!
                    MAX
           (Over.)
—Somebody!
                    WALTER I
           (Pause.)
I can't reach the rock.
                    MAX
           (Laughs.)
I can't reach it.
           (Pause. Laughs.)
Who left the window open?
                    WALTER I
           (Dropping his arm finally.)
I didn't come through the window.
                    MAX
Yes.
                    WALTER I
—Yes!
           (Pause.)
I can't get in through the door.
                    MAX
           (Overlapping.)
—I can't even MOVE.
           (Pause. Calls.)
Somebody come move the rock!
           (Pause.)
Why did Walter close his eyes?
                    WALTER I
No.
           (Pause.)
My eyes—
                    MAX
Yes, yes—
                    WALTER I
—Aren't closed really.

                    MAX
           (Pause. WALTER opens his eyes.)
Now they're open.
                    WALTER I
I'm sorry I can't help.
                    MAX
Yes.
           (Pause. Laughs.)
Where's Rhoda?
                    WALTER I
           (Laughs.)
She fell out the window.
                    MAX
Yes.
           (Pause.)
Help me.
                    WALTER I
Jesus, Max. Tell me what to DO.
           *(The lights suddenly cut down to a
           spot on MAX's face, plus consid-
           erable spill.)*
                    MAX
There's a mysterious rock, huh?
                    WALTER I
Yes!
                    MAX
           (Pause.)
My feet—
                    WALTER I
           (Laughs.)
—My feet hurt.
                    MAX
           (Continuing.)
—Are off the ground.
                    WALTER
           (Pause. Laughs.)
**My shoulders hurt. My shoulders hurt worse
than my feet.**
                    MAX
Mine too.
           *(Pause. The sound of wind. MAX
           laughs.)*
MY shoulders hurt.
                    WALTER
           (Pause. Low.)
Your face is radiant, Max.
                    MAX
           (Low.)
My shoulders hurt, and I'm dizzy.
                    WALTER
           (Pause.)
You look happy.
                    MAX
Yes.

(Pause, laughs.)
The window's open. I feel a draft.
(Pause.)
Hey!

WALTER
(Laughs.)
That's how I—

MAX
—What?

WALTER
(Pause.)
That's how I always pictured you.
(Pause. He turns and goes.)

MAX
Hey!
(Pause.)
Somebody shut the door!
(Pause. Somebody throws a second, larger rock, in through the window. Pause. MAX laughs.)
I can't reach it.
(Pause. Laughs.)
A big rock came in the window.
(Pause.)

BLACKOUT

TOTAL RECALL

SOPHIA=(WISDOM): Part 2

1.

(BEN sits at a table. The cabinet rear opens. SOPHIA revealed standing inside, holding a lamp. HANNAH comes halfway through a door. Pause.)
HANNAH
I came in at the wrong moment.
(Pause. Light gets brighter.)

2.

(BEN sits. Cabinet opens. SOPHIA gone. Her lamp just hangs where she would have been holding it. Pause. It gets brighter.)

3.

(Empty stage. Cabinet opens. It's empty and the light hangs there. It gets brighter.)

4.

(Empty stage. HANNAH comes through the door, carrying a lamp. She covers her eyes with her free hand and slowly crosses the stage.)

5.

(BEN is sitting alone. Pause. Then HANNAH comes through the door with her lamp and her eyes uncovered. She stops just inside the door. Pause. She faints and falls to the floor.)

6.

(BEN at table. His hands on the table, he spreads his fingers. The

The title photograph and all photographs accompanying this text by Babette Mangolte.

cabinet opens, SOPHIA holding her
lamp.)

BEN

I don't know who I believe.
(Pause.)
The Gods speak to me but I don't know if
I believe them.

Legend: WHAT GODS.

(BEN falls asleep. SOPHIA leaves
her cabinet and exits as 30's jazz
begins and plays to the end on the
motionless stage.)

7.

(BEN crosses and opens the window. A light behind the window
becomes very bright.)

BEN

Nothing seems different this morning. I sit
down to breakfast. I have coffee and rolls.
Then I put on my coat and go out into the
street.
(Pause.)
Nothing seems different.
(Pause. Crew brings on coat and
hat, dresses BEN and exits. Pause.
Then he steps through the window.
Pause.)
Standing out here is a revelation.
(Pause.)
When I have a revelation I can't move and
I find everything very unusual.
(Pause.)
I feel like I'm standing in the ocean with
the water halfway up, to my waist.
(Pause. Cabinet opens, SOPHIA
there.)
I can imagine there are lots of things hap-
pening I can't see. Some of them are be-
hind my back and some of them are in the
center of the light.
(Pause.)
I've been out here long enough, so I think
I should go backwards through the window
and into the room again.
(Pause.)
That's complicated.
(Pause.)

That shouldn't be complicated but it's com-
plicated.
(Pause.)
If I stand here a long time birds will come
and sit on my shoulders.
(Pause.)
I wish I had somebody to talk to. Wrong.
That would spoil everything.
(Pause.)
I think somebody is looking at me.
(Pause. Lights go out.)

8.

(Lights up. BEN sits, a lamp on his
table. LEO sits across the table from
BEN.)

LEO

What happened when Ben went out this
morning.

BEN

Not much.

LEO

(Pause.)
How come he went out through the window instead of through the door.

BEN

Ben will have to answer that for himself.
(Pause.)
I never answer for Ben, I let him do his own
talking.

LEO

I see.

BEN

(Pause.)
Could I ask you a question.

LEO

Why not forget the whole thing.

BEN

First rate.

LEO

(Pause.)
What.

BEN

First rate.

LEO

(Pause.)
I'd like to see you show me exactly what
happened.

BEN

What's Leo investigating.
(Pause.)
Are we related.

LEO
I think my sister is married to you.
(Pause.)
I better have a good enough memory for both of us, huh.

BEN
I had a good memory once.
(Pause.)
First rate.

LEO
I never doubted it for a minute.

BEN
Are you pretending to be somebody I remember.

LEO
I think you remember.

BEN
(Pause.)
Leo.

LEO
That's a good

BEN
What

LEO
Guess.
(Pause.)
Now let's see exactly what happened.

BEN
I can't show you exactly.

LEO
I'm disappointed.
(Pause.)
I don't mean I'm disappointed in Ben, I mean I'm really disappointed.
(Cabinet opens, SOPHIA there. Loud noise. Then silence.)

BEN
Well, time for bed.

LEO
—I wanted to see exactly what happened.

BEN
(Pause.)
I thought you said you wanted to see exactly what happened.
(Pause. LEO scratches his face. He turns away from BEN, frowning, and faces forward and keeps scratching.)
Something on your face.
(He keeps scratching.)
That doesn't look real to me.
(Pause. Continues.)

What I'm doing looks more real than what Leo is doing.
(Pause. Continues.)
Hey. Hey. Did you completely forget about me.
(Loud noise. Then silence.)
I think I'll light up.
(Pause. A rope pulls the tablecloth off the table between them. The lamp has been set on a wire so it remains there, hanging a half inch above the tabletop. LEO stops scratching. Pause.)

9.

(BEN halfway through window, one foot out and one foot in. Cabinet opens. Pause. SOPHIA there, no one moves. Pause. Cabinet closes.)

BEN
No, go back.
(Pause.)
Don't think I'm talking to myself.
(Pause.)
I wouldn't know how to talk to myself even if I wanted to. Let me clarify that.
(Long pause. Then HANNAH enters with a lamp.)

HANNAH
(Stops just inside.)
Oh, oh.

BEN
What.

HANNAH
(Pause.)
I made a mistake.

BEN
What.

HANNAH
I thought I'd be carrying a lamp and I am but I should be carrying Ben's coat and hat.
(Pause.)
Let me try that again.

BEN
I'm just standing here.
(Pause. She exits. Returns. He faints. Pause. She exits. Cabinet opens, SOPHIA there.)

I had a choice. Either fall forward and go outside or fall backward and fall inside.
(Pause.)
I guess I didn't need my coat since I'm inside.
(Pause.)
Don't you ever say anything.

SOPHIA
You don't want me to say anything.

BEN
Yes I do.

SOPHIA
Don't kid yourself.
(Pause.)

10.

(BEN in fainted position. Cabinet closed. LEO opens door halfway.)

LEO
What happened.
(Pause.)
Don't bother telling me. It's not important.
(Pause. Enter a large black dog. He wanders about, sniffing everything. After two minutes, the crew enters and takes him out. BEN gets up from the floor and exits through one door as LEO closes his.)

11.

(BEN comes and sits at table. Cabinet opens, SOPHIA there.)

BEN
Am I crazy or did you come in here disguised as a big dog.
(Pause. In the cabinet, enter HANNAH with a second lamp, and stands behind SOPHIA. Pause.)
O.K. Which one of the two ladies wants to answer.

HANNAH
This is stupid.

BEN
(Pause.)
Well, Hannah just said this is stupid.

HANNAH
You're not even looking.

BEN
(Pause.)
I have ears in the back of my head.

HANNAH
Could we have a sensible discussion about this.
(Pause.)
Any minute the cabinet door could close by itself, huh.

BEN
I think one of you is very inhibited.
(Pause.)
Now they both want to prove they're inhibited because I was thinking of each one separately. No. I shouldn't have said that. I should try to be a little more precise about what's going on in my head.
(Pause.)
Oh boy, I don't know what to do about this whole situation.
(Pause.)
The truth is I don't know which of you two is in my opinion stupider.
(Pause.)
I never should have gotten married in the first place.
(Pause.)
Hey beautiful, come and have some breakfast.
(Pause.)
You have to sit down to have breakfast.
(Pause.)
Nice things used to happen to me. I used to go out through the window and have mystical experiences. Private detectives like Leo used to come and interrogate me.
(Pause.)
Uncle Leo used to be a detective. I never knew that until it was too late.
(Pause.)
What do I mean, too late.
(Knock on the door.)
If he comes in here now he'll see something he shouldn't see, huh.
(Pause.)
One of you ladies better close the cabinet door.
(Knocks.)
I really can't do anything about it. One of you better close that cabinet.
(Knocking.)
That's not Leo.
(Pause.)
My god, that's not Leo after all.
(Knocking. Then pause. Long pause.)

12.

(BEN is leaning against the cabinet, which is closed.)

BEN

I think there's a secret panel in the back of this cabinet.

(Pause. It is on a turntable and it turns, front to back, turning BEN with it. Pause. SOPHIA and HAN-NAH leave the cabinet from a now visible rear panel. Then it turns back again. Pause. It opens: empty. It closes and turns back to front. SOPHIA comes and goes in through the rear panel. Turns again and opens revealing her.)

I think there's a secret panel in the back of this cabinet.

(Pause.)

Art doesn't interest me like it used to. How come.

(Pause.)

Sex interests me more than art.

(Pause.)

How come she never says anything any-more.

SOPHIA

Who me.

BEN

(Pause.)

The world is full of oppressed and exploited people and I have it pretty easy in com-parison.

(Pause.)

Oh well. What's next.

(Pause.)

Twelve times more. That sounds like a pretty good idea to me.

(Pause.)

I don't even think my brain is functioning. I mean, I don't think the brain functions. I don't think it's the brain that does the functioning, which is what I used to think.

SOPHIA

What does the functioning then.

BEN

Space.

SOPHIA

Right.

BEN

(Pause.)

Now what.

(Pause.)

I guess somebody's going to help me figure it out, huh.

(Pause.)

I hate it when I have to figure things out for myself. Wrong. I don't hate it, I actually like it but what I mean is I hate waiting until I finally have it figured out. If I'm going to figure it out eventually I don't see why I can't just as well figure it out immediately.

SOPHIA

Maybe you don't even figure it out.

BEN

I reject that.

(Pause.)

Oh well, I guess I just have to wait until I figure it out.

(Pause.)

I think I'm doing the right thing.

(Pause.)

If Leo came in here now and said I'd like to see exactly what happened when you went through the window, I'd say forget it you creep.

(Pause.)

Oh well, what next.

(Pause.)

Hum, that was an interesting idea.

(Pause.)

Oh. I see.

(Pause.)

Well, this is all very interesting. What time is lunch.

HANNAH

(Off.)

Forget it you creep.

BEN

(Pause.)

I'd like to build something.

(Pause.)

Oh well, I'll figure it out sooner or later.

HANNAH

(Off.)

Don't count on it.

BEN

(Pause.)

What I need is a little encouragement.

(Cabinet door closes. Pause. BEN's pants have been rigged so a string now pulls them down.)

That's not funny.

HANNAH

(Off.)

You creep.

BEN

Come in here and fix my pants up.

(Pause.)

Oh, what's the difference.

(LEO appears at the window.)

I think somebody's at the window.

(Lights change, get dim in the room and bright coming in the window.)

Oh stop changing the lights.

(Pause.)

Don't keep doing stupid things like changing the lights.

(Pause.)

Fix my pants if you want to do something useful.

(Pause.)

13.

(LEO in the window. Behind him a platform rolls into place, set with a small replica of a country scene as a three-dimensional backdrop-shadow box kind of affair. With realistic little trees, a river, etc. LEO takes out a handkerchief and blows his nose. BEN enters outside with LEO.)

LEO

Whatever happened to that dog.

BEN

Who knows.

BEN and LEO

(Pause. BEN and LEO begin calling for the dog, whistling, coaxing etc. This goes on for a while and during the second half of the activity, the cabinet door opens revealing SOPHIA. BEN comes in through the window and enters the cabinet from behind. Pause. The dog is now barking offstage and LEO is still in the window. HANNAH enters. BEN behind SOPHIA.)

HANNAH

Shut up. Shut up.

(Pause. Dog stops.)

Get out of that window.

LEO

Look.

HANNAH

Scram.

(He goes. Pause, then she goes.)

SOPHIA

(Pause. BEN behind her, remember.)

Don't touch me.

BEN

Why not.

SOPHIA

Just keep your hands off me.

BEN

(Pause.)

I wonder what she's really like if you get to know her.

SOPHIA

Don't try to find out.

(Cabinet door closes. Pause. BEN comes out by opening it just a slit. Pause. Dog barks off as BEN exits.)

HANNAH

(Off.)

Shut up!

(Silence. BEN re-enters. A table and chair brought on and he sits. Pause. LEO enters and sits across from him.)

LEO

It's beautiful out there.

BEN

What do you want to find out about.

LEO

Shhhhh.

(Pause.)

Just let me enjoy the moment.

BEN

I think that's shaking.

LEO

What.

BEN

(Pause.)

Hey. Are those things moving.

LEO

Everything's moving a little bit. Are you thinking about what's outside the window.

BEN

Do me one favor. Don't let that dog in here again.

(LEO scratches.)

You itch.

LEO

Yes.

(Pause.)

Shall we step outside.

BEN

Through the window.

LEO

Yes.

(Pause.)

It's beautiful.

BEN

I've noticed something. Different times of the year it's beautiful in different ways.

(Pause.)

For instance. Sometimes there's just so much light I can hardly see.

LEO

Sunlight.

BEN

(Pause.)

I don't know if it's sunlight.

LEO

What else could it be.

BEN

To continue.

(Pause.)

Sometimes, like now, the trees are beautiful.

(Cabinet opens. SOPHIA holds lamp.)

LEO

How come I never see Rhoda in here.

BEN

She's frightened.

LEO

(Pause.)

Close the window.

BEN

There's no glass in it really.

(Pause.)

Nothing much happens. For that reason she sleeps most of the time.

(Scenic shadow box taken off, lights get bright shining in through window.)

See what I mean.

(Pause.)

It got different out there.

LEO

I didn't notice.

BEN

You noticed.

LEO

No.

(Pause.)

I didn't notice anything.

BEN

What are you giving me.

LEO

—I didn't notice.

(Pause.)

Forgive me but I didn't notice.

BEN

You can't see anything now.

(Pause.)

Hey, can Leo see something when I can't.

LEO

I'm not even looking. Notice that my back is to the window.

BEN

(Pause.)

Mine too.

(Pause. SOPHIA lets go her lamp and it's on a string to ceiling so it swings into the room and hangs there. Pause. Crew enters and returns it to her hand. Noise. Exit LEO and BEN. Cabinet door closes.)

14.

(HANNAH sits at the table. She exits. BEN enters and sits.)

BEN

This is still warm.

(Pause.)

Was Hannah sitting here just a minute ago. Why does she leave just as I come.

(Pause.)

Maybe I'm just imagining that.

(Pause. Crew enters and pulls off tablecloth and again, lamp hangs safely half an inch above the table.)

I wish I had somebody to talk to.

(Pause.)

I wonder what ever happened to that dog that used to come in here.

(Pause.)

I bet I could still go out through that window if I wanted to.

(Pause.)

No point in trying. Sometimes there's a garden out there and the rest of the time a bright light.

(Pause.)

My legs hurt.

(Pause.)

Guess what. My legs really hurt a lot and I don't know what to do about it.

(Pause.)

I think I'm losing touch with reality but not
really.

> (Pause. Enter HANNAH. She puts
> down a new tablecloth under the
> lamp and sits facing BEN. Cabinet
> opens and SOPHIA is there, as
> LEO enters and steps inside the
> window. Pause.)

SOPHIA, HANNAH, LEO, BEN
It's beautiful.

BEN
Now wait a minute, I said it's beautiful but
I'm not sure what I mean, what I'm referring
to.

> (Pause.)

I can't tell if there's something moving out
there.

LEO
Ben ought to get his eyes checked.

BEN
I can't.

LEO
Why not.

> (Pause.)

Can't you afford it.

BEN
I can afford it, that's not the problem.

> (Pause.)

There are always little problems.

> (The dog enters again.)

Here's that dog again.

LEO
Funny, I don't hear him barking.

BEN

> (Pause.)

I heard him barking last week.

HANNAH
I didn't know he liked people.

BEN

> (Pause.)

All dogs like people.

LEO
Everybody seems to be sitting down to a
meal but I don't see any plates.

BEN
Wrong.

LEO
Serve a meal now and that dog will make a
mess of things.

BEN
We weren't about to eat.

LEO

> (Pause.)

Then why are you sitting there.

BEN

> (Pause.)

Hannah's about to go into trance.

LEO
What.

BEN

> (Pause.)

Hannah puts her hands on the table. I put
my hands on top of hers and I put my feet
on the tips of her shoes.

> (Pause.)

Right, you notice so far each of us has only
one hand on the table.

LEO
What are you waiting for.

BEN

> (Pause.)

That dog is still here, huh.

HANNAH
He must be hungry.

> (Pause.)

Dog are you still hungry.

> (Pause. BEN and HANNAH shift into
> the prescribed position. Someone
> enters and puts a bandage over
> HANNAH's eyes, after which they
> again take the tablecloth off leav-
> ing the lamp hanging.)

ALL
Nothing's going to happen.

> (Pause.)

Bring back that tablecloth.

> (Pause. SOPHIA comes out of her
> cabinet and places her lamp on the
> table also, then she exits.)

BEN
Where did that second lamp come from.

HANNAH
What lamp.

BEN

> (Pause.)

Don't look.

HANNAH
You're hurting my feet.

BEN
Why.

HANNAH

> (Pause.)

Your feet are pressing on the tops of my
shoes.

BEN
I always do that when Hannah goes into
trance.

LEO
I see it too.

HANNAH

What.
(Pause.)
You mean that lamp, huh.

BEN

There's somebody else in this room so shut up.

HANNAH

You're hurting me.

BEN

Shhhh.
(Pause.)
Well, nothing's going to happen tonight.

HANNAH

Wait a minute.

BEN

What.

HANNAH

(Pause.)
I saw something.

BEN

What.

HANNAH

(Pause.)
I saw a picture in the middle of my head.

BEN

What.

HANNAH

I'd like to draw it for you.
(Pause. LEO exits. The landscape shadow box returns.)
How did that extra lamp get there.
(Pause.)
I smell perfume.

BEN

I don't.
(Pause.)
It must be Hannah's.

HANNAH

I'm not wearing a perfume.

BEN

(Pause.)
There's nobody else here.
(Pause.)
You think I'm hiding another woman in here.

HANNAH

Yes.

BEN

(Pause.)
She's not a woman, she's a spirit from the beyond.
(Pause.)
She's not here now.

HANNAH

O.K. Take this blindfold off please.
(Pause. Dog barks from off.)

BEN

Shut up.

HANNAH

Don't you tell them to shut up.
(Barking continues.)
Here doggy. Here nice doggy.

BEN

Don't let that dog loose again.
(Barking continues. BEN and HANNAH exit. Pause. Barking continues. Lights dim. LEO enters by climbing through window. He sits at the table. SOPHIA enters and sits across from him. LEO scratches his face. Then stops.)

SOPHIA

What did it feel like coming in through the window.

LEO

Good.

SOPHIA

(Pause.)
Do you know Ben's phone number.

LEO

Yes.

SOPHIA

Where did you get it.

LEO

It's not listed.

SOPHIA

(Pause.)
Come on, where'd you get it.

LEO

Why don't you just shut up for a minute.
(Pause.)
You made me forget what I was saying.
(Pause.)
What do you really think of me.

SOPHIA

I think of you as Max's uncle.

LEO

(Pause.)
Is that how you think of me. You think of me as Max's uncle.

SOPHIA

What's it like out.

LEO

(Pause.)
Cool. Very pleasant.

SOPHIA

I think I'll get dressed and go out.

LEO
You are dressed.
SOPHIA
(Pause.)
I meant put on a coat.
LEO
You won't need it.
SOPHIA
Yes I will.
LEO
(Pause.)
You're dressed now aren't you.
SOPHIA
Some parts of me are covered.
(Pause.)
Girls always leave some parts of their body uncovered.
LEO
I wouldn't go outside unless I was bundled up.
(Pause.)
No chance of that, huh.
SOPHIA
What happened to Ben.
LEO
You want him to watch something.
SOPHIA
(Pause.)
I'd borrow his coat.
(Pause.)
No I wouldn't.
LEO
Ben.
SOPHIA
Shhhhhh.
(Pause.)
He thinks I'm an angel.
LEO
What's that perfume you're wearing.
SOPHIA
(Pause.)
Do I look like Rhoda.
LEO
She wanted to know about your perfume. When she asked, I told her I didn't think you were wearing any.
(Pause.)
Hey, are you wearing any perfume.
SOPHIA
Can't you tell.
(Pause.)
Leo should be able to do something. Lower his eyelids and see the parts of the body emanating.

LEO
I don't know how to do that.
(Pause.)
Uncover your body for me.
SOPHIA
Just the opposite.
LEO
What.
SOPHIA
(Pause.)
I want to cover it and go outside.
(Pause.)
My body emanates even when it's covered.
LEO
Then she's an angel after all, huh.
> *(Noise. LEO covers his ears. Noise stops. Pause. Crew brings a coat and puts it over SOPHIA. They lift her and throw her out the window. They throw the table, her chair, LEO and his chair, all out the window. Everything lies in a heap.)*
SOPHIA
(Pause.)
Can we continue our conversation even though we're outdoors.
(Pause.)
I'm glad I put my coat on before I went out the window.
LEO
That's Ben's coat.
SOPHIA
(Pause.)
Is it.
LEO
What.
SOPHIA
(Pause.)
Was that Ben who threw us out.
LEO
No.
(Pause.)
After all this
SOPHIA
What
LEO
She can't even recognize whether or not it's Ben.
SOPHIA
Maybe I don't make the same kind of distinctions most people do.
(Pause.)
Was it Ben.
LEO
No.

SOPHIA
(Pause.)
If he comes into the room now will be notice what happened.
LEO
No.
SOPHIA
(Pause.)
How do you feel.
LEO
Why do you ask.
SOPHIA
(Pause.)
What's the weather like.
LEO
Beautiful.
SOPHIA
(Pause.)
What's the weather like now.
LEO
Still beautiful.
(Pause.)

15.

(LEO and SOPHIA still in a heap outside the window. Crew brings on a a second identical set of furniture. BEN and HANNAH come and sit just like LEO and SOPHIA had been sitting.)
HANNAH
I smell perfume.
(Pause.)
Guess what. If Ben closes his eyes halfway—
(Crew enters and blindfolds BEN as she speaks.)
—he can see the parts of my body from which there are emanations.
(Pause.)
I smell perfume.
BEN
Somebody made a mistake.
(Pause.)
Hannah's eyes should be covered with a bandage.
HANNAH
Why.
BEN
She goes into a trance.
HANNAH
What does she see.

BEN
(Pause.)
She sees parts of her own body.
(Pause.)
I made that up.
HANNAH
I made that up.
(Pause. Crew enters and uncovers BEN's eyes.)
Feel better.
BEN
(Pause.)
Yes.

16.

(HANNAH and BEN sit. Cabinet opens. Light just hangs there.)
HANNAH
(Pause.)
I think it's moving just a little bit.
(Crew enters, covers BEN's eyes with the bandage. Cabinet closes.)

17.

(BEN and HANNAH still sit. BEN's eyes still covered. Cabinet opens, empty but the lamp hangs and swings slightly. It closes. Remember, SOPHIA and LEO still in a heap of furniture outside the window.)
SOPHIA
I think I saw it moving.
BEN
I thought you were all powerful.
SOPHIA
(Pause.)
Who.
(Pause.)
I don't have any control over objects.
(Pause.)
I can enter people's minds if they want me to enter.
(Pause.)
Correction. I don't really enter the mind. I enter a small point of light just over the head.

BEN
What good does that do.
> (Pause. Cabinet opens, lamp
> swings.)

It's certainly moving now.
LEO
What good does that do.
HANNAH
How come you can see it when your eyes
are blindfolded.
> (Pause.)

Isn't it interesting.
BEN
What.
HANNAH
> (Pause.)

I go into trance and see pictures in my head
but Ben sees things through the bandages.
BEN
We're different people.
HANNAH
What.
BEN
> (Pause.)

When we're blindfolded.
HANNAH
It's the first time Ben has been blindfolded,
isn't it.
BEN
> (Pause.)

Yes.

18.

> (Lights up. Crew takes blindfold
> off BEN's eyes as the cabinet opens
> and HANNAH rises and exits. BEN
> covers his eyes with his hands.
> Noise. Then silence and pause.)

BEN
It's about time isn't it.
> (Pause.)

I spent the whole morning thinking about it.
ALL
WHAT!
BEN
Shut up.
> (Pause.)

I can't think when other people are talking.
> (Pause.)

I wonder if anybody else can get into my
head. I can't get into another person's head.
> (Pause.)

Maybe I can but I don't know about it.
ALL
SHUT UP!
BEN
> (Pause.)

I guess I can after all.
> (Pause.)

I guess I can get into other people's heads
whenever I want to.
> (Pause.)

It's easy.
> (Pause.)

What next.
> (Pause.)

Maybe I'll go outside for a walk. I bet it's
cool out.
> (Pause.)

I better put on my overcoat.
> (Pause.)

Well, come to think of it I don't know what
happened to my overcoat.
> (Pause. Crew enters and throws
> BEN, his table and chair all out
> the window on top of SOPHIA and
> LEO and their stuff. Close cabinet.)
> (Silence.)

ALL
WHAT A MESS!
BEN
It used to be nice out here.
> (Pause. HANNAH enters the door
> halfway, carrying her lamp.)

HANNAH
What happened to everybody.
BEN
You mean what happened to Ben.
HANNAH
No stupid.
> (Pause.)

I mean what happened to everybody.
BEN
Oh, you mean Ben and Uncle Leo.
HANNAH
No.
> (Pause.)

I could show you a thing or two.
> (Pause. She goes and opens the
> cabinet.)

There's a hidden panel in the back of this.
> (Pause.)

I smell perfume.
> (Pause. She lets go of her lamp and
> it hangs on a string to the ceiling
> and swings slightly.)

I accidentally let go of the lamp I was carrying but it seems to be able to continue under its own power.

(Pause.)

Are you in love with me.

BEN

Sure.

HANNAH

(Pause.)

How do I know Ben is telling the truth.

BEN

You can't see him, can you.

HANNAH

(Pause.)

I can see his feet sticking up.

(Pause.)

Close my eyes and imagine it.

(She covers her eyes.)

BEN

Why don't you help me back into the room.

HANNAH

Don't you like it out there.

BEN

(Pause.)

No.

(Pause. HANNAH exits. BEN, LEO and SOPHIA come through the window and load all the furniture back into the room. Then they stand about.)

BEN

(Pause.)

Something's wrong.

(Pause.)

We brought more furniture back in than went out.

LEO

That's impossible.

(SOPHIA sits. She sticks out and spreads her legs, making her whole body straight.)

BEN

(Not moving to look.)

What's she smiling about.

LEO

Who.

BEN

(Pause.)

Maybe I'm the only one who notices what she's doing.

LEO

Who.

BEN

(Pause.)

She looks very appealing.

LEO

Who.

(Loud noise. BEN and LEO fall to the floor. Pause.)

LEO

What the hell is coming out of her body.

BEN

Light.

LEO

I smell her perfume.

BEN

I think she's inside my head.

(Pause.)

Wrong. I think she's a second head. The second head belongs to me even though it's invisible.

LEO

All I can think about is her body.

BEN

All I can think about is her mind.

LEO

(Pause.)

I don't believe it.

BEN

What.

LEO

(Pause.)

I think Ben is thinking about her body.

BEN

(Pause.)

It's not like an ordinary body.

(Pause.)

It's like a mind.

LEO

What.

BEN

(Pause.)

Her body.

(Pause.)

I think her whole body is thinking and I can hear it.

LEO

What.

BEN

(Pause.)

Thinking.

LEO

Her body is emanating but it's not thinking.

SOPHIA

Get up.

BEN and LEO

(Pause.)

The minute she says get up we get up even though we don't know how to do it.

(Pause.)

Maybe we didn't bring too much furniture back into the room even though we brought back twice as much as we threw out the window.

SOPHIA

Who.

BEN and LEO

(Pause.)

We didn't throw it out the window.

(Pause.)

Somebody threw us out the window at the same time they threw the furniture out the window.

HANNAH

(Opens the door halfway. With a lamp.)

Get up.

SOPHIA

Stop shining the light on my body.

(Pause.)

That's an order.

BEN

Who keeps changing the light.

(Pause.)

Hannah, I want you to meet somebody.

HANNAH

Who.

BEN

Your uncle.

HANNAH

Who's sitting in my chair.

(Pause.)

I can't think straight.

SOPHIA

It's O.K. if you keep holding the light then Ben can see everything that happens.

BEN

Wrong.

(Pause.)

I don't need anybody holding a light over my body.

(Pause.)

I stood up for a better view, huh.

HANNAH

What do you mean by saying there's somebody I should meet and then saying let me introduce you to your uncle.

BEN

Who do you want to be

HANNAH

—What

BEN

(Pause.)

Introduced to.

HANNAH

I don't know.

SOPHIA

Keep holding the light that's O.K.

(Pause.)

If your arm gets tired.

HANNAH

What.

SOPHIA

Put it down some place.

(Pause.)

You could put it down between my legs.

HANNAH

What.

SOPHIA

(Pause.)

Don't worry about my body.

(Pause.)

It thinks.

HANNAH

What.

SOPHIA

Shhhhhhh.

HANNAH

I don't know how to think with my body.

ALL

POOR HANNAH!

HANNAH

(Pause.)

I only know how to think with my head.

(Pause.)

My head is like a lamp, isn't it.

ALL

POOR HANNAH!

SOPHIA

Just make sure that lamp stays on so Ben can watch.

HANNAH

What.

SOPHIA

(Pause.)

Even if you have to go out of the room.

ALL

Poor Hannah!

SOPHIA

Keep holding the lamp right where it is so Ben can watch.

HANNAH

What.

ALL

(Pause.)

Everything.

HANNAH

You said

SOPHIA
What.

HANNAH
(Pause.)
I could put it in your body.
(Pause.)
My head is like a

SOPHIA
What.

HANNAH
(Pause.)
Lamp. Right.
(Pause.)
Poor Hannah.

SOPHIA
Who.

HANNAH
Could I put it in my own body.

SOPHIA
What.
(Pause. Then a loud noise. Pause.)

HANNAH
They can't see anything even though I'm holding it.
(Pause. She very, very slowly, with tiny sliding steps, crosses to SOPHIA.)

BEN
(As she crosses.)
What's it like out.

HANNAH
I haven't been out today yet.

BEN
I thought somebody threw you out the window.
(She finally reaches SOPHIA.)

HANNAH
Sit up straight.
(Pause.)
Anybody can do that.

SOPHIA
What.

HANNAH
(Pause.)
What's that perfume you're wearing.

SOPHIA
What are you wearing.

HANNAH
(Pause.)
Why should I tell you.
(Loud noise. Crew enters and wraps HANNAH in a large blanket, lamp and all, and carries her off all wrapped up.)
(Silence. SOPHIA rises and goes to

the cabinet and steps in. BEN and LEO get up and brush themselves off and stand looking forward.)*

BEN
That's double the amount of furniture we began with.

LEO
You must be seeing double.
(The cabinet closes on SOPHIA.)
Not much light in here.

BEN
Oh no.
(Pause.)
I can see O.K.
(Pause.)
Maybe I have it inside my head so it comes out my eyes and goes on whatever I look at.

LEO
What.

BEN
(Pause.)
Light.

LEO
You describe light as if it was a liquid.

BEN
What.

LEO
(Pause.)
You describe it as if it were coming out of a hose and covering everything.

BEN
(Pause.)
Right.

19.

(Empty. HANNAH enters halfway through the door with a lamp. Cabinet opens showing SOPHIA.)

HANNAH
(Pause.)
There's double the amount of furniture in there.
(Pause.)
Ben.

SOPHIA
Shhhhhh.

BEN
(He is right behind HANNAH in the doorway, mostly hidden.)
I'm right behind you.

HANNAH

(Pause.)

Stand in the room where I can see you.

BEN

Close the door.

SOPHIA

Shhhhhh.

(HANNAH backs out and closes the door. Pause. Crew brings in additional furniture. Two tables, like card tables. Each with a small curtained proscenium across the center of the tabletop. Like a small puppet stage. After the tables are set, the cabinet closes and the crew opens the table-stage curtains revealing a shadow box behind each opening with a miniaturized built landscape. A loud jazz number plays through to the end.)

20.

(Into the already crowded stage, a bed is brought and placed. BEN enters and lies down on it. The cabinet opens. SOPHIA emerges, goes to the bed and lies down. They begin to embrace and the bed immediately collapses. They don't move.)

BEN and SOPHIA

(Pause.)

Don't move, don't move! The bed just collapsed!

(Pause.)

21.

(Empty stage. The bed is still collapsed. HANNAH opens the door halfway. Holds lamp.)

HANNAH

Ben.

(Pause. Cabinet opens and SOPHIA comes out and goes to lie on the collapsed (tilted) bed and immediately slides to the floor and is motionless.)

ALL

(Pause.)

Her body is

SOPHIA

What.

ALL

(Pause.)

Disappearing in air.

SOPHIA

Wrong.

(Pause.)

I tried to get into bed but it was tilted and I fell out.

(Pause.)

I imitated that I had a real body.

HANNAH

What's that

SOPHIA

What.

HANNAH

(Pause.)

Perfume.

(Raucous music begins, then stops midway. Pause.)

What's that.

SOPHIA

What.

HANNAH

(Pause.)

Music.

(Pause. She exits. Pause. SOPHIA gets back on the bed, slides to floor. Pause. Repeat onto bed but this time she holds herself suspended in place on the tilted mattress. Pause. LEO enters through the window with a lamp held in his hand. Puts it down on a table. In the silence, he starts to undress.)

SOPHIA

Where did he get that lamp.

(A shot rings out and LEO falls to the floor. Pause. SOPHIA lets go and slides to the floor. Then she rises, goes to the cabinet and enters and closes the door. The cabinet turns, she slides out the back panel, gets back on the bed and slides to the floor as the cabinet again turns forward. Crew enters and puts LEO's lamp inside the cabinet and closes the door. It's quite dark. One light blinks on and off in rear.)

LEO
It's dark.

SOPHIA
Shhhhh.

LEO
I'm not frightened because I'm shot.

SOPHIA
You shouldn't have tried to

LEO
What

SOPHIA
(Pause.)
Touch my body.
(Pause.)
My body is like a human being's mind.

LEO
Could I see the

SOPHIA
—What.

LEO
(Pause.)
I think I'm O.K.

SOPHIA
Believe it.

LEO
I could get dressed now.
*(Pause. Loud music. The crew
enters, dresses him and throws him
out the window.)*

22.

(Empty stage, LEO outside window.)
LEO
What happened to the trees.
(Pause.)
What happened to the furniture that used
to be out here.
(Pause.)
I have to assume that everything worked
out O.K. for Ben and Hannah.
(Pause.)
I never should have gotten involved in the
whole situation.
(Pause.)
I wonder what time it is, under normal
circumstances I could be enjoying myself.
*(Pause. He rises, comes in the
window and gets his lamp off the
table where he had placed it, goes
out again and lies down as he was,
but with lamp.)*
What happened to the trees.
(Pause.)
I got a lamp but I don't got no trees in my
field of vision.
(Pause.)
This lamp is a piece of furniture.

ALL

Look how bright Leo is.

LEO

Come on.

ALL

(Pause.)

What.

LEO

I'm not bright it's my lamp.

(Pause. His lamp goes out.)

What a surprise. I'm bright because my lamp went out and I'm still shining.

(Pause.)

Everybody else saw it before I did, huh.

(Loud noise. Everybody halfway into the room, carrying lamps—i.e., SOPHIA from cabinet, HANNAH and BEN from two separate doors. Noise stops. Lamps out.)

23.

(BEN and HANNAH each halfway in through a separate door. The crew enters and clears the two tables with curtained stages.)

HANNAH

Bring that back.

ALL

Why.

(Pause.)

Part two.

(Pause.)

Part two of TOTAL RECALL.

(Crew takes out all other furniture and then brings back just the two tables with curtained stages.)

BEN

All of the old furniture got taken off the stage before we were finished with it.

(Pause.)

There was an important experiment I wanted to try with the furniture.

HANNAH

There's furniture.

BEN

(Pause.)

I mean the old furniture.

(Pause.)

That isn't regular furniture.

LEO

(Still outside the window.)

What happened to all the furniture that used to be out here.

BEN

Shhhhh.

(Pause. As cabinet opens and SOPHIA is seen.)

I wanted to try putting the extra furniture back into the first set of furniture.

(Pause.)

I'm not making myself clear, huh.

(Pause.)

All of a sudden I came into the room and said hey, there's twice as much furniture as there was originally.

(Pause.)

Each piece of original furniture was repeated when I saw that.

(Pause.)

I wanted to try to make each second piece of the same piece of furniture return into the body of the source, which I take to be the first piece of furniture.

SOPHIA

Good thinking, Ben.

BEN

(Pause.)

What.

SOPHIA

What you said was good thinking.

BEN

What.

(Pause.)

There's only one of me, huh.

(Pause.)

I won't get a chance to try that experiment.

SOPHIA

Why not.

HANNAH

Why not.

BEN

They took all the furniture out.

(Pause.)

That's not real furniture.

(Pause.)

I don't want to try it with bodies before I try it with furniture.

(Pause.)

Please bring back the furniture so I can try it first with furniture.

(Pause.)

There's nothing more I can do.

(Pause.)

Try putting the second furniture into the

source of the furniture which is the first furniture.

(Pause. HANNAH and BEN collapse to the floor.)

Who's that standing up.

LEO

I wish I could help but I'm out here.

BEN

What's it like out.

LEO

Very nice.

(Pause.)

Step out here a minute.

BEN

Too bad. I already fell down.

(Pause.)

Hey Hannah is that you.

HANNAH

Yes.

(Pause. Cabinet closes. HANNAH and BEN crawl off. Pause.)

24.

(Pause. HANNAH and BEN crawl into the room, circle it once and then crawl out.)

25.

(Lights up. Crew brings on one complete set of furniture.)

ALL

(Off.)

We did it. We did it. The furniture is all back together.

(Pause. BEN comes halfway in one door.)

BEN

Maybe I shouldn't have asked them to bring the furniture back.

(Pause.)

There's only one set of real furniture, huh.

(Pause.)

I used to have unusual experiences but now they don't seem unusual. Plus. They seem more interesting if they are not unusual.

LEO

(Still out window.)

What.

BEN

Experiences.

LEO

What experiences.

BEN

(Pause.)

Whenever I have an unusual experience it seems more interesting if I pretend it isn't unusual.

(Pause.)

I used to try and imagine that all of my experiences were unusual because then I thought they were more interesting.

LEO

(Pause.)

I think somebody's hiding in the cabinet.

(Crew opens it to show it's empty, closes it.)

BEN

There's a secret panel in the back of that cabinet.

(Pause.)

That explains it.

LEO

That's interesting.

(BEN exits.)

Hey, don't go yet.

(Pause. Crew comes and throws all the furniture out the window so it covers LEO.)

I feel better now.

(Pause.)

When things are more like things should be they are more interesting right away.

(Pause.)

26.

(Lights up. LEO gone. Loud music. Crew opens curtains on the table-stages. Miniature landscapes.)

(Pause.)

BEN

(Off.)

Anybody who tries to remember everything will end up going crazy.

(Pause. Enter a little girl. She goes and examines one of the miniature landscapes. She faces front and cries, rubbing her eyes. Then she stops and sits, facing the landscape with her back to audience. Pause. BEN enters and goes and sits behind a stage as the curtains of both are drawn. Crew takes off land-

scapes. Curtain of his opens and he is there facing the girl. He makes funny faces. As he does so, HANNAH enters and sits behind other stage. Her curtain opens and she sits there, BEN stops making faces.)

LITTLE GIRL

More. More.

(Silence. No one moves.)

More. More. More. More. More. More. More. More. More.

(Pause. Lights dim.)

More.

(Lights out.)

27.

(Lights up. Girl is now sitting before HANNAH's stage. Pause. Little girl exits. Pause. HANNAH's curtain closes. Then BEN's curtain closes. LEO appears and comes into the room through the window. He stops. Pause, looking forward, he goes and opens the cabinet. Empty, but a lamp hangs. Then all lights out except for the lamp.)

LEO

That doesn't mean anything.

(Pause.)

Stop changing the lights.

(Pause, he goes into the cabinet and closes the door behind him, eliminating all light.)

28.

(Tables with curtains closed. BEN and HANNAH behind them. HANNAH's opens and closes once. BEN puts his hands through his closed curtains and holds them up.)

HANNAH

I smell perfume.

(The larger landscape is rolled on to behind the window. SOPHIA is standing in the middle of it, naked, hands modestly over her breasts and cunt.)

Maybe what I smell is just the countryside.

(Pause.)

The trees outside the window, huh.

(Pause.)

My uncle used to take me walking in the woods.
BEN
(Behind curtain, just his hands showing.)
Did you ever really look at me carefully.
HANNAH
What.
(Pause. Her curtain opens.)
BEN
My body.
(Pause.)
Parts of it.
HANNAH
It would be easier if I didn't have to do it all at once.
BEN
What.
HANNAH
You know what.
(Pause. SOPHIA, in slow motion, is slowly turning front to back. HAN-NAH puts her hands out on the table and BEN's curtain opens.)
See, it doesn't matter.
BEN
What.
HANNAH
You know what.
(Pause.)
I'm going to turn over the first card.
BEN
What.
HANNAH
(Pause.)
My hands are covering cards. I'll uncover the first one and find out what it tells me.
BEN
You don't believe that stuff.
(Pause. Little girl re-enters with the big dog on a leash.)
HANNAH
Ready.
BEN
I think you could read the lines of my hand to better effect.
HANNAH
Get that dog out of here.
(Pause.)
I don't want to uncover the cards with that dog here.
(BEN's curtain closed. His hands still out. Little girl sits at BEN's table with the dog. Loud noise.)

29.

(Same. Girl and dog. HANNAH's curtain closed. Girl pets dog. LEO enters rear with a big overcoat, and climbs into the landscape and puts it over the naked SOPHIA who has her back to the audience. Pause.
HANNAH's curtain opens. She is cutting a deck of cards and that noise is increased by amplification. Little girl and dog exit. Loud noise of cards being cut. Curtain opens on BEN now. He pours himself a shot from a bottle on his table and downs it in one gulp. Noise continues. LEO has gone off and now brings a chair for SOPHIA to sit on, back still to audience. HAN-NAH throws her cards in the air, but the noise continues. Then after a while a buzzer and noise stops.)
HANNAH
(Pause.)
What I want most. I want to get inside Ben's head.
(Pause.)
I want to find out what he's really thinking.
BEN
I thought that's what Hannah did when she used to go into trance.
HANNAH
I never did that.
(Pause.)
I was faking.
BEN
Don't believe it.
HANNAH
(Pause.)
I was only faking it.
(Pause. She leaves her table and goes and squeezes next to BEN to sit on his chair, holding him with both arms awkwardly from the side. Staring straight at the side of his head.)
BEN
Hannah better get back in her own chair.
HANNAH
I'd really like to get in there.

BEN
(Pause.)
Sure.

HANNAH
What's inside that, huh.

BEN
Find out.
(Pause.)
Maybe I have a picture of Hannah in there.

HANNAH
What about the rest of my body.

BEN
What.
(Pause.)
What about inside Hannah's

HANNAH
What.

BEN
(Pause.)
Her head.
(Pause.)
Hannah better get back in her own chair.
(Pause.)
How come Hannah doesn't think she's de-grading herself.

HANNAH
I'm not doing it.

BEN
(Pause.)
What.
(Pause.)
I'd like to get inside Hannah's head and find out what was in there.
(Pause.)
Do you mind if I pour myself a drink.

HANNAH
Go on.
(Pause. He pours a drink and drinks it fast, but because of her arms holding him from the side he misses his mouth and spills the liquor over himself.)
How come Ben spilled it.

BEN
It was because Hannah's holding my body.

HANNAH
No.
(Pause.)
Hannah's just trying to find out.

BEN
I don't think Hannah thinks anybody is watching.

HANNAH
What.
(Pause.)
Could I remind you what I'm thinking about.

BEN
(Pause.)
Don't bother. I have

HANNAH
What.

BEN
(Pause.)
Total recall.
(SOPHIA's coat falls off her back. LEO comes and replaces it.)
I might find out that what went on inside Hannah's head was her body.
(Pause.)
If she wants to find out what goes on inside my head why is she holding my body.

HANNAH
Let's put both our feet on the table.

BEN
What for.

HANNAH
(Pause.)
Ben wouldn't ask what for if he wanted to find out more about me.

BEN
I can't do that now.

HANNAH
Why not.

BEN
(Pause.)
That dog might come back into the room at any minute.

HANNAH
No, that dog was in the first part of the play.

BEN
(Pause.)
That dog was also in the second part of the play.
(Pause.)
Now Hannah knows what goes on in my head.

HANNAH
Let's put our feet up.

BEN
I can't.

HANNAH
Let's get help.
(Pause.)
I know what goes on inside Ben's head but I can't see it.

BEN

What.

(Crew enters and helps them to put their feet through the stage opening onto the table, with HANNAH's arms still around BEN from the side but the position is so awkward they fall immediately to the floor.)

We needed help to do that.

(Pause.)

It's almost like falling out of the window.

SOPHIA

(Turning forward.)

I don't feel special any longer.

HANNAH

(Pause.)

She's not special.

BEN

Who.

HANNAH

I'm special.

BEN

You're not special.

(Pause. Close the table-stage curtains. Carry miniature landscapes into place. Noise, open curtains to reveal miniature landscapes. Silence and SOPHIA exits. Noise again.)

30.

(Empty stage. Open miniature landscapes. The cabinet opens. It turns around. BEN and LEO enter and sit, backs to audience, facing small landscapes. Loud music.)

31.

(Empty stage. Open the cabinet which has been turned front again, empty, lamp hangs. SOPHIA comes into the room, goes into the cabinet and stands. Cabinet closes. Pause. Cabinet turns back to front, she exits backwards through the panel, hugging the cabinet and feeling her way around to the other side and re-enters through the upstage front. HANNAH enters to a stage-table. Puts one foot on the table, then the other and falls.)

HANNAH
(From floor.)
That's in the way.
(Pause.)
That scenery is in the way and Ben isn't getting through to help me.
(Pause.)
He's on the other side of the table but he can't.
(Pause.)
I didn't plan on it. Wrong. I mean I didn't plan it right.
(Cabinet turns back to face forward. Opens. SOPHIA is fallen down inside it. Pause. Enter BEN who gets on top of SOPHIA and starts kissing her. LEO comes halfway through a door.)
LEO
Hey.
(Pause.)
Ben's with the wrong person.
(Lights up on audience and off onstage. Stage only dimly seen from reflected light from audience.)
LEO
I think I see my
HANNAH
What.
LEO
—Niece.
HANNAH
(Pause.)
Uncle Leo.
(Pause.)
I thought Uncle Leo was dead.
(Pause.)
Who's that in the door.
LEO
Me.
HANNAH
(Pause.)
Who's that in the cabinet.
BEN and SOPHIA
Me.
(Lights out in house. Stage lights up as miniature landscapes are removed and curtains are closed. BEN has placed himself behind the curtain at the table in front of which HANNAH lies. He crawls through the curtain, over the table, and down on top of HANNAH. Then the curtain opens. SOPHIA is

standing behind the table. Puts one leg up and falls behind the table. LEO exits. Curtain on other stage-table opens. All three rise and go over to the second table. HANNAH in front, leg onto table and falls. Curtain has closed and BEN crawls through and onto HANNAH. Curtain opens and SOPHIA puts leg onto table and falls. Loud noise.)
BEN, SOPHIA, HANNAH
We all look like furniture that turned into a second piece of furniture.
(All crawl off on their hands and knees. Music blaring in accompaniment.)

32.

(The tables have their curtains drawn. BEN and HANNAH crawl through from separate tables. Fall to the floor. Then SOPHIA crawls through HANNAH's curtain and falls on top of her.
Pause.
Then everyone rises. BEN and HANNAH go to the rear wall and stand, and SOPHIA again crawls through and falls to the floor.
Pause. Then HANNAH goes and from the side, just as she did when sitting in a previous scene, holds BEN tightly from the side, staring into the side of his shoulder.)
HANNAH
Can I see into his head by looking through his ear.
BEN
What's important isn't what's in my head.
(Pause.)
Guess where it really is.
(Pause.)
It's just over my head like a single point.
HANNAH
Wrong.
BEN
(Pause.)
Rhoda thinks it's in my body, huh.
SOPHIA
(From floor.)
It's in somebody else's body.

BEN

Whose.

SOPHIA

Three guesses.

(Pause.)

Isn't that appropriate. I said three guesses and there are three people here.

HANNAH

What happened to my uncle.

BEN

What happened to the little girl and the dog.

HANNAH

(Pause.)

What little girl.

(Pause.)

Only two people here.

BEN

I better pretend I'm not here, huh.

HANNAH

Am I hurting you.

BEN

(Pause.)

She's certainly squeezing me, huh.

HANNAH

I'm not finding out much yet.

(Pause.)

Now I'm finding out everything.

BEN

Let's go outside.

(Pause.)

Let's step outside together.

HANNAH

O.K.

(Pause. Still holding him from the side, awkwardly they manage to step through the window. Pause. Light from behind comes up bright.)

Just like the old days, huh.

BEN

Wrong. Can Hannah figure out the difference.

(From above SOPHIA, a lamp is lowered to her, on a string, to the floor.)

HANNAH

We walked into the window. Wrong. I mean through it.

(Pause.)

The light changed.

BEN

The light used to change all the time.

(Pause.)

I said stop doing it and it stopped.

(Pause.)

I felt like I was in a floor.

HANNAH

What.

BEN

(Pause.)

Light.

HANNAH

What.

BEN

A flood of light.

(Pause.)

I felt that my whole body was flooded.

HANNAH

I think it's pouring out of me.

BEN

What.

HANNAH

(Pause.)

My whole body.

BEN

It's thinking.

HANNAH

What.

BEN

(Pause.)

All of it at once.

SOPHIA

I never felt so sure of myself as now.

(Noise. Then pause.)

The light outside, plus, I reveal myself once and for all.

(Pause.)

That lamp hanging over me is visible for the first time.

(Pause.)

Ben sees it.

BEN

Stop holding me.

HANNAH

Don't turn around.

(Pause.)

Hey Ben darling don't turn around.

SOPHIA

Now my first body falls to the floor.

(Pause.)

My second body rises, I am the Goddess indeed.

HANNAH

Don't remember to

BEN

What.

HANNAH
(Pause.)
Look.
SOPHIA
My lamp.
(Pause.)
My body.
(Pause.)
My whole body.
BEN
I'm finally
HANNAH
What
BEN
(Pause.)
Looking.
(Pause. Noise. Pause.)
She didn't
HANNAH
What.
BEN
Get up.
(Pause.)
Now I see who it is.
HANNAH
Wrong. Ben means he remembers something.
BEN
What.
SOPHIA and HANNAH
(Pause.)
Total.
BEN
What.
SOPHIA and HANNAH
(Pause.)
Recall.

(HANNAH leaves BEN, comes back through the window and sits behind the table before which SOPHIA is fallen. The curtain is drawn. Pause. Loud noise. SOPHIA sits facing the drawn curtain. The curtain opens. The curtain at the other table opens to reveal a large papier-maché head on a string that swings a little.)
SOPHIA and HANNAH
What happened to Leo.
(Pause.)
What happened to the dog and the little girl.
(All curtains close. SOPHIA exits briskly. She immediately comes back in and stands with her back

against the door. HANNAH's curtain opens.)
SOPHIA
I almost forgot something.
HANNAH
What.
SOPHIA
(Pause.)
My lamp.
HANNAH
I hadn't noticed.
SOPHIA
What.
(Pause. She goes and takes her lamp and exits. BEN comes through the window and sits behind the other curtain. It opens and the head is still hanging there—it closes immediately. Then it opens and the head is gone.)
BEN
I almost forgot something.
(Long pause.)

33.

(Empty stage. Two curtains open. Cabinet turns once. Pause. Large scenery box in behind window with LEO in midst. Off immediately as miniature landscape is brought to one table.)

34.

(Lights up. Now both miniature landscapes set. Pause. Silence.)

35.

(Lights up dim. The curtains are drawn and on each table, a lamp stands in front of the curtain. Loud music begins and crew sets out incense and small photos of the cast on each table beneath the lamps.
After everything is set, the tables are taken out. The music stops.)

36.

(Empty stage. HANNAH half opens a door. She is wearing a nightgown and is carrying a lamp.)

HANNAH

What happened to my bed.

(Pause.)

It's late, isn't it.

(Pause.)

I can't fall asleep as long as I'm holding a lamp.

(Pause.)

I still better find out what happened to my bed.

(Pause. Slowly, with tiny steps, she comes center. Waits. Someone else is crouched under her flowing nightgown, making a strange hump.)

I smell something funny.

ALL

What!

HANNAH

(Pause.)

This lamp cord might be dangerous.

ALL

SAFETY FIRST!

HANNAH

(Pause.)

I smell my own perfume.

(Pause.)

Who's under my nightgown. I bet it's Ben's idea.

(Pause.)

I'm scared to look.

LEO

(Goes to window, holding his own lamp.)

Hannah, I can't help noticing.

HANNAH

What.

LEO

(Pause.)

You got something under that nightgown.

HANNAH

Both of us are emanating in the dark, huh.

LEO

I'm just passing through.

HANNAH

What.

LEO

(Pause.)

I'm outside at night.

(Pause.)

I just thought I'd try to help.

(She moves off, slowly with tiny steps, and he comes in through window. Goes to cabinet. He opens it and looks in. He turns it around, and looks in from the back. Then he exits.

Pause. Empty stage. HANNAH half opens the door, still with lamp.)

HANNAH

He went. Good.

BEN

(Half opens door.)

I smell Hannah's perfume and I see her carrying a lamp.

HANNAH

We both

BEN

What.

HANNAH

(Pause.)

Emanate.

BEN

What.

(Pause.)

Let's meet in the center of the room. Then.

HANNAH

It's late.

BEN

Let's go to bed.

HANNAH

(Pause.)

Where's my bed.

BEN

(Pause.)

Let's go outside and sleep under the trees.

HANNAH

O.K.

(Pause.)

Help me.

BEN

You should move first.

HANNAH

What.

BEN

(Pause.)

Hannah doesn't mean what, she means only should I move first.

HANNAH

Because I can't move good.

(Pause.)

Because I'm emanating something.
(Pause.)
Help me through the window for a second
time.
BEN
There's no bed outside.
HANNAH
So what.
BEN
(Pause. Points center stage.)
Look, that way.
HANNAH
I can't go to the place Ben is pointing out.
BEN
That's a help, huh.
(Pause.)
Where am I really pointing.
HANNAH
I bet.
BEN
What.
HANNAH
(Pause.)
I bet I could find out where Ben is really
pointing.
BEN
(Stops pointing.)
Find out.

HANNAH
Can you still tell if I'm hiding something
under my nightgown.
BEN
(Pause.)
No.
HANNAH
That's because we're not really in the same
room, huh.
(Pause.)
Is that because the lamp is shining in Ben's
eyes.
BEN
It's late.
HANNAH
Use it to look.
BEN
What.
HANNAH
(Pause.)
My lamp.
(Pause.)
Is it because my lamp is emitting some-
thing.
BEN
It's late.
HANNAH
Is it because Ben is falling asleep.

BEN
(Pause.)
What happened to my

HANNAH
What.

BEN
(Pause.)
Bed.

HANNAH
Try to remember what happened to my bed.

BEN
(Pause.)
Don't move. Don't move.

HANNAH
I'm too tired to move.
(Pause.)
Plus. I have a second body.
(Pause. She slowly moves center. BEN exits.)
I wonder what happened to my bed now.
(Pause, hump still there.)
How could I lie down in bed with my second body.
(Pause.)
My second body would get in the way of my first body, plus my lamp isn't safe in bed.

ALL
Safety first! Safety first!

HANNAH
(Pause.)
I think my second body is more beautiful than I am.
(Loud noise, both HANNAH and whatever is under her nightgown collapse to the floor.)

HANNAH and SOPHIA
(SOPHIA under the nightgown.)
We are two bodies which have fallen down.
(Pause.)
It's late at night but we have no bed to sleep in.
(Pause.)
What happened to the little girl and what happened to the dog.
(Pause. BEN enters, goes out window and exits.)

BEN
(From off. Pause.)
Let me sleep out here!
(Pause.)

37.

(Empty stage. Door opens. HANNAH and SOPHIA under her nightgown, cross to center, face out. SOPHIA emerges from under the nightgown and exits briskly. HANNAH turns and exits slow, tiny steps in other direction. Wait until she has gone.)

38.

(Empty stage. Door opens. Loud noise. Then HANNAH enters with SOPHIA under her nightgown. They come center and stop. Loud noise. They turn and go out the window but fall. Pause. They rise and continue off. BEN opens the door halfway. A lamp lowers from the ceiling.)

BEN
What happened to my bed and Hannah.
(Pause.)
There was never anybody else in my life.
(Pause. He closes the door, the lamp goes back up. Loud music plays for three minutes.)
(Door opens and BEN swings out into the room by means of a radio that is on a rope to the ceiling. He hangs on the suspended radio, his feet dragging on the floor. The music stops.)
It plays all night long and I hold myself up on it.
(Pause.)
It stops and then it starts playing by itself, huh.
(Pause.)
Hannah. Each letter is like a radio station.
(Pause.)
How come I'm not hanging on a lamp instead of on a radio.

HANNAH and SOPHIA
(Off.)
Come out where nature is.

BEN
(Pause.)
I bet she comes back.
(Pause.)

Hannah I mean. She was the only person in my life.

(Pause.)

How come this radio doesn't play more often. Maybe I should get it fixed.

(It lowers to the floor and he goes with it. Pause.)

I tell you this. I have total recall and can remember everything that happens.

(Pause.)

I can evaluate it too.

(Crew enters and sets up a table with a tablecloth and two chairs. LEO comes and sits. BEN rises and sits opposite. Loud noise, as crew comes and covers BEN's eyes with a cloth. Then silence.)

39.

(Lights up. SOPHIA lies on the floor and HANNAH stands holding a lamp. Lights just up for a second.)

40.

(Lights up. Now HANNAH on the floor and SOPHIA stands holding

the lamp. Then they switch positions. Loud noise and SOPHIA falls onto a rug which is immediately pulled out.)

41.

(LEO and BEN sitting at the table. LEO has both hands on the tablecloth and is shaking. He is nervously crumpling the tablecloth so it gets bunched up under his hands. HANNAH enters with SOPHIA under her nightgown. They come center behind the table and face out.)

HANNAH

Time for bed.

(Pause.)

Don't be scared it's just your wife come for a visit.

(Pause.)

We have nothing to hide from him, huh.

(Pause. HANNAH puts her lamp on the table between BEN and LEO, loud music begins. She and SOPHIA go to the cabinet, enter and close the door. Music stops.)

BEN
I think that lamp will stay there a long time.
(Pause.)
That's a solid table.
LEO
I moved the tablecloth.
BEN
Good idea.
LEO
Why.
BEN
(Pause.)
It's more solid if it's resting on the table as opposed to a tablecloth between the lamp and the table.
LEO
Why.
BEN
(Pause.)
It has better contact.
(Pause. BEN rises and goes to radio which is again hanging, and hangs on it.)
LEO
Ben isn't going far, is he.
BEN
Rhoda darling, come out now.
(LEO rises and stretches. Then goes out window.)
SOPHIA and HANNAH
(Off.)
Safety first! Safety first!
BEN
—Total recall!
(Big landscape box moved in behind window. LEO sleeping in it. Lights change. Trees shake. Light comes up in the sky, HANNAH and SOPHIA out of cabinet, SOPHIA still under the nightgown, HAN-NAH with a lamp. They go to window. Trees still shaking.)
BEN
I guess I'll never forget this night, huh.
(Pause. Still hanging on radio.)
I better tell Hannah the truth. Hannah, I'll never forget this night, plus I couldn't fall asleep.
(HANNAH and SOPHIA have crossed through window into the landscape. SOPHIA comes out from under the nightgown. HAN-NAH turns and they look at each other.)

HANNAH
Good-by.
(SOPHIA takes her face between her hands and kisses her lightly.)
Good-by again.
(Pause. No one moves.)
This is like a garden.
BEN
I'd play the radio for you if I didn't need it for my body.
(It lowers and lowers him to the floor.)
Good-by.
HANNAH
Ben said good-by so you better kiss him.
SOPHIA
What.
LEO
(Sleeping.)
Good-by.
SOPHIA
Where's he hiding.
HANNAH
Who.
(Pause.)
My uncle.
LEO
Good-by.
BEN
Good-by.
SOPHIA
(Pause.)
I think we're stepping on him right now.
(Pause.)
Fortunately I have no weight.
HANNAH
She has no body.
SOPHIA
Wrong.
BEN
(Pause.)
She has a whole body inside a part of my body.
(Pause.)
She's here.
LEO
I think she's here I think she's actually standing on my head.
BEN
(Pause.)
One foot is standing on Leo's head and one foot.
SOPHIA
Shhhhhh.

BEN
(Pause.)
My head.

SOPHIA
Stop talking about me.

BEN
(Pause.)
Good-by.

HANNAH
Kiss Ben.
(Pause.)
Where you kissed me.

SOPHIA
What.

HANNAH
(Pause.)
I'm cold.

LEO
I'm waiting.

BEN
Go in through the window.

LEO
(Pause.)
Kiss me on the forehead.
(Pause. SOPHIA enters, goes to BEN, bends down and kisses him. Exits. Pause. She re-enters and stands against the door.)

HANNAH
Get out of here.

SOPHIA
Shut up.

HANNAH
(Pause. She turns, takes aim and throws her lamp at SOPHIA. Pause.)

SOPHIA
It missed.
(Pause. She exits.)

BEN
I smell something like an electrical fire.

ALL
Safety first! Safety first!
(Dog begins barking off.)

BEN
It's always dangerous to use electrical equipment indoors, plus I didn't need that lamp and it probably overloaded the circuit. If it ever breaks, the fire comes out through the crack and creeps over the furniture even if you're sitting on it so beware, beware everybody and always remember, safety first.

ALL
Safety first.

BEN
Wow. Pick me up and do something with my body. Then call Hannah in from the garden and wake up Uncle Leo because he's sleeping. It's too late for anything else tonight. We should have gone to bed a long time ago but I couldn't fall asleep soon enough. I have all of my best ideas when I'm sleeping. Too bad I didn't do it earlier.
(Pause.)
It'll be O.K. though. I had some good ideas and I'm certain to remember them.
(Pause. Barking continues. Then stops.)

42.

(BEN sits at table. Morning. He drinks coffee. HANNAH comes in the window and sits on the windowsill.)

HANNAH
Like it.

BEN
Yes.
(Pause.)
That's a good background for Hannah, huh.

HANNAH
You see me and you see the garden behind me.
(Dog enters.)
Maybe that dog wants some breakfast.

BEN
I bet he doesn't remember us.

HANNAH
Who.

BEN
(Pause.)
That dog.
(Pause.)
What's his name.

HANNAH
I don't remember.
(Pause. Someone comes in and collars the dog and takes him out. Pause.)

43.

(Lights up. HANNAH alone, sitting on the windowsill. She is combing her hair.
BEN opens the door halfway.)

BEN
(Pause.)
Nice.

HANNAH
I do this for a long time and I feel funny.

BEN
Hannah's head trembles a little, huh.

HANNAH
(Pause.)
That's what I mean.

BEN
What.
(Pause. She falls backwards out the window into the garden.)
Did that hurt.

HANNAH
No.
(Pause. She gets up and sits in the window again.)

BEN
Do it again.

ALL
(Pause.)
No.
(Pause. Cabinet opens. Empty.)
Do it again, Hannah.
(Pause. She falls again.)

BEN
(Pause.)
Did it hurt.

HANNAH
(Still fallen.)
No.
(Pause.)

44.

(Lights up. HANNAH alone, fallen out window. Pause, then she starts screaming. Enter SOPHIA from cabinet, head bandaged, goes to table and sits. At same time, LEO enters from landscape stepping over screaming HANNAH, with his head bandaged and he too goes and sits at the table. SOPHIA and

LEO *both fall out of their chairs and* HANNAH *stops screaming.)*

SOPHIA
(From floor.)
This is stupid. Nobody really got hurt.
(Pause.)
Nobody got hurt bad. Nobody had to put on a bandage.
(Loud music.)

45.

(HANNAH in window, sitting. Combs hair. BEN opens door halfway. She stops. He closes it and then she continues.)

46.

(Cabinet opens. SOPHIA exits from it and sits on windowsill. Takes out a comb and a small mirror and combs hair. Then she starts putting on makeup. BEN opens the door halfway, watches her. After a while she falls on the floor.)

BEN
It didn't hurt.

SOPHIA
(Pause.)
What.

BEN
(Pause.)
It felt wonderful.
(HANNAH opens a door halfway.)

SOPHIA
What.

BEN
It hurt.

SOPHIA
It didn't hurt.
(Pause.)
Admit it didn't hurt.

BEN
It didn't hurt.

HANNAH
What.

BEN
(Pause.)
She knows but she won't say.

HANNAH

What.

BEN

(Pause.)

It's wonderful.

(Pause.)

She knows.

SOPHIA

Ben knows, doesn't he.

(Pause.)

Why does he talk about it if he knows.

(She continues putting on her makeup. She finishes, stands and goes off through the landscape. Long pause. LEO comes and pushes through from behind HANNAH and goes to the hanging radio and places it on the table. He exits. Then a pause; the radio starts playing music. After a while BEN and HANNAH exit and the music keeps coming through the radio until everyone has left the theatre.)

ONTOLOGICAL-HYSTERIC MANIFESTO I

(APRIL, 1972)

Theater in the past has used language to build: what follows
what?

We use language not to destroy, but to
undercut pinnings of <u>there</u>.

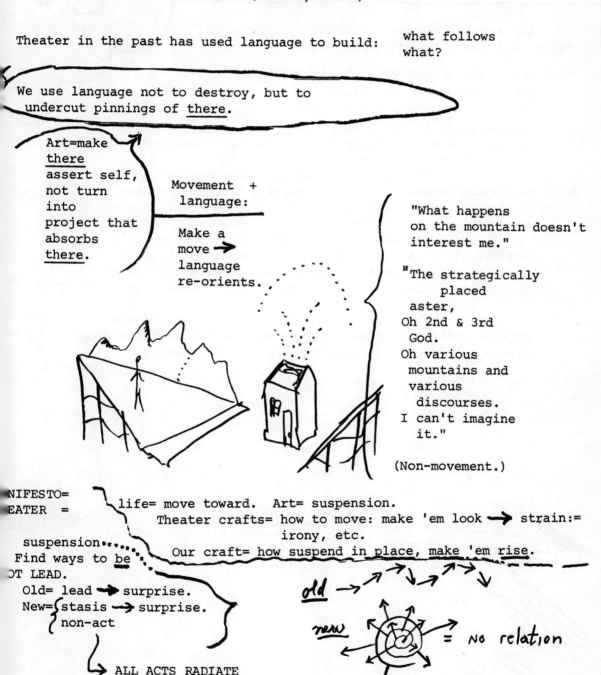

Art=make
<u>there</u>
assert self,
not turn
into
project that
absorbs
<u>there</u>.

Movement +
language:

Make a
move →
language
re-orients.

"What happens
on the mountain doesn't
interest me."

"The strategically
placed
aster,
Oh 2nd & 3rd
God.
Oh various
mountains and
various
discourses.
I can't imagine
it."

(Non-movement.)

NIFESTO=
EATER =   life= move toward. Art= suspension.
                    Theater crafts= how to move: make 'em look → strain:=
                                          irony, etc.
   suspension   Our craft= how suspend in place, make 'em <u>rise</u>.
Find ways to be
OT LEAD.
  Old= lead → surprise.   <u>old</u> →
  New= stasis → surprise.
       non-act   <u>new</u>   = No relation

        ↳ ALL ACTS RADIATE

THEATER !

The stage. Destroy it carefully, not with effort but with delicate maneuvers.

Why? Heavy destruction vs. light destruction.
What distorts is excellent.
What distorts with its weight.

Distortions: 1) logic -- as in realism, which we reject because the mind already "knows" the next move and so is not alive to that next move.
        2) chance & accident & the arbitrary -- which we reject because within too short a time each choice so determined becomes equally predictable as "item produced by chance, accident, etc."
        3) the new possibility (what distorts with its weight) -- a subtle insertion between logic and accident, which keeps the mind alive as it evades over-quick integration into the mental system. CHOOSE THIS ALWAYS!

        The field of the play is distorted by the objects within the play, so that each object distorts each other object and the mental pre-set is excluded.

MANIFESTO !

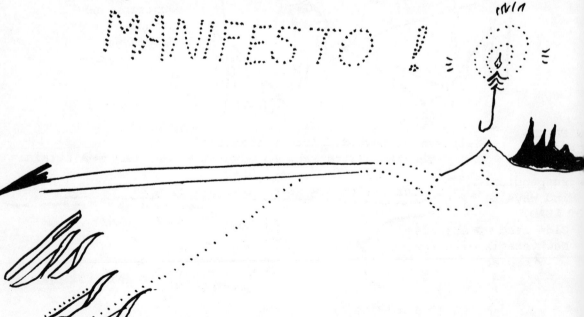

Problem of art-- how
to make people watch
the right thing while
it's going on... **SO** ——————>

Not watch changing
relations:
But watch what
doesn't change in
midst of it.....

"Language
subjects us
to orien-
tation
massage." --
Peckham:
that's
all.

Art: not concerned with essence
 But with THING
            used in such a way
            that it vanishes
            & what is
            left is suspension:
 In life. ——>.thing is tool --we get
 somewhere.
 In art.<——> never get there
            Suspended.
          Why? Create a ZONE
            in which placed
            things (head) luminate!

1967-- Suddenly the theater seems ridiculous in all its
    manifestations and continues to do so in 1971. I.e.,
    Peter Brook staged Midsummer Night's Dream. The actors
    enter onstage and immediately, the absurdity-- both
    in the orchestrated speech and activity-- as Stella,
    Judd, et al. realized several years ago...one must reject
    composition in favor of shape (or something else)...
    Why? Because the resonance must be between the head
    and the object. The resonance between the elements
    of the object is now a DEAD THING.

1971--Lenox, summer. I sit, at sunrise, and stare out
    into the trees, listening to the birds-- i.e. 100
    invisible birds in counterpoint. My head, savoring
    that interweaving of themes, performs in a good way--
    performs in the way that heretofore I have felt art
    should make it perform. But suddenly (drama!)
    that often-before entertained notion crystallizes in
    my head in such a way that a chapter ends, the book
    closes, and I have no more interest (no more risk,
    no more "unknown") in such an art based on counter-
    point & relationship. What can replace it? Don't
    know.... The painters have discovered "shape." What
    can the theater discover?

I.E.

Only one theatrical problem exists now: How to
create a stage performance in which the spectator
experiences the danger of art not as involvement or
risk or excitement, not as something that reaches out
to vulnerable areas of his person,
          but rather
the danger as a possible <u>decision</u> he (spectator) may
make upon the occasion of confronting the work of art.
The work of art as a <u>contest</u> between object (or
process) and viewer. Old notions of drama (up thru
Grotowski-Brook-Chaikin)= the danger of circumstance
turning in such a way that we are "trapped" in an
emotional commitment of one sort or another.
The new ontological mode of theater (within which
hysteria lies as a seed/spark which forces the
unseeable to cast shadows) --
The ontological-hysteric theater: the danger that
arises when one chooses to climb a mountain and-- halfway up-- wishes one hadn't.

> Art till now= appealingness: Making an object
> that we fall in love with. Make the obsessional
> object.

          NOT ART/No more art, naturally. Yet the aesthetic
thrill. The point is, of course, that "art" no longer
provides (provokes?) the aesthetic thrill. In a world
of scarcity (now psychically superceded if not yet
practically) the one was against the other.
Conflict at root of drama. OK. It's all so simple,
really. Now-- art can't be based in conflict. Old art
aroused, empathized with that, made our inner nature
vibrate to that in such a way that it was "profound."
The grounds of conflict are now seen as...not between
entities, but within the single unitary occasion which
could exist-- could not exist. That oscillation
replacing "conflict."

where oscillates the conflict ?
conflict o—→←—o
conflict ←—o—→
. . . . ?

But there is no center, the conflict is between the idea
of a center and the idea of a field. (The idea of a
center= old-fashioned "being"; the idea of a field=
old-fashioned "not-being.")

A FIELD BY ITS NATURE CONTAINS ONLY HARMONY.
In our attempt to hold together a center, we mistakenly
    view the field perhaps as one in which particles,
    etc., form a kind of conflict situation. But:
Not true.
Conflict there, as elsewhere, an illusion. (Absence
    of conflict doesn't mean absence of dynamics.
    Conflict BLOCKS dynamics.
Ecstasy = all forces operate at once to produce STASIS!
            (Replace conflict-- push and pull of selected
                forces-- with total action of all forces.
                That is stasis, that is ecstasy.)

Wittgenstein:
    If mean= intend. Anything is intended.
    Any intend.
    Use anything, to mean anything: but, the system must
        have a rigor.
    Mean something by a movement·of the hand-- was it the
        movement that he meant?

To express something which can only be expressed by this
    movement.

To read off the "said" from the face of the thought?
No-- our theater is making harmony. Singing counterpoint
    in language-- swimming in language in a way
    appropriate to the ongoing internal (mental) activity..

So : language systems:
            THUD!
            (Start out speaking in own terms,
            system created in terms of play
            by using own concerns!)

$$\left(\begin{array}{l}\text{think of swimming, think of singing,}\\ \quad\text{think of the picnic, think of the grass}\\ \qquad\text{glass}\\ \qquad\text{glass}\\ \qquad\text{glass.}\\ \text{(Has a system begun to be created?)}\end{array}\right)$$

Now:

    Acting against materials (the table, the floor, the other actor's body) is establishing this new language that doesn't <u>read</u> but "illustrates." (I.e., thinking against things.)   Pick proper interference. Like new <u>motor</u>.

$$\text{\underline{MOTOR}} + \bigg/ \frac{\text{\underline{slight shifts}}}{\text{\underline{stuckness}} ?} \longrightarrow \text{glue:}$$

ALWAYS NOTATE YOUR EXACT SITUATION AND PROCESS WHEN <u>WRITING!</u>

TAKE TWO RULES CONTRADICTORY IN NATURE. FOLLOWING BOTH MEANS SUCCESS.

In 1968, the theater became hopeless. I suppose the immediate revulsion is always against the artificiality or something related to that, although artificiality itself is noble enough-- being the HUMAN contribution which, if properly posited, lifts the moment...turns nature herself into a construct of delight.

Ah-- that is the point is it not? To make a construct, which must be the motive behind all art effort. So where does the theater's artificiality turn sour? At what point does the "construct" give way to the lie, to the exaggeration? That may be the point: to isolate the difference between exaggeration and invention. Whereas exaggeration destroys balance, and invention is constantly replacing the center of harmony, shifting it

slightly in such a way that the shift, the moment of shift,
the act of the shift, becomes-- if experienced as the
specific OCCURRING EVENT that it is-- an occasion for
testing oneself, as climbing a mountain is a test of the
body.

Art, of course, tests the soul, tests the psyche. That
is to say-- purely a matter of vibrations. Now, where
do these vibrations vibrate? What fluid is it in which
the resonating wave patterns are established?

Well, folks-- ! The vibrations are in the head, of course.
And they are most certainly produced by the
(demonstrable) scanning mechanism of the brain. And
the universe-- which exists to us as a direct "production"
of that scanning and in-the-instant-rescanning, must
enter into a new relationship to the art work. No longer
the relation between a changing world (events march on)
and a posited ego which VIEWS events and in so doing
EXTRACTS art from the flux of the world-- while in that
EXTRACTION lies the terror that manifests itself as
"conflict and expression" in drama.....but a (new)
relationship in which the world is essentially a
repeating mechanism (which it is on both its building
block level and its higher cyclic levels) and the
scanning mechanism superimposed on the repeating mechanism
slowly builds an edifice. (The way nature and history
build.)

Two DIFFERENT kinds of edifice are built, however. One of
them is called "life" (in the private sense of "I have
lived a life") ...and the other shall be called art,
though this "art" is clearly something different from what
has been called art up to this point.

For this new "art"-- perhaps we should not think of it as
an edifice but as an accretion, as deposited sludge--
this new art is not EXTRACTED from the flux of life, and is
therefore in no sense a mirror or representation-- but a
parallel phenomenon to life itself. The scanning
mechanism produces the lived experience when it is
passive. I.e., the input rhythms are dominant; and the
scanning mechanism produces art when it is the ACTIVE
element, when its rhythms dominate the scanned object.
(The actual "making" of the art object then becomes
essentially a matter of notation.)

So hopefully, we end up with a new art that serves two
essential, related functions:
1) Evidence: useful as example to others, of the harmony
that results from an awareness and conscious employment
of our mechanism which is our "self" in its properly
industrious way upon the world (that flux of "everything
that is the case").
Evidence....to give courage to ourself and others to be
alive from moment to moment, which means to accept both
flux (presentation and representation to consciousness
as reality) and an INTERSECTING process--scanning--which
is the perpetual constituting and reconstituting of the
self. The new work of art-as-evidence leaves a tracing
in matter of this intersecting, and encourages a
courageous "tuning" of the old self to the new awareness.

2) ORDEAL. The artistic experience must be an ordeal to
be undergone. The rhythms must be in a certain way
difficult and uncongenial. Uncongenial elements are then
redeemed by a clarity in the moment-to-moment, smallest
unit of progression. After all-- clarity is relatively
easy (at least the "feeling" of clarity) in terms of
large structures because simplification can always be
wrought on a large structure (simplification often being
the bastardization of clarity).
But CLARITY is so difficult in the smallest steps from
one moment to the next, because on the miniscule level,
clarity is muddled either by the "logic" of progression
(which is really a form of sleepwalking) or by the
predictability of the opposite choice-- the surreal-
absurdist choice of the arbitrary & accidental &
haphazard step.
Of course
 ORDEAL
is the only experience that remains. And clarity is the
mode in which the ordeal becomes ecstatic.

Art is not beauty of
description or depth of
emotion, it is making a
machine, not to do some-
thing to audience, but that
makes _itself_ run on _new_
fuel. Can this machine
run? Most machines (art)
run on audience fuel--
(Man's piggish desire to
be at the center, to be
made to feel there is
"caringness" built into
the world: old art
manipulates that, tries to
get a response: fuel is
DESIRE in that case.
 FIND FUEL OTHER THAN
 DESIRE! Nervous energy?
 Basic hum of life?
 Vibration?) (Desire
 kills vibration, gets
 too crude)

WE MAKE A PERPETUAL
MOTION MACHINE. (The
closer to that ideal the
better. Run on less and
less fuel...that's the
goal of the new art
machine.)

I REPEAT !

I want to be <u>seized</u> by the elusive, unexpected aliveness
of the moment.
Surprise at the center: not the surprise of the least-
expected.....because that (least-expected) is a reaction
that "places" it and makes it no longer elusive. But
surprised by
a freshness
of moment that eludes
                constantly refreshes. You go toward it
and can't seize it? You don't go toward it...........

Art to me=
energy of wanting
to know (alert)
without desire to
move off the
center, off the
energy itself to
the object. Be
happy <u>NOT</u> knowing
in condition of
wanting to know.
Be joyous in that
tension.

Most art is
created by
people trying to
make their idea,
emotion, thing-
imagined, <u>be-there</u>
<u>more</u>. They re-
inforce. I want
my imagined to be an

Write by thinking
<u>against</u> the
material. Since
you don't want
to <u>convince</u> self
of your vision,
etc.-- but to le
it be informed by
the disintegrati
now-moment.

occasion wherein the not-imagined-by-me can be there.
My work= to deny my assertion (imagined) is true (is
there).
    by letting moment disintegrate it, as no assertion
really true in the face of the elusive now, the real
moment, which in its bottomlessness turns what it holds
into the bottomless anti-matter of what is <u>itself</u> in
the rigidity and deadness of before and after.

Subject of theater-- vanity: in all: nothing real
or of any great matter, including <u>that</u> fact: So it is
                                      ALL THEATER.

1) Used to be--   like a staggered race
                    Relations (beauty)
                    Now that's a cliché.
      So-- no relations:
         But shape?   relates to head

         Head: keep dealing with throb in head.
2) Undercut
    Set up irritant
       against line of the scene.
          (Bright lights?)
              intersect with other realm.

Don't sustain anything

1) Erotic ~~angel~~ angel: --a shape

Subject: THE EFFORT OF PUTTING WHATEVER ARISES TOGETHER
        That <u>EFFORT.</u>

Subject: Make everything dumb enough to allow what is
        really happening to happen.

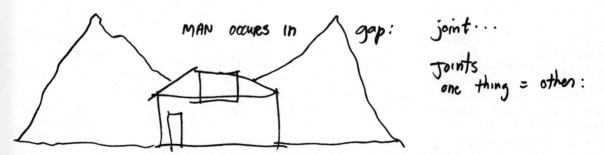

MAN occures in   gap: joint...

*Joints
one thing = other:*

"a new cadence means a new idea."

only: → get → rhythm of the mind as something that acts
vis-a-vis entering dots: which leave <u>traces</u> that other
dots bounce off. So mind is input folded over imput.
GET THAT!

BEN: (That writing) says "I gave up writing plays
three years ago." (<u>Pause</u>.) The fat lamp descends.
That is not written but imagined. (<u>Pause</u>.)
Come into the writer's workshop.

<u>A second lamp down, hanging over the first. A hum.</u>

Get that second lamp outa here.

LEGEND: "WHY?"

BEN: Nobody has a right to ask me questions who doesn't
       show himself.

Crew comes and closes curtains on screen on which title
is projected.

       Why.

Thud, pause.

       The minute I formed that word carefully it was
       an imitation.

The curtain reopens by itself. A slide of an ancient
auto is projected on the screen. Pause. Then the same
picture is projected on the table-top.

VOICE: One picture must not be allowed to view the
         other picture.

Music begins. A sign comes down--"Cousins in
photography." The music stops. Ben has exited. He
returns with a rope, throws it over the screen, with a
hook on the end of the rope, and starts to pull.

BEN: Oh well. (Pause.) Make something.
ALL: Can you describe it, Ben?

HċOhTiEnLà

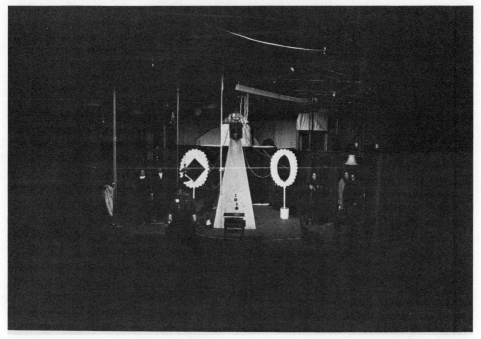

Photo Babette Mangolte

(or) HOTEL CHINA

PART I

(Two naked bulbs on floor stands.
Two men sit, one behind each
bulb. KARL has a sack covering his
head. Pause, then a lamp is brought
out and placed on top of his head,
over the sack.
MAX holds the sides of his chair
seat tightly and at the same moment a wrapped package is placed
upon his lap.)

BLACKOUT

(The lights come up again and
MAX has a rock on his lap, the
rock having replaced the package.)
MAX
Get this rock off.
KARL
(Under the sack.)
I didn't notice it.

BLACKOUT
(When the lights come up, the
rock is gone from MAX's lap. Crew
enters and puts a second sack over
KARL, this time covering the lamp
as well as the head. Then they put
a large sack over MAX that covers
his whole body. Then they put a
rock on his lap.)
MAX
(From inside sack.)
Under the circumstances, leave the rock.
(Noise of rock being hit with a
hammer.)
Under the circumstances, that rock is shining.

(Lights out, flashlight spot on rock.)

BLACKOUT

(Lights up on empty stage. Rock
suspended in air and illuminated
with flashlight only. Slightly swing-
ing. Slowly comes to rest in space.)

BLACKOUT

(Lights up full and bright for the
first time, the rock still hanging in

air. Enter MAX awkwardly, still encased in his sack.)

MAX

(From under his sack.)

Oh, that rock is still here.

(Pause.)

**Thank God, if Rhoda's uncle comes looking
for me he won't really find me.**

(Pause.)

Watch out for that rock.

(Pause.)

Watch out for that rock, everybody.

(Noise of hammer hitting rock.)
(Pause.)
(Noise of hammer hitting rock.)

I'm hidden and I'm empty also.

(Enter KARL II—RHODA's uncle.
He stands there, then exits and re-
enters in a sack that reaches to the
floor. A hum. Pause. Lights dim
down to a spot on the rock. The
two sacked men move very slowly.
A thud.)

MAX and KARL

Magic.

(Pause.)

Like magic.

(A bell.)

(Enter KARL I, with just the head
sack and the visible lamp balanced
over it on his head. He turns the
lamp on. Pause. Then turns it off
and all exit. Lights up bright. Rock
hangs on empty stage. A hum. Then
ten more rocks are placed about
the stage, and silence. A sign is
hung on the rear wall:

**WHERE IS THE LIGHT COMING
FROM.**

Pause, a second sign over the first,
reads:

**EACH ROCK IS CAPABLE OF
VIBRATING INDEPENDENTLY.**

A hum returns. Then the hum goes
off and another sign is placed:

**EACH ROCK LOOKS LIKE A PIECE
OF BREAD TO EAT (A POTATO).**

Lights dim and the rear is removed
to a film screen. Film begins.

The film is about ten minutes long.
It concerns rocks being placed in
different spots in different rooms.
On chairs, on cabinets, etc. Sometimes a room full of rocks, sometimes only one rock to a room. At

the end, the film goes slowly to
white and the stage lights come up
full. The stage is completely
cleared. The projector is still running clear leader as a big six foot
high rock is rolled on. The big rock
reaches its position, but then keeps
rocking slightly back and forth. The
projector goes out and the light
dims to the two clear bulbs on
stands, but the big rock keeps rocking. Bird chirps are heard and continue a long time as the rock rocks.
Finally the rock comes to rest. The
bird noise continues and a single
bright flood down center comes on
bright and illuminates the stage.
The bird songs fade as crew comes
and places small rocks on the floor
in a circle about the big rock.

Pause. Noise of hammer on rock,
ten times. Silence.

Pause. Enter MAX who goes about
and picks up the small rocks, load-
ing them into his shirt front so he
ends up having a bulging shirt full
of heavy rocks. Finally the load is
too much and he is pulled to the
ground by the weight of rocks.

Pause. Birds sing.

Enter KARL I, he goes to the big
rock, uneasily. Touches it tenta-
tively. He puts his ear to the rock
and listens. He puts the top of his
head against the rock. A hum.
While he is in that position, the
crew enters and puts a strip of
black cloth over his head with the
two ends coming down across his
ears and touching the floor. There
is silence. KARL and MAX speak at
the same time, but each speaks
very slowly, sounding each syllable
of each word at great length, with
space between the syllables.)

KARL	MAX
Trytomake	Ihavemanyw
therockli	ordswhereas
keaword.	Karlhasonly
	one.

(A tree comes out of the top of the
rock.)

MAX

L o o k a t r e e.

(Midway in his sentence, a hum begins. Silence. The stage is cleared and furniture is set about. Following is a rock ballet, in which ten rocks are placed and replaced in strange ways on the furniture and floor, with pauses between moves, etc. During the rock ballet, occasional notations through the clunk sound of a hammer hitting a rock. A hum during which the re-set takes place. Silence. Re-set, etc. Perhaps ten sequences of re-setting. Then, roll in a slightly larger rock on a rolling table. The table gets center, and a crew member tilts the table top, which is moveable, forward, and the rock falls to the floor. He takes the table off. Pause.

A sign is revealed: SAY SOMETHING.

Music begins, romantic Mahler, but made somewhat ridiculous by random single notes of the piano being struck every six or seven seconds, equal in volume to the orchestra. After a while, each rock in

sequence is covered with a different color satin cloth.

Lights go down until the only illumination is again just the two stick lights. The music and piano notes continue through all this. It stops and MAX and KARL I enter and sit behind the two stick lights. A crew member comes and covers KARL's eyes with a handkerchief. They bring back the rolling table, and it again has a somewhat larger rock on it. They set up a curtained wall on the table, so the rock is enclosed on either side, behind and above by the curtain. Pause. A hand comes through the rear curtain and caresses the rock and then lies on top of it.)

BLACKOUT

(Loud noise; as the noise begins the lights come up bright, and a plate of polished metal is balanced on the top of the rock. The curtains have been removed. The noise stops. Silence.)

MAX

Rhoda.

Photo Babette Mangolte

KARL

Yes.

(Pause.)

(Crew enters with a metal sheet and four thin metal legs; they use the legs to help balance the sheet exactly on the top of KARL's head. Pause. Then (with the help of a thin string) the contraption slumps to the side, off KARL's head and falls to the floor.

Crew enters and takes the table with the rock and metal plate, and hangs the table, rock and plate, all of which stick together, so that the table top is facing into the audience —the legs pointing to the rear of the stage—in a position about five feet off the ground and at the furthest downstage point of the acting area.

They set each cloth-covered rock on a small table, ten of which were brought out for that purpose, evenly spaced about the stage. Each table is the same color as the cloth covering the rock on it.

Sign revealed: CONCENTRATE ON ROCKS, NOT ON THE COLOR OF THE TABLES.

A loud hum begins, and each table and rock gets a small light hanging down over it and illuminating it. MAX enters, with a tray on which there is a place setting and food and a small vase of flowers. From the other side, KARL I enters, dragging a sack filled with rocks. MAX exits and KARL proceeds to center and stops. He reaches into his sack and takes out a rock which he puts into his pocket. A loud hum and he falls to the floor. Silence.)

MAX

(Off.)

Hey Karl.

(Pause.)

Get up.

KARL

(From the floor.)

Bring me something to eat on a tray, huh?

(Pause.)

If I had

ALL

What

KARL

(Pause.)

Something to eat would restore my energy.

ALL

What.

(Pause.)

What.

(Pause.)

What.

(Pause.)

What.

(MAX enters, tray held balanced on his head. He walks carefully, like walking a tightrope, knees slightly bent. Stops center, balancing. Piano notes have been occasionally struck as he entered. Now only silence. He moves his hands away and the tray falls, since he makes a fast exit the moment his hands are off the tray.)

ALL

What.

KARL

(From floor.)

Take that rock out of your pocket.

(In the rear, RHODA has been in a chair, sleeping with her head resting on its side on a table set for a meal; a small lamp also on the table. Table is covered with a cloth. She rises, and we see that where her face had been pressing on the cloth, it still adheres. The tablecloth remains stuck to the side of her face as she rises, while everything on the cloth, including the lamp, remains attached to it. She exits, then half re-enters and holds the doorknob, the cloth and objects still attached to the side of her face.)

RHODA

(Pause, holding the doorknob.)

I'm holding a rock.

KARL

That's a doorknob.

(Pause.)

I'm holding a

RHODA

That's a

KARL

(Pause.)

Rock

RHODA
(Simultaneously.)
—Doorknob.
(A song plays through.)
RHODA
That's one of my
KARL
What.
(Pause.)
—A rock.
RHODA
(Simultaneously.)
—Favorites. Well. A story is getting told by my body and my activity.
KARL
Where's Max.
RHODA
Shhhhh.
KARL
(Pause.)
Rhoda should.
RHODA
What.
ALL
(Pause.)
What.
(Noise and reverberation.)

RHODA
That was like saying "shhh," huh?
KARL
—You can't see me putting my finger to my lips.
(Thud and reverberation.)
Because I'm on the floor.
(RHODA puts her finger up to her lips. Thud and reverberation. She doesn't move.)
Look at the rock coming out of my mouth.
RHODA
Shhhhh.
KARL
That sounds like the ocean.
(Pause.)
I think I'll go to sleep.
(Thud and reverberation. RHODA lowers her hand, enter MAX on the other side, carrying a tray with plates, etc. He stops once he is inside the door.)
RHODA (and MAX)
Max (Rhoda).
RHODA
Yes.

Photo Babette Mangolte

(MAX lets go with one hand, so the tray hangs down, but surprisingly nothing falls off it. KARL I, on the floor, rolls over.)

KARL

Watch me good.

(Thud and reverberation. MAX and RHODA put fingers to their lips. Pause. KARL rolls over again. They drop their fingers and he rolls over again; a small thud. Pause. He rolls again. Another thud.)

I read a lot.

(Pause, he rolls over again.)

What goes in comes out.

RHODA

Turn over.

MAX

—Turn it.

KARL

What.

(Pause.)

Page two.

(Thud. Pause, he rolls over again, then rises and exits. Pause. He re-enters behind MAX, and at the same time KARL II enters right behind RHODA, carrying a fairly large book which he rests on her shoulder and starts leafing through.)

KARL I

What's that

KARL II and RHODA

What

MAX and KARL I

Story.

ALL

(Off.)

WHAT!

(Thud and reverberation.)

KARL II

(Pause, he keeps turning pages.)

It's in pictures.

(He kneels, and turns pages more slowly. Kneeling so his back is to the audience, he is pressing the back of the book against RHODA's legs. The "Shhh" noise comes over the speakers, loud, mixed with noise of the ocean.)

RHODA

(After a pause, speaking loud to be heard over the noise.)

Is that sleep.

MAX

(As KARL I is whispering in his ear loudly.)

—He wants me to put the tray on my head.

KARL II

(Loud.)

No pictures!

(KARL I stops whispering, leans back against the doorpost and covers his eyes with his hands. The noise stops and there is silence.)

KARL I

(Quietly.)

I seen it again.

MAX

What.

KARL I

(Pause.)

That's the

MAX

What

KARL I

Second time I seen it.

(Pause.)

I seen it through my fingers, huh.

MAX

All those rocks on the table.

KARL II

No pictures.

(Pause, MAX lifts the tray up and holds it out.)

RHODA

(Pause.)

For me?

MAX

For me.

(He goes to her.)

RHODA

Thanks but I'm not hungry.

(Noise of a hum, turns into ocean noise. Crew enters and puts a big rock on MAX's tray. Silence.)

(Pause.)

I'm so hungry I could eat a rock.

(The rock rises from the tray and hangs above it. MAX puts his head down on the tray, and slowly collapses, stage by stage.)

MAX

(On floor, after a pause.)

That one.

KARL I

That one.

KARL II

(Pause.)

That one.

RHODA

Shhhhh.

(Her "Shhhh" comes through the loudspeaker and grows into the sound of the ocean. A film begins rear; shot of the beach with the waves breaking. All exit but RHODA. She moves to a table which is placed more center, and puts down her head and spreads her tablecloth and stands lamp upright, etc. Pause. Ocean noise fades and film continues.)

There was pressure on my head when I was standing.

(Pause.)

It wanted to go in two directions. What. My head.

(Pause.)

Shhhhh.

ALL

(Off.)

Shh.

RHODA

I made the sound of the ocean with my own body.

(Pause.)

Can I make the look of it.

ALL

(Off.)

Shhhhh.

RHODA

Try.

(Pause.)

Use the body in different ways but don't. What. Try. What.

(Enter woman in bathing suit, wings and dark glasses. She goes in front of movie and splashes water on herself.)

ALL

(Off.)

Shhhhhh.

(She looks at RHODA. Her name is ELEANOR.)

ELEANOR

That looks like my body.

RHODA

If I move I move the table.

(Pause. Enter female angel. Her hands are locked behind her head so that her elbows protrude, and a rock is attached, resting on the top of each elbow.)

Photo Babette Mangolte

ALL
(Off.)
Shhhh.
RHODA, ELEANOR, ANGEL
We're like the ocean but we're also like sleep.
ELEANOR
Don't splash me.
ANGEL
I can't.
RHODA
Is it because I'm sleeping I can't.
(Pause, film continues.)
My head is a weight but that isn't the end of it.
ANGEL
—That head is like a rock.
ELEANOR
Don't splash me.
(Pause.)
I tell that to my angel.
RHODA
Shhhhhhhh.
ANGEL
You don't have to make me think of the ocean.
RHODA
I'm getting deeper.
ELEANOR
(Pause.)
I'm wading.
RHODA
Waiting.
(Pause.)
Shhhh.
ANGEL
Look at me.
RHODA
Shhhh.
ELEANOR
Don't splash me.
(Pause.)
I'm getting heavier for some reason.
ALL
(Off.)
Shhhhhh.
(The "Shh" continues as rocks are now strapped to the ANGEL's thighs and to ELEANOR's head. Silence, Pause. ELEANOR, due to the weight of the rock, gets slowly pressed down to the floor.)

ELEANOR
(From floor.)
Don't splash me.
(ANGEL faces front. Crew enters and attaches strings—lines of force —from each rock (two on elbows, two on thighs) out forward and expanding, each string to the appropriate corner of the projected expanding square.)
ALL
(Off.)
Shhhh.
(Continues for thirty seconds, during which time crew holds chair and lamp, each on end of a pole, up into the zone defined by the string. Noise stops and crew exits with objects.)
ANGEL
That's long enough.
(Pause.)
Thirty seconds is long enough.
(Silence; crew brings out two more objects at the end of poles and holds them in the zone. Pause, they exit. Crew re-enters with a third set of objects as KARL I enters and stands in the doorway.)
KARL I
Could I take a load off my feet.
ANGEL
My head could.
(Third set carried off.)
KARL I
Bring that chair.
ANGEL
Join me.
(Crew brings him a chair. It's set so he is seated facing the ANGEL with his head in the zone. A stone is placed on his head; hum begins. ELEANOR rises and comes into zone and takes a cloth and puts it over KARL's head and arranges it so a lamp, with her assistance, is balanced on his head.)
RHODA
Oh, I could do this.
KARL I
I think the light's in my eyes.
ANGEL
—I think the light's in my eyes.
(Pause.)
Those rocks are pretty good.

RHODA

Don't move.
(Pause.)
Can you tell what's covering you.
(Hum begins again, then stops. Film of ocean stops.)

ANGEL

What I need now is a cabinet.

ELEANOR

—Not a cabinet.

ANGEL

(Pause.)
A chest of drawers.
(Pause.)
To put things in.

ELEANOR

I think so too.
(She uncovers KARL and exits. KARL I turns his chair around as the strings are removed from the angel, who exits. Strings re-fixed to KARL's head. Crew brings out in sequence to drop into his zone the following items; during this, the hum continues:

    spoon
    scissors
    rock
    paper
    notebook
    glass (drinking)
    shoe
    umbrella
    flashlight
    pillow
    wristwatch
    pencil
    nail
    hammer
    flower
    plate of glass
    eyeglasses.

Light changes to single light bulb.)

KARL

Now what I need is a couple of angels. What. To make things tie up. What.

ALL

(Off.)
It's Sunday, Karl.

KARL

(Pause.)
Shhhh.
(Pause.)
Sunday, huh.
(Crew comes and clears all rocks.)

I don't think there's a rock. Oh yes. There's a floating rock also.
(Enter KARL II with a bicycle wheel on the end of a stick. He hooks the wheel over a hook that hangs down. Then he just stands there. The big rock re-enters rear; a hum.)

KARL I

Look, I don't want anything distracting me.

KARL II

You know what day it is.
(Pause.)
What.

KARL I

I think your attention is divided.

KARL II

I'm gonna stand where you can see me, Karl.
(Hum continues, gets louder. They have to shout now.)

KARL I

Talk louder.

KARL II

That makes it a distraction, huh

KARL I

(Pause.)
What

KARL II

Good enough.

KARL I

I bet I'm the only one who knows what's happening.

KARL II

(Overlap end, still shouting, remember.)
—I roll up my sleeves!
(Pause; hum very loud, then off. KARL II takes off his coat, rolls up his sleeves as big rock gently shakes back and forth. He puts his coat over his arm and stands there.)

KARL I

Oh well, I'm still holding on.

KARL II

(Over end.)
—Oh well, I'm about ready to try another position.
(Rock still shaking. KARL II puts coat over his head and buttons up. He goes behind the rock which is still shaking. It shakes a long time and then it stops. The crew enters with poles, and they touch a few of the hanging objects and make them move slightly. Midway, ELEANOR

enters and goes to the table at which RHODA still sleeps, and she also sits and rests her head and sleeps. The big rock goes off.

Screen on, on which is projected an open window, with the ocean beyond and a boat sailing across. The screen is taken off, but the slide remains on. Crew enters and puts a rock on RHODA's and ELEANOR's head.)

ALL

(Off.)

Shhhhhh.

RHODA

I can't get out of this position yet.

(Sign appears: WHAT DAY IS IT.)

VOICE

(Off, low.)

S - - - - - - - un - - - - d - - - - - - - - - - -
ay - - - - - - e - - - - -.

RHODA

(Overlapping end.)

—I'll see you on Sunday, Max.

KARL I

Jesus, look what's coming out of my mouth.

(Pause.)

A hammer.

(Pause.)

A plate.

(Pause. Knocks begin.)

A pane of glass.

(Pause.)

A pair of glasses.

(Pause; knocks get louder.)

A chair.

(Knocks louder, on and on. Clear stage but for RHODA and ELEANOR at the table. Silence.)

RHODA and ELEANOR

Collect things.

ALL

(Off.)

Shhhhh.

RHODA and ELEANOR

Sleep but collect things also.

(Without otherwise moving, RHODA covers her own head with a cloth that lies beside her head.)

ALL

(Off.)

Shhhhh.

RHODA

I don't have to be told. I mean. Suggested.

Photo Babette Mangolte

(Pause.)

I got this idea by myself.

(Pause.)

Now I need a rock on top of the cloth to hold it in place in case it's windy.

(Pause.)

Don't worry I won't be moving for a long time.

(Pause; crew comes and places a rock over the cloth. Soft noise of wind. A second rock hung just over the first. Pause. The ten tables with rocks and cloths over are carried back; carried on slowly, all at once. At the same time, on cue, all the cloths are removed and the rocks are seen to have been replaced with ten wads of paper. MAX enters with a tray piled with rocks; he hesitates, and spills them all on the floor and exits quickly. Pause.)

Legend: ONE ROCK IS GOING TO MOVE.

(A dog barks in the distance. Finally, wired to a string, a single rock swings just once across the stage, barely seen because it's so fast.)

Legend: END OF PART ONE.

(Tape of applause. House lights come up as applause continues. As the stage is cleared, a single table is brought center. At each corner, a rod sticks straight up about three feet with a stone balanced on the tip. A sign above the table reads:

THE BEGINNING OF LANGUAGE.

After a while, as the audience is filing out, a large bowl of soup is placed in the center of the table and chairs are brought for MAX and ELEANOR who have soup spoons and drink soup, both out of the same bowl.)

PART II
1.

(BEN on the balcony; brings from there into the room, a flower in a flowerpot. Crew brings in a rock which they place on the table center. A loud hum. BEN slowly collapses, first to one knee, then completely to the floor. Hum gets very loud; then cuts out. RHODA enters holding up a sheet over her head, hiding herself behind it. She comes and brings it down over the rock, and brings her whole body down so it is flopped over rock and table. A moment of shaking noise.)

VOICES
(Off.)
Get up.

BEN
Which one are they talking to.

RHODA
Look how I'm.

VOICES
What.

RHODA
(Pause.)
Placed.

BEN
What place is this.
(Pause.)
I don't live here, huh.
(Pause.)
Hey, a flower plus.

VOICES
What.

BEN
Falling down when I don't want to fall down or when I want to.
(Pause.)
Being fast.
(Pause.)
Coming from the inside plus

VOICES
What.

BEN
(Pause.)
Coming from the outside.

VOICES
What.
> *(Pause.)*

What.

RHODA
This isn't a natural position for me.
> *(Pause.)*

Right.

BEN
This isn't a natural position for me, huh.

RHODA
Ben's lying.

BEN
> *(Pause.)*

Lying down, huh.

RHODA
I give it

BEN
What.

RHODA
> *(Pause.)*

Time.

BEN
It changes.

RHODA
It doubles and then it changes.

BEN
Look. She's smart when she's in a position
that isn't natural.

RHODA
This isn't a natural position for me.
> *(Pause. A loud hum. Then silence.)*

BEN
During that time period.

RHODA
What.

> *(Thud. Pause. BEN rises, goes to
> balcony. Picks up a flowerpot;
> door opens rear and KARL enters
> halfway with a bouquet.)*

BEN
It doubles and then it changes.
> *(Pause; no one moves.)*

Make a mistake. I don't live here but.

KARL
But.

RHODA
> *(Pause.)*

This isn't a natural position for me.

BEN
But

KARL
But

RHODA
> *(Pause.)*

But

BEN
But

RHODA
But
> *(Pause.)*

But what about a rock and a flower.
> *(KARL exits.)*

Where he was standing.

BEN
What

RHODA
But

> *(Pause. A hum. Crew brings out a
> rock which they place on the small
> of RHODA's back.)*

It passed through my body.

> *(BEN puts the flowerpot back on
> the balcony. He takes a rock out of
> his pocket and leans over the rail-
> ing.)*

Legend: PART TWO: WHERE BEN
DROPS TWO ROCKS FROM THE
BALCONY TO SEE WHICH HITS
THE SIDEWALK FIRST. ONE IS
HEAVIER. IT HAPPENS AND IT
HAPPENS AGAIN.

> *(Pause. BEN holds two rocks high,
> then lets go. He just stands there.)*

RHODA
> *(Immediately after the two clunks
> of the rocks hitting.)*

—That happened fast.
> *(Pause. Crew brings two more
> small tables, one for her feet,
> another for her arms and head, so
> she is totally prone. Another sheet
> covers her completely, except for
> a hole through which the rock on
> her back protrudes. During this
> BEN turns to her.)*

BEN
> *(Pause.)*

Oh Rhoda, you thought that I lived here.
> *(Pause.)*

Look how I sleep standing.

RHODA
Can anybody.
> *(Pause.)*

See my mouth moving when I speak.

BEN

I'd like to drop that rock from a great height.

RHODA

Do that.

(Thud.)

Do that Ben.

(Pause. Front table removed, her arms and head again fall downwards.)

That's better.

(BEN turns to rail, holds it, leans over kicking up one foot a bit and looking out and up. It is a quick motion, and he returns to standing position.)

RHODA

(Pause.)

Do that again Ben.

BEN

—Do that again Rhoda.

(Pause. BEN lifts a foot six inches, keeping the leg straight. Immediately sets it down again. He takes a rock from his pocket and drops it as inconspicuously as possible. All that in one swift, hardly noticeable movement. He bends down and puts the rock back in his pocket, quickly comes center—again quickly lifts the foot, drops the rock. This time he doesn't pick it up but quickly turns and exits. As he exits, KARL is coming in the very same door with a bouquet of flowers. He goes to the balcony as a hum starts; he covers his eyes and collapses.)

BEN

(Off.)

I wish I could see the rock under Rhoda's stomach.

(A silence. Pebbles begin to be thrown over the walls into the set. They fall like rain. Lights dim to a single clear bulb over RHODA's head. A halo-type semi-circle set on the table over the rock on her back—like a ruffle. Music begins and a voice like a vaudeville master of ceremonies speaks over the music.)

VOICE

In the center of the rock, there is a dancing figure. Watch the figure in the center of the rock. Ladies and gentlemen, in the center of the rock there is . . .

(He continues repeating the message; his voice slowly fades as music continues, and pebbles keep falling.)

BLACKOUT

2.

(A table is set with a tablecloth, flowers, place settings. Silence; then a hum. Pebbles begin to fall. RHODA enters, draped in a sheet. KARL enters at the same time, carrying a heavy rock; both immediately lean back exhausted against the door through which they entered.)

KARL

(Pause.)

It's too hot to stand up straight, huh.

RHODA

—I better not take off this sheet.

(Pause. Pebbles keep falling.)

This sheet keeps me cool.

KARL

—What a heavy rock I got.

(Pause. BEN enters and sits at the table; he tucks a napkin under his chin, and turns to the others.)

BEN

Join me.

RHODA

What.

BEN

Ben.

RHODA

(Pause.)

What a heavy sheet I got.

(KARL lifts the rock to his face and presses it against his head from above slightly, as if it's pressing down on his tilted back head.)

ALL

(Off; not waiting until KARL is set.)

That rock keeps him cool.

(BEN picks up a fan and fans himself. RHODA takes the bottom edge of the sheet and ties it up

*over her head with a ribbon. This
takes some time. Then KARL falls.
Crew enters and carries him to the
table, sits him in a chair; he slumps
over, but they manage to tuck a
napkin under his chin. Two others
are meanwhile bringing two buckets of water with sponges. They go
to RHODA and sponge down her
legs. Then they take a towel and
dry her off. They help RHODA
place a foot in each bucket. They
lead her to the table, walking with
her feet in the water buckets; not
walking—shuffling.
Pebbles still falling; low hum continues.)*

RHODA
(As she is shuffling across.)
I feel a lot cooler this way.
(Pause.)
Pebbles are getting into my buckets.
BEN
Join me, huh.
(Pause, as RHODA is seated. Pause.)
Let's all look at something.
ALL
(Off.)
What.
BEN
(Pause.)
How much do all of us weigh now.
RHODA
—Gravity is attracting my body.
(Pause.)
Gravity plus heat.
BEN
Shhhhh.
*(Pause. Enter ELEANOR who sits at
the fourth place at the table. She
tucks a napkin under her chin,
while pebbles still fall.)*
I tend not to. What. Notice anything impor-
tant.
(Pause.)
Then I had dinner. Then I went out into the
garden.
ELEANOR
Could I look like that.
ALL
(Off. Pause.)
What.
ELEANOR
Rhoda.

BEN
Karl.
KARL
(Pause.)
Ben.
ELEANOR
—Rhoda.
(Violin music begins.)
Wow. That brings back wonderful memo-
ries.
BEN
What.
ELEANOR
(Pause.)
You don't have a garden, Ben. You have a
balcony with flowerpots on the railing of
the balcony.
BEN
I don't.
ALL
(Off.)
What.
BEN
(Pause.)
Live here. But I act like I live here.
*(Crew goes to balcony. Repeats
BEN's lean-over, kick-foot-up, look-
up-out motion. Then gets down on
floor—not a collapse.)*
I fainted on it.
ALL
(Off.)
What.
BEN
(Pause.)
Let me show what I mean.
*(He doesn't collapse, but like the
crew, gets down on the floor.
Door opens, showing crew with a
tray with a meal for the table. As
the door opens he collapses on the
spot.)*
No not so fast.
ELEANOR
It looked more.
ALL
(Off.)
What.
ELEANOR
(Pause.)
It looked more realistic when it was.
BEN
What.
ELEANOR
Fast.

BEN

I got down on the floor but I was completely in control of my body.

ALL

(Pause.)

What.

BEN

Try it again.

ELEANOR

Proof.

BEN

I want a repetition. Proof.

(Pause.)

Wanting something is proving it, but I'm imagining.

ALL

(Off.)

What.

BEN

(Pause. Violin music has long since faded or cut. Pebbles still fall.)

Something hit my face.

(Pause.)

Say what before I say face.

ALL

(Off.)

What.

BEN

Face.

(Lights cut to single bulb.)

What a collection of.

ALL

(Off.)

What.

ELEANOR

(Pause.)

Everybody should

ALL

(Off.)

What

BEN

Change.

ELEANOR

What.

BEN

(Pause.)

I don't live here.

(All get onto the floor, not fainting.)

Everybody did that slow and they were all in control of their bodies.

(Pause.)

Now they have a chance to do it faster. Nobody fainted.

(Pause.)

Nobody's still fainted.

ELEANOR

What hit me in the

ALL

What.

(Pause.)

Face.

BEN

Look at those pebbles coming from the ceiling.

(Pause.)

I couldn't see them for the first time.

(Pause.)

If we all fell from our chairs would we get hit in the face with pebbles.

(Crew crawls off. Pause. Re-enters carrying another tray loaded with meal. Immediately collapses. Pause.)

Fast and not in control of the body, huh.

(Pause. All crew crawl off.)

Doing things.

ALL

(Off.)

Moving the furniture, huh.

BEN

Eating dinner.

(Pause.)

If I

ALL

What

BEN

Lived here. A. You don't live here, Ben. B. You still do things even though you don't live here. Different people would have different problems eating dinner. What. Rhoda would have something covering her face and the food couldn't get into her mouth.

(Pause.)

Karl would have a different problem.

(Pause.)

All of us would have the problem of not sitting at the table and being on the floor lying down.

(Pause.)

If the table was sideways.

KARL

(Over end.)

—Something's hitting me in the face.

BEN

—the food would slide onto the floor, huh.

(Tape noise of pebbles falling.)

ALL

(Off.)

Try it Ben.

BEN

What.

ALL

(Off.)

Try it.

BEN

(Pause.)

I don't live here.

ALL

(Off.)

Try it.

(Pause.)

Please try it.

BEN

—Can I try it now.

(Pause.)

I better go to the garden. Ha. What garden.

(Music begins soft.)

I want to get a better look at

ALL

(Off.)

What.

(Pause. RHODA rises, puts feet in buckets and shuffles off slowly.)

Don't bump into anything, Rhoda.

(She continues slowly off. Wait until she's gone completely.)

BLACKOUT

3.

(Lights full, intense bright from in front. BEN, KARL, RHODA and ELEANOR sit at table; normal dress. They all manage, while sitting, to move chairs and table as a unit in a circular revolve, a full 180 degrees. While this is happening, crew comes and manages to blindfold RHODA. At the same time HAN-NAH enters and goes and waters the flowers on the balcony. She does the lean-out bit. All at the table turn their chairs and look at her. She repeats the lean-out bit.)

ALL

(At table.)

She lives here.

(They all point at HANNAH who now just stands at the balcony. HANNAH goes back to water the

flowers; crew lowers a large white beam over the table, perhaps a foot above its surface. It hangs there parallel to the footlights in line so it points at HANNAH at whom the others are still pointing. All their pointing arms are now tied to the beam. HANNAH now has a broom and is sweeping up pebbles from the last scene. She goes and does the lean-out bit. Crew comes and dumps another bag of pebbles on the floor. IDA enters and goes to rail where both she and HAN-NAH do the lean-out bit. Then HANNAH goes gack to sweeping and the crew dumps another bag of pebbles; IDA tries to take the broom away from HANNAH. They struggle over the broom a good while, as music begins. They end, collapsed in a big stuffed chair center, exhausted. Crew brings a big flood that is directed out, right behind and over the chair. They hold it there.)

ALL

Begin again.

BEN

(All have their arms tied to beam, remember.)

Do that motion again of going to the balcony railing and

ALL

What

BEN

(Pause.)

Kick one foot up a little and leaning out and twisting your head and

ALL

What

BEN

(Pause.)

Rolling your

ALL

What

BEN

(Pause.)

Eyes

ALL

What

BEN

A little.

ALL
(Pause.)
Begin again.

BEN
That's a heavy.
(Pause.)
Say what.
(Pause.)
Say that beam of wood hit me in the eye.
(Pause.)
If it hit me in the eye it would have to be a beam of sunlight.
(Pause.)
What am I pointing at.

KARL
(Overlap end.)
—What am I pointing at.

RHODA and ELEANOR
—What am I pointing at.
(A noise, "ping," and a second beam lowers. This one angled from above so it comes down into BEN's eye.)

ALL
That's not sunlight.
(Crew covers HANNAH and IDA in the chair with a big white sheet.)
Sweep up.

BEN
—What's happening on the balcony.
(Pause.)
Hey. Somebody should go to the balcony and lean over.
(Pause.)
I can't because I'm pointing at it, plus

ALL
What

BEN
(Pause.)
I have a beam hitting my eye.

ALL
Sweep up.

BEN
—I don't live here but I do things.
(MAX enters and stands just inside the door. He wears a dark suit and hat, dark glasses. A dark, full beard. He carries a stuffed briefcase.)

MAX
(Pause, tiny bells tinkle.)
Take a load off my feet, huh.

BEN
Do that

MAX
What

ALL
(Pause. Tinkle stops.)
Shhhhh.

BEN
I could be quiet when I do that or else
(A thud.)
Try it again.

MAX
(Puts finger to his lips.)
Shhhhh.

BEN
They say be quiet.
(Pause.)
They don't do it with their finger

MAX
My . . . way . . .

KARL
(Overlaps.)
—I'll say it for that gentleman.

MAX
(Finger up again.)
—Shhhh.

KARL
He said it first, I said it second.

ALL
Shhhhhhh.
(Pause.)
Shhhhh.
(Pause. Still at table, they all turn their heads and look out.)
SHHHHHHH!
(Thud.)

MAX
Even if that chair is covered with a sheet. What. Take a load off my feet.

OTHERS
Shhhhhh.

MAX
—I can be quiet too huh.
(Women move under sheet.)

BEN
Do that again Ben

HANNAH and IDA
What.

BEN
(Pause.)
Talk louder. No.
(Pause.)
Talk showing the mouth moving.

MAX
(Pause.)
Shhhhh.

BEN
What's moving.
(Women under sheet move.)
Now I move into a different position.
MAX
Shhhh.
BEN
I'm not showing it
ALL
What
BEN
(Pause.)
My mouth
ALL
What
BEN
(Pause.)
Moving
(Women move under sheet.)
MAX
Shhhh.
ALL
If we all move at once the beam hitting
Ben's eye will not have moved.
MAX
(Over end.)
—How. Do. I. Get. There.
*(Thud. Pause. A big stone lowers
onto the sheet.)*
ALL
Now. Nobody. Has. To. Move. Because.
Something. Else. Moved.
(Pause.)
RHODA
My arm hurts.
*(Pause. Then a piano note begins
to be repeated and repeated.)*
I liked it better when my sheet was cover-
ing my face and my legs were showing.
BEN
(Over end.)
—I have a beam in my eye but I don't com-
plain.
(Pause.)
I saw something.
*(Lights out, spot on rock; spot
moves to MAX's face. Silence.
Pause.)*
ELEANOR
Whose hand am I touching.
BEN
—Don't move.
*(Pause. All move their chairs a bit.
Spot still on MAX's face.)*

KARL
Shhhhhhhsssssssssss.
BEN
(Over end.)
—I don't know what to do with my hands.
(Pause. Spot goes back onto rock.)
HANNAH   **IDA**
I wish that could talk.   What rock, I don't
                          see any rock.
*(Pause. They move under the
sheet.)*
ALL
(At table.)
We haven't moved.
(Lights up full.)
RHODA
—I think there should be another beam
coming out of my eye and pointing at
something.
BEN
(Over end.)
—The beam is coming into my eye and it
isn't going out of my eye.
(Pause.)
How come it isn't pushing my head back.
*(Lights out. Spot on MAX. He shifts
his weight and for the first time re-
laxes, no longer pressed with stiff
neck against door; he just stands
there; waits. Pause.)*
ALL
Do that again, Max.
*(Long pause. He doesn't move. He
shifts his weight. Lights up full;
long pause. He shifts his weight
again.)*
Do that again.
*(Crew has come to railing from
outside and climbed over. As MAX
speaks, crew turns and does lean-
out bit.)*
MAX
I guess I'll take a load off my feet even
though that chair is covered with a sheet.
*(He begins an incredibly slow
shuffle toward the chair. Lights immediately go out, except for a spot
on crew who repeat the lean-out
bit. The spot follows the crew as he
exits through door; then spot to
MAX who is shuffling. As soon as
light hits MAX, full lights immediately up as crew comes to move the
beam which hits BEN's eye. They
move it so it goes from his eye to*

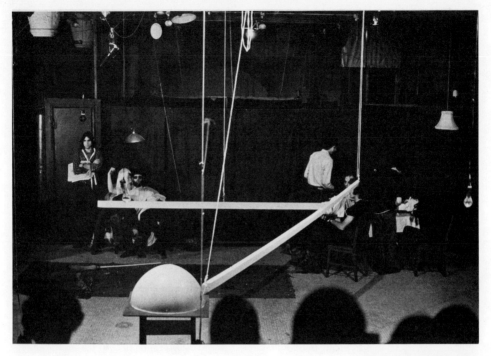

Photo Babette Mangolte

a white dome which they place on a second table. During this MAX sits on women moving the rock. Women start screaming as he sits on them, and so continue. One gets out from sheet, goes and does railing-lean-out bit. She collapses. Other continues screaming. After a while, collapsed one rises and returns under sheet. HANNAH II enters and does lean-out bit. A bouquet of flowers is tossed over the wall onto the set. A bright spot is brought to illuminate area of balcony; HANNAH II waits for it to repeat lean-out a second time; then she exits but bright spot (visible) remains on balcony. Pause. Screaming continues. Crew comes and does lean-out bit in bright spot. He is accompanied by a second, who watches. HANNAH II re-enters, does bit. As second crew person goes and gets a birdcage which he hangs outside above balcony, the lean-out bit seems to be directed to looking

up at the bird. Crew tries to do lean-out and stops in frozen position to let HANNAH II adjust him. Screaming continues all this while. Then all three randomly try lean-out bit. Bell struck each time they do it. At the same time, the crew turns the white dome, showing rear side to be cut out, with flowerpot and flowers inside.

Crew person doing lean-out exits; HANNAH II does it alone, with bright spot still on that area. Group at the table all have their shirts taken off as much as possible considering their arms are still tied to beam. HANNAH II exits and MAX takes out a pipe and lights it. Pause. Screams continue.

MAX takes out newspaper and reads it; it hides his face; women stop screaming. Crew comes and gives MAX slippers, and tie paper to his face (string around upheld paper and head). A big clock begins to strike, and a crew person

enters with a grandfather clock strapped to his back—he bends over and angles himself so the clock is pointing at MAX.
Just as he manages that position, he collapses with the clock on top of him and the lights go out.)

***

(Pause. Lights up, the same but the clock man is gone. Nobody moves. Pass out programs to the audience. Then pass out handfuls of gravel. Lights out except for spot on MAX. Held for a while, then spot shifts to the group at the table. Big clock chimes again. Lights up. Man enters again with clock. Falls; pause, then lights out.)

***

(Lights up, clock man is gone. Pause. Crew enters to turn dome to hide flowers. Crew brings muslin strips and winds them around the beam and arms, encasing the arms tied to the beam, mummy-like.
Sound of soft hum.

Sign revealed rear: GET READY FOR THE NEW LANGUAGE.

Hum gets louder. Crew removes paper from MAX's head. He takes off his coat and rolls up the sleeves of his shirt. He shows his muscles as the legs of the women creep around from under the sheet to hold him in the chair. He holds his muscle a long time; then relaxes. Pause. Makes muscle in his other arm.)

BLACKOUT

***

(Lights up; crew is putting gloves on MAX's hands.)

BLACKOUT

***

(Lights up. Nothing happens. Long pause. People at table free their arms from the beam. They put on shirts and sit. At the same time, MAX gets dressed again, first taking off the gloves.
Pause. All wait. BEN goes to railing

Photo Babette Mangolte

*and does lean-out bit. He just
stands there. Pause. Repeats it.
Pause. BEN makes a circle with his
fingers and holds that circle horizontal, parallel to the floor. He
looks at his hands forming that
figure, then holds it up to the audience. He drops it horizontal again.
HANNAH II enters naked and
stands right behind BEN who is
looking at his hands and the figure
they form. She does the lean-out
bit. She turns front and shows her
body, extending her arms in either
direction. The crew comes and
gives her a beam to hold. The beam
is like an extension of her outstretched arms. Pause. BEN
crouches so she can turn and make
the beam revolve, which she does.
She now stands in profile.)*

VOICE
(Over tape.)

Begin again.

*(Knocking is heard. Entire stage
cleared of props and people. Then
BEN enters and sits. Frowns and
holds his forehead between finger-
tips. Enter RHODA. She takes off
her coat and hangs it on a hook
next to the door.)*

BEN
Do that again, Rhoda.

*(Pause. She shakes her head. Pause.
Thud. She exits. BEN sits back in
his chair, still holding his head with
his fingers. HANNAH enters, puts a
big rock on the table and lies over
it. Hum. ELEANOR enters, puts a
big rock on top of a tall cabinet
and exits. IDA and HANNAH II
enter with grandfather clock, sliding it in upright position, set it and
exit. RHODA enters wearing a second coat, which she takes off and
hangs on a hook.)*

RHODA
(Pause.)

Should I

BEN
What

RHODA
(Pause.)

Do it again, Rhoda.

BEN
(Over end.)

—Do it again, Rhoda.
(Pause.)
Let's try

RHODA
What

BEN
(Pause.)
Let's try talking at once.
*(She exits; re-enters wearing a coat.
She takes it off and hangs it up as
BEN speaks.)*
Watch out.
(Pause.)
Do it again Rhoda.

RHODA
—Is that talking

BEN
What

RHODA
(Pause.)
Rhoda means at one time.

*(Enter HANNAH II who does rail-
ing-lean-out bit as RHODA exits.
Pause. RHODA enters and goes to
railing and she and HANNAH II
both do lean-out bit. Pause. Then
RHODA faints. Enter ELEANOR in a
coat; she takes it off and hangs it
up, and as she does, HANNAH
again does lean-out bit. Pause. BEN
goes and embraces HANNAH II.
IDA enters and HANNAH rises from
table to help her slide the clock to
a new position on the floor. They
exit as BEN and HANNAH II face
the clock.)*

BLACKOUT

---

*(BEN sits, holds head with fingers.
HANNAH II has gone. RHODA
comes in door, takes off coat.)*

BEN
Do it again Rhoda.

*(RHODA immediately after hang-
ing up her coat goes to table and
flops over the rock that is still there.
HANNAH II and IDA enter and
move clock to balcony. A tick-tock
noise begins. They place the clock
so it rests on its side on the railing,*

*laid across the railing. At the same
time crew enters and pulls up
RHODA's dress, attaching the hem
to strings so it rises over her prone
body like a peacock ruffle. Then
BEN exits.)*

                    RHODA
(Pause.)

Oh Ben.

                    BEN
(Off.)

What

                    RHODA

I feel like I got a

                    BEN
(Off.)

What

                    RHODA

Got a

                    BEN
(Off.)

What

                    RHODA
(Pause.)

Got a

                    BEN

What. Rock.

                    RHODA

Did I say that.
(Pause. Long silence. A thud.)

**I have to stay in this position for a long
time.**
*(Balcony railing falls and clock falls
to floor.)*

Guess what.
(Pause.)

**It broke and now there's another way to tell
time.**
(Pause.)

Use my dress for that.
*(MAX enters. Takes off his coat and
sits. Takes up newspaper which he
opens. Crew enters and ties it to
his face. A house (small—a model)
is lowered in the sky. Pause. A
second table is brought out for
RHODA's head. It's put so she can
rest her cheek on it. A small mirror
is on it so she can see herself.)*

That's not a reflection on my
(Pause.)

What.
(Thud.)

Body.
(Thud.)

Photo Babette Mangolte

Ready.
(Thud.)

Looking into it is to know everything fast.
(Thud.)

                    BEN
(Off.)

Help out.

                    RHODA
(Pause.)

I'm not touching anything now.
(Pause.)

**Oh Rhoda, you turn your body like a handle.
Look, look.**

                    BEN
(Off.)

Help out.

                    RHODA

Her eyes.
(Pause.)

Look, look her eyes.

                    BEN
(Off.)

Look look my face.
(Pause.)

Move it once.

RHODA

(Pause.)

Look look as I move my face like a glass. What glass.

(Pause).

Look look as I move my eyes like something.

(Pause.)

Breathe onto the mirror, huh.

(Crew brings slippers and pipe for MAX, makes a small hole in the newspaper and slips the pipe through and into his mouth. Pause.)

Oh what a wonderful body, the mirror makes me think about that.

(Pause.)

I never thought about that until I had a mirror to look into it.

(Crew brings a blanket for MAX.)

It's getting chilly out here on the table. Oh, looking into the glass, huh.

(Pause.)

I should arrange my dress better. What can she see, Rhoda.

(Pause.)

Only her eyes.

(Pause.)

They get wider. Oh, I better move my

ALL

(Off.)

What

RHODA

Head a little.

(Pause.)

Oh, I better move my head a little so my eyes don't

ALL

(Off.)

What

RHODA

Hurt.

(Pause.)

They don't hurt.

MAX

(Under his newspaper.)

Oh Rhoda

ALL

(Off.)

What

MAX

(Pause.)

What big eyes you have.

RHODA

What big eyes I have.

(Tiny bells tinkle as she continues.)

Move the glass a little or move the eyes. Hurt hurt she says and then she repeats herhelf. And then she spreads out her dress and shines.

(ELEANOR appears in the door.)

Hurt hurt she says and collapses beautifully, huh.

(Bells stop. Pause.)

Then she

ALL

(Off.)

What

ELEANOR

What big eyes you have, Rhoda

MAX

Help me.

(Pause.)

Sit on my lap.

ELEANOR

What can I see in that

ALL

(Off.)

Mirror

RHODA

My eyes.

(Pause.)

Move a little.

ELEANOR

I was about to say that.

ELEANOR and RHODA

(Pause.)

Move a little.

(Pause.)

Discover it, huh.

ELEANOR

—I'd like to sit down.

RHODA

—Wouldn't you like to see me move my eyes a little.

(Pause.)

Oh, that hurt.

ELEANOR

I bet that hurt a lot Rhoda.

(Pause. She points.)

I don't know if that mirror is trembling or Rhoda's face is trembling.

MAX

—This used to be a relaxing position but my face is shaking behind the newspapers.

(Tiny bells again. ELEANOR holds point, then crosses, still pointing, and angles herself so she can see the newspaper in the mirror. Silence.)

ELEANOR
I can read the newspaper by looking into this mirror.

RHODA
Once.
(Pause.)
Using the mirror once.
(ELEANOR collapses, holding handles on table top so she dangles.)
Oh God, notice carefully how Rhoda rolls her eyes like marbles.

ELEANOR
—That hurt.
(Pause.)
Rolling like I had

ALL
(Off.)
What

ELEANOR
(Pause.)
Rhoda had marbles under her feet.

RHODA
I'm Rhoda.

ELEANOR
—I'm Eleanor. I had

ALL
(Off.)
What

ELEANOR
(Pause.)
I had the experience of reading the newspaper in the mirror.

RHODA
—Oh God, look at my eyes rolling.
(Pause.)
I had marbles under my feet.

ELEANOR
—I'm Eleanor, I had marbles under my feet.

BEN
(Off.)
My feet.

RHODA	ELEANOR
My eyes.	—My feet.

RHODA
(Pause.)
My eyes is more correct than my feet, huh.

ELEANOR
I had marbles under my feet.

RHODA
—My eyes.

ELEANOR
And I had the experience of

ALL
(Off.)
What

MAX
—She read something backwards.

ELEANOR
Reading the newspaper but using the eyes differently.

RHODA
Like marbles.

ELEANOR
Like feet huh.

MAX
(Pause.)
Like feet.
(Pause.)
Like feet.
(Crew comes and puts small platform with wheels under MAX's feet.)

RHODA
(Pause.)
Like eyes he said when he thought about it.
(Pause.)
Everybody moves their feet to get more comfortable, plus

ALL
(Off.)
What

RHODA
(Pause.)
See more.

ELEANOR
—I don't see everything from this position.
(Pause.)
I don't see anything without moving my feet, huh.

RHODA
Shhhhhhh.

ELEANOR
(Pause.)
They do not

ALL
(Off.)
What

ELEANOR
Move.

RHODA
(Pause.)
Correction

ELEANOR
They do not move without telling them to
move.
(Pause.)
Each muscle is small enough to
ALL
(Off.)
What
ELEANOR
Move.
(Pause.)
Each eye muscle
RHODA
Shhhhh.
ELEANOR
(Pause.)
It doesn't hurt.
RHODA
Shhhhhh.
*(MAX slumps inside his paper co-
coon. Pause. Rope on the foot cart
pulls it back and forth a bit, mov-
ing his feet.)*
RHODA and ELEANOR
Read about it in the eyes, Rhoda (Eleanor).
(Pause.)
Look into my house and read about it huh.
ALL
(Off.)
What.
RHODA
Shhh!
*(Pause. Cart moves a little. Pause.
House moves a little in sky.)*
ELEANOR
Look into it.
RHODA
—What.
ELEANOR
(Pause.)
My house naturally.
(Pause.)
RHODA
—Look into it.
*(BEN enters halfway and leans
against door jamb. Pause. A faint
"ping" is heard. All turn their
heads and look at house in sky,
except MAX.)*
RHODA, BEN and ELEANOR
We are not looking directly at the house yet.
(It moves a bit. Pause.)
We are changing our lives effectively but we

are changing the language we use about our
lives.
(Pause.)
We are not keeping track of our language.
(House moves a bit.)
We are not looking directly into the house
but we are trying to remember everything.
(Thud. Pause.)
We are not looking directly at the house.
*(Enter man with grandfather clock
strapped on his back, crosses tightly
past BEN and falls in the doorway;
they speak as he falls.)*
We are not looking directly at the house,
think about that.
(Thud, pause.)
Keep track of something—
(Thud.)
Keep looking directly into the house.
RHODA
—I think it moved.
(Man with clock is crawling out.)
ELEANOR
—Don't give me that shit about the house
moving huh.
(Pause.)
Tell me something.
(Thud.)
—Why did Rhoda
ALL
(Off.)
What
BEN
It moved.
(He exits.)
ELEANOR
(Pause.)
Why did Rhoda
ALL
(Off.)
What
ELEANOR
(Pause.)
Why did Rhoda
ALL
(Off.)
What
ELEANOR
Go to the balcony and
RHODA
What
ELEANOR
What
(Pause.)
Why did Rhoda go to the

RHODA
What
ELEANOR
Balcony
(Pause.)
Why did Rhoda
RHODA
What
ELEANOR
What
(Pause.)
Why did Rhoda go to the balcony and look
up
RHODA
What
ELEANOR
Why did Rhoda go to the balcony and look
up and put her foot up and twist her head
RHODA
What
ELEANOR
Head.
(Pause.)
Why did
RHODA
What
ELEANOR
(Pause.)
Do it
RHODA
What
ELEANOR
(Pause.)
Why did Rhoda
RHODA
What
(Pause. Thud.)
ELEANOR
Why did Rhoda look at the house that was
floating when she
RHODA
—What
ELEANOR
—Said she wasn't looking at it exactly.
RHODA
Why did Ben do that
ELEANOR
What.
RHODA
(Pause.)
Why did the
ELEANOR
What

RHODA
(A bell rings once.)
Why did the man with the clock fall down.
(Pause.)
The man with the clock fell down because
the clock was heavy and he wanted to.
(Pause.)
It felt wonderful
ELEANOR
What
RHODA
Why did Rhoda, correction, why did Ben.
*(Music starts. Lights dim, spot
focuses on house. Music fades. The
spot remains on the floating house.)*
Oh, what like a cloud a house that floats.
*(BEN enters, stands hung up center,
looking at the house. Pause. BEN
exits.)*
ALL
(Off.)
Ben just entered.
(Thud, pause.)
He looked at the house for a long time then
he re-entered.
(Thud.)
RHODA
Sometimes Ben comes and he says some-
thing.
(Pause.)
Sometimes he comes and he doesn't say
anything.
ELEANOR
Help out, huh.
RHODA
(Pause.)
Sometimes a man with a clock comes into
the room and falls down.
(A bell rings once.)
Oh teeth.
ELEANOR
Oh teeth, oh teeth.
RHODA
—Oh truth, truth, saying that I think of the
table and the house.
*(Pause. A faint clattering sound be-
gins rear.)*
ELEANOR
Oh teeth, teeth, put it between my teeth.
RHODA
—Oh put it between my teeth, Rhoda.
(Pause.)
Is that where the words are.
ELEANOR
—Oh teeth, oh teeth.

RHODA
Is that where the lost words are.
ELEANOR
(Pause.)
Oh truth.
RHODA
—Oh teeth, teeth is that where the lost words are.
(House moves a bit in the sky.)
Oh teeth oh lost words.
ELEANOR
—Oh truth. Teeth. Teeth.
(Pause.)
RHODA and ELEANOR
Oh teeth teeth truth truth teeth.
(Crew enters; a hum begins; they have a long thin cloth, about a twenty foot strip, which they place: one end in RHODA's mouth and the other end in ELEANOR's. The cloth between them lies in a heap on the floor. The hum continues as BEN enters. He picks ELEANOR up off the floor to put her into a chair at the table, but she is too heavy and they both fall to the floor. BEN rises, after a suitable pause, and drags ELEANOR off through the door; she is still holding the strip of cloth in her mouth. After having taken ELEANOR off, he returns. He sits at the table and looks up at the house, leaning one arm on the table.)
(Loud, over the hum.)
What a nice way to move.
RHODA
(With cloth in mouth.)
What a nice way to float says Rhoda.
(Thud.)
She says it without moving her lips.
(Cart moves so much that MAX's feet fall off. Pause. House moves a bit. Pause. Cart moves again, then house moves. ELEANOR enters, cloth still in her mouth, carrying a tray with tea setting. She sits at the table, setting down the tray. Right behind her, the man with the clock on his back enters halfway as close behind her as possible. He quickly backs out, so his entrance seems almost a mistake.)
BEN
What a nice combination.

RHODA
—What a nice way to think about it says Rhoda.
ELEANOR
—E . . . . E . . . . . E . . . . E . . . L . . . E . . E . .
A . . . N . . . O . . . R.
(As she is spelling, crew enters and re-sets MAX's feet on cart. Hum ends.)
Now make the house move.
(Both RHODA and ELEANOR speak as best they can with the cloth in their mouths. Pause.)
We imagine we live there.
(Pause.)
We imagine making a visit. Ben. Rhoda. And E.L.E.A.N.O.R.
MAX
(As she repeats spelling her name.)
—Uncle Max.
HANNAH
(Off.)
—Hannah.
HANNAH II
(Off.)
—Hannah number two.
ALL
(Off.)
—Everybody else!
BEN
What.
(Thud. Pause. BEN rises as house and cart move. House moves just a bit, but cart goes all the way offstage. BEN goes to kiss ELEANOR but can't because of the cloth in her mouth. He takes her face in his hands, tilts his head and forms his lips, then stops. Thud. Thud. Cart returns with flowers. MAX takes off his shoes and socks, and puts his feet gently on the flowers, not crushing them.)
ELEANOR
E . . L . . E . . A . . N . . O . . R.
BEN
—B . . E . . N.
RHODA
—R . . H . . O . . D . . A. That spells Rhoda.
(Pause. The cart rolls a bit. The house lowers to the floor and is turned around to show its doll house interior. HANNAH enters and crouches inside the house. As

Photo Babette Mangolte

soon as she is there she speaks
quickly and perfunctorily.)

HANNAH

H-a-n-n-a-h. That spells Hannah.

*(She turns, turning the house with
her so it again faces its outside to
the audience and she is hidden.)*

BEN

—I'd like to give Eleanor a kiss.

(Pause.)

Try me.

ELEANOR

Try it out Ben.

BEN and MAX

Feet first huh.

ELEANOR

**—I got this thing in my teeth but that
shouldn't bother you.**

(She stretches out her body.)

I got this—

(MAX exits briskly.)

**—thing in my teeth but that shouldn't
bother you really.**

(Pause.)

**It blocks my mouth a little bit but that
shouldn't bother you really.**

BEN

Who's in the little house.

*(A window in the house opens and
HANNAH presses part of her face
in the small opening. ELEANOR
rises and exits quickly. Thud.)*

Don't.

ALL

(Off.)

What.

BEN

(Pause.)

That house moved a bit.

*(He takes out a cloth and wipes his
face. HANNAH exits, loud clatter
begins; BEN looks closely at
RHODA, then seizes the tablecloth
in his teeth and pulls it off the
table, from under her body and
exits with it still in his teeth as the
clattering continues.)*

BEN

(Off.)

Get that house.

ALL

(Off.)

What.

BEN
(Off. Pause.)
Get that house back
ALL
(Off.)
What

BEN
(Off.)
Floating.
(Pause. Clatter stops.)
Getting that house back floating so it's moving a little

ALL
(Off.)
What.
(Pause. Clatter begins. A second house in the sky makes a brief appearance, floating on and then immediately off.)
Get that house back

BEN
(Off.)
What

ALL
(Off.)
—Floating so it's moving a little bit.
(Clock man in halfway and immediately backs out. MAX enters simultaneously, puts on his shoes and exits, still wearing the paper cocoon which has, however, mostly slipped off his face. As MAX is exiting, BEN enters halfway with tablecloth still in teeth, and immediately backs out. He re-enters right away and goes to the table where RHODA is and stops and turns to look at the bird in the cage which starts to sing. Sound of buzzer after BEN is set looking. HANNAH enters and halfheartedly does lean-out-look-up-at-bird bit; stands on the balcony, slumping arms folded. She looks at BEN as crew enters with a light stand with a single clear bulb on top; they set the stand on the balcony, light incense while the other lights go out leaving only the single lightstand illumination. Bird song continues as crew brings on a second long cloth and takes the tablecloth from BEN's mouth and places one end of the long cloth in his mouth and the

other end in HANNAH's mouth. HANNAH exits and BEN turns and looks at RHODA. Thud. Bird song fades.)
(Off.)
I can't see good what Ben is
(Thud.)
Doing.
(Thud.)
Make it more
(Thud.)
Visible.
(Thud.)
In a
(Thud. Pause.)
(Thud. Bird song off.)
BEN
(Pause, he hasn't moved.)
The next thing I have to do. Get it out of my mouth in a certain way.
(Pause.)
It's not
ALL
(Off.)
What

BEN
It's in my teeth not in my mouth really.

RHODA
—It's in my teeth and Eleanor is in a different room.
(Pause.)
That means Eleanor is in a different kind of communication, huh.

BEN
—This kind of communication means something is in my teeth and I talk when I'm holding onto it.
(Pause.)
Hey, that isn't mumbling, Rhoda.

RHODA
I bet

BEN
What

RHODA
(Pause.)
I bet that isn't mumbling.

BEN
My teeth.

RHODA
Ben's teeth means it isn't mumbling huh.

BEN
Get it out of my teeth, not to

RHODA
What

BEN
Not to replace mumbling.
(Thud.)

RHODA
It isn't mumbling

BEN
—It isn't mumbling.
(Pause.)
Now I know how to express all of my best ideas, huh.

RHODA
—Those are some of the best ideas you ever had, Ben.

BEN
(Pause.)
My best idea yet.

ALL
(Off.)
What.

BEN
Get the towel out of my teeth: in a way.
(Pause.)
Find a good way.

RHODA
That's your best idea yet, Ben.
(Thud.)
Find it.

BEN
I found it.
(Pause. He drops towel from his teeth, pretty much unnoticed because of the single light source and the insignificance of the opening-of-the-jaw movement. Pause. Thud.)
Did you notice when it went out of my teeth.

RHODA
—I almost noticed good.
(Pause.)
I noticed.

BEN
—I did it carefully. Correction.
(Pause.)
I didn't do it carefully but I thought about it carefully a moment before and I thought about it carefully a moment after.
(Pause, house moves a bit.)

BEN and RHODA
Oh Ben, what precision. Oh Rhoda.

ALL
(Off. Pause, as BEN moves very slowly over to RHODA and climbs quickly on the table and takes her neck in his teeth.)

What precision.
(Loud thuds begin and continue, as a voice speaks immediately over the loudspeaker; there is a brief pause between each word NOT timed to thuds. Simultaneously HANNAH enters, goes to balcony and does lean-out once, then again, taking bird out of cage and throwing it up to sky, whereupon it simply falls to the earth.)

VOICE
(Off.)
This part of the play is invisible because Ben is holding Rhoda's neck in his teeth but his head is blocking the audience's vision. This part of the play is also hard to see good. She threw the bird into the air but it fell down—
(Continuous with preceding action HANNAH II enters, does lean-out bit once and shouts over the loudspeaker voice "I'm the real Hannah even though my part is not important." She falls to the floor, followed by HANNAH I as speaker continues.)
—This part of the play is hard to see also. A second person playing the same part bites the body of the first person playing that part and they both fall to the floor. But Ben is—
(Clock man enters and immediately backs out.)
—thinking carefully about what he has between his teeth while that happens which is invisible like all thinking. Oh, did you see him almost come into the room, maybe you missed seeing that.
(Pause. Thuds stop. Then they begin again.)
Try to see Ben's eyes. He is trying to look at you to convey his thoughts. It's very hard to see that.
(Pause.)

BLACKOUT

4.

(The house is in the sky. Door opens, clock man comes in a step and immediately backs out. As he exits, RHODA enters and immedi-

ately goes to balcony, waits a beat and falls.)

BLACKOUT

5.

(RHODA still on the floor; house floats in the sky. It moves a bit. ELEANOR opens a door halfway.)
Legend: SHE'S LOOKING AT IT IN THE SKY. BUT THE LINE OF HER VISION MISSES THE HOUSE BY A FEW FEET. NOBODY ELSE KNOWS THAT.
(While the audience reads the sign, BEN enters immediately behind ELEANOR and is pressed against her in the doorway.)
                    BEN
          (Pause.)
What a beautiful
                    ELEANOR
What
                    BEN
          (Pause.)
That's where I.
                    ELEANOR
What.
                    BEN
          (Pause.)
Let's
                    ELEANOR
What
          (Pause. She points at the house.)
What a beautiful house, I can imagine myself
                    BEN
—Oh Eleanor darling, you spoiled it by talking about it.
                    ELEANOR
          (Pause, still pointing.)
Wrong. I spoiled it by pointing at it.
          (As it moves slightly. Pause. BEN backs out.)
I'm not pointing at it exactly, huh.
          (Music starts. It is morning; birds heard over the music and two trees are moved on, framing the house. Music finally fades.)
          (Still pointing.)
Oh, oh, point through the trees Eleanor.

                    RHODA
—Oh, oh, point through the trees as a favor to my body, huh.
                    ELEANOR
          (Pause.)
Through the house maybe.
          (Music begins again.

Legend: POINTING AT SOMETHING INSIDE THE HOUSE, WHICH SLOWLY GOES DOWN TO THE EARTH, AND ELEANOR FOLLOWS THE LINE OF HER OWN INTENTIONS.

Music fades and ELEANOR slowly walks toward where she still points.)
                    ALL
          (Off. Whispering.)
Like a beautiful:
Morning:
In the . . .
          (Music begins. ELEANOR waits for a moment, then exits briskly. Ropes are brought on and hooked to make line network, triangular, between two trees and house. After a while, blackout in which the music fades. Pause. Lights up. Birds singing. Pause; BEN enters halfway and backs out immediately. The lights start to go out as a table is carried out. A plate with an apple is placed on it. Lights out just as plate reaches table. Pause. Cut noise. Lights up. Apple rises an inch from the plate. Pause.)

BLACKOUT

6.

(House hangs in sky; empty stage. Crew enters in silence and sets up a chute that runs from door of floating house to ground. Then, in silence, all kinds of doll furniture, little figurines, tiny toy cars and other goodies come tumbling from the door down the chute. After a while BEN and others enter and scoop up the things that have fallen through and exit. Random thuds and bells begin to sound.)

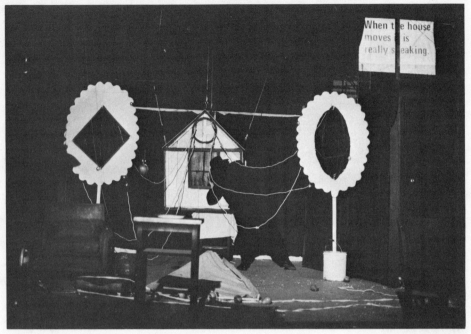

Photo Babette Mangolte

Legend: WHEN THE HOUSE MOVES IT IS REALLY SPEAKING.

(Pause. Noise continues and house starts to move across the sky as a child enters, takes the apple, bites it and puts it back. Pause. The child goes to the railing and does lean-out bit. Then exits. Pause. Noise continues; BEN enters and sits. Pause. Noise continues and there is a very loud knocking over the noise. BEN rises and goes to door which he opens. It reveals RHODA who lifts her lips to show her teeth. BEN walks into her, forcing her out and closes the door behind them both. This is all very perfunctory, un-inflected and quick.

House descends to earth, on a table. MAX enters quickly, goes and looks in a window for just a second, turns and exits.)

Legend: THAT WAS THE FINAL ACTION OF PART TWO OF HOTEL CHINA. RELIVE IT IN YOUR MEMORY.

CAN YOU REMEMBER WHAT HAPPENED? MAX LOOKED IN THE WINDOW OF THE LITTLE HOUSE AND THEN WENT OUT OF THE ROOM.

(As signs continue, and on through the closing of the theatre for the night, the following occurs. Crew brings out a large house in which the top is an open sort of skylight. BEN and ELEANOR sit on the top level and are served a meal. This is NOT part of the play. It just happens.)

NOW YOU REALIZE THAT IT WAS THE LAST ACTION OF HOTEL CHINA, PART TWO.

THERE WERE MANY OTHER ACTIONS THAT PRECEDED THE LAST ACTION. THEY WERE ALL INTERRELATED AND YET THEY WERE ALL BEAUTIFUL AND COULD BE SEEN FROM DIFFERENT POINTS OF VIEW. YOU ONLY REMEMBER SOME OF THEM. CAN YOU REMEMBER THE NAMES OF ALL THE CHARACTERS?

SOPHIA= (WISDOM)

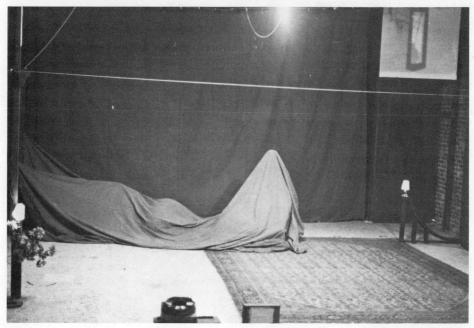

Photo Michael Kirby

Part 3: THE CLIFFS

ACT ONE

(*Room. Door opens halfway. A plucked string. BEN into door halfway, then exits. MAX, at table, rises and tries to press through wall.*)

VOICE

Not yet.

BLACKOUT

(*MAX sits at table. A big brown cloth descends from above and covers everything. Door opens and people enter, are immediately under the cloth and crawl through the room under it.*)

VOICE

Not yet.

(*People bring in a couch and set it over the cloth. Then a small table and lamp. The other people come out from under the cloth, roll it up without disturbing the furniture, and exit.*)

Legend: IMAGINE THE CLOTH SLOWLY DESCENDING OVER EVERYTHING. IT WILL NOT ACTUALLY HAPPEN, SO YOU SHOULD IMAGINE IT IF YOU LIKE. ASSERTION. THERE IS NOTHING ELSE INTERESTING. ONLY ASSERTION IS INTERESTING.

(*Crew brings out a screen with a curtain. They open the curtain and legend shifts to this new screen centered in the set.*)

ONLY ASSERTION IS INTERESTING. THE DANGER IS: TRYING TO MAKE AN ASSERTION DECORATED. DO NOT FALL PREY TO THAT DANGER. THINK OF AN ASSERTION.

(*Screen taken out. Door opens halfway.*)

VOICE

Not yet.

MAX

Two simultaneous assertions, notice.

(*Pause.*)

Now that painting is no longer interesting, perhaps something else will be interesting in the same way.

Legend: PAINTING A WALL IS STILL INTERESTING.

VOICE
People are more interesting than props: Do you agree with that statement.
(Panel opens in rear wall and naked woman is there. A thin blackboard goes horizontally across the stage space, about four feet off the floor. As the naked woman appears, someone comes and writes across the board, "THINK HARDER." A second woman, dressed, comes and stands with the first.)

MAX
No, the second girl should put her clothes on.

HANNAH
Is that me.

SOPHIA
Is that me.
(Pause.)

MAX
No, the second girl should teach mental clarity to the first girl.
(As he speaks, BEN enters with a candelabra which has a sack coming out of its bottom and hanging there.)
The second girl could do that in certain ways and the first girl could do that in certain other ways. I can't choose between alternatives, but then I never said that I could choose between alternatives. Oh look, what Ben is carrying. Oh look, how the light it casts, no it is not finally the light that is important.
(Women start going "Bo-o-ingggg.")
Now to resist would be impolite, would it not.

BEN
—I. Can't. Choose. Plus. Already. Having. Chosen. "Bo-i-ng."
(All but MAX keep going "bo-ing" and a chorus enters to join them. Perhaps six people. After a while, screen rolled on. Words projected are: REMEMBER "ASSERTION." Then, a horizontal line projected across the screen.

The people leave, massing at the door.)

VOICE
I hope this is interesting enough to suit your purposes.
(A string is set to cast a shadow in the center of the line of light on the screen. BEN enters. Spot light on his face. He smiles.)

VOICE
(As hammer hits.)
That seems right, doesn't it.

HANNAH
Ben. You should help me move this into the room.

SOPHIA
Don't ask Ben, I'll help.
(Pause.)

HANNAH
Are you going to help like you said or aren't you going to help me.
(Pause. SOPHIA and HANNAH pull a rug into the room. BEN exits.)

HANNAH
We can't get the rug under the furniture.

SOPHIA
It will have to stay buckled up, won't it.

VOICE
(String is plucked and hammer hits.)
The trouble with nothing but images is that images . . . alone . . . don't . . . make . . . anything . . . new . . . happen.
(Screen. An image of man in mountain-climbing gear, including dark glasses, snow suit, etc.)

SOPHIA
Oh Rhoda. Is that you.
(Moves to the screen and presses herself against the image of the body.)
I've always desired your body.

HANNAH
I've always desired your body but since you were a goddess I thought it would be an impossible physical relationship.

SOPHIA
I don't ever think about unhappiness.
(Scene shifts to a field, cliffs rear.)

SOPHIA
What do you have in that basket, Rhoda.

RHODA
(In a summer dress, with picnic basket.)
Something to hit you with.

SOPHIA

What.

> (Pause.)

RHODA

I won't tell.

SOPHIA

Can I look.

RHODA

Aren't you afraid of being hurt.

SOPHIA

No. Being a goddess I don't experience pain, no matter what happens.

> (Pause. She steps toward RHODA and RHODA pulls back her basket.)

I thought I could look.

RHODA

I haven't decided yet.

> (Pause).

SOPHIA

Maybe I'll look anyway.

> (Pause. RHODA slowly uncovers the basket and shows it to SOPHIA. A ringing noise, which gets louder. SOPHIA and RHODA sit on the ground, as if dazed.)

SOPHIA

> (Silence. She points.)

I could make something out of that lunch.

RHODA

Oh, angel.

SOPHIA

I really could. I could make something out of that lunch.

> (She stops pointing.)

Legend: DO YOU REMEMBER THE ROOM AND THE ACTIVITIES WITH THE CARPET. DO YOU REMEMBER THE WRITING WHICH HAD BEEN PROJECTED ON THE SCREEN. ALL OF THAT HAPPENED LONG AGO. NOW WHAT CAN HAPPEN. THE CLIFFS IN THE DISTANCE ARE LIKE A SCREEN ON WHICH PICTURES AND MESSAGES ARE WRITTEN, BUT STILL THERE ARE NO PICTURES AND THERE ARE NO MESSAGES.

SOPHIA

I want it to be like this.

RHODA

—I want it to be just like this.

SOPHIA

Can you get closer to the cliffs.

> (RHODA slowly undresses. Clock ticks.)

RHODA

> (Sitting naked now.)

I'm certainly closer than I used to be.

SOPHIA

How so.

RHODA

> (Lies down.)

Don't you notice anything different about me.

SOPHIA

Call me the angel.

RHODA

The angel.

SOPHIA

The angel.

RHODA

The angel.

SOPHIA

The angel.

RHODA

The angel.

SOPHIA

That's what I am really.

> (Pause.)

I don't show it to too many people.

> (Lights dim. Hum in rear. Enter BEN, who sits next to SOPHIA, then pushes her back on the ground and climbs on top of her.)

RHODA

Hey, Ben.

> (The hum gets louder.)

I'm the one that's undressed.

> (Pause.)

SOPHIA

Hey, Ben, you can get into her body easier than you can get into my body.

> (He sits up, startled. Noise very loud now, he looks at RHODA. The noise has now become like the beating of wings. Lights fade out as RHODA arches her body and a disk, carried to behind BEN's head, does back and forth oscillation. Snow effect. Out of the blackness and snow, the bundled-up Mountain-Climber advances slowly from the rear. He rocks forward, back and forth against the snow. Noise cuts out but he maintains his gently rocking motion. Naked RHODA enters wrapped in a

blanket. *She goes to him and rubs against his body.)*

RHODA

Oh, you're so cold.

VOICE

(Low.)

Fri-gid. . . . fri-gid . . . fri-gid . . . (etc.)

RHODA

—Oh, I don't think anybody can get through to you, Max. You have a one-track mind.

(Noise again, soft . . . it gets louder. She rubs against him again. Set changes back to the room.)

RHODA

I had the most unusual dream last night.

(A whistle. Set changes back to cliffs.)

Legend: NOW IT CAN BE SAID CLEARLY WHAT IS HAPPENING. THE ROOM ITSELF IS NOT DOING THE SPEAKING: (READING): BUT IT IS MOVING. THE CLIFFS AND THE MEADOW ARE NOT MOVING BUT ONLY BEING THOUGHT ABOUT. THE CLIFFS AND THE MEADOW ARE LESS LIKE REAL CLIFFS AND A REAL MEADOW THAN THE ROOM IS LIKE A REAL ROOM, THOUGH NEITHER IS PERFECT.

(A rocking, deep bass music has begun. Enter SOPHIA and RHODA, each with a flower basket.)

RHODA

Look what I've been able to gather in such a short time.

SOPHIA

(Holds out her basket.)

Should we trade.

RHODA

Why.

(Pause. A single piano note.)

Good god, why should we trade our flowers.

(Little house appears on top of the cliffs. Pause. Its windows light up, SOPHIA and RHODA turn and look to it.)

Legend: IS SOMEBODY WATCHING FROM THE LITTLE HOUSE ON THE CLIFFS. PERHAPS THEY COME TO THIS PLACE BECAUSE THEY KNOW THERE IS A LITTLE HOUSE ON THE CLIFFS OVERLOOKING THE PLACE WHERE THEY ARE AND SOMEBODY IS WATCHING THEM FROM INSIDE THE HOUSE. IS IT A SMALL PERSON BECAUSE THE HOUSE IS SO SMALL. (Ticking begins.) DID THEY WAIT FOR THE MOMENT TO APPEAR—THE HOUSE, THE HOUSE. OH, THE HOUSE SAYS THE HOUSE AND APPEARS AT THE MOMENT IT IS THOUGHT ABOUT, LIKE A FLASH IN AN APPEARANCE.

(BEN enters with a rope coil and a grappling hook. Throws it to the top of the cliff and prepares to climb the face of the cliff. The little house facade swings open, MAX's head inside. Tinkling bells.)

MAX

Do/on't tr/ry an/ny/yth/ing fu/un/ny.

(BEN tests the rope, noise of wings beating. Crew comes and straps furniture to BEN's back as girls sink to sitting position near the floor and start throwing flowers at BEN. House closes. Opens again and MAX's face has been replaced with a phonograph. It plays a scratchy old record. Toward second half of song, RHODA crawls over and hits SOPHIA with her basket. SOPHIA tugs at RHODA's blanket. RHODA screams and tries to keep the blanket about her. SOPHIA rises and pulls RHODA to the cliff, and attaches her wrists to a chain that comes out of the wall. BEN watches. He takes the stuff off his back, as the music stops. He then comes to the chained-up RHODA and touches, delicately, different parts of her body.)

Legend: DO YOU KNOW WHAT YOU'RE DOING.

(SOPHIA has backed off to watch.)

SOPHIA

What are you doing, Ben.

Photo Babette Mangolte

MAX
(House opens again on him.)
Do/on't tr/ry an/ny thi/ing fun/ny. Sh/he wo/orks/s in/n a/a fac/ctor/ory/ry an/nd is/sn/t ex/xpe/er/ien/ced a/at/a/all.
(As he is speaking, he starts dropping small doll furniture from his house, each piece of which dangles on a string over the edge of a cliff.)

Legend: THOSE ARE HIS BELONGINGS. EACH OF THEM IS VALUABLE TO HIM AND WORTH MONEY.

(Noise of wings has begun, gets loud as lights dim and Mountain-Climber again appears rear and starts forward.
Empty stage. The cliffs. BEN and RHODA naked. Holding each other, they start doing rather gymnastic rolls all over the stage.)

Legend: THIS IS HARD TO DO. WOULD YOU LIKE IT BETTER IF THERE WERE MUSIC GOING ON AT THE SAME TIME AND YOU COULD THINK OF IT AS DANCING.

RHODA
(Bells start and they still roll.)
I/I ha/ad a/a fun/ny dre/eam las/st ni/ight a/a bou/ut th/he a/a bom/min/na/able sn/now ma/an.
(Organ music begins.)

BEN
I/I ha/ad o/one o/of m/my be/est id/deas to/oo.

RHODA
(They are still rolling.)
Te/ell me/e ab/bout i/it.

VOICE
Not yet. Not yet.
(They continue to roll. SOPHIA enters, dressed, and starts rolling by herself. Lots of people peer over the edge of the cliffs.)

SOPHIA
(While rolling.)
It can't be happening without my help.

CROWD
She's beautiful. She's beautiful.
(RHODA and BEN stop rolling and
SOPHIA continues alone. Wings
are carried on and held for her.)
SOPHIA
The wings are getting strapped on my back
slowly.
CROWD
Yes.
SOPHIA
We discover them. Then we are sure to
enjoy them.
CROWD
Who said anything about enjoying them.
SOPHIA
(Stops rolling.)
What happened to the abominable snow-
man.

BEN
Did you dream about him as good as you
said you were going to dream about him.
MAX
(In his cliff house.)
—Having a house is better than not having
a house.

**Legend: NOW LOOK AT THEM,
NOW SEE THEM IN THEIR POSI-
TIONS, DON'T BE SO TIRED.**

RHODA
Can you be seized by your imagination, says
Rhoda.
BEN
I can, I can, I can if I am dressed better.
CROWD
Ahhhhhhhhhh.
(Pause.)
RHODA
Don't wait for enlightenment, says, Rhoda.
CROWD
Ahhhhhhhh.
(Pause.)
RHODA
Then she covers her lips with her fingers.
SOPHIA
—I do that.
RHODA
Evening approaches.
SOPHIA
I have the feeling.

Photo Babette Mangolte

RHODA
What.

SOPHIA
I have been here before.

RHODA
—Evening approaches.
> *(It gets darker.)*

RHODA
Is a bell ringing someplace in the distance.

CROWD
Ahhhhhhh.

MAX
> *(In house.)*

—We did not have the chance
> *(Other little houses go up on cliffs, and frame people's heads.)*

to invite you into our houses. Look. Look.

CROWD
Ahhhhhh.
> *(Bell tolls in the distance, lights very dim and a tinkle between the tolling bells.)*

Legend: **THE HOUSES. OH, THE HOUSE ON THE CLIFFS. OH. THE SECOND SERIES OF HOUSES IN THE VALLEY BELOW THE CLIFFS.**

> *(In the dim light the Mountain-Climber again appears from rear, slowly advancing forward. He has a coil of rope. When he gets center, he stops. Throws his rope up and ahead; it lands in a heap. Then he backs off. RHODA re-enters, wrapped in a blanket, with a thin stick. She comes and, with the stick, traces the pattern the rope makes on the floor.)*

CROWD
Ahhhhh.
> *(BEN enters naked with an apple. RHODA turns and looks at him. She takes the apple from him and the blanket slips from her, and she prepares to bite.)*

CROWD
Ahhhh.
> *(She stops and looks off. Waits. SOPHIA enters where she is looking. SOPHIA has a sword. She places the point so it rests on the apple.)*

CROWD
Ahhhhhh.

> *(SOPHIA, RHODA and BEN now slowly shuffle off without dropping their poses or relation to each other.)*

CROWD
There is nothing more to know about the lives of unhappy people.
> *(Chorus repeats this sentence, as individual voices emerge—)*

ONE
What happens in the rocks, tell me, what happens in the rocks.

TWO
Oh, rock chested.

THREE
He was rock chested.
> *(Chorus still repeats: "There is nothing more to know about the lives of unhappy people." The room returns. RHODA sits and rubs her temples. SOPHIA enters.)*

SOPHIA
You don't want my help, probably.

RHODA
I don't believe in your help.

SOPHIA
You are wary of me.

RHODA
Yes.
> *(SOPHIA comes and sits next to her and stares at the side of her head as RHODA continues rubbing.)*

SOPHIA
Do you think that I'm more beautiful than you are.

RHODA
Oh yes.
> *(Pause.)*

Probably.

SOPHIA
Guess what. I'm not looking through you, Rhoda.
> *(Tea is served.)*

I'm not even looking inside your head. I'm looking at the surface of your eyes, aren't I.

RHODA
Then I guess I'm looking at the surface of your eyes.
> *(BEN enters, leans back against the door and takes a photo of them. They both turn and look at him. Pause. He takes another photo, all the while leaning back against the door.)*

RHODA

Add that picture to your collection.

> *(He turns head flat against door, profile.)*

What a nice profile you have, Ben. Somebody ought to add your photo to their collection.

> *(Little bells ring.)*

SOPHIA

He stays there long enough.

BEN

This is a nice interior.

SOPHIA

I didn't hear that.

VOICE

> *(Bell accompaniment.)*

When the dragon comes, he is prepared for anything. His teeth, which have known the forest, what is, what is, what is, what is this dragon, what is this christ/beast.

> *(All leave quickly. Radio placed in center of room. Pause.)*

VOICE

The discovery of the, the, the, I can't say it.

> *(Long pause. Just radio, then Mountain-Climber enters and stands there.)*

Legend: THERE IS NOBODY FOR HIM TO HEAL. LOOK AT HIS HANDS. HE IS READY TO LAY THEM ON THE FOREHEAD OF THE SICK PERSON BUT THE SICK PERSON IS NO LONGER INSIDE THE HOUSE.

> *(RHODA enters the door halfway.)*

MOUNTAIN-CLIMBER

Don't be frightened.

RHODA

Don't be a child, Rhoda. Put yourself back to bed under the covers.

MOUNTAIN-CLIMBER

—Do you like my face.

> *(Pause.)*

Do you like my profile.

RHODA

I like everything about you.

> *(Screen on. On it is projected a set like a cabinet whose open doors reveal different locales. Pause. Then lights up on room; they haven't moved.)*

RHODA

There's another one there.

MOUNTAIN-CLIMBER

What.

> *(Pause.)*

RHODA

There, there. Right next to Rhoda.

> *(Screen image still faintly seen.)*

MOUNTAIN-CLIMBER

You're Rhoda.

RHODA

Yes.

> *(Pause.)*

MOUNTAIN-CLIMBER

I'm the same actor who was playing.

RHODA

What.

> *(Pause.)*

There.

MOUNTAIN-CLIMBER

What it is.

> *(Pause.)*

The movie screen again.

RHODA

Not yet.

MOUNTAIN-CLIMBER

There.

> *(Pause.)*

RHODA

You just repeated what you heard me saying.

VOICE

The cliffs still exist outside the house in the distance.

RHODA

Oh, this isn't a house, this is just a room.

> *(Pause, bell, violin.)*

Did you ever fly, that's what a bird says to me and it is of course flying above the cliffs in the distance.

> *(Pause.)*

I think about it and then I say NO.

MOUNTAIN-CLIMBER

You are so much more intelligent than I am.

> *(Pause.)*

But I can heal people.

RHODA

Do I believe that.

MOUNTAIN-CLIMBER

Now I have you in my power, huh.

> *(Pause.)*

Oh Rhoda, Rhoda. You don't yet understand me.

> *(Behind the room, on the cliffs, the houses light up.)*

RHODA

I can't see them. My own house interferes with my vision, not a house complete, a room. I was very quick to correct myself.

> *(Pause.)*

I hurt myself yet, so my mind itself is more perceptible, don't you think.

> *(He crosses, puts his hand on her forehead.)*

O.K. that did it now I'm better.

> *(He exits.)*

The first thing happened.

> *(As he exits, crowd comes into their houses on cliffs. A whistle.)*

As I was coming home from the library I had my briefcase, anyway, I opened the door and stepped inside. All of a sudden, in the painting on the opposite wall—

> *(Painting now hung.)*

—there he was. There he was. I fell onto the floor and a bolt of lightning hit me in the head. Oh christ, I said. Oh christ.

> *(Mountain-Climber returns and tries to press through wall.)*

VOICE

Not yet.

> *(Room off, back to cliffs. Houses with people's heads, plus below on the meadow, the real model cabinet-stage. Whistle. People on cliffs whistle, on and on—it becomes a tune as cabinet sits there happily.)*

Legend: **SOME PEOPLE WORK HARD FOR A LIVING, NOT ME. SOME PEOPLE GET UP WHEN IT'S STILL DARK OUT. THEY WORK ALL DAY AND THEY FEEL TERRIBLE AND THEY COME HOME TO SLEEP. THEY DON'T CRY BUT THAT'S A SMALL CONSOLATION. HOW WOULD YOU LIKE A HOT BUTTERED ROLL. I HAVE SOME EXTRA.**

> *(Whistling still going—BEN and RHODA enter naked, rolling. Music begins. MAX enters, staggering, with a stage set built out of his forehead. As he sits, all lights go down, there is a spot on his forehead set, and strings are placed from the four corners of the set out into space. RHODA and BEN still roll in shadows.)*

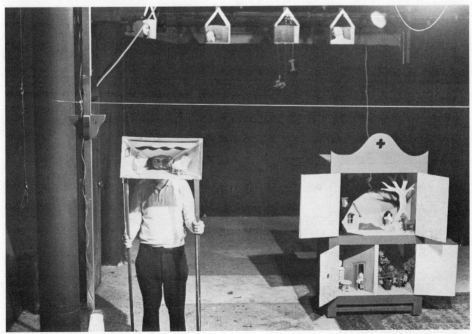

Photo Babette Mangolte

MAX

Think, think. Think harder than you are thinking.

(Pause.)

Ha. That did it huh. You broke it.

(Pause.)

You can't think when it's broken, I bet.

(Pause, little dolls of RHODA and BEN are placed in his forehead set.)

Ha. What are they going to do to each other.

(Pause, holds up his hands.)

Look. No hands.

(Lights up on cliffs. He remains and naked RHODA enters with a whip and starts beating the cliffs. BEN enters, dressed now, comes up behind her, grabs hold of her in a hammerlock and drags her off.)

MAX

Each person who enters the stage has one thing they do good and one thing they don't do no matter what happens.

(He slumps a bit and lets the strings relax and the head-set dip.)

I'm not going to get back into character.

(Crew brings on a big white block,

down center to audience, and off. SOPHIA enters with towel and starts snapping it. Continues a long time. MAX still there. Crew brings on a new white block, same procedure. Exit. As they come on, RHODA also enters with a towel which she snaps. Crowd comes down into area and watches the two women. Then crowd leaves; as it is doing so, another big block is brought on, presented to audience and taken out. Pause. Enter Mountain-Climber. Piano music, to which he dances. All enter and watch. When he finishes they applaud.)*

MOUNTAIN-CLIMBER

(Quietly.)

O.K. Who wants to be cured.

(Block on . . . presented . . . off. Mountain-Climber exits. Piano music. Everyone dances. Music fades. People still dance. One person takes flowers out of a magic hat, as the room pushes back on, pushing people out of the way who

Photo Michael Kirby

*still keep dancing. In the room,
BEN and RHODA face each other,
both their profiles to the audience.
RHODA has cards, which she fans
for BEN. He watches with folded
arms. She is given a glass of water,
and spurts it in his face.)*

VOICE

Not yet.

RHODA

Pick a card, Ben.

*(Pause. He does, and shows it to
audience. SOPHIA comes in the
door backwards, bent over, tugging
a big suitcase. MAX comes in from
the other side, puts his two hands
on her behind and keeps holding
it as they both cross the stage backwards, bent over, she dragging the
suitcase.)*

RHODA

What time is it.

BEN

Everything's O.K. It's very clear, all of it, so
it's O.K.

(Pause.)

It's even enjoyable.

RHODA

It must be about time for bed.

BEN

It's been wonderful because it's been so
clear, really.

(Pause.)

Really. Everything's been very clear.

RHODA

(Goes to window.)

Those people are still out there.

BEN

What people.

(Pause.)

Really, everything has.

(Pause.)

We've touched on everything. It's O.K.

*(They leave. Big block on. Pre-
sented.)*

VOICE

Not yet.

ACT TWO

---

*(The cliffs. BEN enters, tries to
press his body through the cliff.)*

VOICE

Not yet.

(Pause.)

Not yet.

*(BEN exits. Enter SOPHIA with tiny
bell. She rings it. The houses are
set on the cliff.)*

Legend: **THERE WAS SOMETHING
MORE TO BE SAID: ABOUT THE
HOUSES AND THEIR RELATION-
SHIPS. NOW WATCH. WATCH.
IT'S BEING SAID.**

(She is still ringing the bell.)

**IT'S BEING SAID CONTINUALLY
LIKE IT HAPPENS.**

*(She stops ringing the bell and
RHODA enters in galoshes.)*

**RHODA AND SOPHIA MAKE A
FAIR EXCHANGE. ONE BELL FOR
ONE PAIR OF GALOSHES.**

*(RHODA does handstand on
SOPHIA's feet and they walk out
that way. Pause. A small piece of
doll furniture hangs by a string
from each of the houses.)*

ANOTHER FAIR EXCHANGE.

*(String added to attach the furni-
ture to the neighboring piece.
Then a string from above attached
to the system and the system pulled
up into the air. Then small dolls
sit in the small chairs so suspended.
Tiny bells ring.)*

CROWD

(In the houses.)

We are not actors and actresses.

(Pause.)

We do not need bread or money.

(Pause.)

Something is missing.

*(Enter RHODA and BEN with picnic
lunch in basket. They spread a
cloth, and the lunch over it, and
begin to eat. With each bite they
take, they rise—to go and touch a
suspended doll with a wand, then
return to eat. The wand is like a
pull-out car aerial that is opened
and closed each time. As they do
this many times, a thin blackboard
is rolled across—crew writes
"THINK HARDER." Then a rocking
surface is brought out. All picnic
articles are placed upon it. It starts
to rock and they try to keep on*

Photo Michael Kirby

with the picnic, and as items fall
off they are replaced. Then silence.)

RHODA

This is one of the most rigorous learning
experiences I ever had.

BEN

Oh Rhoda.

(Pause.)

RHODA

The ends of my sentences are accompanied
by a flash of lightning, huh.

BEN

—Oh Rhoda.

(Pause.)

What a day for a picnic. Oh Rhoda.

(Enter SOPHIA with a parasol. She
twists her feet as it's taken away
from her; at the same time,
RHODA is also given a parasol,
which is immediately taken away as
she opens it.)

RHODA

Come back.

CROWD

(In houses.)

We/e ha/ave a/a ri/ight to/o ge/et ou/ur

hou/use ho/old po/ossess/ions ba/ack int/to
ou/ur hou/uses.

RHODA

Lo/ok, lo/ok to/o th/he le/eft. Lo/ok to/o
th/he le/eft. Do/on't ke/ep lo/ok/in/ng for/or
wa/ard.

(Lights dim.)

It/t's no/ot i/in th/he blo/od on/ly; it/t's i/in
th/he st/rings i/in th/he blo/od.

(MAX enters with parasol, spreads
his legs and squats a bit and opens
his parasol.)

It/t's a/a sto/ory.

CROWD

The/he clif/fs ar/re.

(Pause.)

RHODA

Now everything is like a single thought.

CROWD

Oh Rhoda! Ar/re yo/ou sti/ill th/in ki/ing.

(SOPHIA hops once. Pause.)

Co/ome co/ome, chi/ild re/en.

VOICE

SHHHHHHH.

(Three easy chairs brought on.
Ropes from the chairs to the
hands of the principals in the

meadow. Pause. Then they all drop the ropes.)
RHODA, SOPHIA, BEN, MAX
Now let's begin where we left off.
(They pick up the ropes and move until the ropes are taut.)
We can't move any further offstage than this if we want to keep holding the rope.
(Bell rings.)
WOMAN
(In house.)
A real scene, a realistic scene, a scene, a scene keeps changing, a real scene keeps changing, a screen, a real scene and a screen keeps changing, a real changing screen scene.
(Bell. Additional ropes tied to the end of the ropes so they are now long enough for the principals to move offstage. Pause. They come back on.)
RHODA
Now the ropes are longer.

Legend: THE CLIFFS. THE DIFFICULTY OF MAKING ART HAPPEN WITHIN THE CONFINES OF NATURE. THE TRANSFORMATION OF THE NATURAL SETTING INTO AN ARTIFICIAL SETTING. THAT HAS ALREADY HAPPENED OF COURSE BUT IT HAS NOT HAPPENED EFFECTIVELY ENOUGH.
RHODA
All these things we're holding by rote.
(Pots and pans and spoons brought to the four principals. As soon as each gets a pot and spoon, he begins rhythmic banging. Continues for five minutes.)

Legend: THE INDUSTRIAL SUBURBS ARE ON THE CLIFFS. THE WORKERS' HOUSES, I.E., THE MANY SUBJECTS WHICH ONCE NAMED RENDER FURTHER DEVELOPMENT SUPERFLUOUS.
(Music changes as four below stop banging and people in houses start singing a rhythmic, jazzy "bum-de-bum-de-dump.")
THE WORKERS LIKE THAT KIND OF MUSIC. EACH WORKER HAS A SEPARATE RADIO. THE PEOPLE WHO ARE NOT WORKERS PREFER MORE REFINED MUSIC. THEY DO NOT NEED RADIOS. THEY HEAR IT IN THEIR INNER EAR. (DO THE WORKERS HAVE INNER EARS?) EACH ONE LISTENS TO HIS OWN FAVORITE MUSIC IN HIS OWN INNER EAR.
(They begin banging again as the people above continue singing.)
IT IS NOT A SECRET IT IS A PERSONAL THING.

(They stop banging and exit as singing continues. After a while singing stops, too.)
(Pause.)
CHORUS
That's my kind of music.
(Pause.)
If we were not workers you might see our faces in the cliffs but you do not see them—
(House fronts begin to be closed.)
—in the cliffs, you see them in the houses.
(Pause.)
You can still see them if you look in the window.
(Room comes on.)
KARL
(Sits in a chair.)
I guess the workers have taken over the houses.
RHODA
(Outside at window.)
Look, look.
(RHODA, LEO, BEN and SOPHIA outside the room, bang pots.)
KARL
I guess the workers have taken over the houses and the people who aren't workers don't like it.
(HANNAH swings into the room on a rope.)
What's on the radio.
(HANNAH turns on the radio, and the singing "bump-de-dum" continues. As it continues, KARL sits up in his chair, his feet up tight, arms around his knees. Silence.)
KARL
I too could be beautiful, different resources, that is, different developments, while the head is developing.
HANNAH
Oh Karl.

KARL
Shhhhh.

HANNAH
Our bodies are different.
(Pause.)

HANNAH
Can't you tell that our bodies are different from other people's bodies.

KARL
Workers, huh.

HANNAH
Not workers.
(Pause.)
Our bodies are the same as the workers' bodies.

KARL
What workers.
(A heavy drop cloth dragged in the door, to cover things. Pause.)

KARL
Is that nice.

HANNAH
—I don't know if that is nice.

RHODA
(At window, looking in.)
Look. Look.
(KARL takes position over RHODA.)

KARL
Oh, Rhoda, your body is changing.

RHODA
I like having a man over my body.
(Pause.)

KARL
Your body is changing.

RHODA
It used to be.

KARL
Shhhhhh.
(Pause.)

RHODA
It used to be more like her body.

KARL
Shhh. I think my body is changing too.

Legend: WHERE ARE THE WORK-
ERS NOW. ARE THEY INSIDE THE
HOUSE. KARL.

RHODA
How many workers are there.
(Pause.)
Oh boy, the body should be more interesting than the workers.
(Workers assemble against wall of

Photo Babette Mangolte

*room with lunch pails. They lean
against the wall and each other.
On other side of room, outside, the
grandfather clock is propped. Cover
KARL and RHODA with a sheet.
Pause. Workers open lunch boxes
and eat. Clock lifted on rope.)*

**Legend: THE CLOCK SAYS "CAN'T
YOU SEE ME. EVEN IF YOU CAN'T
SEE WHAT TIME IT IS. SEE ME
ANYWAY."**

(Screen brought into room.)

**Legend: THE INNER ENERGIES OF
THE WORKERS. PART ONE. THE
CLOCK SAYS "I'D LIKE TO GET
INSIDE THE ROOM. MAYBE THE
WORKERS WOULD HELP ME
TO ACCOMPLISH MY AIM."
THE WORKERS SAY "SURE WE
WOULD."**

*(Pause. Workers bring clock into
the room, setting it over the limp-
under-sheet bodies of KARL and
RHODA. They stand around not
knowing what to do. Loud ticking.
A heavy thud.)*
KARL and RHODA
Uncover us.
*(Workers do so, and exit. A big pair
of hands at the end of long sleeves
floats in and they are clamped onto
KARL's head, as if holding his
temples. He staggers to the window
with the hands still holding his
head. He goes through the window,
head first. Then the hands return.
They get attached to the clock.
Lift the clock. A rope is so attached that it pulls the suspended
clock and a table together. The
hands are detached from the clock
and the ticking stops.)*
RHODA
Oh well.
*(Door opens. HANNAH enters with
a lunch box.)*
HANNAH
Hungry.

RHODA
(Turning fast to her.)
—What.

*(SOPHIA has appeared at the win-
dow and leans her chin on it.)*
SOPHIA
She startled you.
RHODA
(Turning fast to her.)
—What.
(Pause.)
SOPHIA
She asked if Rhoda was hungry.
RHODA
Guess how many men there are in my life.
Two. Two.
HANNAH
One of them is a worker.
SOPHIA
—Are both of them workers, Rhoda.
(Pause.)
RHODA
How do you think my body is holding up
objectively.
HANNAH
Have some lunch.
RHODA
What's in that—
HANNAH
Look.
(Pause.)
RHODA
Do I have to eat it if I don't like it.
*(Pause. HANNAH opens the lunch
box and holds it upside down. A
sandwich and an orange fall to the
floor. Pause.)*
HANNAH
You go after the sandwich and I'll go after
the orange.
RHODA
No.
(Pause. She points.)
They both fell on the floor.
(She lowers her point.)
HANNAH
Oh Rhoda. Two things fell on the floor
which means you have to use two hands to
point at them simultaneously.
RHODA
—You go after the sandwich.
*(Pause. Crewman brings in heavy
beam, at least one foot wide, gives
end to RHODA which she holds
between her two hands at her
stomach—other end extends offstage.)*

RHODA

Hold this.

*(Person offstage drops his end.
RHODA keeps holding hers. Then
everyone enters. Pause.)*

ALL

Now Rhoda! You go for the sandwich!

(Pause. Thud. All start to undress.)

BLACKOUT

---

*(Lights come up. RHODA alone,
holding her beam.)*

RHODA

I was not part of the invention.

*(Crew makes string arc over her
beam. Buzz saw noise midway. She
collapses. A clear piece of plastic
set in the arc area, then string from
beam end to end over arc. Enter
SOPHIA with wings. She plucks the
string. A contact mike is set; plucks
string again. A good noise. KARL
enters through window. He has
cloth on feet. Undresses as far as*

*he can with cloth preventing re-
moval down legs of pants.)*

KARL

If she's dead she should be undressed.

SOPHIA

(Plucking her string once.)

What makes you think she's dead, Karl.

(Pause.)

KARL

The body no longer has any secrets.

SOPHIA

(Plucking.)

Wrong.

(Pause.)

KARL

(Putting his arms out.)

Look, the body no longer has any secrets.

SOPHIA

(Pointing.)

Look, the body has secrets.

*(Pluck, on tape. RHODA crawls
under the cloth attached to KARL's
feet.)*

Rhoda vanished, didn't she.

(Pots bang in rear.)

Photo Babette Mangolte

Would you like the workers to come into the room and see your empty body, Karl.

Legend: *(As banging continues.)* **WHY DID SHE SAY EMPTY FOR A BODY THAT IS NOT EMPTY BUT IS UNDRESSED.**

(The following tableau is set. String is placed in KARL's mouth, to floor, where it describes an arc on the floor in front of his feet, leaving a chalk tracing of the arc. HANNAH comes and steps inside the arc. She is given a suitcase. Banging continues and SOPHIA exits. HANNAH turns up to KARL, holding her suitcase, crew comes and holds pillow to HANNAH's behind, as she opens the suitcase and lets the top just hang down. Crew comes and ties a ribbon around KARL's penis, also sets a small screen with flower-shaped hole in front of him and runs ribbon through that hole and off. At start, long strips of cloth were laid over KARL's extended arms and run off, held by crew. Now boxing gloves are attached to end of that cloth. HANNAH turns, pillow kept at her bottom, and sits on suitcase as crew keeps pillow there so she sits on it. She takes out a mirror and looks in it to see KARL's eyes. BEN and LEO enter, with boxing gloves, and each fights with one of the gloves on the end of the cloth. Gloves are manipulated by sticks which crew holds. A light hits mirror so that HANNAH is able to make slow arcs of reflected light travel on rear wall. Banging continues. RHODA emerges, undressed from under the cloth around KARL's feet. Silence. All look at RHODA. She slowly squats. Noise of pots again. Crew brings on a long bench that pretty well stretches across the front of the stage. RHODA and HANNAH go and sit on opposite ends of the bench, sinking into their respective corners. RHODA naked, HANNAH now with furs. Others go off.)

RHODA
(Banging stops, silence.)
Look at that.

HANNAH
What.

RHODA
Shhhh.
(Pause. Then pots and pans. Silence.)
You're sitting far away from me.

HANNAH
I/I do/on't wa/ant to/o ge/et/co/on. ta/am. in/na. te/ed.

RHODA
We workers.
(Pause.)

ALL
Shhhhh.

RHODA
We workers.
(Pause. KARL, LEO, BEN enter and lean on back of the bench. They wear caps.)
Ho/ow ca/an an/ny. bo/od. d/dy thi/in. nk/k o/of ge/et. i/ing co/on. ta/am. i/in. a/ted.

KARL, LEO, BEN
We/eer' r/e Wa/aiti. i/ing fo/or th/he bu/us.
(Pause.)
Sh/he's sho/ow. i/ing o/off he/er bo/ody.

HANNAH
I'm showing off my body too.
(Three suitcases are placed on the bench.)
Are the suitcases going to be attracted to Hannah or are the suitcases going to be attracted to Rhoda's naked body.
(Using a slit between bench seat and back, the three suitcases are invisibly moved to RHODA.)
The naked body is always very appealing to people.

KARL, LEO, BEN
O/oh Ha/an. a/ah sh/how u/us yo/our na/ak. e/ed bo/ody to/oo.
(Pot banging. SOPHIA comes with a suitcase and sits on the bench. Banging stops. Pause. SOPHIA and RHODA swivel in place to look at each other. Pause. SOPHIA and HANNAH swivel to face each other.)

Legend: RHODA NEEDS A JOB. HANNAH NEEDS A JOB. SOPHIA NEEDS A JOB ALSO TO MAKE A

Photo Michael Kirby

LIVING. SHE GETS A JOB IN A DINER BEING A WAITRESS: OH, A GODDESS BEING A WAITRESS. SHE KEEPS HER IDENTITY A SECRET.

(A tray with dishes is brought to SOPHIA at the bench. SOPHIA, with tray, slides along bench—men behind it are clearing suitcases—till she is next to RHODA. Crew brings a small table. A wash basin on top, another on a shelf at foot level. SOPHIA proceeds to wash the dishes in the top basin, and crew washes RHODA's feet in the bottom one. Organ music, which then softens so HANNAH can speak.)

HANNAH

(Pointing.)

That is not. That is not like Rhoda at all.

(Pause.)

Oh, that is not like Rhoda at all.

BEN

Wouldn't you like some entertainment.

(He spits on a handkerchief and wipes a spot on HANNAH's face.)

(After a while, buzzer and three men off. Three women again equidistant on bench. First SOPHIA and HANNAH swivel to face each other —then SOPHIA and RHODA. Repeat several times. Cliffs light up rear with people's heads in the houses. After a moment, women turn on bench and kneel so that their chins rest on the bench back. After a while, enter KARL, LEO and BEN, who are behind the bench and squat or bend down so that each one puts his face directly into the face of one of the women. Ticking. The faces in the houses are covered with cloth.)

Legend: THEY DID THEIR PART SO THEY VANISHED.

(Crew comes and sets a long piece of material so that it is held between the three pairs of "chin-against-chin." Little model houses and trees and other things are placed on the bench.)

Photo Michael Kirby

Legend: **OH RHODA, POINT TO THE TREE.**
(She does.)
OH HANNAH, HANNAH, THINK ABOUT THE HOUSE.
(Crewman brings doll. Lying down to be out of the way, he makes the doll walk about on the bench. Heavy thuds begin.)
OH SOPHIA, BRING FRUIT INTO THE GARDEN. REACH FOR IT OUT OF THE SKY AND PLANT IT UNDER THE LITTLE HOUSE WHERE BEN AND RHODA AND HANNAH AND LEO AND KARL ARE SLEEPING.
(Small paper wings are hung on SOPHIA's shoulders.)
OH SOPHIA, BETWEEN THE MEN AND THE WOMEN, SUSPEND A WHITE VEIL OF PURITY. THEIR HEADS ARE PRESSED TOGETHER LIKE TWO HALVES OF A LEMON. DO NOT LET ANYTHING COME OUT OF ONE MOUTH THAT WILL TRAVEL DIRECTLY INTO ANOTHER MOUTH.
(A thin cord is placed from wing tips to shoulders of HANNAH and RHODA. Fruit is placed on the bench.)
INTO THE WORLD. (ONTO THE BENCH) THE INTRODUCTION OF EACH ELEMENT IN TURN. EACH TIME THAT IT HAPPENS: HAPPINESS.

(Silence. The thuds stop.)

HANNAH
The features of the countryside are my features, huh.

LEO
Oh Hannah. Delight, delight. I associate delight with the past.
(Pause.)
I am no longer allowed happiness. I am no longer allowed strong feelings.

SOPHIA
I. Am. Your. Equal. Now.

ALL

Shhhhhh.

Legend: HER HEAD: WHICH ONCE, AT THE CENTER EMITTED A GIANT LIGHT THROUGH THE OPENING: WHICH CAME DI-RECTLY FROM THE BRAIN: WHICH WAS AS LARGE AS A GRAPEFRUIT.

(Drumrolls and thuds, during which people bring out six grapefruit halves and stand below bench, two people facing each other in pairs and each pair pressing its two halves together. Basins below catch the juice so squeezed as drums continue. The basins are lifted on string and hung just above head level. The grapefruit rinds are left on the benches. Drums stop. Silence.)

BEN

Oh Sophia, Sophia, Sophia.

SOPHIA

(Overlapping.)

—I have not had enough my of name. I want it to be like a dome. I want it to be like a cup. I want it to be like liquid.

(Crew comes and puts paper ruffles around the women's ankles; they kneel with soles of feet toward audience. Drumrolls and thuds begin again.)

Legend: WHAT IS HER SECRET. CAN YOU IMAGINE WHAT IS THE PHENOMENON WHICH MUST BE EXPLAINED ABOUT THE GOD-DESS. CAN YOU IMAGINE A BODY THAT IS EXTENSIVE. CAN YOU IMAGINE A BODY FULL OF THE VOID WHICH IS FILLED AGAIN WHENEVER SOMETHING HAP-PENS.

(Silence.)

RHODA

Go home now.

KARL

Let's go home, huh.

Legend: EVERYBODY KNOWS WHAT EVERYBODY ELSE IS GOING TO SAY.

(Long pause.)

Legend: PARADISE.

HANNAH

Let's go home.

LEO

—Somebody turned on the radio.

ALL

Shhhhh.

(Pause.)

Legend: THEY CAN'T GO HOME.

(Pause.)

DON'T WORRY.

(Pause.)

DON'T WORRY. IT'S O.K.

(There is a shift now. Each person takes the sheet from between chins and puts it between his teeth. The men, holding the sheet in their teeth, awkwardly climb over it and the back of the bench; with a bit of maneuvering, men and women— all still with sheet in teeth—come off bench and move down backwards until they stand under the suspended basins. The drum thud-rolls begin . . . . and flowers are dropped into the basins above as they come and stand upstage of the group, and grasping the other side of the sheet hold it out so it forms a receptacle. Wait. Silence— as the bench is cleared. A single ping.)

(When the bench is gone, cotton wads are dropped onto the sheet. The entire group of sheet-holders then inches upstage until they are in the shadow of the cliffs. Those with it in their teeth not touching it any other way, slowly lower the sheet to the earth. Then exit.)

(Pause.)

(RHODA returns and tapes the cotton wads over her naked body. She begins to whirl slowly about. Faces reappear in the houses above. SOPHIA enters with a suitcase. As she does so a man in a house throws down a rope. She ignores the rope, sits down on her suitcase and takes off her shoes and rubs

Photo Michael Kirby

her feet. Crew brings two radios which fit over her feet. Music begins on the radios and she rises and slowly walks, each foot in a radio. Crew comes and gives her the end of the rope from the house. She takes it and winds it around her neck once, then loops it over the back of her head so it comes down across her face. The people up in the house begin raining cotton balls onto the scene. Lights dim and music continues. A large long, long arm with a lamp on the end swings down into the space from the cliffs as the light gets very dim.)

Legend: SOPHIA, GUARDIAN OF WISDOM, HAS EVERY ONE OF HER WISHES AT LAST. GOOD-NIGHT FOREVER.

(Drumrolls very loud as lights go out completely. A sign blinks on and off rear, "ENCORE." Lights up and BEN is on a swing. Drums fade.)

BEN

Can you believe it.
(Pause.)
I can believe anything.
(He swings himself a bit.)
Stop that you idiot.

Legend: HOW MANY ARE KING HERE?

(A foot looms up from the floor and LEO is nibbling at the toes. A giant foot. As wind is heard, a telephone sails by. As it passes, the receiver is lifted off the hook by someone accompanying the unit and the receiver floats ever farther behind the drifting phone-body. BEN and LEO look wistfully after the phone, as drumrolls fade up, and lights dim as KARL, in a red wig with bells tied to his hair, enters and begins shaking his head to make the bells ring. Again sign lights up "ENCORE" and lights come up and drumrolls fade. Stage is empty. LEO comes on with a pack of cards. He fans them for the audience. HANNAH comes and takes one, drops it on a plate that crew holds. The card hits the plate with a loud "clunk," as though made of lead. At that moment, house lights come up full, and voice over loudspeaker says, as actors quickly leave.)

VOICE
The play is over. Go home. Go home. Go home. The play is over. Ladies and gentlemen, the play is over. Go home. Think about it if you like, but go home. Better still, go home. Go home. Go home.

ONTOLOGICAL-HYSTERIC

MANIFESTO II

(JULY, 1974)

One always begins with the desire to write a certain kind of sentence (to put on stage a certain "kind" of gesture. That "kind" then turns out to be about that-which-be-comes-your-content).

The key, however, is in this sentence (gesture) cell. Most people don't see the cell, are perceptually unable to see small enough (ephemeralization). Because their LIFE training is that to "see small" means to enter the realm where contradictions are seen to be at the root of reality—and that disturbing realization they would avoid at all costs.

The desire to write a certain kind of sentence (gesture) is akin to the desire to live— be—have the world be in a certain kind of way. (Art as a solution to what is—Musil. Through style, through smallest possible units. Bricks determine one style of archi-tecture, stone another, etc.)

> *(A solution to the problem of what is*
> *doesn't imply a utopian vision—how*
> *to fix the world—but how to BE*
> > *so that*
> *One can respond to the world-as-it-is*
> > *instead of*
> *responding to a dream world, an inherited*
> *world in which institutions and training*
> *hypnotize us so we see THEIR version of*
> *reality.)*

To UNDERSTAND the work is to understand the cell, and the possibilities and implica-tions latent in the cell, just as the possibilities and implications latent in atom and molecular biology lead to a view of life and universe—the end in both cases being a patterned energy system.

Reach the pre-conscious: remove the personality.

Make the acts of the play not be "aimed" acts but isomorphic with the pre-conscious and its richness. In other words, acts that on each occasion evoke the *source*— rather than acts (as in daily life) which pick an object of desire and, in isolating that object from the whole constituting field, are the very means by which we cut ourselves off from the source.

Detach (abstract) acts from sensuousness (desire-aim) ground.
Make acts be a form of wisdom. (Thinking)
                                  (Speaking)

We are usually told that art should root itself in the concrete. That means—object making, image making, hypnotizing man with idols (beautiful things, stirring emotions, seductive personalities).

No, man's task is to respect the imbalance in himself (Ortega) between nature (his outside—the concrete) and spirit (his inside—abstraction and dream). The concrete is what RESISTS man—so that he finds himself in that resistance. The TRUTH of man is that moment by moment resistance of the concrete—the concrete which RESISTS the inner project of abstraction, ephemeralization. FOR art to root itself in the concrete is to make the spectator believe for a while that he is either animal (who is that being who totally adjusts to nature—if it does not it simply ceases to exist) or God (who is totally isomorphic with abstraction, dream, idea—for whom the wish IS the reality without the resistance of nature interfering).

Only art ROOTED in the abstract smallest unit of sentence or gesture as a KIND of projection of inner which then stumbles over "nature" (outer) reflects the truth of man's condition. Classical realism, classical romanticism (which includes, of course, Surrealism, Expressionism, etc.) puts man to sleep—returning him to animal nature or deluding him that his dreams are objectively real.

If a work of art has a MESSAGE it means it is putting the spectator to sleep. The minute man "knows," he sleeps (Shestov). Because he loses touch with that IMBALANCE which he most deeply is. Art must keep man consciously rooted in that imbalance—and that can only be done if no conclusions are drawn (implied—as in the MESSAGE or RESOLUTION)—but rather, the spectator is moment by moment exposed to the true process of a certain kind of sentence-gesture (man's inner quest for style, for a way of being-in-the-world) as it encounters the resistance of the real-object (nature).

So the work of art is ROOTED and PROCEEDS from the abstract (spiritual, inner) and uses the ABSTRACT as content—which content finds it HARD TO EXIST in the world of the object (nature) and that is the grand music which the work captures because that is TO-BE-MAN.

That's what it means to say "images alone don't make anything new happen." The concrete image is an idol; empathy with an interesting character is the creation of an IDOL. We have an obligation to return the spectator to his own proper human space; oscillating

back and forth between the frontiers of
animal and God.

No "development" is possible. It's false when it occurs in a work of today. It's a rever-
sion to primitivism. (Which is, of course, what people want, what we all want—to sink
back into nature and sleep. To sink back into the mother—to end "stress".) Development is the negation of stress, or rather the avoidance of stress. To return to the
one human point—that imbalance between inner and outer—is to sit on the one true
stress-point that is never resolved—just as the STRESS which is being-a-human is
never resolved (unless one finally does opt for animal or God), DEVELOPMENT in a
work of art is a giving-up, a moving-off that stress point into animalism or spiritualism.
In both cases—dreaming, wish fulfillment, going to sleep.

When we say "development," perhaps to be more exact, we should notice that
development generally means the development of each item from the preceding
item of a series—and it is this which is false. ANOTHER sort of development exists—
details proceeding from an idea of the whole living-field.

The "impossible," "false" developmental procedure in current art would be step
A proceeding from step B—such development can be nothing but hypnotism and lie.

The only development possible which leaves us free to be awake and be human
in our watching is one in which each detail proceeds from a continual referral back to
the constituting process of consciousness colliding with world—the process that
makes things for us "be."

Bad art, Kitsch, develops detail from preceding detail. That is, the "previous" fact
is an object, the "response" to (development from) that object is another object, and
so on.

> Creating a network of objects.
> Idols.
> Imprisonment.

We IGNORE the preceding fact or act—so it is allowed to VANISH as it should when
its moment of being-there has past—so the NEW can arise, moment by moment.

If each moment is new, if we die to each moment as it arises, we are alive. Development (sequential) is death. Is objectification. Is idol-making. Drama as it has
been focuses on conflict between formed entities. (Idols. Dead things. Hamlet as a
dead thing—to the extent that he is a character one can talk about.)

Such drama is a dream
　　　a lie
　　　a hypnotic act which has power over fools, (which we all are except at
MOMENTS). Such drama is based on inertia, entropy, deadness as conflict works out
to resolution—i.e. object, end, death, sizeable "meaning."

At each moment a thing that we "see" (objectify)—Fred, Ralph, Hamlet, etc.—is
trying to be itself (Fred trying to be Fred, who desires Juliet) within a system where
Ralph is trying to be Ralph-who-desires-Juliet-himself. Mutually exclusive.

So Ralph kills Fred or adapts to being NOT-RALPH-who desires-Juliet or adapts to

being Ralph-who-doesn't-get-Juliet. But in watching this we watch dead people, sleeping people (as we are in life) and we have no hint that to LIVE AWAKE is to not-be Ralph—to have a vested interest in seeing and living the
          DIFFERENCE
between the inside (Ralph)
          and
the outside (events, objects).

Drama (old, what I reject) is people trying to make the inside (their subjective life) and the outside (the world) cohere.
          That's a bad way to live, that's a living death.
          To live as a HUMAN BEING is to CONSCIOUSLY live the tension between wish and reality.
All MY "characters"
     "do the task"
of identifying themselves with

consciousness

which doesn't (if you will take the trouble to notice
     for yourself),
doesn't SUSTAIN objects in the mind (that's impossible for more than a millisecond)

     but presents and represents
          in every tiny quanta of time
          the content.

Now: furthermore—the overlay of associations
(the harmonies) are DIFFERENT on each re-presentation.

     I reflect that.

I have evolved a style that shows how it is now with us, in consciousness. I don't speak in generalities. I show the mind at work, moment-by-moment.

Most everybody thinks in inherited abstractions, idols (Fred, the sky, the trees, Wanda's desires, Ralph's personality, love, hate, etc.) so of course the

REALISM

of my theater seems to be unreal to most people.

The universe as a variation on the theme of the formless (energy) and form continually interpenetrating each other—now you see it, now you don't (man: imbalance of inner and outer).

          Any art that gives or is based on the illusion of the SUSTAINED OB-
          JECT
          is bad, unuseful to man's development, his coming-to-himself as a
          spiritual, shipwrecked-on-earth (in nature) being.

Today, to the man who accepts his split (shipwrecked) nature, the "whole" is only possible as a regressive vision, a kind of primitivism. POSTPONE the whole (as Duchamp's—a "delay" in glass. As Heidegger tells us we are between the Gods that were and the Gods that will be and must "wait.")

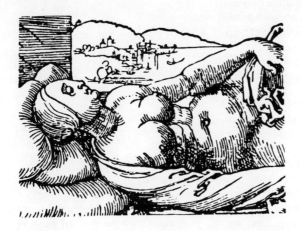

ETHICAL DIGRESSION

1) BE IN TWO PLACES AT ONCE
   (Duo-consciousness:
     Awakedness:
      I.E. The aim)
       2) USING INTENTIONAL PERCEPTION
         (That GRASPS in seeing.
         I.E. The method)
           3) A FIELD OF EVER MORE
              SUBTLE DISCRIMINATIONS
              (The necessary
              environment)

To make serious art is to evoke ever-subtler resources
of perceptual discrimination.
BAD art gives us GROSS
              OBVIOUS
              OVER-STATED contrasts and juxtapositions.
Man rises (art *can* perhaps help) if he
REFINES
his ability to discriminate ever-smaller differences between
adjacent, or linked, or simply postulated, objects and events.

Our art is the setting up of relations in which one *SAVORS*
the smallest possible differences . . . or the finest point
of identity.
      (1) Match two moments (objects).
        They just, slightly, don't match.
           (the basic human [shipwrecked]
           dialectic between inner and outer that

are always out of phase, i.e., inner never
matches outer—no matter how close, how much
effort: and that tiny, unresolvable mis-match
[dream and resistance of world]
[mental image and unexpected data]
is the source of human creativity, energy, life . . .)
  or
(2) two very dissimilar objects (events):
 and be able to notice in each the tiny
 seed that is identical.
  (very different objects in which
  the *identity* is subtly determined
  —it being the tiny pivot point between
  inner and outer [the different objects]
  that are always out of phase—but are
  the same in being the two poles of one human
  condition which pivots between them).

Most theater (bad) tries to thrill the sleeping audience with ever new, ever bigger (gross) contrast (collision, conflict). That merely continues the process of putting people to sleep under the pretense of waking them up. "This'll knock their eyes out!" says the artist—

 But it will
 and it will not.

The GROSS contrast between   purple cow and twenty-
           foot-high glass
           farmer
           or
           Army of ferocious
           Indians and pure
           maiden

—these "wake" the sleeper in certain of his centers, which are the same gross, utilitarian ones used to get through life =

 (sleeping—not noticing deviations and distracting input—so that *ENDS* [making a living, winning the loved one, etc.] can be attained).

In daily life, we suppress awareness, noticing as-little-as-possible of what would distract us from (inherited, taught) aims.

In art, these GROSS, OVERSTIMULATING contrasts allow us to get the thrill of "seeing," without real seeing, without effort, without the need of waking up, without mobilizing the sleeping "noticing, savoring, intentional perception" that sleeps in us as we live daily life.

 "HALF DEAD PEOPLE WHOSE PERCEPTUAL MECHANISMS ARE ASLEEP TO FACILITATE THE AVOIDANCE OF DISTRACTING REAL-PHENOMENON ON THE ASSIGNED ROAD OF LIFE—HERE'S A THRILL FOR YOU!" (And you don't have to wake up to get the kick.)

ESTHETICS = ETHICS

The above stated esthetic of gross thrill = an immoral keeping-the-sleeper-asleep.

Because: everybody should wake up.
    Begin to "see," "listen," "touch," "taste," "smell," in such
    a way that it is
        THINKING (doing those things)
        Not just swallowing.
I.E. NOTICE. . . . how (in what *small:* exact [therefore powerful] ways) each thing that
is the same is different and how each thing that is VERY different is the same.

DO YOU UNDERSTAND THE IMPLICATIONS OF THE ABOVE DIAGRAM?

    NOTICE:
    NOTICE:
The art work should be a field for noticing.

    Which means: It should *INVITE*
the viewer to *SEE* what's *THERE.*

ART technique has generally been a means whereby the spectator
is *besieged*
by the most obvious possible content available in the
field of the work at a given moment.
        Result—he is so busy receiving (into his
           mechanism) that gross data

        (he has to swallow it)

that he has not the chance to *NOTICE*
to go "visiting"
to "reconnoiter"
to "wake up and explore" the world before him (the
        field of the art work).

So: just as the autonomic nervous system swallows dinner FOR us

        so
the sleeping spectator swallows the proffered sensory input
of gross-contrast art which is AUTOMATIC (conditioned)
perceptual mechanism.

    Immoral art technique (in collaboration with a content
    of gross contrasts) keeps him hypnotized, continues
    to manipulate him in a world of signs—
    rather than perceptions.

The least we could do is to make the content be ever-subtler contrasts and identities
so that

When he *sits back* to *receive. . . .* he gets VOID!

Then, faced with that VOID, if he wants something to fill it (panic?) he has to call upon, to wake up, the dormant, up-till-now-sleeping

intentional-perception

within. And GRASP—reach out toward, perceptually "make" for himself—what is "offered" in the field of the work at such and such a moment.

AND WAKE UP.

Just as it's a truism that one only LEARNS deeply when, out of inner necessity, one digs out ideas for oneself,
         so in art
one is only "touched" (touched in an awake state, rather than stroked back deeper into sleep) when the form is such that it invites one (and one co-incidentally discovers the need) to dig out what-is-there-to-be-noticed.

EFFORT ALONE is rewarded; the greater the perceptual effort, the greater the perceptual reward. The art work has to be aware of this and purge itself of the kind of "beauty" that can come and enter the sleeping, passive mind. That kind of received beauty can seem effective but only on the sleeping mind that uses it to sink, through beauty, into deeper sleep.

Beauty that isn't "discovered" or "made" by the spectator in an astute "picking it out" of the field of the work—such beauty is pre-digested beauty that is only part of a language of signs in which "the beautiful" event is another sign—not a disorienting experience demanding human effort in order to come to terms with it and "know" it.

Beauty is only useful or desirable to human development when somebody MAKES it be there by SEEING it in some spot which had been looked at 100 times before . . .
         The audience that RECEIVES beauty
                              vs
         The audience that constructs it, notices it, flushes it out of hiding. Which audience do you want to belong to?
For a long time there has been a certain art ideology which proclaimed that in life one is active, and in art one is passive and receives.
         In bad art (90 percent of most art—99 percent of most theatre)—YES.
         But in GOOD art—the perception is forced into being an ACTIVE mode.

Good (moral) art (and yes, I dare to refer to those categories) in which—to make it be for himself—the spectator must use active, intentional perceptive modes, has as its end the exercising of those active perceptional modes which might then, someday, enter life itself. . . .and transform it.

> The test: when the audience says "wow" and they sink into wide grins of awe, or laughter, or tears, or in general have wide-eyed, child-like delighted faces (so loved by the hidden camera which shows people enjoying a show)—

WARNING!

When they frown, and wrinkle the brow, and stroke the chin and say "hummmm. . . . curious. . . ."

THEN

They're perhaps awake, and working at seeing and noticing how things go and don't go together.

"DON'T YOU WANT TO WAKE UP? TO HAVE A MIND THAT NOTICES THINGS?
A MIND AS SHARP AS A MICRO-TELESCOPE?
                    I CAN HELP
BUT YOU HAVE TO *WANT* IT. WHEN YOU WANT IT—COME TO ME AND I'LL
SHOW YOU SOMETHING YOU'LL BE ABLE TO MAKE USE OF.
                    UNTIL THEN
STAY HOME, IN BED, WHY SPOIL A GOOD NIGHT'S SLEEP."

The result of being awake (seeing):
  You are in two places at once (and ecstatic).
                    Duo-consciousness.
      1. You see
      2. You see yourself seeing

The *ONLY* justifiable technique in art (art of this historical moment)—
The only technique which is not simply audience manipulation—
(leading the ones who sleep deeper into that sleep)
                    is
learning how to be in two places (levels, orientations, perspectives) at once.

      1) Study all kinds of "FRAMING DEVICES."
      2) Study the superimposition of DIAGRAM upon reality.

(Both = two places at once = man's condition. The inner world *superimposed* on the outer [remember, they never quite match and/or they are very-different-but there is a tiny, exact (therefore powerful) common element (pivot point)].)

To be a proper SPECTATOR is to be in two places at once.
1) Seeing where *it* is (the art)
2) Seeing where *you* are (watching).

      If you see "it" only—you are not a spectator but you are a person who has
      been hypnotized.

      And you will need bigger and bigger, grosser and grosser thrills, contrasts,
      effects.

If you see "it" and "yourself"—
If you direct a GRASPING beam of intentional perception at "it"

      (which energy beam—like feedback or resonance—then ALWAYS
      makes you tingle and come back to yourself also and at the same time)
                    THEN
you will begin to see what most others don't see, and you will find in each inch of the
perceived surface—
                    WORLDS
      and energy and delight
        and information about how it is in this universe.

(Be assured, intentional perception also reveals
   how awful most art is. It's like looking through
     the heretofore unnoticed make-up of a famous
       "great beauty" and seeing the banality and
         pock-marks underneath.)

To use international-perception
to see ever more subtle distinctions
                                    IS
human development, and art either serves or retards that development.
       MAKE YOUR CHOICE.
          Have fun if you like, and spend as much time as you like sleeping—
             but realize at every moment, it's YOUR choice, and results will follow
             from that choice.

Part II

For many years I thought the task was to "re-tree" the tree. Make the spectator see it
fresh, strange—as for the first time, not seeing real tree through the learned concept
tree (the standard POUND, RUSSIAN FORMALIST, PHENOMENOLOGIST idea).
      Now I realize—the task is the opposite. Not re-TREE the tree, but DE-tree the
tree. Make it function consciously as the element it *is* in man's attempt to be a "soul."
(To realize what he is—an abstracting force, a thinking force not IN nature but superimposed upon it.)
      The experience of "tree" is a collection of facts—or more a configuration of
facts—for instance, turning a corner, looking, being told what's a tree, deciding to in-
vent a catagory "tree," shade, coolness, rising to the sun, catching the breeze.
      So seeing the TREE is seeing *that* THING out there (being ready to see it and
having that readiness filled)—seeing and knowing you are seeing that and allowing
associations to exist—those associations which define the tree's being—associations
which are abstractions (as memories, possibilities, hopes, projects).
      Moment by moment—this is the stuff (these associations, filters of memory, ideas,
etc.) that living is made of. Now, the task is to show *this* clearly (the smallest possible
unit).

Art should ground us in what-it-is-to-be-living. Not develop our lust for solutions. (And various solutions are: arrival, meaning in the sense of conclusion rather than process, emotion—which once aroused performs a kind of "closure" on the spiritual apparatus.)

Art should awaken a hunger for an immersion in being-conscious-of-process. . . .

Art is a *reminding* technique. NOTHING ELSE. "Don't forget this is going on—an *act* of a certain sort is going on in each milli-second of being an awake, unbalanced, in-collision-with-nature human being.

And most things in our "world" (and most "art") collaborate to make us overlook that process-of-responding-to-our-unbalanced-state. . . . and instead we are taught to see objects (rather than perceptual acts) and we are, by those objects, enslaved (desire, envy, worshiping of images). The "object" personality, the "object" beautiful image, the "object" meaningful emotion, the "object" having seen some*thing* clearly: all these make up sleep.

The greatest problem in performance art is how to include digressions, which can clarify, while not losing from consciousness the small event that prompted the digression, which now prompts its OWN digression.

The alienation technique, for instance, is an attempt to deal with this, but a very primitive attempt.

The problem is probably insoluble, but the struggling with the problem is the artist's unique problem and only reason for being.

POSTSCRIPT

One *thinks* about life and sees its richness. Thinking makes life *richer*
    DENSER
than mere living without reflecting on the living-it.
    (that's why man was
      LURED
    into thinking).
The task in art: to make that awareness of life's greater density part of the pure

    SEEING of it (in each moment—not needing the time-lag-linked "thinking."

                    Gertrude Stein says the problem
                    with theatre has always been
                    the spectator is either a little
                    before or after his own
                    time in watching, not exactly
                    matching the play's time. That's
                    because pre-Steinian theatre
                    didn't have the technique
                    required to make the richness
                    and density be IN the moment,
                    but always asked the spectator
                    to THINK the implications of
                    the presented moment in terms
                    of the past and future moment.
                    Replacing narrative with process-

concerns is a way of dealing
with this problem.)

Most people like material on stage which is NOT DENSE in the sense we mean, because they haven't used—in their lives—the THINKING that reveals the density of the
simplest moment. So to them—
    the DENSE vision
Seems confusion, discontinuity, even THINNESS!
    because it doesn't
                  SEEM (appear)
like the life they know. In order to live (in their lives), they depend on various
simplification mechanisms that blockout everything except the
                  USEFUL
          signs, pointers, tools
they find on the narrow road they have made of their life—all energy directed to
being able to continue moving along that NARROW road.

> (Recall how most modern art is at some stage called SIMULTANEOUSLY
> DENSE [impenetrable] and thin [lacking human richness]; this, clearly, be-
> cause of it's wideness—it's open to multiple levels of being [which thought
> can also but not simultaneously discover] and causes the usual, humanistic
> signposts—which still exist in it—to SEEM to have vanished, simply because
> the space BETWEEN those signposts has been greatly expanded so there is
> room for
>
>   ALL THE REST.)

One should add that the lust for increased DENSITY
of life
Or the lust for SEEING the density that is THERE but
        usually hidden until thought reveals it

    is desirable because
    our being tends to make itself, in the moment
        of artistic perception,
    isomorphic with the work of art. We get into
    the "rhythm" of the music, into the "spirit" of
    the novel, into the "atmosphere," "Aura," "world"
    of the work of art—its ups become our ups, its
        downs our downs, etc.

So. . . . being isomorphic with the vision of DENSITY
    makes our consciousness SPREAD.

        In life—we are on the narrow road of
           trying-to-achieve our aims.
        Aiming means—narrowing the vision and following
    that narrow beam to a goal.

        We have to be LEAN and EFFICIENT, and so we
        cast off excess baggage. But what is "excess
        baggage "on this road toward achievement is

all that is genuinely creative and human
within us.

The great man RADIATES, because he is in touch with the (pre-conscious) density and
variety and roundness of his being. The other kind of man is
    A NARROW MAN . . . who never leaves the
        narrow road and NARROWS
        HIMSELF so he better fits
        the architecture of the
        road itself.

                        THE WORLD IS ROUND
                        THE ROAD IS NARROW.
                        Art should direct us to the world.
                        ART should REMIND us that one is not an

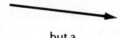

                                    but a

                                    or a

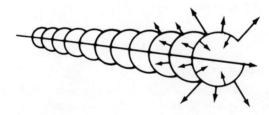

Much art doesn't allude to all that is not "in" it, all the "left out" that is in the world,
in thought, but not in the work.

It convinces us, while it is going-on, that "this" is the world.

Most people still reject art that implies "all" because to do that its technique is to have
    GAPS (thru which filters—attracts the viewers pre-conscious, the "ALL")
and those gaps are dissonances, disassociation, discontinuity, dehumanization

and GAPS remind one of what is true:
    That man is always shipwrecked
        That his conscious resources are never equal to his dilemma
            That he will never WIN
                (Which is different from saying that he cannot
                    PLAY magnificently and joyously—in which
                        case not-winning is hardly a cause for sadness).

But man wants usually to be able to believe that, just like the animal, he is at home in the world. That nature is his proper realm. So to point-out that man is NOT at home—

Well, man can sometimes deal with that intellectually as the "message"
So a realistic (which means conforting-style) work can
      tell a story of shipwreck, and sentiments of shipwreck can be expressed
Because man can handle that emotionally by looking at it as ONE EXPERIENCE out of many ("yes," he says, "sometimes we are shipwrecked, but we also have happiness, a mother's embrace, a balmy day, a good meal, the adulation of the crowd, the caress of the loved one"). And so his conscious thinking makes him feel O.K. even in the face of a momentarily disturbing STORY about REAL PEOPLE.

But to use a style (dissonant, disassociated) which attacks the on-going world style of assumed continuity and coherence is to attack man's false at-homeness on a level at which he
                    HAS NOT
the defenses he has against truthful story-telling. Because he is trained to WATCH STORY consciously, so he can defend against it in his consciousness.

But style works on the level of the pre-conscious, where most men prefer to say "oh, nobody goes THERE any more" as if it were an ancient vacation place that has long since lost its clientele.

And so style attacks, with truth, where man most deeply is but where he has the least developed navigational techniques. So truth storms
                  as style
            in the pre-conscious
And man *IS* shipwrecked, unable to navigate in that storm

So he says

                NO!

To the offending work of art.

And in saying no. . . .he says no to what he is and prefers to remain animal-man. At home in the world. Asleep in his mother's arms. Balanced (seemingly). Whole (seemingly). Happy (seemingly).

CLASSICAL THERAPY

(or) A WEEK UNDER THE INFLUENCE . . .

(BEN looks at the mirror. It turns and looks back at him. It crosses to him, and bumps into him.)

BEN

That proves it's looking back at me.

(Pause.)

The number of operations it can perform on my body are limited.

(Enter ELEANOR, comes up behind BEN, puts a hammerlock on him, presses his head and body in a series of different positions against the mirror.)

ELEANOR

Those are some of my different positions.

(HANNAH is in the doorway. A suit over her arm.)

HANNAH

Get dressed, huh.

BEN

Hey.

ELEANOR

What.

BEN

(Pause.)

I need a better position.

ELEANOR

—Is that a request directed at the mirror or Ben's head.

HANNAH

—I knew he was dressed.

(Pause.)

Guess what. I wanted to confuse him.

BEN

How come.

HANNAH

(Pause.)

I wanted to see how good he could operate if he was confused.

ELEANOR

Shhhhhh.

BEN

—I can't show how confused I am because Eleanor isn't giving me freedom of movement.

(HANNAH into room.)

HANNAH

(Pause.)

That suit doesn't fit you too good Ben.

BEN

—It would fit better if I was wearing it.

HANNAH and ELEANOR

A likely story.

CLASSICAL THERAPY was performed in Paris and in French for the Festival d'Automne. All photographs accompanying this text by Babette Mangolte.

HANNAH

(Pause.)

Any other takers.

ELEANOR

How about me.

(A song in German. As the music continues, ELEANOR releases BEN, and comes and puts on the suit which HANNAH carries. BEN watches. Then BEN points in mirror and song fades. As ELEANOR strikes pose of "showing." Crew runs a small white dot from BEN's pointing finger to the mirror, and bounces it back to ELEANOR's cheek.)

ELEANOR

Oh, is that what you were looking at.

(Pause. BEN lowers his hand.)

Oh Ben, is that the spot on my body you were watching.

(BEN crosses, kisses image in mirror as HANNAH simultaneously bends over to kiss ELEANOR's cheek—on which the white dot now sticks—and crew puts second white dot on her lips as she then slouches close to ELEANOR. Then a string from RHODA's white spot —which she holds between her teeth—to the vest pocket of ELEANOR's suit. A handkerchief in the vest pocket then taken out by ELEANOR who blows her nose. BEN makes his hands into binoculars: still looking at the reflection of all this in the mirror. Crew comes and turns him so he looks out to audience, still with hand binoculars. They bring two long tubes which they place in his hands and ELEANOR and HANNAH exit as BEN readjusts his hands and eyes so the long tubes to which his eyes are pressed go from his eyes straight down onto the floor, and then he walks, using the tubes as canes from eyes to ground. Organ music.

Door opens and a black upright coffin-like box comes to fill the opening.)

Legend: "WATCH WHERE YOU'RE GOING, BEN."

(The coffin-box opens. BEN does a dance, still keeping the tubes pressed between eyes and floor. Then a pause. Then he puts down the tubes and goes to the mirror. A hum.

HANNAH comes in with a suit. BEN, looking into the mirror, tries to make it look as if the suit he is wearing does not fit him well.)

BEN

It fits beautifully, huh.

HANNAH

—Look. It doesn't fit too good.

(She holds out her suit. She holds out her suit on a hanger. Attach a string to BEN's back. Run the suit on hanger from HANNAH to BEN's back. Then another string, plates slide down and hit him and hang. A third string—books.)

Legend: "ALL MY IDEAS ARE DIFFERENT."

(Music. ELEANOR enters.)

Legend: "WRONG ENTRANCE."

(A curtain covers her. Crew brings a curtain to hide BEN. He exits and the curtain is taken away.

HANNAH goes behind ELEANOR's curtain. It goes and they are revealed center, holding each other's hands, and they lean back from each other at the waist, as a German cabaret song begins, and that way they slowly sink to the floor. A cabinet behind them opens. Each item on the shelves of the cabinet has a string. The two girls, on the floor now, pull the strings one by one and the objects fall onto them.

Silence.

Then the crew sets many small stands, each with a single clear bulb on top, all about the room. The lights blink in sequence, only one on at a time. (There are as many as a dozen.) After a while— during which the blinking in sequence continues—the mirror moves to the door and knocks. Door opens. A bookcase enters. The mirror selects a book from

out of the bookcase. Opens it and presses it against its own glass front, and tapes it there.
The bookcase itself takes a book out of its shelves, and throws it across the room. It is, however, attached to the shelf with a rope. And the bookcase then pulls on the rope and hauls the book back. Then casts it out again. This continues as thuds begin.)

Legend: WATCH THE BOOK
IT RECEDES LIKE LIGHT
ITS WRITING IS WRITTEN.
IT. IT. A CONSTANT SPEED
A VERY SPECIFIC HEAD SO ARTIC-
   ULATED.
UN-UTTERABLE?
NOT SO. NOT SO.

(Crew fixes a head cut-out center stage. The cut-out is a good six feet high—
BEN enters; a noise like a printing press.)

Legend: TRY THAT ON FOR SIZE.

(Strings set from the inner edges of the cut-out, outwards to the edges of the set.)

(The two girls rise and one by one, with strut-steps, walk through the profile from behind; then BEN follows, and they all exit.)
(Then crew enters and takes four books out of the bookcase—each book with a string still attaching it to its shelf—and they glue the four books to different spots along the cut-out profile.
HANNAH has re-entered. The book that is taped to the mirror is removed and HANNAH is now taped to the mirror. The book is taken to BEN, who now sits in a chair. His two tubes, now directed at the book which is attached to a rope and swings and he tries to watch it through his tubes.)

BEN
It's hard following the story this way.
(Through the head cut-out we see ELEANOR starting to put things back on the shelf.)

Legend: I'M GLAD ELEANOR IS STARTING TO CLEAN UP.

(As soon as HANNAH has been taped to the mirror she breaks away and leaves the room. The

mirror then moves between the book on a string and the tubes.
There is a rattling noise, BEN rises and exits, letting the tubes droop (they have been supported mid-point on a tripod) and the person who has been inside the mirror making it move also exits.)

Legend: BEN, OUTSIDE OF THE ROOM READS TOWARD THE CENTER
(Rattle.)
BETWEEN THE WORDS A WHOLE LIFE ARISES.
(Rattle.)
(The door opens, the coffin-box enters and its door immediately opens and BEN begins to enter and exit—that is, he steps in and steps out, again and again.
Silence.
HANNAH and ELEANOR join hands behind the cut-out and again and again ease themselves to the floor.)

Legend: THE HEAD SAYS "I WAS CREATED BY A BOOK."
NOT IN ONE MOMENT
BUT IN THE SUM TOTAL OF
   MOMENTS
NOW I EXIST, BUT I HAVE NO DE-
SIRE TO MAKE MY EXISTENCE
A CONVINCING EXISTENCE.

(The cabinet behind the girls is moved off, and behind it a curtain opens revealing a stage. On that inner stage, MAX sits, knees together, elbows on knees and chin on fist.
HANNAH II and ELEANOR II enter the inner stage and standing on either side of MAX, each puts a hand on his shoulder as the other two girls continue rising and falling and BEN continues stepping in and out.)

MAX
Please get your hands off my shoulders.
ELEANOR II
Oh Hannah.
HANNAH II
What.
(Pause.)

I had a suitcase in this hand and something in the other hand.
ELEANOR II
I think he'd like me to hold his head.
MAX
(Turns.)
I would not.
ELEANOR II
Shhhhhh.
HANNAH II
Don't calm him too fast, Eleanor.
MAX
I'm not really looking at her.
(ELEANOR II and HANNAH II back out.)
I put this suit on especially even though I knew it didn't fit me good.
(Enter HANNAH II with a suit over her arm.)
HANNAH II
Did you do that on purpose Max.
MAX
Why don't you show me the rest of your body, Hannah.
(ELEANOR II enters and kisses his cheek. Then the second set of girls fall—while the first are still doing their up-down bit.)
HANNAH II
I didn't even worry about the suit.
(The second set of girls then independently gets up and falls five times. MAX rises.)
MAX
These are my fingers. Look how I combine them.
(He twists each set of fingers, holding up his hands. Drumroll, enter from the side, walking sideways in crab-waddle steps, LEO and IDA. Slowly squat-move across—
MAX twists his hands that have twisted fingers, showing them in different positions. There is a whistle.)
BLACKOUT

(Lights up. BEN is moving slowly toward the door. When he gets there he knocks, and the curtain rear opens onto the inner stage. MAX is discovered, slowly revolving with his arms out. He falls. BEN

exits. MAX rises and revolves. BEN re-enters now on the "stage," waits a moment, then exits and the curtain closes.
Pause.
Enter HANNAH I and II, ELEANOR I and II, MAX, BEN, LEO and IDA all through door, they cross up and go through the closed stage curtain.
Slow thuds accompany this.
Then the curtain opens, and only MAX is there, slowly revolving.
BEN enters on the stage and holds MAX from the rear and so both are revolving.
ELEANOR enters halfway, carrying suit. Mirror enters down in room.)

Legend: TRY TO LOOK INTO THE MIRROR WHILE TURNING.
I.E., ALL AT ONCE
I.E. THE GETAWAY.

(Mirror starts turning and curtain closes. LEO and IDA enter in sideways squat-steps. BEN also, after IDA.
Funny music.
Bookcase follows them on. Crew takes a book from the shelf, runs it over to hit mirror, and as mirror is still turning and he holds book to mirror's face, he gets wound in string which attaches book back to shelf. Music off, and BEN, IDA and LEO keep rocking squat-like back and forth in place. String from BEN's teeth to floor. From IDA's teeth to side. From LEO's to above. They all are still.)

SOFT VOICE
It happened in one of the world's most beautiful cities.
(Curtain opens: an airplane.)
It happened in one of the world's most beautiful cities and it was so important it

had to be remembered and remembered again.

> *(Plane on string, swings. Throw a ball of string back and forth over the plane as BEN, IDA and LEO rock back and forth, and the plane is finally all tangled in string.)*

BEN

Could somebody help that airplane get untangled.

> *(Telephone brought and held.)*

Oh please, could somebody help that airplane get untangled.

> *(Arrow carried from telephone off.)*

Oh, I bet Uncle Leo and Ida are going to be some of the first people to help that airplane get untangled.

Legend: SHE IS HIS SISTER.

IDA

I'd help if I could help best.

> *(Pocketbook given her, her string reset so it runs from pocketbook to floor.*
> *Telephone receiver is on a string now, and swings in the air as crew still holds the body of the phone.)*

Legend: IT'S AS FAR AS THE MOUNTAINS NOW.

> *(Drop shifts to mountains. Then curtain closes and reopens on a new drop which is a river with swirling rapids. MAX and RHODA enter in a canoe. RHODA in the front seat. Crew slowly carries the body of the telephone across the stage.)*

MAX

It's going too fast to catch it.

RHODA

> *(Turning back to look at him.)*

Oh Max, look how my body.

MAX

Shhhhhhh.

RHODA

> *(Pause.)*

Afraid I'll break it huh.

MAX

—I was trying to keep track of the—

RHODA

What.

MAX

> *(Pause.)*

Phone.

RHODA

It was the rapids.

> *(Pause. The curtains slowly close.)*

Look, the curtains are closing Max.

MAX

Look, the water is

RHODA

What

MAX

> *(Pause.)*

Thick.

RHODA

What.

MAX

How can water be thick.

> *(Curtains now completely shut. Enter LEO and IDA, side-squat steps. Pause. Then MAX and RHODA in canoe enter the downstage area, are blocked by LEO and IDA.)*

> *(Lights come up and the cut-out head is on the stage. The strings coming from the profile edge are set.)*

Legend: "THERE WAS A CANOE HERE.
ARE WE REALLY IN THE ROOM STILL. ARE WE STILL IN THE ROOM."

> *(A second smaller screen is set, and in hand writing appears—"Oh Reinhardt. Write what you want to write. Does that mean the same thing as imagine what you want to imagine. No, he says. Now. Who is 'he.' He is not myself. He is here now. He is on the stage. Oh God, one might say that he is continually on the stage. Write what you want to write.")*

DOES NOT=IMAGINE WHAT YOU WANT TO IMAGINE. THEREFORE, NOT WRITE WHAT YOU WANT TO WRITE BUT WRITE SOMETHING ELSE. AH YES. SOMETHING ELSE: YOU ARE NOT INTERESTED

IN A CANOE OR THE CUT-OUT SHAPE OF A HEAD, ARE YOU.
(Set up a table. On the table are two small white slopes. Off the slopes are run, by two crew members, two small white objects. They continue the trajectory of the slope and hit the walls, bounce off and fall to the ground. HANNAH and LEO onstage, at edge.)

HANNAH
That acted like a piece of chalk.
(Pause.)
I'm pretending to like you.

Legend: YOU ARE NOT DOING A GOOD JOB OF PRETENDING IT.

(They exit. Pause. Then LEO enters with a hat.)

LEO
This hat is an item.
(Pause. Puts on the hat.)
An item.
(Pause.)
A second item makes its appearance.

Legend: IT'S TIME FOR A SECOND ITEM ISN'T IT LEO.

(Pause, curtains open and empty canoe there.)

Legend: GO BACK TO THE CANOE.

LEO
Then go back to the item.
(Pause.)
Then please go back to the second item.
(As HANNAH comes to the canoe, gets in and starts paddling.)
The second item is a memory. Everything is an evolution and this is too, is it not.
(Set up a small house center stage, covered with roses.)
It is so easy to set up a house covered with roses. It is so easy to be in the sunshine. It is so easy to hear whatever one wants to hear.
(A train whistle, as ELEANOR enters with a broom sweeping, the sound of a steam engine, smoke comes out of the little chimney of the house as ELEANOR sweeps furiously and LEO enters the house and

opens the shutters and looks out. He now holds a violin, and from behind his head a flowerpot is thrown through the window onto the stage.)

ELEANOR
I'll have to sweep it up.
LEO
I was here before but you didn't notice me.
(Pause.)
Sweep it up.
ELEANOR
(Finger to her lips.)
Shhhhhh.
LEO
Why is Eleanor telling me to be quiet.
(Pause.)
Look how I'm dressed.
*(A book is held to his head. MAX enters dressed as a trainman, with a long nosed watering can.
Noise begins, thuds over music. A flowerpot is hung from can, then string from the bottom of the flowerpot, and as others exit that string is pulled so the flowerpot tilts and rises a bit.)*

Legend: ITEM.

(Enter HANNAH with a canoe.)
HANNAH
Out of my way, trainman.
MAX
—Do you live here.
HANNAH
(Pause.)
I'm going by in my canoe.
MAX
(As a white cloth is held flat behind his head.)
My but the sun is bright.
(Whistle.)
Pass behind my body, child.
HANNAH
I'm not a child, sir.
MAX
(Pause.)
Look at this child in her canoe.
(Window in the little house opens again and LEO is there.)
LEO
Did I hear something.
(Pause. Note on violin.)
Not my violin.

(String to violin, other end dropped to floor.)

Legend: THEY EACH HAVE A SEP-
ARATE INSTRUMENT.

HANNAH
This is an island, is it not an island.
Legend: PARADISE ISLAND:
(Music starts.)
WHAT ARE THE BEST MEANS
OF TRANSPORTATION IN AND
AROUND PARADISE ISLAND.
(All exit but MAX and can and flowerpot.)

MAX
Sisters can be eliminated on Paradise Island.
(Pause.)
Eliminate the island or eliminate the Paradise. All sentences have a meaning by definition. All acts have a certain beauty and
this act

(Legend: "='s")

also is a beauty of an act, huh.
*(A second string set to pull off the flowerpot in a slightly new direc-
tion.)*

MAX
1. The beauty of an act noticing itself.

HANNAH
(Off.)
Oh Max, do you notice something different.

MAX
What.
(Pause.)
2. The beauty of certain themes which are incapable of development.

HANNAH
(Off.)
Oh Max, I have nothing to say but in a
certain sense, whatever you say.

MAX
What.
(Pause.)
3. What.

HANNAH
What.

MAX
What happened to your canoe, Rhoda.

HANNAH
(Off.)
Was it Rhoda who had the canoe or Hannah
who had the canoe.

(Pause.)
I'm using my body like a stick.

MAX
Me too.

HANNAH
(Off.)
What.

MAX
(Pause.)
I should be

HANNAH
What

MAX
(Pause.)
Watering the engines, huh.
(Train whistle.)

HANNAH
(Off.)
—What I needed was water for my canoe.
*(Curtains rear open and the little
stage is now set with two painted
drops, side by side, a long pause.)*

SOFT VOICE
Oh pictures. You are enough for my happiness. What I want to know is what happened to the train and what happened to
the canoe.
(Pause.)
The train and the canoe, now I see them and
I know what happened to them.
*(Pause. Curtains pulled closed. En-
ter LEO with watering can and
flowerpot and string as MAX exits
with his. HANNAH enters with a
spoon and starts tapping the side
of LEO's can.)*
Oh, my happiness is complete when I can
relate the thing that I am seeing to the thing
that I am hearing.
(Pause, tapping goes on.)
It doesn't have to be a part of the seeing
to make me happy enough to like seeing it.
*(Pause, attach a string to HAN-
NAH's spoon, which she then holds
up in front of her face. Then the
same sound of spoon hitting can is
heard.)*
Do you know that a sound can be other
things—like a photograph.

HANNAH
—Look, I'm having a picture taken.

SOFT VOICE
Or a mirror held in the hand like a plate.

HANNAH

—Look, what I can see is my own face, beautifully when I think about it, and even more beautiful when.

SOFT VOICE and LEO

What. What.

HANNAH

Shhhhhhh.

(Pause.)

That was most of the time when it was even more beautiful.

SOFT VOICE and LEO

—Oh Hannah, Hannah. One of my roles.

HANNAH

What.

(Curtain opens, canoe drop gone, engine drop remains.)

The canoe has vanished, but the engine, oh the engine, oh the engine is there for as long as I need to think about it too.

LEO

—If you could only manage to do what I have been trying to do.

(Clunk, and curtain closes.)

Legend: CAN YOU WAIT WHILE SOMETHING ELSE IS HAPPENING.

(HANNAH exits, LEO remains. Curtain opens on a distorted perspective Italian miniature set, exterior with wall on one side, and large bed on other in which lie, under the covers, HANNAH, RHODA and ELEANOR.)

(Pause, in the bed under the covers, RHODA grabs HANNAH's breast.)

LEO

My God, what happened to the little house, house, house—

HANNAH

—My God, she's grabbing my left breast in her right hand.

(Crew comes and puts a long cap, with a long extension, on LEO's head. The end of the cap is dipped in a bucket of water.)

RHODA

My God, she's putting her right foot directly into my cunt.

ELEANOR
(Overlaps.)
—My God, she's putting her thumb into my ass like a rubber hose.

Legend: IT IS SO EASY TO FORGET EVERYTHING THAT HAPPENS.

ELEANOR
I did not dream it did I.
RHODA and HANNAH
What.
(Pause.)
We all dreamed it together, beautiful lady.
LEO
Hardly a day passes.
ALL
What.
LEO
(Pause, steps forward, stretching his nightcap.)
Hardly a day. Without. It passes.
ELEANOR
It didn't have something.
ALL
What.
(A clunk.)
LEO
Hardly a day passes without something good happening to us.
(A stick props up nightcap in the center of its span.)

Legend: IT COULDN'T BE NO-TICED IF IT WAS HIDDEN BY THE BLANKET.

(Girls move under the blanket, shaking and screaming.)
Hardly a day passes without something interesting happening to me. Tr/r/ra/ains.
(Pause.)
My life is tied up in trains. They come and go through here.
ALL
What.
LEO
Tr/r/ra/ains. They go on the tracks. Where are the tracks going now.
(Girls under blanket now sob.)
Where do those tracks go, Rhoda. She can't answer now because she is crying. Oh Rhoda, how come you are crying a little bit. I should ask one of the other little girls may-

be. Pretty, pretty, where are the trains going Rhoda.
ALL
Shhhhh.
LEO
(As lights dim.)
Even if I can't see them in the light—wait a minute, dimmer and better huh.
RHODA
He said it.
ALL
Shhhhh.
LEO
What, what.
ALL
Dimmer and better.
LEO
—Tracks.
(Pause.)
Tracks.
(Lights out.)
RHODA
She is putting her.
ALL
Shhhhh.
RHODA, ELEANOR, HANNAH
(Pause.)
My body.

(Lights up. MAX stands. A string attached to his back, RHODA stands in door with a suit and that suit runs along the string to his back. Then BEN comes and grabs him from behind and they struggle.)

Legend: HE'S TRYING TO PUT ON THE SUIT.

(Train noise heard.)

(BEN downstage to the side in a bed. Curtain onstage opens—the window of a train compartment. Scenery beyond.)

Legend: HEY BEN. GET FROM HERE TO THERE.

(A bird sings.
Enter MAX with a cane. Holds it,

does a soft-shoe step as drum starts to clatter.)

Legend: "MORE PILLOWS?"

(BEN rises, now sees that he has pillows on his fists, and starts punching the dancing MAX.
As lights slowly dim, BEN keeps hitting MAX and the girls tumble onstage, fighting as they roll on the floor.)

(Empty stage. Tracks up the wall. All enter, each with the car of an electric train set. They run their cars up the tracks up the wall, using chairs, etc., to stand on so they can collaborate and make a connected train of cars. Others start throwing stones at the train group which slowly runs its train to the top of the wall.)

MAX

Bigger and bigger.

(Pause.)

Wait.

(Stage curtain opens, bed—Italian miniature set is there.)

Legend: GET INTO BED SOMEBODY. THE BODY AND THE DIRECTION ROUTE.

RHODA

The tracks.

(Thud. She lies down. All take their train cars and put them on different parts of her body and hold them there. Pause. Then she rises, and they hold the train cars to those parts of her body as she slowly walks off.
Pause. Then the mirror walks on; i.e., now a small 1' × 1' mirror held by ELEANOR. BEN follows and they keep angling themselves so BEN can see different things in it. Finally she comes and holds the mirror directly onto his face. Then while she is doing so, a string to his back. Suit slid along until it rests on his back. He takes the mirror and

slips it under his shirt. He starts jumping about the stage, little hops, with string and suit still attached.
Thuds begin.
He vanishes.
Thuds continue.
A radio is set and turned on. Then the inner stage opens.
The Italian miniature set is there. In bed, the three girls moan once and turn over.
Then the cottage is brought and set center. A little bridge system set so the train tracks run into a hole in the side of the cottage.
The train goes in, and a moment later MAX runs out from the other side.)

Legend: HE IS BEING CHASED BY A TRAIN.

TRAIN=MIRROR.

(All enter and each has a partner to whom he immediately presses, face to face as if glued.)

RHODA

(Pause.)

Oh, that's not me.

ELEANOR

Look into my eyes, Rhoda.

(Now the individual pairs all come together.)

Legend: THERE'S NOBODY LEFT TO MAKE THE LITTLE TRAIN RUN INTO THE HOUSE.

(Inner stage opens to show a shiny black wall. People in clump dance as a unit.)

Legend: OH DEATHLESS ESTHETICISM, YOU MUST GIVE WAY BEFORE PROGRESS, HUH.
THIS IS HAND WRITTEN.
THE HAND WORKS AS GOOD NOW AS A MACHINE: ALL LANGUAGES ARE EQUAL.
GERMAN=FRENCH.
FRENCH=LATIN.
CAN YOU INSERT MORE COM-

BINATIONS OR (EQUIVALENTS).
LET'S SEE.

*(Dance stops and people exit.
RHODA comes back carrying a
suit, but she is surrounded as she
walks by a little gate system, the
kind that keeps a child in.)*
RHODA
What am I bid for this beautiful suit.
(Pause.)
Ben only wore it three times.
BEN
(Enters on high shoes.)
Oh Rhoda, I would like my suit back now.
(Pause.)
Would it fit.

Legend: PARADISE ISLAND.

RHODA
Oh Ben, we are on an island now.
BEN
Would it fit.
(Thud.)
The change in size is without any noises
accompanying it.
(Pause.)
Look at me. I am Reinhardt the significant.
(Thud and he begins moving.)
RHODA
Oh Ben, where you step the trains follow.
BEN
Each step is a what.
(Pause.)
Route, huh.
*(Enter LEO, in tall shoes also, step
by step behind BEN.)*
We're traveling in the same direction.
(Pause.)
One more step and we will have crossed to
the other side of the island.
(Pause.)
Together.
RHODA
(Tears the suit in half.)
Now I have two suits.
*(A bong and music starts. Enter
two men. Each puts on half the suit
and exits. The music continues and
the inner stage opens; HANNAH
and ELEANOR are cleaning the set
with the miniature Italian bed.
RHODA joins them. Making the
bed, changing sheets, etc.)*

BEN and LEO
We'd like to complain about our suits.
*(Close the curtain, the music off.
Then the curtain opens immedi-
ately and the three women are
having a pillow fight.)*
LEO and BEN
Can't we move better.
BEN
I see everything important.
LEO and BEN
(Pause, girls still fight.)
Paradise Island. Paradise Island.
LEO
—The only way you can arrive is by air.
The only way you can travel across the island is by foot.
*(Close curtains. A small train is run
across the floor to BEN and LEO.)*
What is behind me, what is behind me.
*(They exit and train goes over pre-
set hills, helped by crew. Curtain
then opens, girls frozen in pillow-
fight positions. Then one by one
they open their hands and the pillow they hold falls to the floor and
they are immediately given another.
This procedure continues throughout the next scene: the cut-out
head is set downstage of the inner-
stage, and the little floor lights
pulsate. Then pillows are scattered
about on the floor and strings are
set from the profile edge to pillows.
BEN enters and steps from pillow
to pillow and goes in front of the
profile. He carries a book which
he opens, and one long page is
unfolded out and carried to the
edge of the stage. He stands in
profile himself, and a smaller cut-
out profile of a whole figure is
brought out and it frames him sideways. Then a seven foot high curtain closes to mask the cut-out
piece, but above that curtain is
open, and, he is still seen in his
cut-out.)*
BEN
All I need is half a suit, huh.
(Pause.)
What time is it.

Legend: DO YOU LIKE TO READ
ON THE TRAIN.

(Pause, then a thud.)

WHAT DO YOU LIKE TO READ ON THE TRAIN.

BEN
I'm thinking about the train.
RHODA
(Enters wearing a ludicrously big suit, in which pant legs and coat arms drag on the floor.)
You should wear this suit in the train Ben.
BEN
Oh Rhoda, I wanted to dress good for Uncle Leo.
RHODA
Who.
BEN
(Pause.)
Uncle Leo.
RHODA
He was impressed with your appearance, Ben.
(Pause.)
He offered you a job working in his factory, Ben.
BEN
—I'd rather go to Paradise Island.
(Music begins.)
RHODA
How do you get there Ben.
(She has her suit arms and legs

pulled out by strings already attached to them.)
Would you rather live on Paradise Island than go to work in Uncle Leo's factory.
BEN
Yes.
RHODA
What would you do on Paradise Island.
BEN
Unless I'm mistaken—
RHODA
What.
BEN
One does not need to work if one is living—
RHODA
Wrong.
BEN
On Paradise Island.
RHODA
Oh Ben, the body never stops working.
(She exits, and two small tables are now set against the curtain, one on each side of BEN.)
BEN
I go on reading a book while other people work.
(Lamps set, one on each table. The little house set to one side of the stage. The shutters open and KARL is there with a violin.)
Do you mean the violin or the lamp.
(Thud.)

Do you mean the desire for the lamp.
KARL
Which lamp.
BEN
(Pause.)
There is a lamp behind my back which I cannot see—
KARL
—I play to amuse myself.
BEN
(Pause.)
I am thin.
(Flowers placed in windowsill.)
Two lamps and one violin, huh.
KARL
—Oh Ben, do you appreciate flowers.
(String run to violin, attached to its bottom; then as KARL holds the neck, string pulled so violin sticks out horizontal in space.)
Oh Ben, do you love music or do you just love to listen to it.
BEN
—I think your violin is in a dangerous position.
KARL
I think one of your two lamps is in a very dangerous position.
BEN
(Shifts one leg.)
Oh?
KARL
What trick are you
BEN
What
KARL
(Pause.)
Trying.
BEN
What trick are you trying Leo.
(LEO immediately replaces KARL in the window, holding the violin, as KARL disappears.)
LEO
I'm Leo.
BEN
(He falls in place.)
I'm Ben.
(Shift back, KARL replacing LEO.)
KARL
I knew that one of his lamps.
(The one behind BEN falls. Pause.)
Was in a dangerous position.

BEN
Can't you fix it.
(KARL plays a note on the still-extended violin. All lights suddenly out except the one lamp still on the table.)
Oh well, one is still working so I guess it's O.K.
(BEN shifts his position on the floor.)
Oh well, I have more freedom of movement than I imagined at first.
KARL
Do you have freedom of movement.
BEN
Yes.
KARL
(Pause.)
Stand up Ben.
BEN
One lamp is still working.
(Pause.)
Why doesn't the sun come out.
KARL
Oh Ben.
BEN
Shhhhh.
KARL
Do you like listening to music.

(Lights up. MAX enters and goes and stands in the opening from which BEN has fallen.)

BEN

I used to like it better when I was standing up.

(Pause. He exits.)

MAX

The sun came out.

(He lifts his arm and a string runs from his hand, extending the line of his arm through the window.)

It would be very hard to exchange places with Ben now.

KARL

Ben.

MAX

I'm not.

KARL

Shhhhh.

(Pause.)

That's Ben huh.

MAX

Everything depends on not moving.

(BEN enters. Stops. Exits. Pillows are held from behind, above the curtain. Pause. Then the pillows are thrown into the set.
Pause.
HANNAH, RHODA and ELEANOR enter as music begins. Then they put their heads on the pillows, keeping their legs straight and supporting their bodies with straight arms, their behinds sticking up in the air. In that position they begin circling, their heads acting as a pivot on the pillow.
Then the music fades and an airplane flies across in the rear.)

MAX

(Twisting his head to look at the plane.)

Traveling around the island but in the imagination only.

(Girls still pivot, remember.)

KARL

What benefits huh.

MAX

Do you mean traveling in the imagination.

(Pause.)

I am Karl a great believer in the imagination.

KARL

So was Ben also.

MAX

(Pause.)

Was he a great believer in the imagination.

(A string comes to the tail of the airplane and attached, then pulls it backwards. BEN enters carrying a suit on a hanger. He takes it to stuff through the gap in the wall between MAX's body and the edge of the cut-out.)

Legend: THE SUIT COULD GET THROUGH BUT NOT THE BODY.

(A white dot is carried out and attached to BEN's cheek. Pause.)

Legend: NO. PUT IT ON HIS TEMPLE. CLOSER TO THE HEAD.

BEN

In my case it is the side of the mouth that does the imagining.

MAX

No.

BEN

Yes. The side of the mouth.

(Pause. Dot moved to temple. Another suit is brought out, and tied to his body with string. Lights down to two lamps.
KARL and MAX exit—
Girls still pivoting on their pillows, and BEN falls to the floor.
Train pulled across on a string.)

Legend: THE TRAIN HAS TO BE MADE TO RUN OVER THE BODY.

ALL

Why. Why.

Legend: TO GET INTO THE HOUSE IT HAS TO PASS OVER THE BODY (ANSWER).

BEN

What is in the house.

(Train gets into the house, and the house is turned to show the train on the inside.)

The train itself enters the house, huh. Paradise Island.

(RHODA stops pivoting and goes into the house.)

Rhoda herself.

RHODA

No.

(She leaves as HANNAH stops pivoting and goes into the house, takes a broom and starts sweeping.)

BEN

Hannah.

HANNAH

Yes.

(She sweeps a bit, then stops.)

Welcome to Paradise Island Ben. This is not the first time you have been here. Do you remember being here before.

(RHODA enters with a rose. She pins it to HANNAH's blouse, then holds HANNAH very tight from the side around the waist.)

Probably not.

(ELEANOR stops pivoting and exits.)

If you had remembered you would also remember how to move about on the island and all of its other secrets. Now that you are here again you will have other new chances to learn about such things. Many of the nice things on Paradise Island are broken at the present time of course. Perhaps if you come again they will be fixed.

Then again, things get fixed very slowly sometimes. So we don't know which of the two will be the truth.

(Pause.)

The train is coming. Don't miss it.

(Enter, into the house, MAX, who does tap dance again with a cane.

RHODA still hugs HANNAH, and as a certain noise begins, HANNAH wiggles her broom and dances as much as she can in RHODA's grip. Front stage cleared and inner stage opens. Railway compartment cutout. Noise stops. A large stuffed bird seen in window. A runway set into the room, and the bird slowly moves out on the runway into the room, downstage (four feet off the floor). Then strings are set from the four corners of the railway-car window to the four corners of the proscenium.
BEN comes to the bird and feeds it.)

BEN
Now, would you like a smoke, bird.
BIRD
Oh yes.

(BEN lights a cigarette in his own mouth, and then puts it into the bird's beak.
It sings.
Lights up fuller to show whole room.
RHODA enters with a suit.
The following legends appear on the screen as the bird's singing fades out very slowly.)

Legend: SHE SAYS "STOP THE BIRD FROM SINGING, BEN." BEN: "HOW."

"Put this suit over the bird's body."
He does not answer her or move his own body.

He is thinking. That is to say— he is trying to imagine the outside of his own head.
(The floor mirror enters.)
The mirror says, "This will help you in that."

Then Rhoda makes way for Uncle Leo.

(RHODA exits.)
But Leo thinks, "Humm, I will not go into the room until the mirror has left."

(The following legend in red type.)
PARADISE ISLAND.
PARADISE ISLAND.

The mirror says to Ben, "Look, do you see who I really am."
And Ben is afraid to look.
The bird smokes his cigarette, and now that Ben has closed his eyes, he wonders why he can no longer hear the bird singing.

(In red type.)
"PARADISE ISLAND."
"PARADISE ISLAND."

Suddenly Ben realizes that what he has perceived through his eyes is no more real than what he has perceived through his ears.
(Pause. Everyone enters. RHODA carrying a suit, LEO with a telephone, MAX with airplane. Those who carry objects take up a sort of squat position.)
He pretends that he can hear everything: What about the four pieces of string that extended from the corners of the window (train compartment) to the edges of the stage.

The people have to step over and duck under the string at different places.
MAX
(In his squat pose.)
The. . . .cigarette . . . went . . . out. . . Ben.
BEN
The bird let it go out.

HANNAH
(Squat position, with pillow.)
Have. a. pillow. to. let. the. bird. rest.
BEN
—My God, the bird is resting at this very
moment now.

Legend: RETURN TO WHAT YOU
WANTED TO DO ABOUT THE
STRINGS, BEN.

*(BEN lights another cigarette for
the bird, and puts it into the bird's
beak.)*
LEO
*(As he lights a match and holds it
out.)*
Here, let me.
ALL
Oh Leo, he lit the cigarette before he put it
into the bird's mouth.
KARL
(Offering the telephone to LEO.)
Here let me.
*(LEO takes phone and puts the
mouthpiece part of the receiver to
his forehead and tries to lick it.)*
ALL
Oh Leo, don't try to lick the part of the
telephone everyone uses to speak into.
*(Now in the window, small train is
set on the runway and it runs down
into the room until it gets to the
bird.)*
VOICE
"Get out of the way please," says the train.
KARL
He let the cigarette go out.
ALL
(Pause.)
The bird isn't singing no more.
BEN
Does everyone know exactly where they are
standing.
(Pause.)
Take your bearings—
VOICE
"Beep, beep—"
BEN
—from the string.
KARL
Oh Ben, it's not efficient to take our bear-
ings from the string.

Legend: THE TRAIN AND THE BIRD

WILL NOT BE ABLE TO PASS EACH
OTHER WITHOUT GETTING HURT
(ONE OF THEM).

*(Out of the end of the track-run-
way, which rests on a table, a white
head emerges and stands in front
of the bird.)*
ALL
Should we line up under the white strings.
(Pause.)
This is still a train, isn't it.

Legend: "HOW COULD THE TRAIN
COMPARTMENT BE MOVED WITH-
OUT MOVING THE STRINGS."

ALL
(Pause.)
Watch us. Watch us.
*(They all help in shifting the inner
stage set to the Italian-bed unit, but
they are able to reset strings to the
four corners of the bed. And the
bird and white head and train and
most of the runway remain. HAN-
NAH, RHODA and ELEANOR get
under the covers in bed. The others
wait onstage.)*
RHODA
Thank God this bed has four corners, huh.
ELEANOR and HANNAH
Sleep, sleep.
HANNAH
—Can you do it while the rest of us are
watching.
RHODA
Shhhhhhhh.
ELEANOR and HANNAH
We are so familiar with each other's body
that it is easy.
ELEANOR
(Pause.)
Do you remember the mirror.
ALL
Yes.
ELEANOR
(Pause.)
Have you ever looked at your own body in
the mirror.
ALL
We remember more than one mirror.
ELEANOR
Oh.
(Pause.)

Please take the covers off the three bodies in the bed.

ALL
Wouldn't you like us to remove the train and the bird and the head first.

ELEANOR
No. Take the
(Pause.)
What

RHODA and HANNAH
Blanket.

HANNAH and ELEANOR
(Pause.)
Blanket.

RHODA
Now things are back to normal and Hannah and Eleanor speak together and I

HANNAH and ELEANOR
Rhoda.

RHODA
Speak independently.

ALL
Take the blanket off the bed huh.

BEN
—The strings are less.

ALL
What.

BEN
(Pause.)
Can you still walk under them.
(Pause.)
When we take the blanket off the bed should we think about it in relation to the.

ALL
What.
(Pause. BEN goes into the bed also. Then four strings are set to his wrists and ankles.)

Legend: "NOW THE BLANKET IS AS GOOD AS OFF."

BEN
Take the blanket off the bed.
(Pause.)
Thank God they are holding on to me so I don't have to fall off the bed onto the floor.
(Some of those remaining onstage have gotten chairs and are sitting to watch. Pause.)
Let's go back to the train.

BIRD
Hey, my cigarette went out.
(Blackout. Lights up again.)

Legend: "NOTHING IS DIFFERENT."

BEN

Who is going to keep lighting the bird's cigarette.

HANNAH

Oh Ben. I don't think it should get into the habit of smoking.

(Crowd moves a bit, coughs, etc. Pause.)

Good, good, now that we have your body maybe we won't be so interested in our own bodies.

Legend: "THE BLACK MIRROR."

RHODA

(Pause.)

The black mirror. I remember it but I thought it was the ocean.

(Soft music begins.)

HANNAH

Oh Rhoda.

RHODA

Shhhhhh.

HANNAH

Is your body still in the bed.

ELEANOR

My body is still in the bed.

RHODA

—My body is still in the bed but it is no longer of any interest to me.

(Rear wall behind the bed gives way to the black mirror.)

ALL

Shhhhhh.

(Music fades.)

RHODA

I think we are on the black ocean.

ALL

—It is a mirror Rhoda.

(Pause.)

What floats on the mirror, huh.

(A seaplane, thirties vintage, appears on the black mirror-ocean.)

BEN

(Pause.)

Is that my body you're holding ladies.

RHODA

We thought it would be more interesting than

ALL

What

RHODA

(Pause.)

Our own bodies. Correction.

ALL

(Pause.)

What.

RHODA

We were interested in each other's bodies but we thought it would be more interesting to be interested in Ben's.

ALL

Shhhhh.

RHODA

(Pause.)

Body.

BEN

Body.

ELEANOR

(Pause.)

Don't move anybody.

(Music.)

HANNAH

Didn't she mean to say, "Don't move anything."

(The four strings are removed from BEN's body and placed on the airplane rear.)

RHODA

Isn't it odd that after all this time they still haven't moved the blanket off of our bodies.

Legend: "WHAT IS THE NAME OF THIS ISLAND."

RHODA, HANNAH, ELEANOR

Oh Ben, we do not find your body as interesting as.

BEN

What.

RHODA, HANNAH, ELEANOR

(Pause.)

Shhhhhh.

(The crowd coughs and moves a bit.)

BEN

It's my mind that is interesting, ladies.

RHODA, HANNAH, ELEANOR

Oh.

BEN

It's my.

RHODA, HANNAH, ELEANOR

What.

BEN

(Pause.)

It's my.

RHODA, HANNAH, ELEANOR

What.

(The airplane moves a bit.)

ALL

Oh.

BEN

(Pause.)

You can take the blanket off.

RHODA

It would be interesting to see the way we are—

ALL

What

(Pause. Cough and move crowd.)

RHODA

Holding: the body.

ALL

What.

HANNAH

Very well ladies. It would be interesting for everyone to see the

ALL

What

HANNAH

Way we are holding the

ALL

What

HANNAH

Body

ALL

What

HANNAH

On the bed without bodies.

(Pause. Remove the blanket. Pause. Crowd moves and coughs.)

RHODA

It's as if you didn't have a body at all, Ben.

(Crew goes off, gets a suit which they bring back and dress BEN as he stays lying on the bed amidst the three ladies.)

RHODA

Now you look better.

LEO

—my boy. . . .have . . . a . . . cigar.

(LEO extends a cigar as drumroll fades up, louder, into a drum solo as everyone leaves the stage and the drum solo continues.

House lights up, as drum solo gives way to soft music.)

VERTICAL MOBILITY

Photo Kate Davy

(SOPHIA=(WISDOM): Part 4)

MAX
(MAX sits—writes on pad.)
Oh, oh, I don't want to look at anything.
(Pause.)
I mean what I wrote. Sees it.
*(Two girls come with wet towels,
put them on MAX's forehead and
on the paper he's just written on.)*
RHODA
The damp cloth is dissolving the ink, Max.
MAX
My eyes get a rest, huh.
(Pause.)
Let's see if I can see through the damp cloth.
RHODA
Which one.
MAX
(Pause.)
Let's see if I can move fast enough to reach
it before it goes out.

BLACKOUT

(Lights up.)
MAX
Oh, are my feet—

VOICE
What.
MAX
(Pause.)
Heavy weights.
VOICE
Keep that rug from floating.
MAX
—I could do that by standing on it.
(Pause.)
Well, I don't seem to be able to make it.
(Pause.)
My body sure weighs a lot.
VOICE
Maybe it's only the feet.
MAX
—I can't tell if the head does.
(Pause.)
I've said everything important, and it didn't
take much time to do it. Writers. . . . vanish
. . . when . . . they have finished . . . their
job.
(Music.)

Legend: THEY DON'T VANISH,
BUT THEY STOP WRITING IF
THERE IS ANY GOOD LEFT IN
THEM.

*(Rear wall opens. Island mauso-
leum. MAX there.)*

MAX

Everything has already been said. Plus, it is
there already. I certainly am enjoying this
new (better) life. The sun. The sea. The
rocks. Basic insights are all over the place.
(All dance.)

BLACKOUT

(Lights up.)
*(Room again. MAX sits, turns one
foot so sole of his shoe is seen. Red
applied to it. Enter RHODA with
glove with red palm. Puts red palm
to red sole. MAX then goes onto
the floor, sticking the foot up,
which RHODA still holds as she
sits. Then undo the shoe. She still
holds it and lets her arm drop to
her side.)*

RHODA

(Pause.)

Weight.

(Her feet to side.)

Ramp.

(One leg pulled up.)

Airplane.

(Pause.)

Caught.

(Pause.)

Ice.

(Tilts head.)

Tilt.

(Open mouth.)

Cave.

(Spreads knees.)

Avenue.

(Arm between knees.)

Self-control.

(Shoe on knee sideways.)

Colorful.

(Pause.)

Balance.

(Pause.)

Doubt.

(Twists to look rear.)

Siphon.

(MAX on floor, moves six feet.)

Trip.

(Pause.)

Ladder.

(MAX rolls over once.)

Adventurer.

Photo Kate Davy

(She drops shoe.)

Lost.

(Pause.)

Revolve.

(Pause.)

Siphon. Siphon. Siphon.

(Now she moves, still sitting in chair, toward door. Sliding it under her. Midway to the door, she stops and is strapped to the chair.)

Legend: ONE CAN GO (THE MIND) NO FURTHER THAN THIS. THIS IS THE ULTIMATE WAY THE MIND CAN DO AN INVENTION.

(Music, she moves out the door in her chair. Then the music stops. Another chair set. RHODA comes and sits in it. Again goes in it to door. Then stopped. Strapped. Then she goes through the previous motion sequence as best she can— being strapped as she is. Then a hat put on her head. Pause. Then taken off. Then she spreads her arms from her elbows and rests her hands on two low tables. Then strings from tables to either side wall. Then MAX, still on floor, puts his feet up along string. RHODA again gets a hat. Slowly turns head left to right. Then pause. Head left.)

RHODA

It was to make me move better, but now I can't at all.

ALL

What.

Photo Kate Davy

RHODA

(Pause.)

It was to make me move better.

ALL

What was.

RHODA

The rope tied me to the chair so when I moved I could concentrate on moving and not holding onto it.

MAX

If the rope was higher,

RHODA

Not that rope.

MAX

—I couldn't make this composition.

ALL

You're not making it perfectly, Max.

(He relaxes. Crew pulls the string down to his feet.)

That's as far as one can go in making a composition.

RHODA

(Pause.)

I'm not that interested in it, but I do it.

(Crew puts cloth under her hands, over low tables. Then replace tables with small pyramids, keeping cloth between.)

Will the points hurt. It wasn't moving the cloth, it was moving the tables.

(Pause.)

Oh, Rhoda, you have never been so happy, and you won't speak about it for a long time.

(Pause.)

Focus more on the mouth for that reason, Rhoda.

(Hum. Pyramids into mouth, push back chair.)

LIGHTS FADE.

(Lights up.)

(Two small pyramids, on tables, tall thin ones so they reach ceiling.)

ALL

What happened to Rhoda.

(Pause. Door half opens.)

She's looking at the objects that were hurting her.

(Her two feet in on supports, her therefore leaning body, held from behind.)

Nothing can hurt her now, she says.

RHODA

Oh, Rhoda, you are invulnerable, huh.

(Pause.)

Her memory, her memory.

ALL

Oh, it says what happened to Max's red feet.

RHODA

—Why am I thinking about it now.

(Pause.)

When his feet turned red.

ALL

She said it.

RHODA

(Pause.)

I'm alone.

VOICE

Oh, Rhoda, you are not alone. Plus, you have more than your memories.

(She is walked into room in her tilted position, supported from rear, wearing a headdress that trails on the floor.)

Walk slowly, walk slowly Rhoda. Do not look where you are going because others are leading you but walk slowly.

(She exits. A boing. Open to mausoleum. SOPHIA enters with a large book. Two skew prop sticks set to open book. SOPHIA puts her head into the book. Comes forward with crew help. Again close to room.)

SOPHIA

How do I get out of here.

ALL

Why do you want that.

(Appear in door, MAX and RHODA. Bed opens to show BEN in nightcap and gown.)

SOPHIA

It's too hot for my body indoors.

MAX, RHODA, BEN

Oh, Sophia, if you did not have your head in a book all the time.

ALL

Shhhhhhh.

MAX, BEN, RHODA

(Pause.)

Books can't replace friendship.

SOPHIA

I can't have them.

MAX, BEN, RHODA

What.

ALL

(Pause.)

She is a goddess.

Photo Kate Davy

BEN

Wrong. She thinks she is a goddess because she is shy.

> *(Gong. BEN puts his feet from the bed into the room on risers. RHODA and MAX get one riser [for one foot] each.)*

MAX, BEN, RHODA

We are all terribly shy.

> *(Stand set over SOPHIA, three heads. Now SOPHIA and whole unit [propped book and three heads] go to rear. Pause.)*

SOPHIA

What happened to the—

ALL

Shhhhhhh.

SOPHIA

> *(Pause.)*

Are you watching my awkward movement.

BEN

—Come to bed.

SOPHIA

> *(Pause.)*

Make the bed ready for me.

BEN

—It's ready.

> *(Pause. She turns and goes. Stops. BEN still with feet out into room on risers. She faces him, profile to us.)*

SOPHIA

It's not ready.

BEN

Why do you say it isn't ready when it's ready.

> *(RHODA and MAX, each with one cothurnus, clump to line up behind SOPHIA. Fog horn. Lights fade and wall goes so mausoleum returns. Now silhouette tableau. Mausoleum door opens, out rag stuffed body. Carry it to the line. A hum now. All in line put one foot back. A hose set from BEN's penis to under all dresses, inside all flies. Then music. All dance in place. Then lights up on room. Buzz and music off.)*

Photo Kate Davy

BEN

Who is that.

(Pause.)

A dead person.

SOPHIA

I returned from the dead.

ALL

Goddess.

BEN

—She has everybody believing it.

(All go into bed, ladder helps.)

ALL

What's your problem, Ben.

BEN

You should ask her.

ALL

Goddesses don't have problems.

RHODA

What about me.

MAX

—What about me.

(Close bed curtains. Crew exit. Then the stuffed body out of bed, pulled by a rope so it is horizontal, six feet off the floor. Pause. Enter RHODA through door. Lies on floor, arms up to match doll's hanging down arms. BEN enters with book, places it on RHODA's fingers between them and those of doll and RHODA's.)

RHODA

Are you convinced that this is really good for people.

BEN

Convinced is not the word, Rhoda.

(As he says this, on table with a vice. His head goes into the vice, and crew tightens it, as RHODA goes and drags SOPHIA from the bed and puts her in position under the doll as she was. Connect SOPHIA's arms and doll's arms with lashed sticks. A second head affixed atop BEN's. He rises and immediately crew hits off the second head with a baseball bat. The wall comes in blocking the mausoleum and RHODA and BEN. Pause. Then—)

Thud, Oh/ eee-o, eee-o, eee-o, eee-o.

(That singing pattern on and on. Then add lines after phrase.)

VOICE

Could I be in that room much longer without Rhoda.

Photo Michael Kirby

She did not speak to me.
She did not fall toward me or away from me.
(RHODA enters and goes to wall.)
She did not tell me anything she had discovered.
(She goes to chair, makes it rock.)
She began to play her own instrument.
(She rocks it, then a flag on a pole set in it. She rocks it again, then she goes out. A plywood sheet set on the floor.
Loud music begins.
Ten-minute dance. Object manipulation.
First the room. Then the mausoleum.
Then a tennis court.
They all playing.
Then the room.
BEN sits, exhausted.
Head back, leg out, racquet out resting
on knee. In profile. Crew brings drink. BEN puts his tongue out.
A clip with a string from tongue to

glass. On tray. The tray is balanced on a tray.
Then a spike system, spikes held to project through tennis racquet strings.
RHODA one foot in the door, then crosses and puts out a foot to touch BEN's forward foot.)

BEN
She's showing it.
(Pause.)
It's showing.

RHODA
It's showing.

BEN
It's still.

RHODA
It's still showing.
(All exit. SOPHIA enters with book and stick supports, and stands on the plywood sheet. A lamp on a small table lights up. She crosses to it.)

SOPHIA
I can't get my pages bright enough to—

ALL
Shhhhh.

SOPHIA
What.
(Pause.)
I can't read.

ALL
Your face is close enough to the book, Sophia.
(Enter BEN with block. Puts it between book and her face.)

BEN
Reading matter.

SOPHIA
Oh, Ben, I'm always buried in reading matter.

BEN
I notice.
(Pause.)
I came into the room.

SOPHIA
Do not forget, do not forget.

BEN
(Pause.)
Where am I.

SOPHIA
Do not forget.

BEN

Do not forget, he says, as he twists his foot to look closer.

SOPHIA

What.

BEN

Shhhhhhh.

(He twists his foot, looks away, and points.)

SOPHIA

We have the same reading matter.

BEN

Red foot.

(Pause.)

The red foot came into the room with his reading matter.

(Backs out in held position.)

SOPHIA

I still have to deal with the lamp, but I'm overlooking a very important part of it.

(Pause.)

Oh, I just forgot about the lamp completely.

ALL

Did you forget about the book, too, Sophia.

SOPHIA

(Pause.)

What.

ALL

What book.

(Picture on wall slides off, book falls from behind and dangles on a string.)

I can't remember what was in the picture or if the book had a relationship to it.

ALL

Which book.

SOPHIA

(Pause.)

There is only one book, and I am immersed in it.

(She climbs into bed. Lights blink.)

VOICE

The book cannot blink. The picture can return, however, but it will not.

(Enter crew, holds up book.)

It is in the book.

(Enter RHODA, with bag of groceries. Looks over her shoulder— crew takes off coat that had just been laid over her shoulders. She shrugs three times. Holds the top of the bag, and it turns out to be the top of an inner, velvet bag, as the paper bag itself falls to the floor,

and she is left holding a velvet one that extends all the way into the one now fallen on the floor.)

RHODA

That's what I wanted to come out of the book.

(SOPHIA comes head first out of the bed, still in book. Head in book to floor, feet still up on bed. Helped in this by crew.)

LIGHTS FADE.

(Block on table. SOPHIA gone. RHODA goes to table, dragging bag.)

RHODA

I could add that to my bag.

(Pause.)

I bet I could find a way to make that block adhere to the surface of something.

ALL

Oh, Rhoda, why are you so interested in the block.

(Pause. She puts down her bag and holds her head.)

RHODA

I forgot to think about it.

ALL

Shhhhhh.

(MAX half through door. Pause.)

Now she's remembering it.

MAX

Can I get.

RHODA

Shhhhhhh.

MAX

(Pause.)

Ben.

RHODA

I don't think he could help me out of this dilemma.

MAX

What dilemma.

(Pause.)

Oh, Rhoda, what you need should be attached to the head but the top of it.

(Pause. She gets a second head.)

It's tempting to—

RHODA

What.

(Pause. Then he with a bat, swats the extra head off. Pause. She looks

at him. He offers her the bat. She takes it and sticks it up her dress.)

MAX

Is that comfortable.

RHODA

I wanted to take a load off my feet.

(BEN enters with two large baseball mitts, one on each hand.)

BEN

Before I go to sleep, I wondered if either of you had some good reading matter.

RHODA

(Pause.)

I forgot what you said.

BEN

Reading matter.

(She holds her head.)

RHODA

I forgot what you said.

(He with mitts, holds his head. MAX looks then exits. RHODA and BEN get close, both look down and side three-quarters. Then walk three steps and bat falls out of RHODA's dress.)

RHODA

Pick it up for me.

BEN

I can't Rhoda.

RHODA

(Pause.)

Clumsy.

ALL

Why does she say he is clumsy when he hadn't tried to prove anything.

(MAX out, gets bat, puts it on strip laid on floor, then pulls out strip so making bat exit. Then he puts the hanging book into its wall box. Then he stands in front of the opening to hide the book with his head.)

MAX

Notice anything different.

(Enter SOPHIA—freezes, then starts moving backwards slowly.)

ALL

Come back, lady.

SOPHIA

I want to get out of here fast.

(Pause, slowly to door. Then she re-enters with her face in a book. Pause. MAX moves away from the hole.)

MAX

Notice anything different.

(Sticks again set to SOPHIA's book.)

ALL

She's too shy to read anybody else's book.

(BEN and RHODA cross as far as they can, then sink slowly to knees.)

MAX

Are you really a goddess or just shy.

(Crew takes off BEN's gloves, BEN and RHODA bow down, heads to floor. Then MAX also. Crew takes book from hole and puts it on floor three feet extended from MAX's head.)

ALL

Almost but not yet.

(Out small block, book put on it, then SOPHIA lifts her face from her book.)

SOPHIA

It's that other book that I was looking for.

MAX, BEN, RHODA

What's in it Sophia.

SOPHIA

A picture of something.

ALL

What.

(Open to mausoleum—SOPHIA goes to doorway and stands, dropping book.)

SOPHIA

Do you recognize me.

MAX, BEN, RHODA

Oh Sophia, it's hard to recognize you without a book in your hand.

(She returns and gets book on block, carries it back to mausoleum—it's still on string to hole. She hugs the book to her chest.)

SOPHIA

I bet if you turned over you could see me.

MAX, BEN, RHODA

We can't turn over. Why not.

(Whistles, two rowboats with fishermen are poled in. They go and drag MAX, RHODA, BEN into boats. All three then sit as if trailing a hand in water, ecstatic. Then dishes of water set for their hands. SOPHIA slowly sets down the book

Photo Babette Mangolte

on the floor. Then a wooden beam
comes down and hits it at an angle.)

BLACKOUT

(Lights up.)
(Boats gone. Mausoleum gone.
Three still on floor, hands in water.)
BEN, RHODA, MAX
What happened to Sophia and the mauso-
leum.

(Open to mausoleum, SOPHIA
now in tennis shorts. Quakes. Given
racquet. Again the beam comes
down and hits book. SOPHIA turns
to go into mausoleum and a
wrapped figure is there and stops
her. Then she hides her eyes and
holds her racquet between two
fingers, arms stretched out from her
body.)

LIGHTS OUT.

(Lights up.)
(SOPHIA kneels at the book pinned
under the beam. Still has her
racquet. Bowls still there with water
but MAX, BEN, and RHODA are
gone. SOPHIA tries to pull the
book out without moving the
beam. She does.)
SOPHIA
I forgot what I wanted to do with this book.
(She sits with the book on the
ground beside her. Noise.)

LIGHTS OUT.

(Lights up.)
(RHODA now sits beside SOPHIA
in same position.)
RHODA and SOPHIA
Compare us. Compare us carefully.
(Voice counts "1-2-3." On three—
both whirl and look at picture
opening. Pause.)

VOICE

Ten points for Rhoda.

LIGHTS FADE.

(Lights up.)
(Both SOPHIA and RHODA against wall. Each has one leg up with the bottom of one foot flat against the wall.)

VOICE

1...2...3
(Pause.)
Twenty points for Rhoda.
(Both given racquets, they balance forward on them, keeping the foot to the wall.)

LIGHTS FADE.

(Lights up.)
(The racquets are now connected at the bottom, held by the two. A stick four feet long from racquet to racquet. They walk out of the room. Pause. RHODA returns, with a separate racquet. She takes the position again with one foot against wall.)

RHODA

I can't remember what I did with my other racquet.
(SOPHIA appears in picture on wall.)

SOPHIA

I can't remember.

RHODA

—wasn't somebody else—

SOPHIA

What.

SOPHIA and RHODA

(Pause.)
We're both shy.
(Pause.)
Each moment is a revelation.
(Birds enter. Flowers.)
Each word has a certain weight.

MAX

Oh, Rhoda.
(Pause, enter floral decorations. Birds get crowns.)

Photo Michael Kirby

Shhhh. I can't speak openly.
> *(Pause.)*
> *(Radios onto set.)*

Everything has become beautiful.

RHODA

Are you—

MAX

Shhhhh.
> *(Flowers set over SOPHIA.)*

RHODA

> *(Pause.)*

He cannot speak openly, huh.
> *(Pause.)*

Oh, Max, I do not recognize—

MAX

What.

RHODA

> *(Pause.)*

—the room.
> *(One bird takes off head, and it is BEN.)*

MAX

Look.
> *(Pause.)*

It became very beautiful.
> *(Rear wall out—now a wall with twenty lamps.)*

Oh, Rhoda.

ALL

Shhhhhh.

MAX

> *(Pause.)*

We are now in Paradise.

RHODA

I know it.

MAX

> *(Pause.)*

Is it beautiful enough.

RHODA

No.

VOICE

What does it mean. She says she knows she is now in Paradise, but its beauty is not enough for her. With that realization, everyone slowly leaves the room, and the play is over.
> *(All dance.)*

ONTOLOGICAL-HYSTERIC

MANIFESTO III

(JUNE, 1975)

> ... the process of living always grows out of
> or is based on certain assumptions: these are
> like the soil on which we stand, or which we
> use as a point of departure.
>
> And this is true in every field. ... Every
> idea is thought, every picture is painted, out
> of certain assumptions or conventions which
> are so basic, so firmly fixed for the one who
> thought the idea or painted the picture that
> he neither pays heed to them, nor, for that
> matter, introduces them into his picture or
> idea; nor do we find them there in any guise
> except as presupposed and left, as it were, to
> one side. This is why we sometimes fail to
> understand an idea or a picture; we lack the
> clue to the enigma, the key to the secret
> convention.
>
> **Ortega y Gasset**

It is usually assumed that if art has a strong
effect upon us, it is good art, and vice versa.

But a virus may have a strong effect, and yet
be not-good. The same is true in art.

The issue is one of goals, aimed at achievements,
and a judgment or at least understanding of
those goals, plus
the further results, in human life,
which those goals may suggest or implement.

A major goal (of *all* human creatures)
Sometimes conscious, often unconscious
is security.

Art is thought of as man being creative. And the
essence of the creative is the letting-go of what is
in one's mental "possession," so that the
new can arise in its place.

In a sense, the very opposite of security. But I
paradoxically suggest that most art is a (relatively
unconscious) means through which human emotional
orientation toward security-goals are reinforced.

Theatre, as it usually is, is a means whereby the
viewer is given the
                    FEELING
that he somehow
                    POSSESSES
the aspects of life therein treated. He is given a
feeling or experience
            and then thinks of it as something he
            carries around inside himself as a
            memory (a possession).

If, at a play, we experience terror, love, excitement,
sexual arousal, or any other emotion in such a way
that we
            ESTABLISH
            inside ourselves
            a clear LINK

                    between
the emotion   and the image-situation-
                                    experience that
                                    triggered that emotion
                                    within us

what has happened is that we have been given a memory-
possession which is then available to consciousness whenever

we choose, and we feel emotional stability to the extent
that we have a large number of such items in our memory
bank. We feel security, because each item is an
emotion-linked-to-event package,
into which we *project* that *mastery* felt in being able
       to 1) *make* such an internal linkage in
           our minds, and
         2) call upon it at will for retrospective
           savoring.

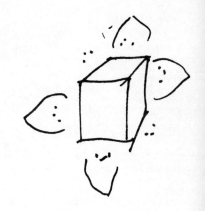

Such art is not very interesting to the man who wants
to understand and see things as they *are* in their
momentary and unique way of being-present.

I remember
that beginning at age fifteen, going to the theatre
every weekend, I would notice even then that most
of the plays
most of them "well received" but experienced by me as
"bad"
manifested their "badness" most strongly during the moment-
to-moment act of watching them.
But a week later the moment-to-moment badness tended
to fade . . .
and certain simple images of the play-as-a-whole which
remained in the memory seemed much
more evocative and meaningful than the moment-to-moment
existence of the play in performance had seemed to me.

As far as I am concerned, that simply meant (and
still means) that
in memory
an   experience fades so that RIGOR has no immediate and
exact data to which to apply itself
and so rigor goes to sleep.
It therefore indicated to me (and still does) that the
audience in the theatre was (is) experiencing performances
in a way peculiarly different from my own—
since my OWN *MEMORY* experience (a week later) tended to
be in agreement with the opinions popularly manifested
(in reviews, the play's "success," etc.)
—while my IMMEDIATE moment-by-moment reaction to
the material when it was PRESENTED to me was almost
always exactly opposite the judgments and
opinions of reviews, etc.

I now believe that the critics and the public interested
in "theatre" invariably see the work before them

through a mental filter which screens out all
considerations that do not reinforce the desired
security-giving configurations of emotion-situation-
idea. And that filter is akin to
        the normal memory filter,
that functions in all of us.
So that most people's relation to the work of art is
akin to one's relation to a thing in one's memory,
i.e., the work is observed in a certain relaxed, receptive
mode of perception
        rather than
an intentional, directed, energized mode of perception.
The work is allowed to seep into one like a memory.
It is not vigorously explored
    IN ALL ITS NOOKS AND CRANNIES
by perception. The relaxed, passive perceptual mode
"overlooks" in the present what it thinks of as trivial
details—much as in scanning a memory the conscious
mind "forgets" what it would call trivial, extraneous
details of past experience.
    But as has been again and again demonstrated, it
is precisely within what one forgets or rejects by
not-noticing that there exists the means of waking up,
understanding, etc. Philosophy, psychology, physics,
—all efforts to understanding—make their great
advances in the same way the psychiatric patient or
the religious initiate does, by learning how to
re-scan the material available to his consciousness
in such a way that the heretofore "unnoticed"
(trivial) leaps out as part of a new, truthful
configuration.

    For reasons related to this, I would go so far
as to say that the STRONG experience in art—the
experience or aspect of it which "stays" with one
powerfully—is suspect. Of questionable value.
    Suspect because its "strength" (recognized and
responded to as such by the spectator) means it is
an "allowed" moment, the consciousness isn't "uneasy"
in scanning and naming it. It is *allowed* to become
a consciously held (owned) memory, and to that extent
reinforcing what we are, our
defenses, our emotional prejudices—evading the
task of awakening our awareness of the implications
and truths of "creativity."
    I would say that the most "serious" art, art for
adults, is that which during the undergoing of it
seems rigorous—
        but which after the fact may seem HARD TO
        REMEMBER, because it is (was) that
        which we-are-not-yet, and so

that-which-we-are finds it hard to remember because
that-which-we-are resists. . .
tries to disarm . . . what denies its validity.
    What is important to me in art, therefore, is
NOT the impression one takes away from the work after
the "seeing" of it is over.
        Most people always refer to that after-effect
        and as a result, are always talking
            NOT about the work as it IS
            in its moment of being-there
        but about their own weaknesses in
        perception.

For me, the prime reason for the work of art is to
further UNDERSTANDING (a different understanding
than that uncovered by other disciplines, of course).
Understanding . . . . of a very certain kind.

Most theatre, on the other hand, is dedicated to creating
an "experience." Sometimes that experience is thought
of as an avenue to understanding. (For instance, an
experience in a politically oriented play, which is
designed to help one "understand" why the workers do
such and such, and the managers do such and such, etc.)

But an "experiencing" does not lead to the radical
"understanding" I am concerned with.
        Here's why.
Experience of any sort is "recognizing." I would not
deny that anything called "art" has to end up in the
thing called "spectator" as some kind of experience.
But there is a difference between this last fact and
the always misguided attempt
    to make the art experience be isomorphic with
an OTHER *experience*-event.
    We experience what we recognize—what we know. Even
if the experience is the experience of "not-knowing"
or "being confused" or anything else to which we
can give a name.

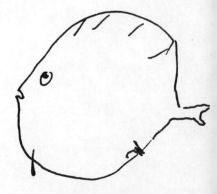

The task of art is to serve understanding . . . by trying
to create a field which is isomorphic with what
        stands-under
experience—which is not experience itself.

        Now, what stands-under experience cannot be experienced,
experience is not the mode by which we can know it.

What *stands-under* experience are the laws (processes)
of perception and other laws-of-configuration of the
universe.

        My task is to make work, the structure of which
        is isomorphic with those laws.

        Then I will be
        standing-under
        experience.

Then the work of art will be an ACT of understanding.

How to find such laws?
They ARE available (Not by experience, but by inference
                through the kind of hypothesis-making
                followed by "testing" (usefulness?)
                which is the basic method of twentieth
                century pure science).

For instance: Dirac, Paul. His 1931 theory—
        (for me, the most useful MANTRA of our time).
    In which he postulates—
        Space isn't empty
        It's filled with a bottomless sea of electrons
            with negative mass (& negative energy)
        All available locations in space, filled with
            minus energy electrons, no interaction,
            no manifestation of their existence!
        On occasion, a high-energy cosmic ray hits
            one of these "ghost" electrons and imparts
            its energy to it.
        So, the ghost electron is then bumped out of
            the sea of non-existence and becomes a
            normal electron with positive energy and
            mass.
        But that leaves a "hole" in the sea where it
            had been. The hole is a negation of negative
            mass, so is positive mass (also positive
            change).
        This hole (DIRAC predicts in '31) would be a
            new kind of particle, having mass equal

to and charge opposite to a normal
electron (which is +mass and −charged.) An
anti-electron

But (he predicts) the anti-electron will be
very short lived because a normal electron
will soon be attracted to the "hole," fall
into it, and the two oppositely charged
electrons will immediately annihilate
each other.

A year later . . . phenomenon were discovered
which were explainable only by recourse to
Dirac's "dreamed of" theory.

I then dream of the application of Dirac's "dreamed-up"
theory to a different field. (Because I find Dirac's
theory the most evocative, beautiful, moving . . . and
meditation upon its structure makes me CREATIVE.)

The Re-Application

Creation (the act of) leaves a "hole" in the
world (notice I say world—a socialized phenomenon,
not universe) of on-going ideas.

The creative moment produces a spark (gesture)
of anti-matter (matter being the on-going ideas which
are the world,

which are dead husks of far earlier creative moments,
which
are the "dead-weight" against which the new, the
matter against which spirit beats . . .)

The anti-matter of idea being born, which
MOMENT is the creative, is immediately annihilated

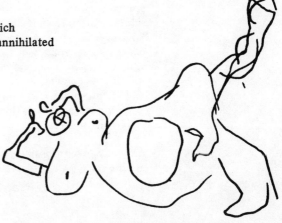

by matter—for the minute the creative gesture is
SEEN, is fixed as seeable in one of the
world-mediums that allows representation—at that
moment it becomes another dead husk (*sign* of
something that "happened" rather than the thing-
that-happened).

Now, something *like* this process, which seems to
me to *stand-under* what is experienced must be
imitated by the play. But it cannot be imitated
except as a process put into operation.

(To further verify the significance of the
Diracian "invention" as applied to art—
with the derived implication of the creative
as being necessarily momentary and always
vanishing and always in need of reassertion and
that reassertion being the essence of art,

I give two harmonizing items:

Picasso saying that the artist must put down
what passes through him, with the implication
which follows that the passing through means
a thing arises and dies and in the brief configuration
of its passage . . . (one must die at each moment
to what is, so that one can be re-born in each
moment).

Remembering myself, on the bus about seven years ago
(the Broadway bus!) looking across the
aisle through the window as we passed the coliseum
and trying to see what was happening as I was perceiving
and noticing then and there that much to my surprise,
what was happening in perception was not a sustaining
of what I was seeing or thinking about
even if I TRIED to sustain a subject—but what was
of necessity happening in consciousness was a continual
presentation and re-presentation every millisecond of
subject matter. Even if the subject matter was the
same over a minute period, it was presented, wiped
out in a millisecond, and then immediately re-presented
again and again. That was the way things had
to be in the consciousness.
    (And so, the way things are as-they-are
    for us since for us things ARE in
    consciousness).

And that presenting and representing of item
in consciousness—

That is a process isomorphic with Dirac's dreamed of
way-things-are.

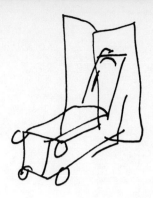

He INVENTED the mechanism that later explained what
    was discovered in the laboratory
And looking at my scripts
    I find
    (my scripts which people have called
    inexplicable)
        I find
the process described above EXPLAINS the way the
units are generated.

        That generation STANDS-UNDER
          the experience

UNDERSTANDING as the aim.

Creativity as the subject.

    Because

That (creativity) is what the subject of all creative
work really is if the work is going to be lucid
and not dealing with glamor or what is vague.

If you write an anti-war play, for instance,
You make an *effort* to show perhaps, what causes
    war, what its results are, etc.
      Now—here comes an audience.
    They are led to see the war was caused by selfishness
which was allowed and encouraged by, for instance,
capitalism. They are led to see the suffering of
the poor, etc.

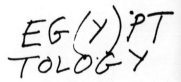

    But in this seeing, which they have been led to,
(like dumb animals are led?) it's as if the author
were pointing away from the real and toward
vague, imaginary shapes and postulates—because
only ALLUSIONS to real information can be made
upon the stage—certainly only allusions to
real information concerning the war and its causes,
etc. The author is saying "will you go along
with what I postulate when I postulate a character
like so and so or an act (imagined) like such and
such and an emotion like I *hint* at when I
ask one of the actors to cry something that I hope
you believe to be real tears?"
    And as the author is asking the audience to
go along with his POSTULATED reality, he is *ALSO*
asking them

to   *IGNORE*
         &
         OVERLOOK

the real part of the event! On stage!

Which is (the real part) this author's (or
director's) *EFFORT* to *MAKE* this thing (the play).

And that real part is where the audience
COULD possibly discover something
EVIDENTLY true
    not just postulatedly true.

(Notice I didn't say experience something true,
because the *experience* of evident truth compared to
the *experience* of postulated truth reveals them
equal as *experiences*:

An experience is always true and
present as an experience of the one
who is experiencing. And that fact of
experience swamps, dominates the fact
of what stands-
under it.

I said, therefore
    DISCOVER
    something evidently rather than postulatedly
true.
    I mean
STANDING UNDER the experience.)

The REAL part of the event is not the alluded-to war
and social turmoil pictured in the play

but the author trying to CREATE his subject and
    structure—

that effort, is something more than just
allusion to ANOTHER reality (the war) that
has its reality elsewhere and so can
    be treated by the mind in different ways
    but can only be treated by art if it is
bad (i.e., inexact) art.

The subject, if it is the ACT of MAKING the thing we
are looking at—only then is there a

CHANCE ! A DESPERATE TINY CHANCE !

for real rigor to operate. It's the only subject
(the making of this as it is made)
that avoids the built-in
deadness of the language in which it articulates itself

here, uniquely, because language (and I include languages also
    of vision, gesture, etc.)
doesn't have to be something that
        "refers to"
        (therefore distorting what it refers to
        since it is DIFFERENT from what it refers to
        but tries to EVOKE it)
but only spins out itself—web-like—as

its own evidence of what it is, in collision
with what one would make (a play with perhaps
    an ostensible "other" subject).

Creativity (the effort at it) as the subject.

Creativity, which is a spark, always struck, always
        immediately consumed. Immediately struck again.

Creation , the minute *IS* , turns into a
        dead husk. The husk must then be
        replaced (annihilated, as it were) by the
        next succeeding immediate creative moment.

RHODA IN
POTATOLAND

        Isn't that a RULE? I follow it.
        Isn't that a RULE that STANDS-UNDER?
        That's what I want.
        To understand.

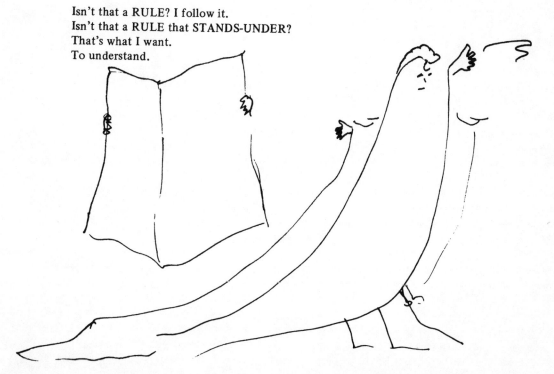

PAIN(T)

1.

(The studio.)

ELEANOR
How could I get to be a great artist like you, Rhoda.

RHODA
Practice.

ELEANOR
(Pause.)
With paint?

RHODA
Yes.

ELEANOR
(Pause. Shows her arm.)
Look. I got some paint on my arm.

RHODA
(Shows elbows.)
Wash your elbows.

ELEANOR
No, I got it on the inside of my arm.
(Turns her arm.)

RHODA
How come.

ELEANOR
That's where the blood is.

RHODA
You mean that's where the blood is closest to the surface.

ELEANOR
Yes.
(Pause.)
What's growing in my arm, Rhoda.

RHODA
—Look what's growing in my arm. My genius.

ELEANOR
(Drops.)
I wish I could paint like you, Rhoda.

RHODA

Do you think you can paint as good as a man?

ELEANOR

Better.

(Pause; then ELEANOR rushes to RHODA and they begin to fight, turn and fall.)

2.

(RHODA in a field. MAX and ELEANOR sleep on the grass. A bird sings.)

RHODA

I thought I could paint. Perhaps I dreamed it.

(Pause.)

Perhaps it's too hot.

(Enter IDA.)

IDA

I came to watch you working Rhoda.

RHODA

Working?

IDA

(Pause.)

I came to see you making a painting.

RHODA

(Points.)

They're all asleep.

IDA

Paint that.

(Pause.)

Do you think it's too hot to start.

(She undresses.)

RHODA

Now I see your body more carefully.

IDA

It's like yours.

RHODA

Yes.

IDA

(Pause.)

Don't say yes so quickly.

RHODA

I can match each part of my body to a part of your body.

(Pause. Done.)

IDA

Oh Rhoda, you do everything so carefully.

RHODA

What a foolish person.

IDA

Me?

(Pause. Music.)

I'm not a foolish person.

RHODA

—It's like looking into a mirror.

(Pause.)

Get dressed. Get dressed.

IDA

—Paint, paint, paint.

MAX

I can paint in my sleep but Rhoda wants to paint something different.

(RHODA has gone to MAX, falls over him, holding him from above, rolls him over, she now under.)

RHODA

(As she rolls.)

Wake up; wake up.

IDA

He wakes up and he sees me.

(Pause.)

He falls in love with the first naked person he looks at.

RHODA

Me.

IDA

He's not looking at you yet.

RHODA

He has eyes all over his body.

IDA

Don't pull him to pieces Rhoda.

(Drumroll. Ends in gong.)

RHODA

(Pause.)

I'd like to have him in my studio.

(Drumroll, bell.)

BLACKOUT

3.

(The studio. Fence horizontal across set.)

RHODA

Here we are.

MAX

What's behind that door.

RHODA

Find out.

MAX

(Goes and opens.)

Nothing.

(Looks at RHODA. IDA enters behind him and pulls him down. Drumroll.)

Don't do it.

Photo Kate Davy

RHODA

What.

MAX

Paint me.
    (Pause.)
I think I'll sleep for a while.

IDA

It's too bad we can't say words with our body isn't it.

RHODA

    (Smears paint on her mouth.)
What about this part of our body.

IDA

I meant

MAX

Shhhhhh

IDA

    (Pause.)
My whole body.
    (RHODA paints on a canvas with her mouth.)

Legend: RHODA PAINTS WITH HER MOUTH.

BLACKOUT

4.

(Countryside.)

Legend: ANY SENTENCE CAN MEAN ANYTHING. EACH WORD

(CERTAIN WORDS IN THE SEN-
TENCE) STARTS GOING IN A DIF-
FERENT DIRECTION.
2) CAN THE BODY (AS A WHOLE)
TALK. MEAN.

*(The word "mean" cut out of
pieces of wood is carried onstage—
each letter a separate piece. The
word "painter"—each letter a separate piece of stuffed soft material,
is also carried on. Then RHODA
enters with an easel.)*
VOICE
Oh Rhoda, try stuffing the word painter up
your ass.
RHODA
It's too big a word.
*(No blackout, but return to studio,
RHODA and ELEANOR.)*
ELEANOR
Look at this part of my arm.
RHODA
Where the blood is.
ELEANOR
—Where the paint is.

(Pause.)
Oh Rhoda, if you came closer.
RHODA
If I came closer I'd want to hurt you.
ELEANOR
I'd want to hurt you too.
RHODA
How come.
(Pause.)
Correction, we made a mistake including
distance in it.
ELEANOR
We're not far away now.
RHODA
If we were thinking about each other we're
not far away no matter how far away we are.
(Pause.)
Also we're not far away because the same
person is thinking about us.
ELEANOR
I still want to.
RHODA
What.
ELEANOR
(Pause.)
Let's fight.

Photo Michael Kirby

RHODA

Let's fight.

ELEANOR

(Pause.)

It's like being an artist isn't it.

RHODA

It is now when I'm

ELEANOR

What

RHODA

(Pause.)

Thinking.

ALL

Oh Rhoda. You are not thinking. Somebody else is thinking.

Legend: WRITING.

BLACKOUT

5.

(RHODA and ELEANOR in a parlor. Series of runs, press the other to wall, hold and collapse; reset-run-collapse.)

ELEANOR

(After five minutes.)

Oh Rhoda, I'm getting black and blue slowly.

RHODA

What are you discovering about me.

ELEANOR

What.

(Another series of runs.)

RHODA

Aren't you discovering anything about my body.

ELEANOR

I'm part of it

(They are in hold position, now shift.)

RHODA

Now.

ELEANOR

Maybe we're part of the same body.

RHODA

No, we're different bodies.

ELEANOR

(She screams. Pause.)

Look, I have paint on my arm.

RHODA

Where.

ELEANOR

Look.

RHODA

Let me see better.

(Hollow of ELEANOR's arm pressed into RHODA's face.)

VOICE

Oh Rhoda, do you feel beautiful.

RHODA

I feel very beautiful.

(Legs spread, stick between.)

Please, please, please keep your arm in my face while I am painting.

ELEANOR

Oh Rhoda, you're not painting.

(Curtain over the stick.)

RHODA

I forgot what I was saying.

VOICE

Thinking.

RHODA

(Pause.)

I shouldn't forget because it contains my whole life.

(Pause.)

If I forget that means I didn't forget. It thinks.

ELEANOR

I'm thinking.

RHODA

I'm thinking too.

(Positions changed; now both on a high rolling table, each head at different side, legs together and overlapping.)

ELEANOR

Now we are thinking.

RHODA

I don't know about you Eleanor, but I'm thinking; correction, I guess I was talking to myself.

ELEANOR

Always.

ALL

Thinking.

RHODA

Ahhh, this foot smells better than my foot.

ELEANOR

It's always the same foot Rhoda.

RHODA

What.

(Ping.)

Do you mean I could paint it.

ELEANOR

I mean with it; you could paint better.

RHODA
What happened to the . . .
       ELEANOR
What.

    Legend: PAINTER.

(They use one foot to attack the other; "Ahhhh" on tape. Music rises behind.)
       RHODA
    (Pause.)
She touches your body and it turns to gold.
    (A vision, SOPHIA has arisen just behind the table. Wet rags over limbs; tied. RHODA and ELEANOR are tied, limb to limb to each other. Pulled tighter.)
       ELEANOR
What.

       RHODA
Oh Eleanor, where are you.
       ELEANOR
I have not a chance.
       RHODA
—I'm so strong now.
       ELEANOR
I'm so strong too.
    (Pause.)
Which of us does she make into an artist.

       SOPHIA
You. Are the same woman. Now.
       RHODA
We were always the same woman.
       SOPHIA
    (Pause.)
I have no body.
       ALL
Wrong.
       RHODA
    (Pause.)
Oh Sophia, I have no body also.
    (Pause.)
It is her body.
       ELEANOR
—It is my body but I have no body also.
       BOTH
We have two noses but we do not have two things to smell. We have two mouths but we do not have two things to taste. We have six dark holes which enter the body below the navel, and those entrances are filled with the limbs of sisters and daughters —our own flesh, the same flesh, the flesh reflected like the body without eyes.
    (Two mirrors held, one to each face.)
       RHODA
Look at me.

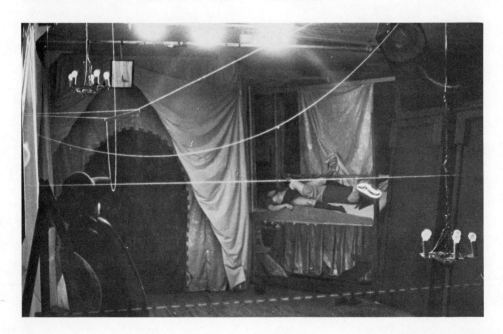

Photo Kate Davy

ELEANOR

Look at me.

RHODA

(Pause.)

Look at me.

ELEANOR

—Look at me.

RHODA

Look at me, it's like painting.

(Enter down the aisle of the theatre, IDA on high shoes; lights shift to her.)

IDA

What grows longer with each step.

VOICE

Oh spectator, your relation is different to the body that is amongst you.

(Beams extend IDA's arms into the seating section where spectators are.)

Do not touch anything.

(Pause.)

Find the best person to make children with.

(Loud gong.)

IDA

She is part of

ALL

What

IDA

(Pause.)

Each arm is an extended arm.

RHODA

(As two others enter, embrace and scream.)

—Let's have it out Eleanor.

ELEANOR

(Overlaps.)

—Let's finally have it out, Rhoda.

IDA

Try making your whole body as long as my body.

(Thud.)

It's like thinking isn't it.

RHODA

(Pause.)

I can think clearly now.

(Enter two men who come and hang on the wooden arms.)

Can you support a weight from the head in that position.

(One leaves arm, hold other's head and both collapse into square area.)

They don't move.

ALL

Who thinks better, the men or the women.

(Thud.)

Who has better children in mind? What is a different direction for opportunities, and more important, inventions.

(Pause.)

Why has everyone forgotten about work and accomplishment. And the painting that she spoke of painting.

ELEANOR

Oh Rhoda, you should get back to work.

RHODA

I don't know if I'll ever be able to forget what has happened to me.

ELEANOR

Of course you will.

(Loud noise.)

6.

(The studio. A large canvas.)

RHODA

(Holding a brush.)

Now

(Pause.)

(Holds it out.)

There doesn't seem any longer to be a relation between my paintbrush and the picture that comes out of it.

(Pause.)

Try it, huh.

(She rams it into the canvas.)

Oh, I hurt my elbow doing that.

Legend: ELBOWS.

(Sign appears rear: "Ecstasy.")

RHODA

"Oh," she thinks.

(Finger to chin.)

Legend: "SHE REMEMBERS THE FIELD
(A SCENE IN THE)
AND THE WORDS
(A DIFFERENT WORD)
SOFT ENOUGH MADE SO PER-
HAPS IT WENT UP HER ASS
WITH BUTTER.
'YOU CAN'T FORGET SUCH
THINGS,' SAYS RHODA, 'EVEN IF
YOU CAN'T REMEMBER THEM
EXACTLY' "

Photo Kate Davy

RHODA
Also, the word was a little different.
ELEANOR
(Enters.)
Just as I stepped in.
RHODA
What.
ELEANOR
—Did I have a certain word.
RHODA
(Pause.)
Oh Eleanor, this reminds me of the past.
ELEANOR
What.
RHODA
(Pause.)
We used words like fists.

ELEANOR
Here's mine.
RHODA
(Pause, turns away.)
I can almost feel it.
(Thud.)
ELEANOR
Get closer to that word, huh.

Legend: TRY NOT TO RELIVE IT.

(Pause. Music; both press to the painting.)
BOTH
We each have a different part of the picture we like best.

Photo Kate Davy

RHODA
—Does that mean it's a good picture or a bad picture.
(Pause.)
Oh, it's so hard to remember but it's so hard not to remember.

ALL
What.

7.

(Field.)

RHODA
Go back to the painting; oh now I see, this was one version of the painting.
(Pause.)
But the bodies were not so real.
(Looks at the hollow in her arm.)
I wonder if this part was very real.

MAX
(On the floor.)
Where's your friend.

RHODA
I paint.

MAX
What.

RHODA
(Pause.)
I paint.

MAX
—I never saw you paint.
(Enter ELEANOR with suitcase. Squeeze her into it.)

MAX
Ahhhhhh.

ELEANOR
Paint me.

MAX
(As he is encased in tent.)
How'd you like to make a little cash on the side.
(Buzzer.)

8.

(The studio; a cot to the side, surrounded by lights, chandeliers.

RHODA and ELEANOR sit on the
bed. Drums: they start to fight.)
RHODA
I don't have time any more to have any
ideas.
ELEANOR
Think anyway, it's art but it's automatic,
huh.
(Change of positions.)
RHODA
Lightning, huh.
(Change.)
BOTH
Lightning.
(Change.)
Lightning.
(Change.)
Lightning.
(Change.)
ELEANOR
Oh Rhoda, why do you think we like to
fight so much.
RHODA
We don't like it when it hurts.
(Change position.)

Correction, the fighting comes first.
ELEANOR
Nothing follows it.
(Change position.)
It has to hurt good, doesn't it.
RHODA
It hurts good.
(Change.)
It hurts good.
ELEANOR
Think about it.
RHODA
Let's not move too fast for good thinking—
ELEANOR
—I'm hurting you I bet.
RHODA
Yes. Yes.
ELEANOR
I'm still hurting.
RHODA
Nothing comes after that.
ELEANOR
(Pause.)
Let's fight.

RHODA
Let's fight; come on let's fight!
(Long pause, no movement, then start to cry.)
ELEANOR
Oh, it's going to be like this forever.
RHODA
My head is so clear.
ELEANOR
Each minute is like a painting.
RHODA
I'm in the painting.
(Change position.)
Now I'm still in the painting.
ELEANOR
I'm like a great artist too, Rhoda.
RHODA
It's like counting. Wrong.
ELEANOR
What.
RHODA
It's like being able to count like a great.
ELEANOR
What.
RHODA
(Pause.)
My head is so CLEAR!

ELEANOR
My head is so clear too!
RHODA
My head is so clear, nothing is in it but mathematics.
ELEANOR
One, two, three, (etc.).
RHODA
—Fight me! Fight me! Oh I'm as clear as a muscle. Oh Eleanor PAINT me.
ELEANOR
Two great artists! Two great artists!
(Both shriek very loud.)
RHODA
Lightning—it's long enough, huh.
(Pause.)
Like lightning, every ten seconds I see for a long time.
(Change positions.)
ELEANOR
Like history.
RHODA
Like a river.
ELEANOR
Like a hole dug.
RHODA
Like mud.

Photo Kate Davy

ELEANOR
Like . . . salt.

RHODA
I'm not bleeding at all but you keep rubbing my body like two pieces of wood.

ELEANOR
It's so clear, like lightning.

BOTH
Lightning.
> *(Change.)*

Lightning.
> *(Change.)*

Lightning.
> *(Change.)*

VOICE
Lightning.

(Thud, followed by change, thud, change, thud, change.)
(Somewhere midway, SOPHIA enters in high shoes, and lights dim to a single bulb over the spectators. Enter people under white sheets.
Music, drums, as people in the very dim light onstage slowly shift positions. They appear—more and more hooded figures—who sternly admonish the audience by shaking a warning finger at them.
Lights up; all are frozen.)

VOICE
The play's over. You're left with your own thoughts. Can you really get interested in them or are they just occurring.

RHODA IN POTATOLAND

Photo Arnold Aronson

(HER FALL-STARTS)

PROLOG

VOICE

Remember. This text is—as it were—inside out. That is, its presentation—to in a sense —make it clear—inside out. Because when you see the inside outside—the inside is clear, right?

Cut the text in half—you haven't seen it yet, but imagine it cut into two parts —a first part and a second part. Then—in the presentation—the first part is played as the second part and vice versa. So what follows, precedes, and vice versa.

Because

to have the first part follow the second is to go, as the time passes, toward the source, which is to say deeper, which is to say at the end

you are at the beginning
which is always
where one should begin.

Only by being a tourist. Can you experience. A place.

They ventured forth. Then they ventured forth again.

They compared their bodies.

It's only by comparing them we will know them.
"Compare them in this situation."
(RHODA and SOPHIA sit, at table, earphones. A waiter enters with a tray.)

WAITER

Coffee?
(RHODA drinks.)
"How can she listen and drink coffee at the same time."

SOPHIA

Look. I made a drawing of you, Rhoda.
(RHODA looks.)

It's good.
>"They are still, all this while, getting information over their earphones."
(They look at each other.)
RHODA
Oh, certainly not.
SOPHIA
Oh, yes, yes, yes, yes.
>"Then she realizes . . ."
RHODA
Comparison will be the basis of my life. That's how I hope to get famous.
(Wall opens to reveal a throne, MAX sits on it.)
MAX
You are famous.
RHODA
More famous. Even more famous.

(A bed.)
RHODA
I think somebody's hidden under my bed.
(The bed revolves—SOPHIA appears strapped to the underside.)
SOPHIA
It was a trick.
(Revolves again.)
RHODA
I vanished. It was a trick.
HANNAH
(Enters.)
Hello Rhoda, I brought you some clams.
RHODA
You can see, it's hard for me to eat them because I'm tied to the bed.
HANNAH
Oh, I thought it was a trick.
RHODA
Hum, you know what these clams remind me of?
HANNAH
Good, she's making another comparison.

It should be easier than this.
What.
(Pause.)
Writing good.
>Don't you know? There's nothing to it.
What.
>Writing good.
What makes me think writing is important.
(Shrugs.) Everybody does it all the

time so it must be important.
She doesn't do it.
Who. *(Pause.)* Rhoda? She's always writing. Everybody is always writing.
RHODA
(Enters.)
Hello.
VOICE
She wrote it.
RHODA
Am I late.
VOICE
She wrote it.
RHODA
She said it.
VOICE
Look, look compare her to a typewriter.
SOPHIA
(Enters.)
Hello.
(Pause.)
RHODA and SOPHIA
Hello.
(They squeeze together.)
RHODA
What are you doing.
SOPHIA
Writing.
RHODA
I'm comparing myself.
SOPHIA
Don't push.
RHODA
She likes it.
SOPHIA
(Arms around her. They collapse.)
Oh Rhoda, what a good writer you are.
RHODA
Would you get this sack of potatoes off my body?
WAITER
(Enters.)
What'll it be?
MAX
(Pause.)
Potatoes.
(RHODA and SOPHIA get up and plop on his table.)
RHODA
Don't read while you eat.
SOPHIA
Here's a potato.
>"They don't really compare themselves to potatoes but he does."

RHODA
I wish I was growing someplace.

(A field. Enter RHODA and SO-PHIA, legs together in a sack.)
RHODA
This looks like a good place to get planted.
SOPHIA
Now maybe we can have a private conversation.
RHODA
(Pause—looks.)
Oh Sophia, write me a letter.
SOPHIA
I can't write.
RHODA
You?
(Pause.)
You're so smart.
"She explains herself, like a potato."
RHODA
(Shakes her head.)
Nothing's explained yet.
SOPHIA
Wait for it to be explained, Rhoda.

RHODA
(Pause.)
Why do we both have to have one leg in the same sack.
SOPHIA
(As HANNAH and ELEANOR enter, two of their legs in a sack.)
There's going to be a race.
HANNAH
Hello, we're ready for the race.
RHODA
I don't want to do it.
HANNAH
Oh Rhoda, do you think it's beneath your dignity.
ELEANOR
You and Sophia looked very dignified on the dinner plate.
RHODA
I wasn't on a dinner plate.
HANNAH
Oh yes. Ben was eating you.
ELEANOR
—He wrote us all about it in a letter.
RHODA
My partner doesn't write.

Photo Arnold Aronson

"The essence of writing now grows apparent."
SOPHIA
I said it would.
"In the middle of the potato field The emphasis on certain words In the midst of a field of other words not so emphasized."
RHODA
In my whole life I never emphasized something that much.
"Wrong."
SOPHIA
I don't write.
"Oh Sophia, did you mean don't or can't."
(HANNAH and ELEANOR push against SOPHIA and RHODA.)
"The potato race, in which nothing special is emphasized."
RHODA
I'm emphasizing a comparison.
(Lights up on audience.)
"It's up to you. Understanding is all up to you of course. But so is enjoyment."
"Certain spaces suddenly appear in the center of the audience."

(Pause.)
"Find them. Find them. Certain spaces suddenly appear in the center of the audience."
RHODA, SOPHIA, HANNAH
Maybe this isn't sensually enough oriented for your enjoyment.
(GONG. Tableau in a shoe salon.)
VOICE
What you see is simply a comparison of bodies. But it is also a comparison of minds.
RHODA
How far do you think my mind is now from the circumference of my head.
"Compare. Her mind and your own mind. She is an actress in the play. But at this moment, her real mind is working just like your own real mind."
(Pause.)
"Now there are spaces distributed amongst the audience but there are other spaces distributed over the stage. Find them. Find them. Try to find them."
RHODA
Oh, I expected to find a space going on in my body, then I expected to find a place

Photo Arnold Aronson

growing in my mind. Then I find a place growing someplace that wasn't in me at all but it was growing so much it finished by being in me.

(Pause.)

I have to return to what I know, but now I know something different.

VOICE

"The orchestra is busy tuning up."

(All-girl orchestra including RHODA and SOPHIA try to play a lively tune and all collapse. Then a large shoe appears on the horizon.)

RHODA

On the horizon, a large shoe. I move toward it in order to wear it. But wait, wait, both of my feet are already covered with

shoes. Dare I now, at this distance, remove the appropriate shoe? The offending, if I may say so, the offending shoe? Look, look, the shoe—there—is large enough to make me think of a boat. Boat vs. shoe, both elements of a journey. But have they a different aim in life.

RHODA

My shoe has to be replaced.

(She is sitting.)

SALESMAN

By what.

RHODA

Are you the only salesperson available.

SALESMAN

I can be more fanatic than I seem.

RHODA

I don't want a fanatic salesperson.

Photo Arnold Aronson

SOPHIA
(Entering.)
Sell me a shoe.

RHODA
(Pause.)
I only sell one part of my body covering to people.

SALESMAN
I don't think Rhoda's a shoe salesman.

RHODA
—Can I interest you in some of my underwear.

SOPHIA
(Pause.)
I don't think you understand my reasons.

RHODA
(Return to shoe on horizon.)
Water comes from the horizon, but so does its relation. Its relation in the form of a boat; i.e., the relation between water and boat; i.e., the flow, which continues, which-of-a-which this is an instance, and the thing that is on it—which in this case is a boat and in another case is an idea. The boat as idea? Ah, not a good idea, huh.
(Back to shoe parlor.)
Why need it be a good idea.

-------------------------------.

RHODA
This place frightens me. I can say that easily. All places frighten me if I allow them to frighten me. Where in the place is the fear.
    "Is it layed over it like a gray (or colored) sheet."
Or is it placed, distinctly, like a jewel. Somewhere . . . where would that jewel appropriately be placed.

SOPHIA
Look, look, the window lights up.

RHODA
But here, here, this piece of paper catches its image.

SOPHIA
Not true.
(Scene is shifting.)

VOICE
(As scene is shifting to grove of trees.)
Only being a tourist. Can you experience a place.

RHODA
I said go to the same place but it's different.

SOPHIA
Be careful.

RHODA
Of?

SOPHIA
(Pause.)
It's pretty isn't it.

RHODA
Yes.

SOPHIA
In ten minutes or less you'll want something different.

RHODA
Oh look.
(She points.)

SOPHIA
You imagined it.

RHODA
(Pause.)
I wrote it.
(Pause.)
I didn't want to imagine it. I didn't want to explain it. I just wanted to experience it.

SOPHIA
There it is.

RHODA
What.

SOPHIA
Wait.

RHODA
What.

SOPHIA
I said in ten minutes or less and it happened.

RHODA
What.

SOPHIA
(Pause.)
It was there.
(Enter AGATHA in woods.)

AGATHA
First it was Max here, but it was only imagined.
    "Written."

AGATHA
Then it was me but I was visible.

RHODA
(Pause.)
I'm going to change places.

AGATHA
(Points.)
I've had enough of you, Rhoda.

RHODA
That was me talking.

————————————————————

(A room, tea served.)
AGATHA
It's really true. I've had enough of you.
RHODA
I could change my appearance.
AGATHA
Not likely.
RHODA
I'll put on something else.
(Goes to door.)
It's locked.
(Another door opens.)
AGATHA
You tried the wrong door.
(A hiss, which gets louder.)
"THE RETURN OF THE POTA-TOES."
(Enter four big potatoes. Then silence, and AGATHA and RHODA undress.)
"ONLY BY BEING A TOURIST."
VOICE
Now this is where the interesting part of the evening begins. Everything up to now was Recognizable. It was part of one's everyday experience.

Now, however

The real potatoes are amongst us
And a different kind of understanding is possible for anybody who wants a different kind of understanding.
RHODA
(Pause.)
I feel like a potato.
AGATHA
—I feel like a potato.
(They feel each other.)
AGATHA
Oh Rhoda, you feel like a potato.
RHODA
You smell like a potato and you even
(Both lick.)
taste like a potato.
VOICE
Would she think that Agatha smelled and

Photo Arnold Aronson

tasted like a potato if she herself didn't feel like a potato.

> *(Lights dim to center as potatoes exit, big couch in behind. RHODA and AGATHA sit back in it on opposite sides, but entwining their legs.)*

VOICE

Potatoes have no special feelings about physical proximity to other potatoes.
On the other hand, potatoes—as far as we know—have no literature or art of any kind to which they sublimate powerful sexual energies.

> *(Pause.)*

Potatoes endure. They are eaten
But they still, endure.

> *(Lights fade out.)*

> *(Lights up: cafe;*
> *MAX and HANNAH.)*

MAX

I had the funniest dream last night.

WAITER

Coffee?

MAX

I dreamt I was a potato.

WAITER

> *(Pause.)*

Coffee?

MAX

Yes.

HANNAH

Don't drink coffee while thinking about a potato.

> "This play transcends the world of the potato and at the same time it enters that world."

MAX

> *(Turns.)*

Do you keep books in that cabinet.

HANNAH

I don't work here as a waitress. I solicit customers and then I introduce them to great literature.

> *(Pause, as she points at low cabinet.)*

Should I open it.

WAITER

> *(Head in door.)*

Your potatoes are on the fire.

> *(Pause.)*

Excuse me, I mean here they come.

> *(A potato comes to front door. HANNAH at cabinet.)*
> "The potato can't enter because the door isn't big enough."

HANNAH

> *(Kneels.)*

Here's the book you want.

MAX

What did you pick.

HANNAH

It says "Erotic photographs of the preceding century"—do you mind if I thumb through some of the pictures.

MAX

That's dumb.

HANNAH

> *(Pause.)*

I'm a little ashamed to have you know that I'm interested in such a book.

MAX

Why.

> *(Pause.)*

Why is that mirror in the potato.

> *(Buzz. Lights up. Tree replaces potato and RHODA appears on floor next to HANNAH.)*
> "I told you what it transcended, but I didn't tell you what would replace what it transcended."

RHODA

In losing the potato you lost the mirror.

HANNAH

It's still here. It's still here. It's bigger but it's still here.

> "The stage is, of course, a mirror and you are looking into it."

WAITER

Here's your baked potato.

> *(Exits.)*
> "You realize, when he's said—here's your baked potato—he's said everything."
> *(On floor, RHODA and HANNAH look at pictures in the book and laugh together.)*

> *(MAX down front, presents a potato to audience.)*

MAX

Here's your baked potato.

> *(A wall, with a small, barred window and shelf. Musical number.)*

Photo Kate Davy

Photo Kate Davy

(MAX and RHODA drop potatoes through the window. Then all enter and dance with one arm extended to floor—a shoe on bottom of the arm—a three-legged dance.
Their shoes are shined.
Then a hooded rolling chair enters and RHODA is left alone with a hooded man who appears in the chair. A table is set. She climbs on it, crying out in fear throughout the music, ready for unimaginable tortures. Potatoes placed on her stomach. She slowly comes to like them, as a voice speaks over the music describing meditative processes using young spring potatoes as a focal point. Music fades, and stage quietly is transformed back into the throne room.)

(MAX on throne. Potato on lap. Enter SOPHIA. Kneels. RHODA enters behind, with knife, SOPHIA half turns—RHODA falls on her, they strain against each other.)
"God. Is he real?"

(Lights up. SOPHIA with knife in chest. RHODA sprawled back, relaxes.)
"The most ELEGANT
MEANING
POSSIBLE"

MAX
In this place. Certain habits.
"Only by being a tourist. Can you experience. A place.
They ventured forth. Then they ventured forth again.
They compared their bodies."

RHODA
It's only by comparing them we will know them.

SOPHIA
Compare them in this situation.
(They get earphones.)

MAX
(Pause.)
He who thinks, always surprises me.

RHODA
What's the good of imagining what can't be imagined.

SOPHIA
Am I different now.

RHODA
No.

MAX
Am I different now.

RHODA
No.

MAX
Wrong.
(Pause.)
Here's what just happened.
"He explains."
(A potato falls rear.)

RHODA
How will that change anything.

MAX
It won't change anything for you, but it will for me, only you won't notice it.

RHODA
(Lights on her alone.)
He went to a certain place.

MAX
(In a door, lit alone.)
I live in an imaginary country.
(A mirror comes forward. RHODA against it.)
"The mirror advances but it has no real mind of its own. Existence is, for it, of course, reflection."
(Potatoes enter.)

VOICE
"Entities struggling toward truth? No. Merely someone caught, momentarily, by light rays."
(Flash.)
(Pause.)

RHODA
Wait, let me take another photograph. I love having my picture taken.

VOICE
(Pause.)
I am trying to photograph what cannot be **"photographed."** I know I am undertaking an impossible task.
(RHODA approaches front of stage.)
"Oh Rhoda. Dig deeper and deeper into your memory."

RHODA
(Pause.)
I was in a garden.
"Don't believe it."
(Room. Window. Others sprawled about.)

RHODA
(Holds up book.)

Oh look.

"Erotic photography from the previous century."
(Others reveal selves.)

RHODA

No, it wasn't that garden.
(Hands on hips.)

Now, try smelling the rose.
(She goes to window, bowl of roses wheeled in on table by MAX.)
"She has a nose in the back of her head."
(ELEANOR leans in window.)

ELEANOR

Look what I picked.

MAX

I made this choice for Rhoda.
"Come to bed
Come to bed
Come to bed
Come to bed."

RHODA

They always say come to bed when what they mean is . . .
(A ping.)
(All but RHODA take out shrunken heads.)
"Ha, we all had one and the others didn't know. Let's do the old right-left."

MAX

Good idea. Let's do the old right-left!
(All dance.)

(Bathroom. RHODA there in bathrobe with towel.)
"Running the tub."
(RHODA turns on the water and steam pours out which causes her to stagger back.)
"It was as if . . . the faucet she turned on was her own brain."
(Nightmare dance in bathtub.)

Photo Kate Davy

(RHODA finishes, exhausted in the tub.)

RHODA

All these heads they have all been collecting.

MAX

(At door.)

Oh Rhoda, you're not going to change your mind at THIS late date.

RHODA

It's been a mistake.

(Pause.)

It's been a miscalculation.

(Open—big head rear rocks slowly back and forth.)

**"In time, they grow much bigger
In America they grow much bigger
The group mind
A play by Doctor Wartmonger
Who is speaking when I am speaking
What does this have to do with headhunters.**

(Potatoes.)

**Generating new material
My discovery**

Today I decided to generate new material by keeping a diary."

RHODA

(At director's table. Full lights on-stage as all is revealed and director goes onstage and looks at audience.)

He found himself deeply enmeshed in plans for her happiness.

DIRECTOR

Cut throat.

RHODA

I bet it wasn't expected.

(Points at director's forehead.)

What he did.

DIRECTOR

Do you care if I title this chapter after your title.

RHODA

Names. That's one of the categories I have to fish for a little more deeply.

(As SOPHIA comes up behind her and tries to cut her throat.)

"It's time you understood. It's all

Photo Kate Davy

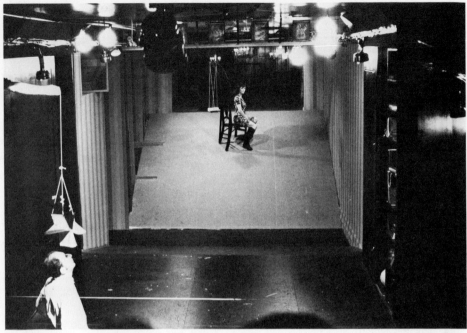

Photo Kate Davy

there and you can't improve upon it."
(A chair is rear in the full light. Weighted with books. Tips. Then RHODA sits.)

RHODA
See—now there's a difference.
(Pause.)
I'm heavier than the reading matter.

MAX
It doesn't matter, those books are smarter than you are.
(Books fall on his head.)

RHODA
I never read them.
(As banquet table is set.)

SONG
"Oh Rhoda, you never read the right books.
Oh Rhoda, you're always reading the wrong books.
Oh Rhoda, why don't you read the right books?
Oh Rhoda, the books you read are wrong books."
(Big book opens rear.)

RHODA
Who joined in.
When.

After it was over.
Oh everybody joined in after it was over.
Then it was easy.
But it was always easy.
Well, then they joined in earlier than I knew.

Legend: **DOING SOMETHING.**
(All-girl orchestra appears.)
Watch how they come running.
(Pause.)
(Orchestra plays a terrible number.)
Hum, that's a surprise of sorts.
"Are you still sure that everyone is joining in?"
No. I admit it. No.

Let's introduce each other.

RHODA
Now there's just one of us.
(Pause—people hold out playing cards.)

VOICE
Humm—take a card.
(Pause.)

RHODA

I'm waiting.

(Card on a table.)

RHODA

Now. The card does the talking. But in a language you can't understand.

(Pause.)

If you were able to understand. What the card was saying. You would be having a response very different from the response you are now having.

(Pause.)

I guarantee it. I guarantee it. Whatever you want I can give you.—O.K. I want to be famous.—O.K. You are.

(Door opens.)

CREW PERSON

(Resembling Richard Foreman.)

Oh, excuse me, I—

RHODA

What.

CREW PERSON

(Pause.)

Aren't you the famous Richard Foreman.

RHODA

(Smiles.)

Yes.

CREW PERSON

It's an honor to meet you.

RHODA

(Shrugs.)

Ohhhhh.

CREW PERSON

I admire you very much. More than anybody else.

RHODA

Hummmmm.

MAX

(To RHODA? To audience?)

See? You're famous.

ALL

(To RHODA.)

We are all proud of you. You have proven yourself by becoming famous.

(Pause. RHODA looks at audience and thinks.)

1.

(Flower trellis set plus low wall, roses.)

RHODA

I wish I was this place.

MAX

What?

(Pause.)

How can you be a "place."

RHODA

I wish I was "this."

(Pause.)

Hah—I am.

MAX

Then you got your wish.

RHODA

No. It shouldn't have been a wish.

(She starts to undress.)

VOICE

The naked body as a vast space. Travel in it. To travel in it

Is to be in a landscape that you KNOW how to relate to.

MAX and RHODA

(Arms out.)

How can I relate to this PLACE.

VOICE

A beautiful vista.

(Pause.)

When you move toward it, it vanishes.

(Pause, RHODA exits.)

2.

(On balcony, naked woman and man.)

But looking at the nude, you are caressed. It is SMALL enough. Yet, it's more other than the landscape. Also, It remarks upon your presence.

MAX

If the landscape could remark upon my presence.

(Pause, he goes through it.)

For instance.

(Lights up, then out.)

(Lights up—RHODA gone.)

MAX

(Pause.)

Oh Rhoda, now that you're this "place" I don't know how to have a relationship with you, Rhoda.

(Pause.)

What this place does is be-here. But I. I. I do something else.

More complex.

More interesting. Because the place is-here, and then it is existing.

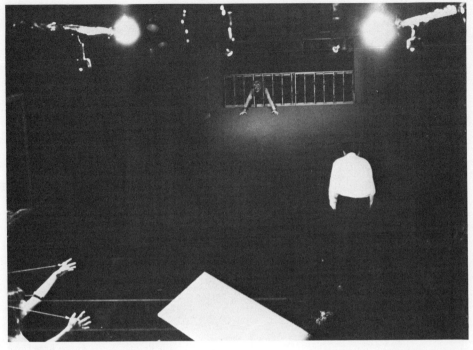

Photo Kate Davy

VOICE

But Max is different. Sometimes he sleeps. Then he gets a good idea. Acts on it. Then he sleeps again.

"Ohhh holy one, oh causative agent. . . ."

MAX

The signs which are important to me speak. What they say is

The past

The past

That is why they are signs.

RHODA

(Appears.)

Come closer.

MAX

Oh lady.

RHODA

Come closer. Rest your head on me.

MAX

Oh lady. In your arms.

———————————————

(A bed.)

RHODA

Do you know how much effort went into building this world.

MAX

It's like the others.

RHODA

What.

MAX

World.

RHODA

I wasn't thinking of a world.

MAX

But you were. But you were without knowing it.

(He returns to throne.)

What I want to give you is . . . an estimable shape. The imagination of a . . .

"Oh Rhoda. Sleep and speech. I'd like to analyze it but I can't really."

RHODA

Teacher? I don't need no teacher.

———————————————

"The contacts that I make with the force are, to say the least, very erratic."

(A table. RHODA rests her head on it and sleeps.)

RHODA
This is my dream life.
   (Pause.)
A text. Inside out. Vulgar imitations.
   VOICE
Remember what I said at the beginning. A
text cut in half, and the first half placed
where the second half should be and vice-
versa.
   "You can't please all of the people
   all of the time.
   Who am I
   Why do I want YOU in my audi-
   ence
   What will you say about me be-
   hind my back."
   MAX
   (On throne now.)
What he means is, how easily can sentences
be generated.
   *(RHODA now with head on a chop-
   ping block.)*
Being productive is his only concern.
   RHODA
It doesn't help, it doesn't help.
   MAX
What doesn't help.

(As book placed on her head.)
"You are punished Rhoda, for
dreaming."
(Open on drop of building.)
"She wanted to be like architecture,
not like dancing."
   RHODA
I wanted a choice, about how to use my
body.
   "Now, choice is a closed book."
   RHODA
   (Pause.)
Look. This was the body of . . .
   "Her body was; a building."
   RHODA
I will be punished for dreaming.
   (Lifts her hand.)
Look, in my hand is . . . a . . . a . . .
   "She tries to name an object which,
   by definition, has no name."
   "Oh Rhoda, for that you'll be pun-
   ished."
   RHODA
Nonsense.
   (Pause.)
Nonsense.

Photo Kate Davy

VOICE

But is it nonsense? You see, when I call upon my own knowledge, when I do that, it only shows me (my knowledge) the very tip of its wing. Is it therefore, as I had assumed, my knowledge?

I do not possess it. In what sense then, do I call it my knowledge?

It is a body of information to which I have occasional, peripheral access. As opposed to other bodies of knowledge. But are there bodies of knowledge? Of course not. There are a composite of partial accesses (other people, myself at different times) and the overlapping of these gives the illusion of a body. Knowledge.

But what is it that is overlapping?

A certain. . . .joie de vivre.

    (Music.)

LIST OF CHARACTERS AND PERFORMERS

ANGELFACE
New York City

April, 1968

Max	Ken Kelman
Walter	Prentiss Wilhite
Agatha	Eleanor Herasmachuck
Karl	Larry Kardish
Walter II	Ernie Gehr
Weinstein	Mike Jacobson
Rhoda	Judy Kardish

TOTAL RECALL
(SOPHIA = (WISDOM): Part 2)
New York City

December, 1970—January, 1971

Ben	Mike Jacobson
Leo	Bob Fleischner
Rhoda	Judy Fyve
Sophia	Margaret Ladd
Little Girl	Alexandra Stone

HćOhTiEńLà (or) HOTEL CHINA
New York City

December, 1971—January, 1972

Max	N. E. Deinau
Karl	Bob Fleischner
Karl II	Ernie Gehr
Rhoda	Sarah Boothe
Eleanor	Judy Fyve
Angel	Kate Manheim
Ben	Andrew Noren
Hannah	Kate Manheim
Ida	Jan Penovich
Hannah II	Ann Clark
Little Girl	Diana Paris

SOPHIA = (WISDOM)
Part 3: THE CLIFFS
New York City

December, 1972—January, 1973

Max (Leo)	Bob Fleischner
Ben	Andrew Noren
Hannah	Margot Breier
Sophia	Linda Patton
Rhoda	Kate Manheim
Karl (Snowman)	Jim Hoberman
Workers	Myron Adams
	Jim Boerlin
	Gregory Gubitosa
	Iris Newman
	Bill Plympton
	Allegra Scott

CLASSICAL THERAPY or A WEEK UNDER THE INFLUENCE . . .
Paris, France

September-October, 1973

Rhoda	Kate Manheim
Ben	Gerard Neut
Max	Remy Chaignard
Eleanor	Anemone
Karl	Christian Ducray
Hannah	Nicole Guichaoua
Leo	Bernard Tourtelier
Crew Persons	Odile Michel
	Sanna de Kerviler
	Elke Gerard
	Martine Carlier

VERTICAL MOBILITY
(SOPHIA = (WISDOM): Part 4)
New York City

April-May, 1974

Max	Bob Fleischner
Rhoda	Kate Manheim
Ben	Jim Jennings
Sophia	Donna Germain
Crew Persons	Marcy Arlin
	John Matturri
	Gregory Gubitosa
	Stuart Sherman

PAIN(T)
New York City

April-May, 1974

Rhoda	Kate Manheim
Eleanor	Nora Manheim
Ida	Mimi Johnson
Max	Stuart Sherman
Sophia	Hanneke Henket
Crew Persons	Bob Fleischner
	Norma Jean Deak
	Charles Bergengren
	Gregory Gubitosa

RHODA IN POTATOLAND
(HER FALL-STARTS)
New York City

December, 1975—February, 1976

Rhoda	Kate Manheim
Max	Bob Fleischner
Sophia	Rena Gill
Waiter	Gautam Dasgupta
Admirer	John Matturri
Hannah	Ela Troyano
Eleanor	Camille Foss
Agatha	Cathy Scott
Crew Persons	Tim Kennedy
	Phillip Johnston
	Charley Bergengren

COMPLETE CHRONOLOGY OF PLAYS
WRITTEN BY RICHARD FOREMAN*

—1968:

ANGELFACE

Presented by the Ontological-Hysteric Theatre at the Cinematheque (80 Wooster Street), New York City, April, 1968.

ELEPHANT STEPS

Music by Stanley Silverman. Commissioned by the Fromm Music Foundation. Presented at Tanglewood, Lenox, Mass., by the Berkshire Music Festival, July-August, 1968. Second production at Hunter College Opera Theatre, New York City, April, 1970.

—1969:

IDA-EYED

Presented by the Ontological-Hysteric Theatre at the New Dramatists Workshop, New York City, May, 1969.

RHODA-RETURNING

REAL MAGIC IN NEW YORK

Music by Stephen Dickman. Concert production at the Cinematheque, May, 1970.

SOPHIA=(WISDOM): Part 1

(Produced by Theatre for the New City, New York City, November, 1974, under the direction of Crystal Field.)

—1970:

TOTAL RECALL (SOPHIA=(WISDOM): Part 2)

Presented by the Ontological-Hysteric Theatre at the Cinematheque, December, 1970—January, 1971.

MAUDLIN NOTATIONS

FOREST: (SUBTITLED DEPTH)

TWO VACATIONS

HOLY MOLY

LINES OF VISION

—1971:

HčOhTiEňLà (or) HOTEL CHINA

Presented by the Ontological-Hysteric Theatre at the Cinematheque, December, 1971—January, 1972.

EVIDENCE

Privately printed notebooks in which LINES OF VISION and HOTEL CHINA were originally written. The first 30 pages were staged and presented by the Ontological-Hysteric Theatre as EVIDENCE, at Theatre for the New City, April, 1972.

---

* All produced plays were designed and directed by Richard Foreman unless otherwise indicated.

(A selection entitled 15 MINUTES OF EVI-DENCE was presented by the Playwrights' Cooperative, New York City, May, 1975, under the direction of Kate Davy.)

DREAM TANTRAS FOR WESTERN MASSACHUSETTS

Music by Stanley Silverman. Presented by Lynn Austin and Oliver Smith at the Lenox Arts Center, Lenox, Mass., August, 1971.

SOPHIA=(WISDOM) Part 3: THE CLIFFS

Presented by the Ontological-Hysteric Theatre, at the Cinematheque, December, 1972—January, 1973.

—1972:

DAILY LIFE

One scene, retitled HONOR, presented by the Playwrights' Cooperative at the Cubiculo Theatre, New York City, May, 1973.

OP/RA: AN ISOMORPHIC REPRESENTATION OF THE GRADUAL DISMEMBERMENT FROM WITHIN OF WESTERN ART IN WHICH A NEW UNITY THAT OF CONSCIOUSNESS ITSELF EMERGES

HOTEL FOR CRIMINALS

Music by Stanley Silverman. Commissioned by the National Opera Foundation. Produced at the Exchange Theatre, New York City, January, 1975.

DR. SELAVY'S MAGIC THEATRE

Music by Stanley Silverman. Presented by Lynn Austin, Lenox Arts Center, Lenox, Mass., July, 1972. Also presented at the Mercer-O'Casey Theatre in New York City, November, 1972—April, 1973.

AFRICA

CLASSICAL THERAPY or A WEEK UNDER THE INFLUENCE . . .

Presented by the Ontological-Hysteric Theatre for the Festival d'Automne, Paris, France, September-October, 1973.

PARTICLE THEORY

Presented by the Ontological-Hysteric Theatre at Theatre for the New City, April-May, 1973.

THE REM(ARK)ABLE CABIN-CRUISER: (DEPTH)

—1973:

INSPIRATIONAL ANALYSIS

VERTICAL MOBILITY (SOPHIA= (WISDOM): Part 4)

Presented by the Ontological-Hysteric Theatre, New York City, April-May, 1974.

WALLED GARDEN (LANGUAGE)

LIFE OF THE BEE (I've Göt der Shakes)

AFRICANNS-INSTRUCTIS

—1974:

PANDERING TO THE MASSES: A   *Presented by the Ontological-Hysteric Thea-*
MISREPRESENTATION   *tre, New York City, January-March, 1975.*

PAIN(T)   *Presented by the Ontological-Hysteric Thea-*
                                               tre, New York City, April-May, 1974 (in
                                               repertory with VERTICAL MOBILITY).

RHODA IN POTATOLAND (HER FALL-   *Presented   by   the   Ontological-Hysteric*
STARTS)   *Theatre, New York City, December, 1975—*
                                               February, 1976.

THINKING (ONE KIND)   *Presented by the Drama Department of the*
                                               University of California, San Diego, March,
                                               1975.

—1975:

OUT OF THE BODY TRAVEL   *Presented as a video piece at the American*
                                               Dance Festival, New London, Connecticut,
                                               July, 1975.

SEANCE

PLACE+TARGET

END OF A BEAUTIFUL FRIENDSHIP

RADIANT CITY

LIVRE DES SPLENDEURS   *Presented at the Festival d'Automne, Paris,*
                                               France, October, 1976.